AETHEROCALYPSE

Mephisto's Magic Online Book Three

CHRISTOPHER JOHNS

MOUNTAINDALE
PRESS

This book is dedicated to a few people, my fans, of course. You all love this series for some reason and that's wild to me and yet here you are. Thank you.

I think most importantly, I would like to dedicate this book to my little sister knowing that she never got to read this far will always bring me to a stop, because I could always count on her to read things and give me her honest opinions and thoughts. I wish you were here to meet my wife at long last. Or my newborn daughter. But life has a terrible way of taking things and people before their time.

I miss you.

ACKNOWLEDGMENTS

There are a lot of you out there who know this, but this last year rolling into this one have been bittersweet to me for a lot of reasons and due to that, I've been throwing myself at my work. Thank you to those of you who have been kind enough to wait for this book. You rock.

THE STORY SO FAR

Seth, Mona, Sondra, and Al got neck deep into the game, Seth and Mona filling in their friends and Mona's mom Emma on what seemed to be happening to them and potentially the whole world.

Having earned their way into the second area within Mephisto's Magic Online, the group contended with a dragon queen, her children, and an insidious scheme to summon demons into the city to disrupt Belgonna's Hold's position in aiding the troops on the front lines.

During this time, Mona discovered that, though she loved him more than ever, Seth's feelings of budding love for her were taken from him in order to awaken his summoning magic. Sensing weakness, the succubus that had killed both Seth and Sondra in the game had picked up the pieces of Mona's shattered heart and promised her revenge on the people who stole her love from her and put her family in compromising positions. Who knew, maybe they would even help her find her father first.

In the aftermath of the fight against the weakened demon, Al decided that he was finished with Seth and Sondra, their priorities eschewed when they should have gone after Mona straight away.

Emma logged out to find that Mona had been taken in the real world, leaving Seth, Sondra, and Emma to figure out what had happened to her, all while preparing for whatever ordeals would arise in game, and out of it.

CHAPTER ONE

SETH

Three goblins crossed beneath my hiding spot, their gazes affixed to the reddish glow of a fire up ahead in the tunnel, not paying attention to the blue aura around the faerie near my left shoulder.

I nodded to him, and Sprinkle launched himself down to freeze the rear goblin's feet in place as I jumped down onto his back and ravaged his exposed neck. Once I had a decent bite, I slipped my elven sword up into the base of his skull, as I'd done a dozen times before, and drained the life from him.

Aether Stolen - Earth Affinity at 53%
23 EXP received.

The other goblins turned and shot toward me, Sprinkle throwing a small ice lance that just looked like an icicle into the lead one's foot as Flicker joined the fight from behind, with Emerald hot on her tail.

Emerald slashed the goblin closest to her along the Achilles' tendons and bashed it in the head with a rock to daze it. Then she turned her sights on the goblin before us.

Flicker clapped her hands to signal for us, my eyes slamming shut as blinding light seared the room, the goblin screeching in agony and confusion.

I plunged my fangs into the back of its neck as Emerald stabbed it through the eyes, nicking my cheek.

9 dmg taken.

Aether stolen - Earth Affinity at 61%

22 EXP received.

"Ouch." I rubbed my cheek, and the blood came away with it. "The object is to kill them, not your party members, Ma."

She sighed; Flicker fluttering close to her illuminated her leather armor and Kitsune avatar. Her fur was matted from the blood, but she seemed fine with it so far.

"My ideal party members would include my daughter, Kyvir." She flicked her wrist and the blood on her Soul Dagger showered the ground before allowing it to fade. "Not to mention, a healer; why is Sundar not with us in this endeavor?"

"She's not sure she should be involved with us while we're working through this, and she got that quest to help prepare for the party tonight, as well."

"So then, why are you not helping her?" Her question was innocent enough, but she already knew why.

"Because I need to work through… all of this," I replied darkly, the shadows of the tunnel that surrounded us as comforting as anything. I hadn't stopped playing the game for more than an hour to go to the bathroom and investigate their house.

As I bent to pick up the loot the goblins had dropped, I thought about our findings at Mona and Emma's home.

Sure enough, the dogs had been tranquilized and Mona's portal left wide open. No signs of a struggle; no signs of anyone else inside the house or the guest house, where both of them had been.

I frowned as I picked up not one, but two, gemstones that looked like opals, then another blood red one like the monster crystals we had collected from the Hell Cat. One of the goblins we killed had been a man-eater.

I slipped that into my inventory and resolved to go and see Ophira to complete a quest I had from her. I lifted my gaze to where Emerald stood, observing our surroundings.

I had to appreciate how easily Emma had been able to adjust to it, her worry and grief quickly fueling into her rage and need to find a solution. All we had for now was to grow strong enough to take the fight to the demons on the front lines and hope we could find both Mona and Albarth to get our shit together.

None of us had bothered to finish leveling up the few levels that we had gained from fighting the weakened Balgrus demon, so we still had that to do. We hadn't taken the time due to the fact that the goblins weren't the brightest enemies we had faced, and with my two summons and Emma, they stood little to no chance against us.

I sighed, and Sprinkle swept closer to me, his expression hopeful. "When is the next time you can pay me some Aether to help me grow?"

"I just gave you some four hours ago; I can't get any back until you leave." He frowned and crossed his arms at me. "I have other Aether, too, but how often can you take it and grow from it?"

"Any time," Flicker announced from her new favorite spot on my shoulder. "The more you give us, the quicker we grow and can evolve."

"You can evolve?" I lifted an eyebrow at them both, and they nodded. "How so?"

"Well," Sprinkle frowned and turned to Flicker, "Do you have a decent example?"

"The dragon queen's friend?" Flicker offered quickly with her hand raised as if it were evidence. "The type of creature he is came about from an evolutionary perk for being close to her. For you, we could be something different from just Faerie. We can grow stronger, and with a little more feeding from you, we can both change, like I did. Aether can affect each of us differently. I will always primarily be a creature of the flame, but now I can develop into more."

It was true, she was a little larger than when I had first summoned her, her wings more impressive than they had been as well.

"Do you get to choose how you will evolve?" They nodded in confirmation, and I frowned. "Okay. Then at least we can get out of here, and then I can feed you all the Aether I have left. Thankfully, you each only took one to summon this time."

"Don't you shoot me that dirty glare, kid." Sprinkle crossed his arms angrily. "She still hasn't gotten back to me about that date."

"Look, I already apologized for that, and I'm not going to again." I crossed my arms in response and frowned at him. "So either you can get over it and we can get out of here so that I can pay you some more Aether, or I dismiss you now and give it all to Flicker."

"Oh! Please keep whining, Sprinkle." Flicker fluttered over to the other Faerie to circle him where he levitated sourly. "I *really* want to evolve sooner rather than later. I think I'll look super cool."

"Oh, shut up, you trumped-up campfire." He rolled his eyes and she stuck her tongue out at him. "Fine, let's get the hell out of here."

Both of the faeries alit on my shoulders, their presences surprisingly comforting as we trudged through the tunnels toward the entrance that exited into the quarry.

"Hey!" someone called as a thunderous crash burst overhead. I quickly equipped my shield, then stilled.

I stiffened as a light rain of rubble clattered down onto my shoulders, and I instinctively equipped my shield onto my left arm and held it up as a large stone collided with the metallic barrier and bashed me, knocking me onto my backside painfully.

13 dmg taken.

"Ow," I grunted as I tried to work the soreness out of the stiffened limb, looking about for the voice that had called out to me.

A dwarven man I didn't recognize jogged over to us and looked me over, his blackened beard swinging before his chest as he dipped closer.

"Sorry 'bout that, Prince; I didn't think 'nyone be in that tunnel on account o' them pesky goblins." He offered me a firm hand up and clapped me on my aching shoulder, making me wince. "Oh! Forgive me, I didn't mean ta do it again, I can be so airheaded at ti—"

I held up my good hand to halt his deluge of information, tersely saying, "It's fine. Just try not to get anyone killed, okay?"

"Well I can't just let that pass, Majesty—nope, not at all." He pulled something from his inventory, a small sheet of paper that he scribbled on with a quill, then passed to me. "Here you be, this is a letter o' recommendation from me to you for a new shield at me family's forge. Give'm that, and they'll see you fairly equipped and at the best possible price."

I nodded and muttered, "Thanks," before setting on my way. Then I stopped and called back, "Where is this forge?"

He blushed and tapped my wrist, the location populating on my mini map. "Thanks. Remember, don't kill anyone."

Emerald was behind me as we went, and before we completely left the quarry, she tapped me on the shoulder.

I turned to find her fixing me with the telltale mom frown of death and disappointment, "That was very rude of you, Kyvir." She shook her head, "I know things are difficult right now; we're both hurting and raw, but your parents and I didn't raise you that way, and you damn well know it."

"I do, but I also don't have time to waste on niceties." I glanced down at the paper.

She folded her arms in front of her, "What have I told you and Mona about 'niceties' in the past?" I remained quiet, and she sighed tiredly before repeating her ideals at me for the millionth time since I was five. "Never burn a bridge unless you're sure you can build your own elsewhere. His family are smiths, or affiliated, and we could use that to our benefit. It's why I've accepted Belgonna's offer to blood me tomorrow."

"That just gives her power over us all," I whispered, knowing what she wanted me to do without her having to say it.

"So what?" She shrugged. "It's power I don't already have, and with that, we are that much closer to getting Mona back, not to mention, she is no longer the acting queen, so she won't order us around unless she truly has to. The perks outweigh the risks. Now, do as you know you should."

I sighed heavily and returned to the dwarf, who had scrambled up the side of the cliff above the entrance to the tunnels we had used and was digging a hole in the stone. "Hey!"

He stilled and turned around, blinking down at me, so I called up, "That wasn't your fault, and I shouldn't have been such a jerk about it, nor as ungrateful. I hope you can forgive me, and thank you for trying to make it right."

He nodded, shoved something that looked like metal piping into the small hole and slid down to where the Faeries and I stood. "It's not a problem. Ta be fair, I'd be bent out o' shape if I were beat on by rocks, too. Mind lending a hand?"

"What do you need?" He glanced at Flicker and then to the pipe, where a small fuse stuck out. "Oh, Flicker?"

She grinned and fluttered up to touch the fuse and watched it burn for a second before coming back down to land on my shoulder.

The dwarf grabbed my good elbow and tugged me back ten feet before the item exploded, bringing the roof of the tunnel in front of us down. I was suddenly grateful he had messed up that last time, and he just grinned at me.

"Name's Cecil." He held his hand out for me to shake, which I did. "You must be Prince Kyvir, right? One o' the ones we'll be feasting with tonight?"

I nodded and smiled at him as best as I could before he stopped shaking my hand. "Go on ta the shop now, and they'll take care o' you proper, I swear it."

"Thanks, Cecil, I will." I turned to leave and found Emerald staring with a slight, wicked grin on her face. "Yeah, yeah."

Both of the Faeries got a portion of my summoning Aether, four each, which was more powerful to them than just fire and ice. That left me with five fire and ice each that I could use to defend myself if necessary. They seemed content with the summoning Aether, and we left it at that.

It took a little bit to get to the location on the map, following back streets and rerouting due to the maze-like structure of the city, but after an hour or so, we found the smithy that Cecil had pointed us to.

The heat here was intense, and it only made Flicker relax even more. I had to send Sprinkle away, which he was happy about.

The outside of the building consisted of metal siding that looked like dragon scales glowing a warm cherry red with a brick base around the bottom. There was no door to this building, just a thin chain-mail-like partisan that I had to shove aside to walk in.

The figure behind the counter surprised me, as I had expected to see a dwarf, but instead found a gnomish man with a handlebar mustache and goatee.

"Hullo!" he greeted politely and put the paper he was working on under the desk he sat at. "How can I help you today?"

"I was sent here by Cecil to see about getting a shield?" The gnome frowned heavily, making me pull the slip of paper out to give to the smaller man.

He read it, sighed, and just chuckled to himself, "Leave it to young master Cecil to injure the royalty." He lifted his head and smiled placatingly at me. "We will help you find anything that you might need, Master...?"

"Kyvir is fine, thank you."

"Yes, Master Kyvir." He rubbed his hands together and slammed them onto the table hard enough to startle Flicker off my shoulder. "Forgive me. I always do that to begin the process of selection; old habits and such."

"That's quite all right," I muttered, a little thrown by the reaction, and followed him into a back room.

The heat intensified. Luckily, I had been blooded by the dragon queen already and was resistant to heat or I'd be dying in here.

The floor was as red as the outside had been and cast an almost infernal glow upon the weapons and armor in the room, where they were neatly arranged by type and height.

I tapped a shield, and it wasn't hot in the slightest, the gnome chuckling, "Yes, it is quite warm in here; however our weapons, armors, and accessories are all well protected against the heat."

"Why is it so ghastly hot in here?" Emerald panted, sweat beginning to pour from her.

"That would be the lava flowing beneath the building that we use as a part of our smithing processes." He pointed to buckets and the forge that looked to be channeling heat.

Flicker perked up immediately. "You have lava here? Where?"

He regarded her oddly for a moment, then motioned to the wall on our left, "In the smithy itself, but I wouldn't venture in there. Master Gretlen does not like to be disturbed when he works."

"I don't care about some stinky dwarf, I want the lava!" She flitted into the next room and was gone.

The gnome launched himself after her and cried out, "Please wait!"

I followed along and came around the corner in time to see her dive headfirst into a stream of lava on the floor as a grumpy-looking dwarf turned slowly toward us.

"Oleg, why did that creature dive into my lava?" His deep voice held a level of threat that made me glad I still had all my weapons and most of my magic.

"Forgive me, Master Gretlen, I tried to stop her!" The

gnome almost cowered and wrung his hands nervously. "Please don't fire me."

I lifted my hand, "This is also my fault. I don't have as much control over my summoning as I should. My deepest apologies." I watched in fascinated horror as Flicker emerged from the lava to float on her back and spit it into the air like a fountain of water before grinning at herself. "What the hell is wrong with you, Flicker?"

"We don't have lava like this where I live!" she cried out in bliss. "It's all taken up by the big guys and girls and other things in between and without. They hate sharing with us; besides, this is almost pure fire Aether for me. I'm gonna get *so big* from this!"

The dwarf growled menacingly, stepping toward her, then stopped and sniffed the air. "Someone smells of metal magic."

He turned and closed his eyes before easing closer to both myself and Emerald as he continued to sniff like a dog following a scent.

He stopped a foot from both of us. "It isn't you two; who is it?"

"My friend; her daughter has a strong affinity for metal," I explained to him, and his eyes lit up. "Unfortunately, she was taken from us by the demons."

His face turned a red so deep, I thought that his nose would start to bleed from the anger. He turned and shouted so loudly, I thought Oleg was going to pee himself as he threw his hammer across the room.

"Fucking *demons!*" Gretlen snarled as he stomped about the room. "I received word from an old friend of mine that said he would be sending someone to me to learn, but they have yet to come, and now another one slips through my fingers?"

"Wait!" I called, and he turned to me just before he upended his massive anvil with a loud bang.

"Trying to bask in lava, here!" Flicker's heated whine fell on deaf ears as the man watched me.

"Was that old friend somehow related to Master Ori Loriander in Iradellum?"

"Yes!" He nodded his head and kicked a pile of tools that had fallen when he had thrown his hammer. "He said they would be here *days* ago!"

"That was my daughter, then!" Emerald exclaimed, and he stilled as he regarded her. "She was Ori's apprentice, but he couldn't teach her about her magic. She was supposed to come see you, but she had to come and get me first, so she had to wait. I'm so sorry."

"It was your daughter?" He raised an eyebrow at her, then shook his head. "Do not apologize. You couldn't help it that she was *stolen* by those infernal *vermin!*"

His head rolled over his shoulders as if he were stretching a kink out of his neck. His face turned toward us, his age finally beginning to show, wrinkles around his eyes and some liver spots just beneath the edges of his beard along his cheeks.

"She was going to be who you trained before you passed, wasn't she?" I asked him politely.

He nodded, finally sitting on the anvil that he'd tipped over. "Aye." He surveyed the damage that he'd done and sighed. "Oleg, would you clean what you can of the shop? I need to step outside."

"Yes, Master!" The gnomish man broke into a sprint to comply with the smith's request.

Gretlen stood, and his back popped with the effort before he made his way past myself and Emerald, motioning that we should follow.

Once we stepped outside, he shook himself out and the light truly lit him for us. His reddish beard was splashed with gray and silver, same as his hair that he tied up in a tight bun on top of his head.

He turned and stared at both of us. "I'll likely die before I get the opportunity to teach her, but I have tomes that I've poured years of my life into that describe my process." He took a deep breath and ran his fingers through his beard, then his hair, letting it free of the band that held it. "If you could bring her to me to train, all the better, but if not, I will give you the tomes to give to her, should you free her. They may prove useful."

Optional Quest Received – Master Gretlen has requested that in some way, either by bringing Mona to him, or his knowledge to her, you pass on his teachings. Reward: Unknown, 1,235 EXP.

Will you accept: Yes / No ?

I looked over to Emerald, and she nodded once, so I accepted the quest. The old dwarf smiled and sighed with relief before raising his eyes to us. "I take it you came in here with something in mind?"

I nodded once and pulled out my dented shield. "I came in to see about replacing this. Cecil said we should come here and see you."

Gretlen looked genuinely shocked. "Looks like I owe the boy a flagon for sending you folks over. He's a good lad, means well, but he takes to science more than metal, and I can't have him experimenting in the shop as much as I did when I was a younger lad."

A scientist dwarf? That was interesting. Then again, he *had* blown up a tunnel entry with a bomb, so there was some definitive evidence for it.

"Have you the shield proficiency yet?" I shook my head, and Gretlen frowned, then shook his own head in return. "Then I would suggest going to get beat on in a training circle by a friend of mine for a little while. She can teach you how to block better than anyone in the city."

"Where is she?" He pointed a thumb over his shoulder toward a massive fort that was connected to Belgonna's Hold. "In there?"

"Ask for Veldora; she's a spirited lass and could teach you well." He grinned and chuckled. "Tell her grandpa says to work hard, and she'll know I sent you. Once you have some proficiency with the shield, come back and I can help you out."

I nodded and he held his hand out. "Thank you both for giving an old man hope again. When you return, I'll have those tomes packaged and ready to take away."

I shook his hand firmly, and so did Emerald, before we headed to the large structure. The guards at the entrance saluted me as we passed through and headed for the open yard, where some of the dwarves and a few humans cheered and hollered.

We edged into the crowd slowly and saw a few of the guards inside duking it out with their weapons drawn. Axes clattering against shields, spears whipping through the air at exposed body parts.

"You lower that damned shield again, and I'll drop kick you into the mess hall for a month!" A woman with red mutton chops and a smattering of hair on her chin roared at one of the soldiers fighting in the ring.

She kept her arms crossed as she watched and must have seen something she disliked, because she sprinted into the circle and planted both of her booted feet into another guard's shield, knocking it into his chin and chest and flinging him backward.

"Get your sorry ass to the mess hall, boy!" She grabbed the shield from his grasp and kicked the dirt next to his head angrily. "And *you*!" I thought she was pointing at Emerald and me, but the soldier closest to my left stiffened. "Don't think I didn't see you exchanging coins. You betting against your brothers?"

He shook his head. "No ma'am!"

I snickered, whispering, "Not the one to lie to."

He turned on me and growled, "Shut your gob!"

I raised an eyebrow at him, but he was gone before he could realize who I was, both of the woman's feet planted in his chest violently enough to send him crashing into those slow enough to have not seen her moving.

"You get your sorry ass to the latrines, and I had better see you for extra duties in the morning!" She snarled as she stood up and dusted herself off, then looked up at me. "Oh, hello there. I didn't know we had royal guests, my apologies—Prince Kyvir, right?"

I offered her my hand, and she bent at the waist and kissed my signet ring, throwing me all kinds of off. "Uh, yeah, that'd be me. Do you know where I could find Veldor?"

"Veldora, your highness," she corrected me politely with a small smile before putting a hand on her ample chest. "That'd be me; what can I do for you?"

I opened my mouth to speak, but she held up a hand. "Forgive me." She turned to glare at the soldiers around us. "Does this look like a damn show? Get lost!"

The soldiers around us scrambled away, picking up gear, and some even sprinted off in a random direction.

"I was told to ask you for help with the shield." She turned and regarded me with a look of bewilderment on her face before I added, "Grandpa said to work hard."

She grinned and laughed, "He would, wouldn't he? All right, we have some time still before the feast is supposed to begin, seeing as it isn't noon yet. How much do you know?"

I grimaced and offered, "Put the shield in front of whatever is coming at me?"

She chuckled and shook her head. "That's mighty good policy, Highness. Mighty good. Come on into the circle."

I did as she asked, and she pulled a shield off the wall behind her to give to me. "There's speculation as to whether the shield is necessary, but I'd say there's no finer thing to use. You get good enough with it, you can attack, defend, parry, and mitigate damage to yourself and others as you please."

She pulled out an axe from her inventory and frowned before tossing it out of the circle, opting to pull out a club instead. She nodded to herself and turned her attention to me. "Let's see what you can do with it for this first pass, eh, Highness?"

"I prefer Kyvir," I offered, and she chuckled.

"Then call me ma'am in the circle, and we'll be all set."

I found myself grinning slightly. "Yes ma'am."

Her smile widened as she launched herself at me. I waited until the last second to raise my shield, planting my feet wide like Sundar had shown me, and took the blow head on, careful to protect my head.

As soon as she would have struck the shield, she danced around it and clubbed me in the back of the leg, my knee buckling.

"Ah!" The involuntary shout of pain made me angrier than the pain itself. *Damn you, Mephisto…*

"You hide your eyes, and you hand the enemy the ability to get you from wherever you can't see." She trotted back out in front of me. "Again. Don't duck behind the shield this time, 'kay?"

I nodded, and she came at me once more. This time, I kept my head above the shield. She hit the shield with her club, then punched me solidly in the nose with her other hand.

"Keep your eyes out, but not your whole face, Kyvir." She smiled at me as I checked my nose for blood. "Don't go too high, nor too low—there's a sweet spot."

She lifted the shield so that just my eyes peeked over the edge in a way that didn't completely ruin my field of vision. "This is the spot right here."

"Great, so that should keep me from getting whacked in the face again?" She laughed at me and shook her head. "I didn't think so."

"From most people? Sure. From me, not likely." She chuckled as she backed away and prepared herself for another attack. "Now, try to keep up. I'll start slow."

She did, for the most part; then she would speed up and clock me over top of the head with her free hand. It was an irritating game of cat and mouse that she enjoyed much more than I did. We trained for half an hour before I got the notification that I was now initiate level one with Shield.

"Good work!" She clapped her hands lightly. "We still have some time, and I have some more I could beat into you. What do you say; wanna go for a bit more?"

I checked with Emerald, who nodded. "You go ahead. I need to go and get Zanjir from the kids, since he should be done sleeping by now. He needs work, and he has levels that I need to apply for him as well."

Veldora took that as affirmation and darted closer to me. "Now we go sword and board; a little extra practice never hurt anyone."

I took out my elven sword, and practice began once more.

CHAPTER TWO

SETH

My body hurt all over from the walloping I took in the training circle with Veldora, her ministrations hardly kind.

"She is fair, though," I muttered to myself as I stretched my aching muscles.

Not to mention, I had increased both of my proficiency levels with the sword and shield by one in the ensuing hour and a half brawl.

I turned and walked into the smithy to find Oleg waiting for me with a smile. "Hello, Oleg. I'm here to talk to master Gretlen about that shield?"

He nodded excitedly and motioned me into the workshop portion, where the older dwarf sat speaking with Flicker while she relaxed in the pool of lava like a queen.

"I was wondering why I hadn't gotten my Aether back," I sniffed at her, but she just shrugged while she leaned against the flooring. "Why don't you go home?"

"Because the longer she sits in this lava, the stronger she will grow," Gretlen stated, as if he had heard it a hundred times, and he likely had. "Not to mention, it does an old man good to have a nice young lady around."

I would've blushed at that if I hadn't already known that someone might be hitting on someone else. I knew pretty well that his granddaughter had been hitting on me the entire time I had been training with her.

"Well, I'm initiate level two for the shield now." I had to sound hopeful, because I did want a decent shield. Even with my two best damage dealers gone, I was still responsible for tanking. I just hoped that my summoning would be able to make up for the DPS we were missing.

"Good!" He smiled and stood, walking into the next room with a wave for me to follow along.

He pored over the shields he had on the wall and picked a couple off to hold up in front of me. One was boxy and square, which I didn't care for as much, but it covered the most space. The other was lighter and circular with a bit of a dome to it, but didn't have as much defense.

"The circular one is meant to attack as well," Gretlen offered, pointing to a slight serration along the lip of the item. "They both will allow for a decent shield bash, but that one will slash and, if wielded well, cut wooden hafts with a couple well-placed strikes."

"Then my hands are tied and I'll take it." I smiled at him, and he grinned back.

"Let's get you a better sword, huh?" He tapped the one on my hip and pointed to the others along the wall. "This one is nice and all, but it needs repairs and even a bit of touch up. I have short swords that will do you well, too."

"Can you repair it?" He looked at me oddly, and I pulled the blade from its sheath. "This one holds sentimental value to me. It was a loaner from a friend."

"Aye, I can repair it, then." He grabbed at the air and I passed him the blade hilt first. He smiled appreciatively, and I turned to look at the other blades he had to offer. "The ones on the left, lad. They're of uncommon quality."

I nodded and moved to the left side of the wall and started to pore over the rack of weapons, finally deciding on one of the short swords with a thicker base that tapered up to a boxier tip meant for stabbing and slashing both.

Short sword
Quality: Uncommon
Base dmg: 7-11 dmg
Durability: 15/15
Worth: 2 gold, 3 silver

The damage was only slightly better than my elven sword anyway, but the blade was made of a darker sort of metal that I liked because it was dull in the light. The shield had been a brass color that I didn't truly care for, so I would see if I couldn't dye it a different color at Ophira's.

Gretlen returned after a few more minutes, and I stopped touching swords that could cost more than everything I owned in the game. They wouldn't even relinquish their stats to me, so that was incentive enough to level up my proficiencies.

"Here you go." He held the elven sword out to me, and I took it gratefully. "The shield and sword, with the repairs, will cost you four gold."

"That's with the discount?" I hadn't been going to complain, but I wanted to be sure he wasn't showing too much favoritism. He nodded, and I bowed my head. "Thank you. Would you also happen to have some repair powder?"

"That garbage?" He raised an eyebrow at me angrily. "No. I don't. If you go to a lesser smith or a general goods store, you'll be able to buy it yourself. Don't insult my craft, boy. I know it wasn't intentional, but a true smith and warrior cares for their weapon correctly."

My mouth thinned, and I nodded. "Thank you, I'll keep that in mind."

He didn't say anything as he watched me carefully. I checked the in-game clock and found that it was closing in on time for me to begin getting ready for the feast.

"Thank you so much for your time, Master Gretlen." I

bowed my head once more before looking back up at him. "Those tomes, are they ready?"

He motioned me back into the lobby and patted a stack of four thick leather-bound books that sat on the desk. "Here they are. All of 'em."

I picked them up, glad that I wasn't a complete weakling of a mage like I had planned to be, for once, and put them into my inventory. The set of books only took up one space, since they were a complete set.

"I will do my best to see to it that she comes to see you before they're necessary, Gretlen," I promised. He patted my shoulder solemnly and walked me to the door.

"We're going to be at the feast, so save a drink for me. Eh?" He winked at me, and I smiled as best as I could, thoughts of Mona and her predicament making my stomach twist and pitch.

"Sure," I managed to say. He grinned to himself and whistled as he walked back into the smithy.

I found my way back to the den, mother Belgonna and now-Queen Sinistella having given us rooms within the building to stay safe from any demonic reprisal for our meddling in their affairs and thwarting them.

The room was more lavish than I felt was necessary; likely something my mother would have enjoyed more than I did. The gold and silver in the room shone pristinely in the firelight, the clothes I was expected to wear to the feast laying on the desk with a note.

Kyvir,

As my newly-found son, I would so appreciate you wearing these raiments of black and red, as I feel they will lend you a little flair. I look forward to seeing you, Sundar, and my new friend at the feast.

Love,

Mother.

I didn't touch the clothes, a bath having been drawn for me already. I rinsed myself off as swiftly as I could, soaped myself up, and rinsed again before hopping into the water. It was warm against my skin, and, after a long day of fighting the heat, was welcome. I washed my horns and hair, the water smelling faintly like roses as it pooled around my shoulders. I dunked myself once and came up to find Flicker floating above the water with a seedy grin on her face.

"Woah!" My hands splashed the water over the side of the tub as I covered myself. "Have you never heard of knocking?"

"Don't believe in it, personally, no." She appeared to be glowing radiantly red with Aether, completely unlike anything I had seen, except for when Belgonna used her powers. Or the creepy person in the hood that had summoned the demon. "I wanted to let you know that I will be returning to my plane now to undergo my evolution. Next time you call to me, I might look different, but I'll still come."

"Do you know how long it will take you to evolve?" I turned to look about for a towel to dry off and found none, so I turned to look back at her.

"It should only be a few hours?" She didn't seem certain. "Once I arrive there, it shouldn't be too long here on the mortal plane. I'll be ready by tomorrow. Oh, I cannot *wait* to see the look on Sprinkle's face when I'm bigger than him!"

I found myself shaking my head, "Then get home and get some rest. Tomorrow, we might go bug hunting."

She grinned and burst into a ball of flames that melted away where it floated.

I sighed and got myself out of the bath to look for a towel, and finally found it on the floor just out of eyesight. But I was curious about something.

I focused my intent and willed my Aether to surround me like a warm wind meant to dry my skin.

It worked at first, but as soon as it came toward my head, I worried I might light my hair on fire and couldn't do that.

I dried my head and hair carefully with the towel and dressed myself in front of the mirror in the room that was at least nine feet tall. The clothes looked great on me, as if they had been tailored to my exact measurements.

The pants were a soft almost-velvet on the inside, with a sturdier cloth on the outside, the black belt and red shirt covered by the double-breasted jacket that I wore. It was comfortable and not too tight. The color scheme was less me, but it wasn't gray and drab, so I could take that.

I took a deep breath and made sure that I had my weapons attached properly, elven sword on one hip and my new short sword on the other.

I wasn't sure if it would be that kind of party, but I would rather be ready than not.

The hall was well lit, and I found Emerald standing outside my room waiting for me in a green dress that fit her as snugly as my clothes fit me.

"You look dapper." She nodded at me with a small, matronly smile. "Though I do wish you had a tie for that coat."

"You know I hate ties almost better than anyone else," I growled in her direction, and she just laughed. Rather than open a menu, I queried, "Where are we supposed to go again?"

"The city square is where I was told to go." She shrugged, and off we went out into the main hall and outside of the den entryway. People bustled by us in a rush with plates of food that were massive.

Some carried tables and carted barrels of sweet-smelling mead and beers with food. It slightly turned my stomach to be bombarded by so many scents at once, but I was okay with it for now. Keeping up appearances was important in this kind of social setting, where our standing served to ease our fight to find and retrieve Mona.

People waved to us and smiled, calling out to save a drink or a dance; even with everything that was going on, it was hard to frown and sulk.

Mona would love this, I grumbled to myself tiredly. I'd hardly slept or tried to do anything else since both she and Albarth had gone. It was strange.

Did I have the right of things? Had I been in love with Mona, and that emotion had been stolen from me? I hadn't had the time to talk to Belgonna about it, and I honestly wasn't sure she would tell me the truth anyway.

"Eyes up, Kyvir," A gruff, feminine voice called out loudly.

I glanced up and found Sundar standing above the crowd. Her purple dress clung to her like the shirts a vain bodybuilder might wear and left *nothing* to the imagination as to what her figure was like.

Her avatar's body was muscular and thick, but it was all muscle and femininity as far as the eye could see. Her hair was tied up away from her face and out of her eyes, a few strands artfully posed for an effect that I appreciated.

She grinned at me. "Looking good there, Vlad."

"Seriously? With the vampire jokes and teasing already?" I rolled my eyes, and Emerald snorted.

"It seems fitting, especially seeing as you've taken to impaling the backs of your enemies' heads with your sword." She leaned down a little lower to stare in my eyes. "That's brutal, and I absolutely love it."

I found myself blushing and looked away. "You almost done with that quest?"

She blinked and stood up, craning her neck to find that both Belgonna and Sinistella had joined us with their Talons, the group of dwarves who assisted in the running of Belgonna's Hold and their various infrastructures.

There were only three of them right now, as both Sundar and I had brutally killed one of them, with the queen's blessing, for betraying her. He and another Talon had gotten it into their heads that they needed to return to their roots and kill their dragon rulers and their sympathizers with the demons' aid.

That had been eye opening for the others in the group. Sundar and I had no compunctions about killing him the way we did. But their reactions to me feeding had been what made me self conscious.

No more. This was who I had become, because I was pushed to this, and this power was a gift from the enemy that I could use to protect those important to me. I'd embrace that monstrous side if it meant that I could have some advantage over what was out there.

We received a notification that Sundar's quest had been completed, and the three hundred EXP was super nice. Which reminded me to make sure I was taking care of my leveling and notifications.

Level up!

I'd gotten two levels from killing that demon, and I needed to apply my points appropriately.

Hmmm… think I'll go ahead and put a point into Strength and Skill. That way, I get five more HP too. I opened my status and made the changes.

Kyvir MagebloodLevel: 13 Race: Kin (blooded)
HP: 175
Strength: 12
Skill: 12
Heart: 12
Knowledge: 11
Serenity: 5
Presence: 5
Unspent Stat Points: 0
EXP to next Lvl: 563 / 1300

I stared at it and smiled; that was good. I also had a running status on how many affinities I had and their progress.

Affinities
Fire – 100%
Ice – 100%
Summoning – 100%
Earth – 61%
Demonic – 90%

Thinking about the blood I'd stolen from the summoner, which had been intended to give the demon its strength, made me grimace; it hadn't been the best, but it was potent, for certain. If I hadn't summoned the vial when I had, we would have likely been watching the city get wiped out.

That also left me wondering how many other affinities were

out there, waiting for me to discover them and bend them to my will. That thought made a small smile creep over my face.

Oh, the mayhem I could sew among the demon ranks with something fun like holy Aether.

"Welcome, all of you—my beloved children—to the celebration of our freedom from the tyranny of those traitorous cretins!" Belgonna's voice fell over the gathered souls like a security blanket.

I wonder how high her Presence stat is… it has to be impressive, because they all just hush when she speaks. Then I thought better of it, if only a little. *Could that be a royalty thing?*

"Today, we celebrate our freedom, the blooding of two fine children, and the acceptance of another." Her chin rose as she searched the crowd until she found us. "Ah, yes, come to me, my loves, so that we might all celebrate and mourn with you as a family."

Heat rose in my cheeks as the crowd turned our way, parting and cheering, with flagons of various liquids raised in an impromptu toast to us.

Sundar's grinning face lowered between me and Emerald, whispering, "Smile and wave for now. We can discuss training and whatnot later on. Appearances are what matters in this moment."

"She's right," Emerald muttered and waved to the crowd with an almost regal mannerism.

I just nodded and focused on getting to where I was supposed to be without embarrassing myself or anyone else.

Cheers erupted once more as we moved to Belgonna's side, her brilliant smile making it all the more interesting.

"Our champions have arrived!" Sinistella shouted to the crowd, a burst of dark fireworks exploding above us in various types of shapes and colors. Some looked like dragons, others demons that were dead. It was quite interesting for a celebration, and despite my current conflicting emotions and thoughts, I found myself wondering what kind of dyes or powders they used to achieve such vivid displays.

I'm going to go and see Ophira tomorrow to get this quest off my list, and then train some more.

"Please, let us all stand together so that we can gift our fine heroes before sharing in this wonderful festival of life and togetherness!" Belgonna bellowed and spread her arms as the crowd exploded with furious calls of support.

"First, to my new friend, I will bestow not only my blood, but my scales." A Dwarven man stepped forward with a plate and presented a long large scale carved like a blade resting on it. The hilt was simple but well-made; the light glimmering off the crimson blade made it difficult to focus on anything else.

Emerald lifted the dagger with both hands and appreciated the weight of it before smiling up at Belgonna. "Thank you."

Belgonna nodded once and moved over to Sundar. "My beloved daughter. To you, I gift this mace equipped with the chitinous armor of one of the large beetles that frequent our plains and fields."

The dwarven man who had presented the dagger to Emerald huffed as he hefted the massive weapon to give to the orcish woman, his arms shaking wildly.

Sundar grasped the weapon, slinging the large spiked ball up onto her shoulder with a grunt. "Thank you, Mother."

She bowed her head and kissed Sundar on her forehead affectionately before moving to me. "And finally, to my beloved son, I gift this set of armor made by one of the finest smiths in the land. It may be some time before you can wear it, but it is yours."

The armor was crimson, like her scales, a beautiful full plate set that made my breath catch in my chest as my fingers touched it.

Minimum requirement: Level 20

That's fair, I suppose. My breathing began again as the dwarf carted the armor to the side so the crowd could see us.

"Let the feast...*begin!*" Sinistella roared loudly. The people in the square cheered together as they rushed to long tables full of food and drink.

There was singing and dancing, riotous laughter, and much embellishment on how the demon had been defeated as the dwarves bickered and battled over who had the right of it.

Father Caltross stumbled up to us at some point in the afternoon, drunk as a skunk, and slurred, "You lit have the bleshing of mine god! Yer sho shpecial to heem, and me, and me church. And me."

He beamed up at us and kissed his fingers, tapping me on the cheek, going for the others before twisting too much and falling down. He no sooner landed on his back than he passed out.

"How much did he have?" Emerald eyed him with consternation.

"A pint," a woman said, shaking her head as she came over and grabbed him by the collar of his robes. "Come on, dearie. Gonna get ya home."

We chuckled to ourselves as we watched the dwarven woman drag the holy man off into the crowd.

"I do hope that this all is not too much in this… trying time." Belgonna joined us, all of us having to turn around to look at her. The more than ten-foot-tall, pseudo-elven woman with flaming red hair and beautiful golden eyes watched us intently, almost sheepishly, which was new.

"It seems to me that your people needed it," Emerald sighed, finding a stool and pulling it over to sit. Belgonna took the cue and summoned three more stools to allow all of us to sit together.

"To be truthful, we do too." Sundar ducked her head, then scratched her ear nervously before looking up at us. "We took a serious blow, and I know damn well that it's weighing on you two. Consuming you."

"Does it not consume you?" Emerald quirked her head at Sundar, as if testing the waters.

"Emerald—no." I shook my head and put a hand on her forearm. "You know Sundar is hurting too, and she's handling it the best she can. We all are."

The set of Ma's jaw and Sundar's could have been the foundation for a brand new house, they were so solid. "I hear that you've been hunting goblins in the mines? I trust it has gone well?"

"Very. We've slaughtered many of them," Emerald answered eventually, her gaze shifting from Sundar to the party around us. "Thank you for your gifts, Bel. The dagger is beautiful."

Sundar and I nodded, the former queen's uncertainty replaced by a radiant joy that you could almost see over her whole body. "Excellent. I am only disheartened that I could not assist you more with your friends. Tell me, have you any leads on where you might be able to find Monami?"

I glanced at the others before shaking my head solemnly. Belgonna's frown bled my heart even more, her hand hovering over Emerald's forearm before finally she pulled back, dejected.

"Bel, you can comfort me," Emerald offered softly, holding her hand palm-up for the other woman to take, as if it were the most precious thing she had ever held. "Thank you."

"We're going to find her." Sundar asserted finally. We all glanced her way. "That girl has been what I thought I'd never have. She's like a sister to me, since there's no one from my unit left who gets me, and I will keep my family with me."

I nodded my agreement and patted her shoulder. "Yes, we are. No matter what has to happen."

"Nobody gets left behind," Sundar growled and flared at all of us. "I know I was doing party shit today—no offense, Mother—but I want to find them, too."

"So, what is the plan?" Sinistella joined us, her hand resting on my shoulder lightly.

"We go and take our search to the demons after we level up some more," I answered and crossed my arms. "I've got a personal quest to turn in tomorrow for Ophira. Then I'll be back, and we can start trying to fight some of the insects from the plains."

"An apt plan." Sinistella paused for a moment, then mused

aloud, "I think I shall send the Herd to ensure that you do not bite off more than you can chew. Sometimes, these insects travel in large groups."

"We would appreciate that," Emerald smiled, and I had to admit, that did seem like it would be smart. She turned to Belgonna and squeezed her hand. "When do we do this blooding?"

Belgonna looked a little uncomfortable, and Sinistella gripped my shoulder slightly before answering, "I petitioned my mother to add myself into this portion of your life, Emerald. While you are her dear friend, she will be unable to control herself if she must make a command of you, and thus worries that it could ruin the good will you share, if that were to happen."

Emerald opened her mouth, but it was Belgonna's turn to squeeze her hand lightly, "So in my stead, Sinistella will offer her blood. She is not as powerful as I am, but her blood is unique and strong in its own way. It has much to offer you."

"I carry no qualms against you, nor do I worry that you will hate me for having to obey my commands." Sinistella's smile looked outwardly serene, and I could almost feel the leviathan-like readying of Emerald's ability to hold a grudge rearing its ugly head.

The woman could be a soul of evil if she wanted to be. She had put entire breeding operations in the ground because she felt that the handling and care of their animals was substandard.

Watching that as a kid had been terrifying.

"I appreciate your willingness to assist in this manner, Queen Sinistella." Emerald stood and bowed her head.

"Nonsense!" The new queen surprised me by laughing. "I feel that ours will be a *very* lucrative relationship, and besides, you'll be able to call me Mother, if you so wish it."

Emerald stiffened terribly, her fur rising a bit, but she bit back the retort that might have escaped, and instead, she smiled. "We shall see. What do you require of me for this?"

"Only that you ingest some of my blood, but we needn't leave the party so soon." Sinistella's grip left my shoulder. "The dancing is about to begin all over again. And soon, you all plan to leave. Enjoy the levity while you can."

Her head bowed as she backed up and turned to pull the Talons away with her, their steps receding and fading.

The music took a turn, and both Emerald and Belgonna stood. They excused themselves before walking off toward the den, and left both Sundar and I alone.

We stayed silent as we watched the dwarves and other citizens of the city join together in celebration of a bitter victory over an enemy they hadn't truly known.

"You know that I want to find them both and bring them back, right?" Sundar asked me as quietly as she could over the music and laughter ringing out around us.

I didn't answer, just turned and pulled her closer to me with a nod, and her relief was enough to let me know she was being genuine.

"You're going back to Iradellum tomorrow, but you'll come back right after, won't you?" Sundar's uncertainty drew my attention to her face. She looked… lost.

"Yeah, of course." I pulled her into a side hug and rubbed her shoulder. "You okay?"

She snorted, "Yeah, no, I'm fine." She tried to play it cool, even as the worry and fear filtered back into her eyes. "Just wanted to know what kind of day I should prep for. Oh, I found this for you."

She pulled a small item from her inventory and pressed it into my hand, the small gem-like feel of it catching my attention.

I looked down and saw that it was a monster crystal. I could hardly retain my composure as she gushed at me and spoke in a low tone. "I found this in a large batch of things that were in the den. It was hidden away."

"You *stole* this?" I whispered back harshly. "From the Queen?"

"I *acquired* gear that was clearly being neglected," she corrected me with a steely tone. "And if it will give you a boost to the quest from Ophira, it should be worth it, right?"

I nodded, and she grinned at last, her features returning to their usual chipper mannerisms.

"I can't wait to get back out there and stretch my muscles again." She stretched as she spoke and stood. "I think I'll go find someone to dance with. Unless you want to?"

I shook my head and motioned to my feet. "Sorry, got two left feet, and I'm all thumbs."

She laughed at me and shook her head before turning and wandering into the crowd. There were dwarves who outright ignored her, but some of the others recognized her for her actions and called out to dance with her in a circle. It was very high school.

I stood and wandered away from it all, content to spend my time in the shadows contemplating what needed to be done. This wasn't going to be easy. Nor fun.

CHAPTER THREE

MONA

My heart rate skyrocketed wildly as we ran down an alleyway, then into a rundown-looking warehouse on the other side of the city.

"Come on, honey, almost there," the man implored me. He was tall, broad-shouldered, and looked like he could bench my car, but he had been completely gentle the entire time he had been with me.

It had only been two hours since I had been forcibly logged out of Mephisto's, but in that time, I had learned that Sean had been working with my father on Mephisto's for years before my dad had some sort of "breakthrough" in getting it onto the market, which made him disappear.

He pressed his hand to a piece of the cement building, and something inside the wall clicked softly before the wall lifted, moved back three inches, then slid to the left. "In here; let's go."

He took my hand and pulled me inside before the door closed. Suddenly, the floor shifted, and an elevator-like sensation of going down made me jump.

"It's okay," Sean whispered softly, uncomfortably close, thanks to the small room.

I bit back a smart-ass retort and held my tongue in check. He had promised answers and that he could protect my mom from the demons that would come for me, since I had been taken by one.

How he had known that happened was beyond me, but it had definitely lent him credibility.

After two minutes, we stopped, and the door behind us opened to a large, sterile-looking environment with monitors and equipment everywhere. The place was a high-tech scientist's dream, and sitting at a large monitor watching me was someone I thought I would never see again.

"Hey, Red." My father's soft, almost-sad greeting brought tears to my eyes. Confusion, pain, and years of just not knowing welled up within me.

He stood out of his chair and started toward me. He had been soft around the edges when I had last seen him, but he looked thinner and much more weary now. Bags under his pale hazel eyes, his balding hairline receding faster, as if he'd been pulling his hair out for a while. His already pale skin-tone made him look like a ghost, but seeing him here, after everything…

I blinked, and suddenly I was in his arms, weeping openly, trying to cough out the words and questions burning through my being for years over what had happened to him.

"I know, baby, I know." He comforted me, petting my hair like he had when I would lay my head in his lap and listen to him tell me a story. "There's so much I wish I could tell you, but we have bigger worries on our hands right now, and I need for you to be patient and brave like you have been, okay?"

I pulled back, nearly hiccuping as I tried to regain my composure, but all I could think about was how had he been so close this whole time and stayed away.

As if sensing my question, he grasped my shoulder. "I've been on the run from the devil, Mona. And it hasn't been kind to me, but I've got a plan to give the world a fighting chance. And I'm going to need your help."

"My help?" I sputtered. He just watched me patiently as the writhing emotions, the hurt and betrayal I'd been holding onto since finding out he was gone, welled up within me. "I haven't seen you in years, and the first thing you want to talk about is what *I* can do for *you?*"

"Sweetheart, it's very complicated, and we don't have much time—" he began, but my right fist connected with his shoulder before he could finish.

"How *dare* you steal me from Mom, tranquilize the dogs that you left, and then ask me for my help for *anyone* else!" I was screaming now. Men and women I hadn't realized were in the room turned to look toward us, but I didn't care. "You abandoned us! Mom found out she had cancer recently; did you know that?"

He opened his mouth to answer, bu, I slapped his arm. Sean attempted to pull me away, but I stomped on the top of his foot, making him cry out in pain before I kneed him in the groin and turned back on my father.

"We mourned you; Mom, Seth and I, and here you are living your dream." Bitter tears stung my eyes as I stared at the computers and monitors as they showed images within the game. "Did you ever care about us?"

"Would you stop with your fucking pity party already?" snarled one of the people in the room. I turned to find one of the women in a lab coat walking toward me, all curves and beauty that made me want to lash out at her. "Jesus, we brought you here to protect you, Mona. Two years, I've had to listen to him wax poetic about how much he loves you and your mom— how he misses you, but had to leave to save you. I don't personally see what the big deal is, now that your ungrateful ass is here."

She crossed her arms and stared at me as if daring me to speak again, but my father raised his voice. "Enough!"

He had never yelled before. Even when I was younger, he

had never even so much as shouted at me or Seth. "Mona Lisa, you will have your answers, I swear to you by everything I stand for, but I need you to pay attention! Put your emotions aside and think of someone else for a moment—the world is at stake, and we're about to lose the only shot we have at staying ahead of the demons!"

I frowned at him, observing him carefully to see if he was just saying anything to stop my anger. Watching him huffing and puffing, shoulders rising and falling from the exertion, it looked like he was trying.

"You have ten minutes—scratch that, five—to tell me what the hell is going on." I glared at him, then looked at the woman and sneered, "You can get lost."

"Nah, I'm here to support the doc, and besides, we're already so well acquainted." She grinned and stepped closer to me.

"Fuck off," I growled in warning, but a hand clapped lightly against my cheek, my father glaring back at me.

"Your mother and I frown heavily on you cursing like that, young lady, and you know it." I blinked at him and frowned, but he spoke again before I could. "I made a deal with a devil. Honestly, I just thought he was a businessman, but he told me all about this wondrous system his company was making, and that he needed a game to make it worthwhile. He heard about the game that I had spent your childhood designing."

He turned and led me to a monitor and pulled up a file, then pulled out a slideshow to play, speaking as the screen flickered. "I had a premise that they scrapped and gave me a new one for, but it was the system that made their pulses race. The magic and NPCs and everything, they imported it all. All I had to do was give them a story that they could use in addition to my system, and together, we would create the ultimate game."

The next slide was of a handsome blonde man standing with an almost forgettable-looking man next to my dad. "I found out some time later that the world and NPCs that they ported into the game? Is real. It's a real world."

I went to interrupt him, and he shook his head, "I know. I found it hard to believe myself, but there was no way that I could make all that many non-player characters without one of the single most powerful AIs still not known to mankind. No, those are the souls of living beings in a world that the demons truly wish to conquer, but that world is dying." The next slide showed the core of the planet rotting from the inside. "Once it is dead, the demons will cease to have a viable source of food and die out."

"Okay, so all we have to do is pull people out of the game and it should be fine, right?" I crossed my arms, confused at what the big deal was.

"You'd think that, but the demons had a plan," the woman added, nodding for my father to switch the slides. This one showed one of the portal pods. "They figured out a way to terraform our planet with their source of magic, Aether. And they're doing something called the Merger."

"So we can stop it, right?" My breath caught as my father's frown deepened, and he shook his head. "Why not? You designed the game: you could force level someone up and drop the equivalent of a magical nuke on them in the game, couldn't you?"

"If it was that simple, we'd have done it, kid," Sean grunted and limped forward.

"The update they have planned for Thursday is to shut us and our equipment out." My father skipped a page in the slideshow and I frowned as the slide read *end*. "If they succeed in kicking us out of the game, then the humans will have to take months and months to learn how to harness and control Aether so that they have a fighting chance against the demons after the Merger. We'll have no way to track their movements and keep them in check, much less staying ahead of them and keeping certain people away from Mephisto and his cronies."

"So then what can I do?" My head was still reeling from the info dump, but it seemed pretty screwed to me.

"What can *we* do," the woman corrected me with a grin.

"That succubus you met in-game, she's taken you under her wing, and as such, you'll be getting closer to the demons than anyone else. Aside from the succubus herself."

"What's that supposed to mean?" I frowned at her, and she shook her head.

"Lira is the Succubus who tempted you in the game, Mona." My father's voice was soft, but clear. "We've figured out a way to make avatars that are demonic and have infiltrated their ranks. They know that we're tricking them somehow, so they don't know how we're doing it yet, but with you and Lira working together, you will be able to impose a patch code in the demons' lines."

I wanted to comment, but didn't get the chance as dad shot a look at me.

"Once the update begins, that line of code will allow us a backdoor into the system that will keep us on the inside," Sean finished, hands still cupping himself as he looked to my father. "Has she always been this brutal?"

"That's come about since he's been gone." I sniffed and raised my chin defiantly. "How are we supposed to do this? I'm a player; the demons will eat me alive."

"Not with a demon whose wing you're under present to assist you." Lira smiled smugly with her arms crossed under her breasts. "Besides, they've been taking in recruits from the players and...possessing them since day one."

I blinked at her, and she nodded. "The people you've seen attacking the elderly, children, and the infirm are in fact demons sent to cull some of the population for the Merger and to bolster the ranks."

"Do they really *possess* people?" My voice was a hoarse whisper.

"They do," my father confirmed solemnly. "If you had found any other demon who had come to that city, you would have likely been possessed on the spot, and your mother would have been killed to get to me."

"So this is all your fault." Not a question from me, a statement of the facts presented so far.

"Yes." His simple answer left me shocked. "I left to make it seem like I didn't care about you all, you, your mother, and Seth, so that they couldn't use you against me, but they're already trying."

"How do you mean?" Was Seth in danger? My pulse quickened again at the surge of uncertainty and anguish that his rejection of me had brought on.

"Mephisto has taken a special interest in Seth, and we don't know why," Lira answered, her smile turning into a thin-lipped frown. "He's put out the order that Seth is not to be trifled with and is to be killed on sight if he can't be converted to our cause. Then again, he's to be killed anyway, because the boy is that much more fun for Mephisto to play with."

"Was that the demon that you made the deal with?" My father nodded, guilt settling on his face. "Could it be because he knows you love him like a son?"

"It could be. However, Seth is resilient, for certain; he will be okay."

"I have to help him." I crossed my arms, and Sean shook his head. "You don't get to tell me what to do, meathead."

"Ouch, name calling hurts, honey." The man frowned and clicked his tongue at me. "If you're allowed to go back to him without being possessed, you'll blow our cover, and we won't be able to help anyone at all. At least this way, we give the world a fighting chance."

"So you're saying I can't go back to the group?" They nodded slowly. "Then I have to tell him that I'm okay."

"Nope." Lira stepped forward once more and shook her head. "They all have to believe you've turned—by the way, breaking that summoning circle with your heel? Genius work, kid. I like that. It's for their safety and everyone else's that we have to have them pursue you. That means no contact, no messages, whispers, or group invites, and sure as hell no booty calls."

Anger rose and fell again, and now it was dad's turn to glare at the woman, who just shrugged as if she didn't care. "Seriously. I'm not risking anything, so buckle up, girly, 'cause this ride is going to get rough."

"What makes you think I'm on board?" I growled after catching myself wondering about Seth again. "And I still have more questions."

"Because if you agree to help us, we can continue answering your questions, instead of locking you away in a deep, dark hole where you won't fuck up our plans." Lira leaned forward and glared into my eyes from a foot or so away.

"Language!" My father barked, making us both flinch. "Enough of this strutting and posturing like animals. Lira, go log in and prepare to have your butt chewed for your failure. It won't be so bad, since you've brought back a prize like Mona, but be ready."

She shrugged and turned to walk away without so much as a backward glance at any of us.

"Mona, you'll need to log in soon, too." I was going to say something snarky, but my dad just shot me a withering glare. "I know you're angry and hurt—you have every right to be, and to hate me—but I know your mother and I raised you better than this. Will you help us save as many lives as we can?"

The question was simple, but the answer was nowhere near so. That was a huge amount to put on a person's shoulders at the best of times, let alone on someone who'd just basically been dumped by their first love. I wanted to lash out. I was so close to doing so. But I had to know something first.

"I have to know." I took a deep breath and stared my dad in the eyes as I asked, "Does awakening Aether really take something from you?"

He stilled and blinked, looking away. "That was a gimmick that Mephisto said made the magic more believable. Giving up something equally as important to the player as the magic was powerful. At first, I was told it would be a potential loss in money, gear, a mandatory quest, or a compulsion to fight something."

His hands worked through his thinning hair as he collapsed into the chair behind him. "Then I saw one of the alpha testers acquire a rare magic that took the memory of his mother away from him. He would stare at a photo of him, his dad, and his mom and just ask who the woman was."

Horror gripped my heart, the blood in my ears suddenly so loud, it took everything I had to remain standing as he continued, "She had died a year before the test, after having raised him on her own once his father had passed when he was young."

So Seth hadn't been lying, and Belgonna did *take away something important to him.* I began shaking as I stepped closer to my dad. "Can you get those memories back? Can you reclaim what you lost?"

"I don't know." His frustration at that answer, bleeding into his mannerisms, spoke volumes. "We've been working on that as well. And we could use the help."

I nodded and decided then and there, "I'm in. Where do I go and log in?"

CHAPTER FOUR

SETH

Grasp the stone and think of where you wish to go that you've been before, I reminded myself as I held the small stone in my hand. This was the upgraded version that Sinistella had given us, and it was much easier to use than the other one.

To look at it, it didn't really seem to be all that special, but the rune carved into the surface, which had been inlaid with silver and red, glowed as I envisioned the street outside Ophira's shop.

I blinked, and a reddish flash of energy surrounded me. Before I knew it, I stood in front of To Dye For.

I blinked, lifting the stone to my face with a start. "Wha— how? What?"

"Kyvir?" I turned to see Ophira, blinking at me in shock from inside the doorway. "How did you get there so fast? I blinked, and you were standing there. You weren't there before."

"I, uh, got a reward for helping out some folks, and it's

pretty awesome?" I smiled at her as she rushed out toward me, pulling me into the shop and closing the door. "What's wrong?"

"You can't just appear like that here, Kyvir," she hissed, looking outside, then locking the door. "That stone, is it right?" I nodded at her, and she shook her head. "You guard that thing. It's very expensive, and someone will steal it if they can."

"Thanks for the advice." I inventoried the stone, then pulled out one of the monster crystals and held it out to her. "Ready to experiment?"

She squealed loudly before pouncing on the item, taking it into her hands and pulling it close to her chest. "Where did you find this?"

"This one? From a goblin." She grimaced, but stared at it in wonder. "So, what do we do now?"

"We make some dye, of course!" She grinned and motioned me over to her counter. The countless hues of all the dyes, phials, vials, and powders around us made me feel more at peace than I had since Mona had left, and I knew I'd likely leave today with some awesome new colors if I could.

She set the core on the counter and pulled out a mortar and pestle to put it in. Muttering something to herself, she began to crush the core until it was powder, then pulled out a small, thin vial of a bluish solvent that I didn't recognize.

"What's that?"

"This is a more powerful solvent that I haven't been able to use before." Her grin was infectious as she unstopped the vial and poured the liquid in.

Once the powder was covered, she set the vial aside and stood back before turning and bum rushing me.

"Ah!" Her arms wrapped around my neck in a fierce hug, her entire body pressing against mine. "What?"

"Thank you so much, Kyvir," she groaned as her hug tightened slightly. "You could have sold that for a lot of gold, but you really brought it to me."

I smiled at that and patted her back awkwardly, my other

hand reaching into my inventory to pull out the other. "Money isn't my concern right now. How about this one?"

She stiffened, her arms loosening so that she could look over at my left hand in shock. She lifted her eyes up to me with her mouth opened wide. "Is that what I think it is?"

"Another monster crystal? Yes." I nodded once, and suddenly her mouth was on mine. "Mmm!"

I fell back a step, my balance completely thrown, then stumbled over something on the floor. I teetered, then tipped onto my butt, with her falling on top of me.

My mouth was free now. "What was that for?"

"You brought me *two cores*, Kyvir!" she gushed, her hands on my chest as tears welled up in her eyes. "You're so committed to this that it's hard to believe! I'm so sorry I attacked you, but I just thought that… well, I was so shocked that I could have just kissed you, and my body moved on its own. I was overwhelmed."

"Tell me about it." I blinked, my lips still tingling and my heart aflutter. I laughed a little more awkwardly than I meant to as she sat up and took the small item from my hand.

She stood carefully and dusted herself off as the light from the many colorful stained windows bathed her in colors so vivid and beautiful that it only added to her bewitching looks. *Should I feel bad?*

Her radiant blue eyes sparkled as she beheld the core, her button nose crinkling excitedly as her long canines flashed in a smile. The glowing beams of color played over her skin in waves that shifted and danced as she moved. Finally, she realized I was staring at her, and her cheeks darkened. "I truly am sorry for being so, uh, excitable."

"Apology accepted, though I would love to help with this one." She leaned down, her multi-colored dress dipping low. I kept my eyes on hers as she offered me a hand.

"I'd love that." She grasped my hand in her smaller one and helped pull me up. She set another mortar in front of me, wiping the residue out of it. "Here you go. You crush it, and I'll add the solvent. That way, you'll still receive some of the crafting experience for it. And of course, that quest will be complete, as well."

I nodded excitedly and ground the crystalline object into as fine a powder as I could make. She pointed out some larger chunks that I dutifully crushed as she prepared the solvent.

"Here, give me your hand." She held her hand out and took mine. She grasped the vial in two fingers, then helped me pour it into the small bowl.

It was enough contact to warm my cheeks again, and with how close she was, it wasn't easy to focus. *Seriously, I should feel bad; why don't I?*

"There! And now we wait." She grinned again and crossed her arms. "I see you're sporting a newer, more colorful aesthetic. What happened?"

I went to tell her about Belgonna, and a notification appeared.

Those who do not know of her cannot know of her draconic nature. This is the law of all of Belgonna's children. Be careful what you say.

"The queen that I went to see rewarded me and Sundar with a special thing I can't talk about, but now, I look like this." I suddenly found myself feeling self conscious. "Is it bad?"

"Red suits you." She smiled at me widely and hopped up onto her counter so that she could sit. "Tell me, have you been keeping up with your dye-making?"

"Not as much as I originally planned; some things have been going on that have required my whole attention." I rubbed my head and sighed deeply before telling her everything that I could without violating that rule.

The entire time, she listened intently, though news of demons trying to take over a city did startle her. "So you stopped them?"

I nodded, and she frowned, "And that cute young lady and the nymph are no longer a part of your party?"

"She was taken by the demons, and he went to look for her on his own."

Ophira dropped off the table carefully, pulling me toward her gently, and gave me a hug. "I am sorry, Kyvir."

I hugged her back, muttering, "You were never this hands-on before."

She leaned back and stared me directly in the eyes as her teeth flashed. "A lady appreciates gifts, and when a man shows that he is committed."

I snorted, and she winked at me, reminding me of Sundar a little. She turned and checked the first dye that we had made. "Oh my! Come and look at this!"

I went over to her and looked inside the bowl to find a darker green, almost goblinoid-type color forming. "This is interesting."

"You killed a goblin for this one?" I nodded, and she lowered her head to look at it from another angle. "That color is very much indicative of their race. I wonder what it will do?"

"You don't know?" She shook her head and shrugged. "I mean, it's a dye, right? So all it does is give the color."

"Yes and no." Her eyebrows scrunched up in thought before finally, she said, "The core of a monster encompasses their experiences and the Aether within them. Not all of them are the same, but it is generally close. The color will be the same, but with that solvent that I added, the Aether within *should* also be brought to the fore."

"So not only will it dye whatever you use it on, but it will make it—what—magical?" My skepticism was met with an excited nod that made me pause. "What are the chances of it working?"

"With my level and experience?" She grinned widely. "High."

We waited and watched the dye forming, and as it did, small brown flecks began to form inside it. "That has to be the Aether." I was sure of it, but she looked at me with a raised green brow. "Goblins have earth Aether."

"Oh," she frowned thoughtfully. "Interesting. Did you fight many of them?"

I ate quite a few, I mentally muttered as I nodded wordlessly.

It wasn't long before it settled completely, and she poured the contents into a large crystal vial. The green and brown of the liquid inside was interesting, but it was the distinct earthy aura that it exuded that interested me more.

"Here." She handed me the vial and smiled. "You get to test it out for me and report your findings."

"You don't want to try it on any old thing?" She shook her head, and I frowned at her. "Why?"

"Because this was something *you* brought me, so *you* should be the one who reaps the benefits." Her easy smile and delight at my confusion just made me even more uneasy taking it. "Seriously, use it for yourself, and just tell me what happens."

"Okay." I shrugged, thinking about it for a moment. The earthen nature of the vial made me wonder… "Let me try something."

I pulled my shield out and thought once more, *Will this be okay?*

"I can buy another, if necessary," I assured myself and poured the liquid onto the metal item.

As soon as the dye touched the shield, the metal darkened, thickening and turning green with flecks of brown, the brown portions slowly growing larger until the shield almost resembled a turtle shell, the sharpened edges still serrated and sharp, but green like a goblin's skin.

"Fascinating!" Ophira hissed and lowered her eyes to the other bowl, frowning deeply. "Oh my gods."

I turned my attention from the shield, my eyes widening as I observed a metallic golden hue within the other dye.

"What the hell kind of creature was this?" Her face rose from the bowl, and I stared back at her in shock. "Kyvir, what was it?"

"I have no idea!" I asserted softly. "Sundar brought it to me because she found it and thought I could use it for this quest."

"This is unheard of!" She stirred the concoction carefully and frowned as the small spoon melted and added itself to the liquid. "Oh, this is bad."

She turned and escaped into the back room, crashing sounds and grunting coming from her as she moved.

"Ophira, am I going to die?" I stilled, staring at the liquid that began to bubble and seethe.

"Don't touch it!" Another loud banging cacophony of something falling rang out from the back as the disheveled woman reappeared with a box in her hands. "Don't you touch it."

The glint in her eyes was enough to give me pause as she advanced carefully from the doorway and opened the box. A mist-like substance filtered out of it, then solidified, until a sort of salamander that took up the majority of the room stood towering over us both.

"Kyvir, my familiar, Jenkins. Jenks, my friend and apprentice, Kyvir." The salamander eyed me, then looked back at her and waited. "I need you to smell this and tell me what sort of creature it came from."

The large animal rolled his eyes, and she hissed at him, "Fine, I'll let you out more, but only if you agree to stop eating my work and scaring away customers!"

The salamander's tail flicked toward the ceiling and he stared longer, "I swear to every god listening that if you don't do as I say, I will summon your father and tell him about the time you ate your sister's tail—not once, but twice. Smell it!"

The massive creature hissed and growled but acquiesced, leaning forward to scent the liquid, his tongue flickering out like a snake's over the nearly-boiling mass.

He sat rigid, panic flickering into his eyes as he looked about, then pawed at the box incessantly, as if to be let back in. His tail thrashed over my head and nearly knocked over pastel hues of primary colors as he hissed and tried to get away.

"That can't be right; there hasn't been a sighting of a gold in more than five hundred years!" Ophira insisted as she opened the box but pulled it away, eyeing him carefully. "You are sure you smelled it right?"

The thrashing tail behind her familiar thumped violently, and powder lifted into the air like a colorful bomb had just burst. "Get in there, you messy thing!"

The salamander filtered away again, and she huffed as she turned to the liquid and produced a jet black vial with a silvered stopper.

She carefully set it on the table, the flat bottom helping it to stay steady as she used tongs to lift the bowl, and upended the contents into the receptacle.

"I don't know what the hell happened, but that was the monster crystal of a gold dragon of some power." Ophira stoppered the lid and wiped her forehead with her sleeve. "Whatever it is, I do not want it in this shop, and you and I will never speak of it again."

I blinked at her and finally got up the courage to ask, "Why?"

Her gaze wasn't hard out of anger, but more worry. "Gold dragons are rare, as you heard me say. To have any part of them is to consign yourself to being hunted by those who would have their power for themselves, the silver dragons."

"So having this dye will make me a target?" She nodded her head. "To silver dragons?"

"Yes." She clutched herself and shivered at the thought. "The gold were the rightful rulers of the dragons. Their lustrous scales and power were a source of guidance to all creatures of sentience, their will that of balance and law. The second most powerful dragons, the silver dragons' avarice and vanity caused them to lash out at their rulers with the aid of the lesser chromatic dragons."

"That's what started the dragon war?" Another nod and shiver. "But I don't understand; what would the silvers gain by killing their leaders if they were…second. They wanted to rule."

"And for a time, they did, but the chromatic dragons took

much of the power of the golds they slaughtered." She slid the vial toward me. "And hunted the silvers into hiding. They work from the shadows and search for powerful prey and remnants of the golds who ruled before them."

I took the vial and reached into my inventory, but she shook her head, "Simply take it and speak to no one of it if you can."

"Do we have any idea what it could do?"

A pensiveness fell over her as she let her gaze fall on the shield. "If it's anything like the other one, this will be some kind of way to enchant whatever it dyes. This is almost unheard of, Kyvir. We tread dangerous waters as it is, but if we could figure out a way to make this more often, then we could turn enchanting on its head! Think of the colors!"

"The profit would help, too, and the power!" I grinned at her, and her smile turned sour. "Think of all the different shades we could find and experiment with if we had money and clout!"

Her smile brightened again, and I sighed in relief. I doubted I could afford paying an enchanter to work on my weapons, and if this was an easier way to do it, then it was what was necessary.

"I knew you were the right one to teach!" She pointed to the vial in my grasp. "Use it or lose it or sell it—whatever you do, I do not want to see it again if I do not have to."

"Yes, Ophira." I put it into my inventory, and she pulled me into a hug. "Hello, again."

She grinned next to my face. "We've made a massive discovery, Kyvir." She put both of her hands on my face. "I've reached master in my profession from just these two things. I could not have done so without you; thank you. What can I do for you in return?"

"Continuing to teach me would be awesome." I grinned as notifications populated in the corner of my HUD. "Other than that, I don't know."

"I do." She smiled and kissed me again, slowly, which made my heart race faster and faster. Finally, she stopped, and I could breathe again. Her smile grew to a grin. "I'll keep teaching you, and we will make many colors together."

"We sure will." I fixed her with a placating smile, the confusion roiling in my head and heart more than a little annoying.

Ophira was a beautiful woman, powerful and prestigious enough that her attention would focus well. Especially with the powerful dyes we could make.

But then there was Thea, her wild and carefree antics fun and exhilarating, and she had been the first one here, other than Trickle, to make me feel truly welcome.

As Mona would say, "It's a game, Seth. These are just computer codes done well. Stop pining over them and move on." Her voice sounded so crystal-clear in my head. *Not to mention the fact that she claimed that you loved her and she loved you back. As if all of this wasn't confusing enough as it was.*

I shook my head as the confusion took over, then sighed heavily as Ophira cleared her throat expectantly. I glanced up to see her concerned eyes watching me. "Don't worry, just some rampant thoughts and other stuff the party is going through. I'll take this stuff and get out of your way. And of course,"—she paused as she was about to speak—"I'll be bringing more cores, if I can find them."

She nodded once and winked at me as I turned to leave. Once I was outside on the street, the draconic dye safely deposited in my inventory, I opened some of the notifications I had received.

Optional Quest Complete – Ophira has imparted a trade secret to you that she hasn't even tried yet in using monster crystals to create dyes. You brought her one to see what happened. No failure condition.

Reward: Increased renown with Ophira, three times profession experience for participating in making a new type of dye, title: Dying One and unknown.

Ongoing quest unlocked – Ophira has asked that you bring more monster crystals to her for dye

making. Reward: Increased profession experience, more renown, other possible rewards.

Quest already accepted.

I blinked at that and frowned, but shrugged and moved on.

Profession: Dye Making

Level: 10 (Basic)

Oh, that's cool! I smiled to myself and looked through everything else.

New brand of enchanting found! As one of the finders, you've been given a special reward: Dye Separation.

Dye Separation – So long as you applied the dye, and still have the original container, you can remove and reuse the dyes you use for an item up to three times. After the third removal, the dye becomes permanent and can no longer be removed.

That was really something too! Maybe I would try it on one of my swords?

I pulled out the new short sword and the jet black vial, splashing the contents on it.

There was a muted flash, then a sort of excitement thrilled through me as a disembodied voice exclaimed, "What in the blazes is this? Who are you? Where am I?"

I turned my head this way and that, searching for the voice's origin, but found nothing.

Until I looked down at the now-golden blade of the sword in my hand.

"Why is there a giant holding me as if I were some sort of…"

I swallowed past the lump in my throat, finishing, "Sword?"

CHAPTER FIVE

SETH

Relax, Seth, you're just in an alleyway with a talking sword; no big deal. I took a few more deep breaths and looked at the weapon once more. "Listen, I know this is hard to believe, but I didn't know that this would happen."

"Do you honestly not think I know that, mortal?" the sword hissed vehemently, vibrating in my hands. "You cannot lie to a gold dragon. I knew from the start that you knew nothing of what you were doing—why do you smell so familiar?"

I blinked at him, and he just growled, "Answer me!"

"I don't know!" I cried. People at the end of the alley turned to look at me, then hurried away, clutching their belongings and children. I lowered my voice to a hiss. "I don't know, okay? I know Belgonna and Sinistella, and Belgonna blooded me."

The sword was quiet for a time, to the point that I worried I was delusional, when finally, the dragon's voice quested, "You were blooded by my mate?"

"Belgonna was your mate?" I wheezed, unable to fully comprehend the level of shit that I would be in if she ever found out about what had happened. Oh my god, she would kill us all. Her revenge would be unimaginable.

"Child?"

I came back from my mild panic attack and gulped, "Yes?"

"I see you worry of the repercussions of this." His low baritone chuckle made me frown. "Fret not; she and I have not spoken since she fled with the majority of my hoard and the eggs from our clutch."

"Then how come she had your crystal?"

"Dragons can divulge their crystal when they are old enough and fear that another will grow stronger for having consumed it." His voice took on a tutorial-like tone, "This was common practice during the dragon war. I hid mine in my hoard so that my mate or my clutch might find it and gain my insight or guidance."

"I can imagine that me finding it was hardly what you meant to happen." I sighed, and a sort of calming sensation emitted from the weapon.

"At least you did not eat me," he admitted. "And since you are Belgonna's child, I suppose that could mean that you are mine as well. Though did you have to put me into such a *weak* sword?"

"I can take you out of a weapon two times, and on the third, you remain there permanently, so I can upgrade your body, or something, I suppose." I could almost sense a frown coming from him. "Or I can try something different, if you want?"

"I am no sorcerer, and this sort of thing is outside my realm of understanding." He huffed and finally added, "Leave me for now. I will guide you if I can, and we shall see what we can make of a young dragonling such as yourself."

"Thank you." I found myself smiling and cleared my throat. "My name is Kyvir; what is yours?"

"No, it is not," he growled, and I blinked, fully realizing he took me telling him that name as a lie.

"On this planet, I go by Kyvir. That is, for all intents and purposes, this body's name." I amended.

A sharp inhale greeted me. "Traveler? Your kind have come at last?"

"Yes, we have, and I am one of them." I sighed and continued quietly, "Things are going to get weird, and I could definitely use some guidance."

"Very well; go to the guild hall," he ordered, much to my surprise. "I do believe you meet the criteria to select a job, if I have the correct feel of you."

"A job?" I raised an eyebrow, trying to recall what that was, since I knew I'd heard it before.

"It is a sort of specialization which adventurers can take upon themselves that will give them unique bonuses and abilities in a fight; not to be confused with a profession." His explanation left much to be desired, but poking and prodding him for more information proved moot.

I made my way to the adventurer's guild, marching through the throngs of players outside still hawking wares, goods, and sending party invites, to the front desk, where I found a large man with orcish features smiling at me in a more than friendly manner.

"Hallo, fren," he greeted me warmly, his enthusiasm making me grin despite my curiosity. "How can Frito help you?"

"Hi there, I wanted to see about selecting a job?" He nodded and reached out his hand. "Yes?"

"Give hand pwease?" He blinked at me, and I gave over my right hand. He set it carefully and gently on the white slate on the counter, and a screen popped into view. "Make choices, let know. I update guildy-thing when done."

He leaned back, clearly pleased with himself, as someone in the rear watched him apprehensively. I couldn't make out exactly who they were, as they hid behind a curtain with one eye peeking through carefully.

I glanced through the choices I had.

Soldier

Knight
Scout
Warlock
Paladin*

The one with the asterisk made me pause, I tapped it and read over the description.

Paladin – A warrior of great power and potential, you've gained the favor of the gods, or their disdain, and have been granted a small blessing.

Requirements: Initiate level with sword and shield, blessing of a holy figure, decide upon a path.

All requirements met.

Optional requirements met: Attention from a dark figure, ruthless murder, ingesting blood of the fallen.

Optional requirements open an alternative job path. Would you like to take it?

"What the hell does this mean?" I asked more for myself more than anything. *It can't hurt, right?*

I selected yes, and blinked as another notification populated on my screen.

Congratulations, you have selected the job of Dark Paladin.

But what does it do? I thought to myself.

Looking at it, it stood to reason that a dark paladin would do whatever the hell they wanted.

Dark Paladin – This Warrior has taken for themselves more than they've given for their gods or their followings, and will continue to do so until their goals are achieved.

"What's the point in taking a job, again?" I looked up at the large orc, who seemed interested and thoughtful for a moment.

"Some jobs give skills, abilities, and sometimes other powers, depending on what they are." The figure behind Frito answered, their voice light and informative, but I still couldn't tell who they were.

I looked and couldn't figure out what they could be. "Is there a way to see, so that you can make the best choice?"

The portion of mouth that I could see quirked up at the corner. "It's expensive to change jobs, since you have to select one in order to see what skills and abilities they offer. Besides, I think you already know what job you'll be selecting to try first."

A chill ran down my spine as I tried to see who was speaking, but as I came closer, they stepped back, laughing, and were gone. I peered up at the smiling Frito nervously. "Who was that?"

"Frito don't know. Said give Frito job if he nice and smart." He scratched his head and smiled. "Frito be good, yeah?"

"Uh, yeah, Frito—thanks." I frowned and wondered if it was the right thing to have selected Dark Paladin as my job, but it was too late now.

"Okay! Frito update thingy thing and…" he frowned and tapped the slate before me, and something happened that made his chipper attitude come back. "There! Dork Paladin is it!"

I snorted at him and tried not to laugh, as he had tried his hardest. "Thank you, Frito. Good job."

"Good luck, mister!" He turned to the person behind me and grinned broadly before bellowing—unnecessarily—"Next for Frito serve!"

I flinched along with every person in the building and just got out of there as swiftly as I could.

I opened my status screen, happy to see that a job tab had been added to my repertoire. Selecting it showed me some interesting tidbits, like a new ability that I had.

Lay of Hands – This can be for good or for ill, depending on the caster's desires. Either siphon health up to the caster's Serenity (5) or heal up to the same amount for any target you touch. No cool down. Only effective per single touch.

Wrathful Smite – Adds fell damage to your next attack, augmented by the amount of Aether spent

since activation. Cool down: 2 minutes. Requirement: Must be made with a melee attack.

That was new. Did that mean if I activated the ability, then spent a ton of Aether, I'd do more damage?

I'd have to test that out. Looking again, I noticed that the job could grow with me, the same growth system as the weapons and skills having been added to it. I was at initiate with it so far, but I wondered what would happen if I got the job to master status.

I grinned as I walked out of the city near the guild and made my way around the stone wall. I used my stone to teleport back to Belgonna's Hold, appearing outside of the den entrance, hoping that it would be okay with my status.

The guards bristled and lowered their weapons, my gaze even as they realized who I was. "Thanks." *Better take a little more cautious stance on that.*

I walked in, checking around to see if I could find anyone, when I heard familiar voices coming from the throne room.

I opened the door wide, finding Sundar standing with Belgonna and Sinistella as they stood next to a small, glowing aura that was so bright, my vision spotted immediately. My eyes instinctively narrowed so that I could still see. "What's going on?"

"She returns from her metamorphosis; the beautiful butter-fly, she shall be." Sinistella glowed the same color as the aura did, but I could actually stand to look at her. "Where have you been, little brother?"

"Collecting my job." I turned to Sundar and winked. "You should get yourself one too, now that we probably qualify for the better ones. Emerald, as well."

"We can go after this." She nodded to the golden energy, which had begun to die down.

I sighed and turned to Belgonna, deciding that I couldn't afford ill will by lying to her, overtly or by omission.

"Mother." She lifted her head immediately and glanced my

way as I motioned her to me. Her head tilted to the side, but she joined me.

"Yes, my love?" Her concern bled into her beautiful features, her eyes intent, and I could tell that she was searching my mind.

I drew my blade and held it in both hands, then allowed the blade to sit on my left palm as I held it out toward her. "There's been an accident."

"Accident? This is beautiful." She touched the blade, her lips curling at the corners in a smile that one might expect of a dragon seeing gold. Her fingertips settled on the blade and her smile faded to a longing so deep, my heart fell to my feet. "It is beautiful, indeed. My mate, Oranthus; you've found him? Where? How?"

"We found a monster crystal when Sundar was helping set up for the feast, and she gave it to me because I had a quest." My head hung, despite the dragon in the blade having offered to help me. "I didn't know—*we* didn't know. I'm sorry."

"I know." She touched my cheek absently. "It has been… long since I have spoken to him. And much the same way that he gave of himself in his crystal, I too shall do the same. I did not know that this was possible."

"Neither did I or my master." I shrugged, and she held a hand up to her mouth to suppress a small smile.

"He wishes to stay with you, but if I might, I would like to introduce him to Sinistella." It was less a request and more that she expected it, and I just acquiesced.

She turned and carried the weapon to her daughter, who took it and scowled, until her eyes widened in shock. Her mouth opened and closed, the normally quick-witted and intelligent new queen floundering for words.

"I know." Belgonna kissed the queen's forehead and held her close. "I'm certain that Kyvir will allow you the afternoon with him, if you ask nicely?"

I went to speak, and she threw me an intense glare that

made me pause long enough for Sinistella to look at me and ask, "Please, Kyvir?"

I didn't trust myself with words as I stared into the raw pain plastered on her face, so I nodded and looked away.

Sinistella turned and began to walk away, then looked back at Belgonna as she stood behind her. "My apologies for not being able to greet her."

Belgonna tilted her head once, and the queen exited the room. It wasn't that there was an oppressive weight against me, or anyone else in the room at the time, it was just the oppression of silent longing building in the air.

Familiar longing ached in my chest, for there to be a return to some kind of normalcy. The gold dragon had been a mate, a father—never having gotten the chance to meet his children before he fell. And here I was doubting myself and wondering if I would ever see a friend again.

I closed my eyes as an emotion I didn't recognize washed over me. I couldn't place it, and the fact that it was so unfamiliar filled me with rage.

My hunger grew with the emotion, and then, as quickly as it had come, it left. In its wake was the monster, ready to consume once more.

I opened my eyes, Sundar and Belgonna standing close, the larger woman hugging her reddish-green daughter and reassuring her.

The blinding light flashed brighter, and then left the room dark. Golden-furred and still glowing slightly, Emerald stood and stretched herself out. She looked like she had been dunked in gold and pulled out to dry, with flecks of crimson scattered over her.

She searched the room, then Belgonna stepped forward. "Due to…unforeseen circumstances, Sinistella had to take some time to herself. I'm certain that she will return and speak with you as soon as she can; for now, take today to train and prepare yourselves for your journey."

I bowed my head with Sundar and turned to leave, walking

to the door, before I glanced back and found Emerald hugging Belgonna as her shoulders shook.

My shoulders hung despite having been able to do nothing about any of that, because I was too good for my own good sometimes, and I headed out the door. Sundar joined me, her mood a little morose as well.

"You okay with her?" She nodded at me, and I sighed. "I didn't mean to rat on you."

She shook her head and smacked my arm, "She said it was an easy mistake to make and didn't blame me. The worst part was that she was sad, and there was nothing I could do."

I understood how that could be. I had been in a similar position with Mona most of my life, but it had been the worst when her dad had left. I growled softly to myself as I tried to eject the painful memories from my head. It seemed that whenever I thought of her, or a memory we shared, I was forced to see it through some kind of film, and it made my head ache fiercely.

"It'll be all right, Sunny. She's more than a thousand years old—she's a big girl and can deal with it on her own, in her own time." My efforts to comfort her just made her face sour a bit more before she let out a tremendous sigh and grinned to herself. "See? There you go!"

"Fake it til you make it, Kyvir; the army taught me that." She patted me on the shoulder sagely. "If morale is low, the gods and staff NCOs take it on themselves to keep the beatings coming until it does improve. I don't want anymore beatings coming from anyone but me."

I chuckled at that. "Sounds fair."

Closing my eyes, I called to Flicker and Sprinkle. My summoning Aether and a single bar of each fled from me as the two of them joined me.

Sprinkle was the size of a small child now, his cool blue skin covered in sections of ice, and he no longer looked to have wings that fluttered on his back. His white hair was shaggier, but not in a bad way, though it clung to his pinched face. "I was wondering if you would call to me again."

His harrumphing and arm crossing was completely lost on me as I turned to look over at Flicker. She was taller by far than Sprinkle, almost to my shoulder, and her fiery essence and aura flared from her like a blazing wildfire. Her skin was dotted with smatterings of red scales, reminiscent of those that covered myself and Sundar. Her body had filled out as well, wreathed in flames that covered all the important bits. She looked more like an adult woman than the sullen toddler-man that was her counterpart.

"Hey, Kyvir!" She greeted me warmly, coming closer to me to show me her backside. I blushed until I saw a draconic tail and wings had grown there. "See what happens when you listen to me?"

"How in the hells did that happen?" Sprinkle demanded in a high-pitched whine. "You fed her more Aether while I was gone, didn't you?!"

"I can assure you, Sprinkle, that wasn't me." I frowned and found my fingers running over her scaled shoulder, checking to see if the heat and scales felt as real as they looked. They did, though she smiled wider, and her incisors were longer and sharper as well. "How do you feel, Flicker?"

"I feel *wonderful,* Kyvir." She breathed my name and eyed me coyly for a moment. "I would love to show you what I can do now."

"As would I, but I think I will require more Aether before I do shit for you!" Sprinkle groused, crossing his arms and raising his chin stubbornly.

"Now, now, don't be that way, Sprinkle," the much larger summoning tutted at the blue-skinned man. "He had no idea that the lava in this city would give me these kinds of benefits."

"Unknowing or not, this is hardly fair, and I will not be relegated to being a lackey to the likes of you." His growl was almost as feral as some of the growls I had heard from wild animals, both back home and here.

"How about you prove yourself today, and I'll give you all the Aether I can." I crossed my arms and glowered at him in return. "I'm not going to give out my strength before our training and fighting has even started."

"Done." He stepped closer to me and held out his thin hand. I shook it, as cold as it was to me, and he smiled. "Where are we going? What are we fighting? More goblins?"

"Nope, bugs." Sundar grinned and both of the elemental creatures shivered in disgust. "Don't tell me that you can't handle a couple bugs."

"They're creepy and crawly and they don't really have too many elemental weaknesses, due to their exoskeletons and carapaces." Flicker grimaced at the thought, then spat angrily. "I hate bugs. If I can kill them, I'm in."

"Then we should get going." Emerald's voice rang out behind us, and I fought not to flinch.

She closed the door to the throne room softly, glancing at all of us. "You kids really know how to step in it."

"Sorry," Sundar stated simply, and Emerald just nodded.

"Let's just go kill some things to get stronger," I grunted, and the others followed along behind me, both Flicker and Sprinkle lifting into the air.

It was interesting to know that Flicker could still fly, but it seemed like Sprinkle only had to do something that made his aura flare, and he abruptly sprouted icicle wings.

Our walk to the gate outside the city was as uneventful as a summoner and prince traveling with two princesses. People waved and smiled at us, calling out to get our attention. More than a few dwarven women grinned my way, and even some of the men tried getting Emerald's attention.

People were polite and courteous to Sundar, but no one vied for her attention in the same way. The two elemental creatures just flitted to and fro as they wished, making children cry joyously as they performed minor tricks.

I made sure no one got hurt, and watched our backs as I could. Once we were outside the city, a small force of the Herd surrounded us, one of their leaders hopping off his goat to come and speak with us.

He smiled and bowed his head. "My name is Lieutenant Frel, and I'll be leading the detachment guarding you today. If you'll allow us, we can take you to our training grounds where we fight and collect from the hives."

"You'll all be staying out of the way, of course?" Emerald leaped toward him and scowled. "We need to be certain we can handle ourselves on the front lines. I don't mean to be too pushy, but we cannot afford to be coddled."

"We will be watching your backs as you fight; you have nothing to fear," he answered expertly.

She was about to say something again, but I lifted a hand and waved it off. "Semantics will only keep us here all day. If they start to get in the way, we order them off." I could tell that the lieutenant was uncomfortable as soon as I said it, and that gave me a small amount of pleasure, only because he had confirmed that I could. Good. "Lead the way, folks."

The dwarves' lieutenant mounted his large goat and thumped it lazily with his boots. "Hup!" The beast lurched forward at an easy pace for us, and we spent a time walking together in tense silence.

Then I remembered the stop we forgot to make. "Shit, we should have gone to the adventurer's guild here!" The ladies looked at me curiously, and I explained, "I got my job; there are things that you two may have gotten the ability to do and train in while you were here."

"We can always go back into the city after a few rounds, Ky." Sundar stretched and brought her massive new weapon out. "I need to work off some steam, and this is going to be the best way to do it."

"I get that, but we're leaving a lot up to chance here by not training our skills, or the ones that we need to be training in order to grow stronger." I tried to come up with a plan, but nothing came to mind.

"We likely have what we need to get a job, anyway. A few extra skills can be learned and trained as we go." Emerald clapped a hand onto my shoulder to get my attention, adding, "I like to look into things, so I know some of it. We come up with a strategy to fight the bugs now, then come back with our jobs to really train."

"Yeah, we don't have to do a full day here—we can split it up and do what we need to." Sundar glanced at me as we moved and sighed heavily. "Listen, kid, I know you want to get out there and find her sooner, but if we rush this, we put her and all of us needlessly in the line of fire. We can do this at our pace and still help her, and ourselves."

I nodded robotically, glad to be at least done with that conversation and on to training.

It took us another twenty minutes of walking to get to our destination, which looked like the entrance to a catacomb-like structure resembling a hive of some sort.

"This is where we come to train." Lieutenant Frel hopped off his goat and herded the others away from the entrance of the hive.

"What do we do?" Sundar asked as I pulled my elven sword from its sheath and put my shield on my arm.

"You lure them out." Frel shrugged and nodded to the entrance. "Going in there is likely a suicide mission, and we don't do it."

"Too many bugs for you?" I raised an eyebrow, and he nodded. "That's fine for now."

I rolled my neck and tossed a glance to Sundar and Emerald. "Ready?"

They nodded as their weapons were bared to the light, and we edged closer to the opening of the tunnel before us.

"Sprinkle, Flicker, I need you two to grab the first bug you see in there and lure it out." They eyed me evilly. Even if Flicker had been keen on me before for the massive dump of Aether that she'd gotten because of the lava, she was bitter now. "I'm not telling you to take any unnecessary risks; all I want is for you two to blast one and bring it to us. Then you can attack from a distance if you like. Sound good?"

They looked at each other, frowning deeply. Then their gazes came back to me, and Flicker answered. "Fine. But we're going to want all the Aether we can get."

"I'll do what I can," I agreed immediately, and they sped off into the darkness below the earth.

"I'm not sure what that means to them, but are you certain you can pay?" Emerald whispered softly.

"Aether and time, I guess." Something akin to motion in the depths of the shadows caught my attention. "Get ready."

Flicker sped out of the darkness with Sprinkle hot on her heels as a massive horned beetle skittered out from below. A weird, hollow chittering sound came from it as it lowered its head.

"Come and get it!" I snarled and slapped my sword on my shield loudly.

The horned head swiveled my way, and it charged. I lowered my head a little behind the shield and prepared. Just as it would have slammed into me, I swept my rear foot out behind me and to the side so the momentum carried me out of the way.

My sword sliced at one of the legs, bouncing off the exoskeleton ineffectively. Fire and ice auras swept over the beetle's head and body as it tried to attack me again.

"I'm going to try sneak attacking it," Emerald called as she sidled around it. "Keep it distracted."

I nodded and banged my sword on my shield again, casting Ice Armor (Full) on myself, just to be safe. Three ice Aether vanished from my bar as the air around me solidified against my armor, giving me another layer of protection.

I closed my eyes and summoned my intent as I closed on it, my weapon sliding back into its sheath as I focused on what I wanted.

As soon as the beetle was almost on me, I slapped my hand into its foreleg and froze it to the ground. My shield cracked against the side of its head as Sundar grunted with effort. A dull *thud* and rasping sound made me pause, then something grabbed me by my collar and yanked me backward off my feet.

15 dmg taken.

I gasped and closed my eyes as the pain ebbed through the back of my head.

"You okay, Kyvir?" Flicker muttered as her figure swam above me.

"Ow." I grunted and hopped to my feet. Surveying the fight, I was happy to see Emerald on the creature's back with her Soul Dagger slashing and piercing as she struck. The beetle tried to shake her off, but it wasn't working.

Sundar attacked with her mace, her swings growing ever faster as the Hell Cat's aura swallowed her in the speed buff.

"Come on, we need to kill this thing." I shook myself out and tried to come up with a better plan.

The shell looked like it was metallic, which gave me an idea —"Flicker, I need you and Sprinkle to super heat and super cool a specific spot on that thing's armor. Can you do it?"

"I think so; does it matter where?" I shook my head, and she smiled evilly. "Hey, frostbite! Attack this spot just behind the head!"

"What did you call me?" Sprinkle roared angrily as a spear of pure ice sped from his fist. "I'll freeze your arms off and club you with them, hot head!"

Flicker giggled and spun this way and that as the incensed ice Faerie cried out and threw himself into attacking the spot she had indicated.

His furious assault froze the area as the rest of us crowded around the beetle to keep it focused on us. My shield bashed and slashed as I stabbed with a sword of pure flame, leaving small burn marks on its jaws and horns as it reared.

"Now, Flicker!" Sundar called to the flame Faerie.

Heat washed over us as her mouth opened and dragon-like flames spewed forth. The ice melted and the shell cracked under her onslaught.

I pressed my luck and slashed at the same leg I had attacked before with the serrated edge of my shield. It carved away just enough to make the limb lean forward.

Emerald lashed out at the weakened spot, and Sundar's mace plummeted onto it.

A loud, shattering crack made me grin as the creature screeched loudly. Emerald stabbed again and twisted her weapon viciously.

Sundar called, "Ky! Alley oop!"

I blanked for a heartbeat, then remembered something from the times we had raided together before, and grinned.

"On it!" I took a knee and braced my shield with both arms above my head. The shield dipped, and I ended up prone for a moment as the orc woman sailed through the air, her battle cry ringing out as her mace crashed into the weak spot again.

The beetle collapsed, the bloodied carapace shattered and crumbling where it had been broken.

"Well done!" Frel and the rest of his guard clapped like they had just seen a nice putt at a golf tourney.

Still breathing heavily, Sundar grunted, "How do you do it?"

Frel shrugged, "We usually just go for the eyes and brain."

His simple answer made us roll our eyes as echoed cries came from within the hive-like structure that made my skin crawl.

CHAPTER SIX

MONA

"Are you *serious* right now?" I muttered to Lira, her succubus tail wagging in and out of my vision as she strutted through a street littered with other kinds of demonic figures.

"Quite serious, Monami." She grinned back at me with a wink. "You're going to learn how to harness all that wonderful ability of yours by picking up a job here."

The city we walked through reminded me of a city on Earth. Streets wove through buildings like a web, their ruined sides eroded and marred with slices and blood splatter.

"How is that even possible? I thought you needed an adventurer's guild for that?" She just waved me off with a negligent flick of the wrist, then tapped her chin with her other hand contemplatively.

She smirked, grabbing my hand and yanking me across the street to enter a small building that could have been just a shop like a deli. As she entered, the humanoid with blazing eyes and blistered red skin looked up at us. "What'aya want?"

"I'm here to see a man about his meat?" She replied lasciviously, and blood warmed my cheeks as she winked at the demon. I could have sworn that she and Sundar would have either been mortal enemies or best friends, based on how she acted here.

The demon eyed her up and down, then looked at me. "Who's the meatsuit?"

"My protégé, meat man, and none of your concern." She grinned wider as he growled.

"You know, I get to pick who goes back to see him, right?" He snarled as he pointed his butcher's knife at her. "You know damn well he don't like meatsuits."

"Who are you to decide that?" she shot back, the pretenses of being coy and appealing gone. "She's a demon in training, and if you don't want her here, fine. Tell your boss that you lost one of his hottest customers."

She snapped her finger at me like I was some kind of small animal to be ordered about with sharp noises, which made my blood boil, but there was a pause, and finally the demon butcher gasped, "Fine, he'll see you. Just get in there, please."

I turned and noticed that he didn't look all right anymore; his skin seemed a bit more pallid, and his eyes flicked about the room as if trying to find something.

"Thanks." Lira giggled and stepped behind the counter, motioning for me to follow behind her.

We crossed through the open doorway, down a thin hallway, and up a flight of stairs to an unassuming office door. Once we got there, Lira stopped me and pushed me up against a wall. "Once we get in here, it's game-face time. No sentiment other than revenge and spite, okay? And whatever you do, do *not* stare at his face." She paused as she went for the door handle, then glared at me again. "I'm going to turn on the charm, okay? Just focus on getting what you need, and don't make any deals you can't come out of."

She didn't give me the time to recover that I would have liked, and instead sashayed through the door. "Vertal, darling! How has hell been treating my favorite dealer?"

I walked into an office room, lavishly decorated with furs and gold that adorned well-crafted chaise sofas and chairs. The place looked like it could belong to a record producer or business mogul. Behind a desk with a long pipe in his hands was a small man, maybe two and a half feet tall, with a stout body. He had a long, hooked nose, severe red eyes that watched us curiously, and the left half of his face was torn asunder, with white bits of skull and red muscle tissue showing.

"I'm doing good, Toots, how about you?" He actually smiled at her, which made the muscles move and contract in a way that was as unnerving as his scowl had been. "Who's the meatsuit? You know I don't care for 'em."

"She's a baby I took under my wing, Vertal." Lira winked at him as she pulled me close to her.

He stared at me, and I did my best to stare back directly into his eyes so I wouldn't look at his face. "You staring at my face?"

I rolled my eyes. "There's nothing else to stare at, is there?" Lira stiffened next to me as he leaned forward. "I like the aesthetic. Very intimidating. I can see why people have to seek you out, and since Lira knows you, it means that you're one of the best."

He raised an eyebrow at me, then narrowed his gaze at Lira. "I hate it when you warn people about what I look like, Toots. Takes all the fun out of it."

"I know you're sensitive about it and all, doll." She winked at him and relaxed markedly.

"You always were the thoughtful manipulator." He smiled a little wider and put the pipe to his lips, stopping just before it passed through his teeth to eye us. "What can I do you for? I got meetings here soon, so I need to be ready."

"We need a job for the kid here; something sexy, since she's a presence type, like myself." Her hands wandered down her body in a way that made my skin crawl, especially since I could see that he was enjoying the show.

"How are we paying for this uh…transaction?" He raised

his eyebrow as he lit his pipe with a snap of his fingers. "Jobs like that are hard to come by, and even harder to secure with the methods we have."

"Vertal, darling, you know I know your methods, and let me just say—they're as fine as you." She grinned and bent forward with her hands over the desk so she could give him a view he found pleasing. "I'd say that the usual should work, should it not?"

"Sounds good to me, but in order to set her up with the right kinds of jobs, I'm going to need to know if she's got the right kind of stuff." His gaze fell on me, and my skin began to crawl even worse than it already had.

Lira glanced back at me, her eyes tight as she smiled. "Oh, she's got the goods; don't you, Monami?"

I stepped forward, heat rushing to my cheeks as I activated Allure, my voice breathy as I whispered, "You bet I do. Want to let me see what you have to offer?"

He turned to Lira and clapped his hands. "She's learning fast. I like this one." He raised his voice, "Fica! Bring me the slate I *acquired* recently. And the demon one, too."

"There's a demon list of jobs?" I found myself wondering out loud, making the little demon grin. "What could they be, I wonder?"

"Oh, there's about as many of them as there are for normal adventurers and travelers." Vertal's knowing smile told me he knew that it might pique my interest. "I also heard that a new one has been discovered and given to someone recently."

"Oh?" Lira looked at him quickly and smiled, "What's that?"

"Dark Paladin." His pipe fit to his lips, and he puffed on it thoughtfully. "Makes me wonder who the recipient was, and how they will grow. Will they support us, or will they use that new job to spite us? It's exciting."

Lira chuckled, "Yes, it is. Who knows? Maybe Lord Mephisto will send me on another recruiting mission?"

I blinked at her, but from the way Vertal nodded sagely, I

could tell he was familiar with some of what she had done. How deep was her cover? What atrocities had she had to commit just to get to where she was now?

An imp of some kind, small, with wings longer than its body, flapped in with two slates in its grip. It looked at me, scowling, then leered at Lira and drooped too low while trying to put the slates on the table. It cracked its head on the table and dropped the slates onto the wood roughly, blood dribbling from its head.

"Fica, you idiot—you eyeballing my guests?" Vertal growled as he stood on the throne-like chair. "Since when has it *ever* been acceptable behavior to stare at my *fucking* guests?"

"Forgive me, master, I just saw how pretty they we—" He hadn't been able to finish his sentence before bursting into flames darker than pitch. "Ahhhh! No! Please, nooooo!"

He burnt to a cinder, the stinking carcass left behind crumbling slowly as Vertal's face steadily regained some of the lesser red color it had before. He smoothed his hand through his hair and huffed, 'Sorry, ladies. Good help these days, and all that."

"You know I don't mind being stared at, doll." Lira winked conspiringly at him, but he just shook his head before she looked at me and motioned to the slates. "Come over and touch them for Vertal, and let's see what you qualify for."

"My thoughts exactly, Toots." Vertal took both slates and put them next to each other. "Left on the black, right on the white."

I stepped closer and did as I was told. As soon as the slate on the right touched my skin, I could feel a sort of suction as the information populated. But when my left hand touched it, it was like touching a live wire that kept you anchored to where you stood. "Agh!"

"It'll be okay; the demon slate is a little more intense." I hadn't expected to hear any kind of sympathy from the little demon, but his low whistle made me grimace. "Oh, kid. You have one that you qualify for from each, but that normy bullshit is a joke compared to this."

I checked the one job I qualified for from the normal slate—it was as a Scout—and shook my head before reading through the demon job.

Harvester – Your ability to take the lives of others, desire for revenge, and to avenge is so complete that you would give almost anything to see that those who cross you and your ideals pay. They will pay.

Requirements: Initiate level with any weapon, a basic understanding of Aether manipulation, and a decision to make those who hurt you pay.

All requirements met.

Optional requirements met: Attention from a dark figure, selfish actions, and betrayal of those who trusted you.

This job is that of a demon, and will require training. Would you like to take it?

"You said that this one is better?" Vertal nodded, and Lira just blinked at me, not being able to see what the job was. "Why?"

"Harvesters are rare, even among demons, so the fact that you qualify as one is crazy." He noticed my impatience and just grinned. "Harvesters have the ability to make weapons imbued with their Aether that can erode the souls of the beings on the receiving end of their attacks. Not only will you be trained to better control and use your own magic, you'll unlock more. You'll be able to create weapons and use them to pull the souls of your enemies into you to make you stronger."

Lira gasped, an intense look of revulsion on her face that made my heart pump wildly until she cursed, "I always wanted to be one of those!" She kicked Vertal's desk as her tail lashed the air sullenly, her lips pouting profusely. "I guess I'll be getting a bonus for this, but dammit, that's such a cool job."

Vertal looked at me. "You haven't accepted it yet; why?"

"Because, although I'm normally a hot head, I want to know more. Like who will be training me?" They both shrugged, so I continued, "What kind of magic, or Aether, will I be unlocking, and at what cost?"

Vertal scowled, glancing at Lira. "Smart kid, Lira, smart kid. You know I hate it when they're smart. Makes deals harder." His scowl turned into a grin as she touched his shoulder. "Look, kid. I would normally make you sell me your soul for something like this, but I owe Lira a favor, so I'll take a small cut of some of the souls you take, in return for giving you the job and what information I can. Sound good?"

I glanced at Lira, who gave me a minute nod in return. "Deal. What can you tell me?"

"The Aether that you should unlock will be Demonic Aether. As to what other kind of power your trainer, or the job itself, will impart on you—couldn't tell you, because most Harvesters keep that on the *real low* down low." He looked out the window in his office that was mostly covered, like he expected to see someone watching or listening in, then turned back to us. "All I know is that you'll be out there taking souls with the best of 'em in no time. Souls are a sort of currency among demons; they give us power and station. I'll only be taking a small cut of yours, so be grateful, huh?"

I tried to smile at him, but that just made me wonder even more what was going on. Was this really something I wanted to do?

Lira's hand clenched my shoulder as she grinned from me to Vertal. "Of course she's going to be grateful! She's going to harvest the shit out of the soldiers on the front lines and become the best little Harvester there is, right, Monami?"

The way she squeezed my shoulder made me grunt a little before I offered a small smile. "Of course I will! I'll take the job."

He lifted the slate and tapped a few things before I received a notification.

Congratulations, you have selected the job of Harvester.

I smiled at him and nodded my thanks before he sighed

heavily, "I wish I could get out there to see you training, kid, but I got other business to do, and I just don't like going outside. Too many mugs to deal with."

"We understand, doll." Lira leaned over and patted his head, kissing her fingertip and tapping him on the nose with another slow wink. "You're always so well done, Vertal. I'll make sure she keeps up her end of the bargain."

She grabbed me, and we strode toward the door, when black flames covered the door handle just before she could touch it. "Not so fast, Toots. I need that in writing."

I turned to see him motion to the desk before him, and a scroll of old paper unfurled with scrawling writing on it in a spidery kind of font. "Typical fare. Every ten souls you collect from any living creature, I get one."

"And when do you consider my debt paid?" I asked as I searched the contract in front of me for anything that might tell me my soul was forfeit.

"After, let's say…five hundred souls?" He offered with a scratch of his chin.

"Two hundred," I countered, and his eyes widened.

"Kid, you'll be getting souls like woah; you sure you want to be stingy?" He eyed me carefully. "Four seventy-five."

"Stingy? Please, it's basic economics." I chuckled at him, and he just stared at me. "I'd have to kill five thousand beings to break even for you, and who knows how long that will take. With the hundred and fifty souls I'll be getting for you while you do nothing but broker deals safely in your lavish office, I'd say you would be making out like a bandit."

He blinked at me, then turned to Lira and pointed with his pipe. "Did I just hear that right?" He blustered at her, then looked back at me. "Did you seriously just cut another fifty off of me?"

"I realized that your generosity was a good thing." I smiled and shrugged. "Besides, power is important here, and I like you. If I have the souls to collect and spend, I know exactly where to come and who to spend them with."

"Four hundred." He narrowed his eyes at me, and I just shook my head with a cool smile. "I could nuke you right here, Monami. Take the deal."

"Meet me halfway, Vertal, and I will." He gritted his teeth, the jaw muscles in the bad side of his face twitching and clenching angrily as I spoke. "Two hundred and fifty souls, and I come to you for any and all deals that I can. You might be able to find someone else to gather souls for you, but you likely won't find another Harvester for a while."

"Three hundred." He crossed his arms, and I just smiled before nodding, making him cry out, "Shit! Hey—this goes nowhere, alright?" I raised an eyebrow at him as he pulled a dagger out of thin air and shook his head. "I got a rep to uphold, and if anyone gets wind that I lost out on two hundred souls negotiating with a damned toddler, I'd never live it down!"

I snorted, Lira laughing uproariously as he waved his hand over the contract to make it reflect. I still saw nothing about my soul being forfeit, nor that of any kind of due date or anything about my friends and family, so I took the offered dagger. "What do I do, cut a vein?"

He scowled at me once more. "And ruin my hard work? Just prick your finger and touch it to the line on the right."

I poked my finger with the tip of the dagger.

2 dmg taken.

I rolled my eyes at the notification and pressed my finger to the right line on the contract as Vertal did the same on the left line. "There we go, we have a deal. You know, as annoying as you might be, this could be the beginning of a beautiful partnership, kid. Don't piss me off, and we could go far together. Right, Toots?"

"He's right." Lira grinned and nodded to the door. "We got errands to run now, Vertal. Gotta get my baby all gussied up to find out who will be training her and where!"

Vertal waved us out of the office, the black flames disappearing as he did. She shuffled me out of the room, and hushed me as my mouth opened, shaking her head and mouthing *no*.

We walked out of the butcher's shop below into the street, and she pulled me along the street until we were a few minutes away before she whispered, "You are clearly fucking insane."

She hadn't looked at me as she spoke, so I just nodded and smiled as I looked around the demon city. "Yeah, I get that a lot. I don't like owing anyone anything."

"You just bartered and got what you wanted from one of the best brokers in the city," she whispered back. "And what the hell were you thinking, risking yourself like that?"

"I'll do what I have to, thanks." I rolled my eyes and stopped walking so that she was forced to stop with me. "My friends are out there somewhere, probably wondering what happened to me, and my best friend lost his feelings for me— you should know this; you were there when I found out. If this is a way for me to get them back, and to make the people who took them pay, then I'm okay with that."

"It was Mephisto who made that rule, Monami," Lira replied tersely. "The other beings who do what they have to in order to give the travelers the powers they need are just as much in the crossfire as we are. They have no choice."

"They chose not to tell him, or any of us, for that matter," I spat angrily, then took a calming breath. "What do I do now?"

"We figure out who is going to be teaching you how to be a Harvester and get you set up so that we can start on our mission." She ran her hand through her hair and sighed. "You can't go around pissing off powerful demons like that. It paid off this time, but he could've easily killed you."

"Any risk worth taking is dangerous." I sighed, then turned to stare at her. "Being here is a risk—my friends and Kyvir are worth it. My revenge is worth it."

"Revenge?" She watched me oddly.

I blinked back; had I said that? "Whatever. Let's go get this over with."

CHAPTER SEVEN

MONA

We traveled through the demon-filled streets for a while, more than one of the annoyingly disturbing creatures stopping to stare at me. They catcalled and whooped at us, but Lira didn't allow me to take my frustration and indignation out on them.

Though one did get too close to me, and I lashed out at it with my chakrams. It cried out and skittered away, the demons around it laughing cruelly and pointing as it fled from me.

"Monami—control yourself," Lira growled at me, my chakrams returning to my hand so I could put them on my belt.

"Only if they do," I spat in response and eyed them all, their disgusting figures leering back. "I'm done playing nice with everyone who pisses me off. If they want to come, they can come, and I'll fight back."

Several demons growled around me, then stopped and bowed their heads, falling to their knees and faces like they were afraid.

"A Harvester, here?" a low voice muttered, as if to itself.

I glanced up and saw a tall, muscular-looking man, blue

skinned and sporting six horns that curved up out of his head toward the sky.

His swirling silver eyes leered down at me as his lips turned up at the sides, sharp teeth flashing in the little light that filtered through the pollution-clouded sky.

"What are you doing, little Harvester?" His head dipped lower toward me.

"Great Abbadon, please forgive us for being in your way. She's new and just learning." Lira bowed where she stood and motioned for me to do the same.

Except, when I thought about it, the last time I had paid deference to someone like that, I had paid for it with the love of my best friend.

I will not bow*!* I roared inwardly until I blinked and saw his smiling face in mine.

"I like this one." His easy-going stance never faltered as he bent to watch me. "She doesn't cower like the rest of you; she stands ready. I could use a Harvester like you."

"Great Abbadon, she's hardly worthy." Lira peeked up from where she bowed, and I just stared, wondering who this guy could be. "Just a bug of a traveler selected at random for her skills."

"And how fortuitous that she just happened to be in *my* way." His gaze flicked to her. "Don't worry, little succubus—you can come too."

She froze, just staring as he turned back to me. "I have a Reaper who can train you. Make you the best Harvester out there—working for me isn't all that bad. That, and I'll give you all the opportunities to get your revenge that you could possibly want."

Now it was my turn to freeze. "How did you know?"

"I know many things, but vengeance clouds the aura, and *your* desire for it is the most intense I've ever seen." His small smile split into a wider grin. "I like that. Come with me."

I found myself glancing over at Lira, but she shrugged to me and motioned that I follow the large blueish being. We didn't walk long, heading down an alleyway that led to what could have been a church at one point. Large steepled roofs rose high above, with stone figures attached to the balconies and small towers like guardians against any well-to-do goodie two shoes that might try to attack this place of unholy might.

That reminded me sorely of an instance in Blood and Gore that both Seth and I had loved for the visuals alone. It didn't matter to us that the gargoyles above and the suits of armor below came to life and tried to kill our characters when we were there.

He and I had two-manned the place a few times, just for fun, when we were high enough level.

I miss that... My lamenting had pulled me from my surroundings for longer than it should have, and I steeled myself to walk into this place.

The doors swung open with a genial gesture from Abbadon. Howls of agonized screaming and the scent of spilled blood engulfed us. As soon as my stomach began to roil and protest, both sensory effects were gone.

"Now that you're inside and in close proximity to me, the wards and enchantments on this place no longer apply to you," he explained with a slight yawn, then led us further into the building. He touched a large door with chains secured in place by a massive lock. The loud, crashing *ka-thunk, boom* of it unlocking and falling uselessly to the ground made my hands fly to my sensitive feline ears.

We continued in as ethereal blue and green figures swooped down toward us—ghastly, ghostly men and women—creatures with little form other than malice and discontent on their partially transparent faces. Once they were within thirty feet of Abbadon, their descent came to a grinding halt, and they sped away.

I had to ask, "What are they?"

"Pets," he chuckled back, reaching up and scratching one of the men behind the ear as if it were some kind of border collie, to come when called, and exist as nothing more than an amusement. "They won't attack my guests; they know better—don't you, my precious babies?"

A ghoulish whine echoed around me that drove my tailbone almost down to the floor. The only thing keeping me standing and not running for the hills was my own stubborn willpower and Lira's close proximity.

Abbadon mounted the pulpit like it was just another place and turned to fall in the large, ornately-carved ivory throne standing like a sentinel before a long altar. With his relaxed demeanor, it was almost enough to say that the man looked like a college-aged frat boy of sorts.

"Monami, welcome to Hell." He waved to the window behind him, and where there should have been stained glass and more beautiful architecture, there were only shattered panels and red skies beyond.

"Thank you, Abbadon." I nodded once, and to my surprise, Lira hissed and actually struck me from behind.

12 dmg taken.

"He is one of the seven Lords of Hell!" she spat as I rounded on her. "If you don't show him some respect, he could kill you and make life very unpleasant for both of us."

"Life in and of itself is always unpleasant, isn't it?" He posed his thoughts carefully, staring at me. "What is the point of life, if it's not what we want? What it could be, if it hadn't been for the betrayal of others? The interference of others. Their whims and wants. Desires."

"You make it sound like anyone who stands in your way is just fodder," I stated as a chill ran down my spine.

"See, succubus? The kid gets it." He laughed and clapped his hands twice, the echoing booms almost shattering my ears as I fell to a knee. "I always forget how weak mortals are—that will change."

I glanced up at him from where I had fallen as he sat up and leaned forward to stare at me intently. "To be concise, Monami, yes. Anyone in my way is fodder; they've just not realized it. Same for you! You can reclaim what you want, what is yours as your right, and you'll be able to do it, with my help."

"Why would a Lord of Hell want to help an insignificant traveler like me?" I said quietly.

His eyes wilted a little around the edges when I spoke so formally. "I don't like that." He frowned and stood to pace in front of his throne. "No, I don't like that at all. I want the fire that you had before in the street. The temper and the desire. Don't think of me as a Lord of Hell; screw all that. Just think of me as someone interested in helping out a like-minded individual."

Why are they all so weird here? What is it with me and these guys?

"Okay, then why would you want to help me, even if I am a like-minded individual?" I shrugged as I climbed to my feet, and he started to smile again. "Don't get me wrong, I appreciate the thought, but what makes you think I need your help?"

He laughed, grabbing his stomach, then wiped a tear from his eyes. "Oh, there it is. I love it." He snapped his fingers, and a goblet of liquid splashed into his hand. "Because, not only do we think the same, but I'm kind of the demon patron saint of revenge and wrath." He held out a hand to stop me when I went to speak. "I'm well aware that, for some reason, you think my brothers and sisters have different things that they like to support and get pissy about. I get it. I'm nothing like them. I couldn't care less about Mephistopheles getting his way, and I sure as fuck don't care about some dumbass war."

"Then why are you here?" I blurted out, and he snapped his fingers again. Something smacked into the backs of my legs and forced me to fall backward onto a chair. "Woah!'

"Take a seat, kid; this is a long story." He held himself up a little higher and seemed about to begin a long tirade when he grinned and said, "Nah, fuck that."

He stepped down the stairs from the pulpit until he could sit on them and look me directly in the eyes before he continued, "I'm here because there's a call for a lot of revenge and wrath on both sides of the field, and I'm not so hungry here. My

Reaper goes out and collects his fill, and then I get mine. It's good for business, and I at least give the slight implication that I serve the greater bad for the demons, so no one, aside from the goody goodies out there on the field and the travelers, is gunning for my throne."

The sound of wings flapping brushed against my ears, and I lifted my eyes in time to see a cloaked figure rush through the window directly behind the throne and alight on the ground behind and to the right of Abbadon.

"What do you want, old man," the figure growled angrily. "How many times do I have to tell you not to summon me like that?"

Abbadon turned a grin on the figure and smirked, "At least six hundred and sixty six more, Bardif." The demon lord motioned to me. "I have a trainee Harvester who I've adopted that needs training in her new powers. See to it, won't you?"

"Fuck you," Bardif spat, literally as flecks of saliva hit the floor next to the demon lord.

Abbadon grinned at us, holding up a single long finger., "One second."

He turned, his arm stretching impossibly long so that he could reach into the cloak and grasp the figure by the throat. Power flared from both figures, wings of ivory bursting from Abbadon's back in a magnificent cascade of feathers, even as twin scythes of darkness formed in the Reaper Bardif's fists and slashed.

They bounced off the demon lord's skin as his wings flapped once, twice, and lifted them both aloft. Bardif's legs swung maddeningly as his blades attacked on their own while he fought to free himself from the blue grip.

Abbadon snarled, "I have put up with your sass and irreverence for millennia because I find it amusing, but do not think so highly of yourself, because I allow it, that you might spit in my presence at a direct command. Am I clear, Bardif? I can take your wings and *stuff* them as an interesting addition to those on my throne."

I found my eyes drawn to the throne and realized that the ivory bars were indeed feathers, and that there were hundreds of them in just the part that I could see.

"Speak!" Abbadon gnashed his teeth closer to the Reaper's face in outrage.

"Fine." The wheezing cough seemed to be enough, as the demon simply tossed the man to the ground below him. To his credit, Bardif landed on his feet.

Abbadon ran his fingers over his horns like a greaser might have tried to comb with his hands; then his normal frat boy pleasantness was back. "There we are. I expect you to devote yourself to her training before the Merge. Things will be quite ugly by then, I can imagine."

"I keep hearing about that; what is it?" I couldn't help the cold curiosity in my voice.

He shook his head and wagged his finger at me mockingly. "I've already given you much. Show me that you can be trusted, and I might be inclined to tell you."

"Fair enough, I suppose." I crossed my arms and sighed. "Annoying that the one guy who tells me that everyone in my way is fodder, is now standing in the way of me learning."

All that did was make Bardif laugh as Abbadon eyed me with mirth.

"Train her, Bardif, and do not fail me," Abbadon ordered, then sat on his throne and waved a hand. I blinked, and it was no longer a red sky greeting us outside the window, but one cloudy and gray. Abbadon was gone, his throne no longer standing at the altar.

"What happened?" I blinked, and Lira looked uncomfortable.

"He transported us all back to the surface from his castle in hell," Bardif grunted and lowered his hood. The man staring out at us had cloudy gray eyes, high cheekbones, and dark skin. He stared at me a moment longer as I took him in before motioning toward the exit. "We should leave; you have a lot to learn and not a whole lot of time."

CHAPTER EIGHT

SETH

Okay, get back in the portal now, Seth. Come on! Food had become so disgusting for me lately that finding the will to eat was just as exhausting as playing as much as I did.

Eating the sandwich and protein shake I had made for myself had been like forcing myself to eat dirt, then drink soap. It had been horrible.

Once I was back inside the city walls, I found Emerald and Sundar already waiting for me. Emerald looked me over and sighed, "Was it that bad?"

I had made the stupid mistake of telling her, and she hadn't believed me at first, but now, with the look of uncertainty she wore—I was beginning to think she did.

"Yeah, it's not getting any better." I shook my head, clearly frustrated. "I'm an *Aether* vampire, right? I devour magic; this is unreasonable."

"It sounds like it." Sundar yawned wildly, smacking her lips afterward. "You ready to go back and train some more?"

"Yeah," I groused, then looked over at both of them, "Did you both get your jobs?"

They nodded, when I heard a bark coming from behind me. I turned to see a massive black dog with heavy jowls and brown eyes staring at me.

"Zanjir!" Emerald snarled, the dog's demeanor shifting to that of total and complete attentiveness. "Hier."

Zanjir trotted around me toward his master, sitting next to her stoically as his head swiveled and observed everything. "Figured we could use a little more back up today, since he's finished growing for now."

She patted him as Sundar's jaw nearly struck the ground. "He's done growing *for now*?" Emerald nodded at her, and Sundar gasped, "Woman, he's the size of a Great Dane and he's still not fully grown?"

"Nope!" She smiled and continued patting the dog's head, his whine for more of her attention adorable. "When they level up enough, they go through a growth spurt and get smarter. It's why he's so obedient now. He recognizes you but is uncertain, because to him, it has been a long time since he's seen you."

She looked down and motioned the dog forward. "Kyvir, you know the process of a dog becoming familiar with you; I need you to show Sundar."

I nodded and stepped forward, extending my hand so that it was palm down and low enough for Zanjir to sniff. He growled slightly, Emerald growling back at him, "Nein! Voran; get the scent, Zanjir."

A cold, wet nose snuffed at my fingers, then the back and fore of my wrist as I looked away. I kept the dog in my periphery, but was careful not to look at him until he was comfortable. His tongue whipped over my fingers excitedly, and he whined happily.

"Good boy, Zanjir," Emerald laughed as his tail thumped against her hips. "Sundar, now you?"

"You guys forget that I can speak to animals." She laughed and knelt down in front of the dog, his tail instantly stiffening, until she started to speak to him. "Hey there, little guy. You wanna be friends?"

His tail went wild as he came close enough to sniff and snuff and chuff at her all over. She laughed, "Hey, what happened to being all badass?"

"Yes, Zanjir, what happened to that?" Emerald raised her eyebrow, and the dog froze before backing up and sitting next to her right leg with his tail thumping the ground loudly. "You big baby."

"So what jobs did you guys get?" I stretched my back out and glanced between them both.

"There was one called Druidic Whisper; it's not like the Druid class is traditionally, but there are some similarities." Emerald smiled at me, and I nodded. "How about you, Sundar?"

"I took the only one available to me: Spirit Priestess." She grinned at my look of shock and confusion. "Having the Shaman mutation is a prerequisite to get this one, and also having a spirit to use as a buff, like the Hell Cat."

"What do they do?" I scratched my head and tried to think of it, but I hadn't even used my own abilities yet as a Dark Paladin.

"Druidic Whisper is a sort of support class, but geared more toward killing things that defy nature's will." Emerald shrugged and focused on something in front of her. "If I get strong enough, I might be able to shift into animal forms! How cool would that be?"

"Pretty damn cool!" I grinned and looked to Sundar as we started to walk.

"Spirit Priestess is basically a stronger healer than my shaman totem is." She lifted her chin toward the sky. "I still have my totem, and I'll get others, too, I believe, but as a priestess, I get more healing spells. Direct healing, if you will. I wish Albarth was here to answer some questions for me, though."

That soured the mood instantly. Him up and leaving, because we didn't instantly go off half-cocked after Mona, had been more than just a slap in the face; it had been uncharacteristic for him. I could see it from me, but that was just odd.

"Yeah, me too." I muttered as we moved along. We made it to the hive entrance and waved to the members of the herd who waited there for us. It had been like this after the first time we left. They weren't going to chance us coming in and doing anything without them like we wanted to.

"Glad to see you lot back again!" The dwarf closest to us yawned and smiled. "Twelve hours of nothing was a wee bit rough on us, you know, and it be nearing dark. Dangerous to be out here in the darkness, lad and lasses."

"Thanks!" I smiled at him, and he just nodded. "But you guys can go back if you like. That beetle was a little tough last time, but we're going in."

"I should think not, Majesties!" He blustered and nearly unseated himself from his mount. "If you go in there, we can't protect you, and the queen will have our heads!"

"The queen knows we mean to get stronger however we can. We took this risk on ourselves." Emerald reasoned with them. "Don't get in our way and get yourselves in trouble, okay?"

"I'll need to confirm this with the queen," he muttered, then turned to the others with him. "I'm riding to the city. Don't let them go in if you can. Violence if you have to."

I raised both eyebrows in surprise as he rode off, leaving four of his men behind as we watched his departure. I watched them turn back to us with a look of patience, which I was slowly beginning to lose more and more as time went on. As if the violence within me was always so much closer than it had been before.

I wondered if Flicker and Sprinkle had finished growing yet with the Aether I had given them both? I had given Flicker permission to go back to the lava, then gave as much of my Aether to Sprinkle as I possibly could. Eight summoning, five ice, and one gray Aether had been a lot for him, and I hoped it was enough. It had worked for them both; I lasted as long as I could in-game, with as tired as I had been, before having to log out and return them both. Though Flicker had all but teleported to the lava once we finished our fight.

I called to both of them mentally at first to see if it would work. This time, both of them took two summoning Aether each and only one of their respective elements.

Oh, boy. I hope I didn't summon them against their will, or this will get ugly. Their powerful auras washed over me, and I got a serious boost to my Evil Eye ability. It was now initiate level 3, and the auras were more intense than ever. "Hey, guys."

A taller and more handsome version of Sprinkle eyed me balefully. "Hello, peasant."

I blinked at him until he snorted and began to laugh as I growled, "Glad to see your sense of humor hasn't changed. What's the deal with the extra summoning cost?"

"It's because I'm now stronger than I was." He looked himself over appreciatively, his hands smoothing down the simple white tunic of frost that he wore. "Once you earn my favor a bit more, I may be inclined to let you summon me for less."

"I'm inclined to do so now!" Flicker's voice made me jump, as she was right behind me.

I turned and noticed her watching me from mere inches away. "Would you like to be my friend, Kyvir?"

I smiled at her. "Yeah, I'd love that."

I reached toward her, and she grinned, but I was able to really take her in at that angle. She was taller now, broader too, as her wings cupped her body like a dress. She stared at me, openly amused, as her tail, longer now with some spikes on the end of it, lashed the air. "You keep staring at me, and a girl might think you have other things in mind."

My cheeks reddened deeply, and I blinked as I looked away bashfully. "So, how do we become friends, so that I can call you whenever?"

"All it takes is a little blood from you," Sprinkle advised as a look of pure disgust fell over his features. "Gross."

I snorted and nicked my thumb with one of my fangs, then glanced at her. She held both her hands out, and I gave my bleeding hand to her.

"Sorry in advance," she muttered and brought the bloody digit to her lips, pressing her mouth over it like it was something to eat.

Despite the fact that the warmth from her was more than a little embarrassing in front of a dear friend and the woman I basically looked at as my mother, it wasn't unpleasant.

Then the heat built fiercely and traveled into the wound. "Gah! What the hell?"

Flicker leaned back, a look of demure pleasure on her face as she smiled. "That was what I had apologized for. It's not always so pleasant."

I looked at the spot that I'd offered up and found that it was gone.

Then I heard her voice inside my skull, *My real name is Vulina. If you use that name to call me, I'll come to you. And when you talk to me like this. Otherwise, just use Flicker. Okay?*

"Okay." The look she gave me said it all, and I was more than glad that it sounded like I had been responding to her previous statement. But I tried to project to her, *Thank you. And it's nice to meet you, Vulina.*

Her lips quirked up at the corners as she ducked her head.

"Well, we ready to head inside?" Sundar glanced around expectantly.

"We can't allow that," one of the mounted dwarves called, his mount stepping between us and the entrance to the hive system. "You'll need to wait until Borin comes back."

"Yeah, no—not wasting daylight for that," I sighed as both Sundar and Emerald stepped closer to the goat.

Both of them began to speak, their voices low, but as soon as they stopped, the goat snapped up and bolted away from the entrance. The dwarven rider fought to regain control, then just to stay on as the animal careened toward the others at full speed.

The others bleated and turned to run in the same direction as the first.

I couldn't help the laugh that escaped as I found them glancing with newfound respect at each other. "What did you tell it?"

"I told her that there was a monster coming, and she didn't believe me at first," Emerald explained as she motioned toward the cave.

"Then I told her it was us, and that if she made a big ruckus, I'd find her and give them all some apples in the morning," Sundar finished with a smug look of triumph on her face as she folded her arms. "Ready, meatshield?"

"Ugh, you know I hate that term." I rolled my eyes and marched forward.

Sprinkle surprised me. "That is quite rude, you know." I was about to thank him when he chipperly added, "I think the term 'damage sponge' is much more what he is."

"You little!" I tried to grab him, but he squirmed out of the way as the rest of the group just chuckled and snorted, as they would.

———

We marched through the cavernous hive, pushing past intersection after intersection of empty passageway.

"Why isn't there anything to find? No corpses, nothing," Emerald wondered quietly as we turned a corner to find a dead end and went back down the path the way we had come. "Not even another beetle. Did something happen?"

I glanced over at Sprinkle. "How far did you have to go to pull one out for us last time?"

"Not this far, I assure you." Sprinkle muttered. "I wonder where they could have gone?"

"Good question, but is it too late to say that I—once again —really hate bugs?" Flicker groaned.

"Stick it out with us, and there could be more lava time in it for you." Her head whipped to me. "Yes?"

"I want to meet the queens." I stopped at her request, eyeing her suspiciously. "I want to feel what it's like to have pure dragon fire breathed on me. I think it might help me grow stronger still."

I frowned, then opened my mouth and closed it. "I'll think on it."

She nodded once, her jaw set, and threw her hands into the air, "Come on out, little buggies; it's stir fry time!"

Still nothing. As the sun was closer to dropping in the sky, we had almost given up, when Sprinkle perked up. "There's something ahead. It's refracting our light."

Sure enough, I saw the shimmer and moved once more ahead of the group as Emerald fell into a stealthier gait and Sundar took her place between us easily with her weapon drawn.

Once we rounded the bend in the stone, we stood in the presence of a huge, crystalline door. The light from my summonings refracted against it and splayed outward in rainbows and differing shades that made me gasp.

"Could this be a dungeon?" Sundar whispered and walked closer to the door.

Her hand reached up, but I grabbed her and yanked her away with everything I had. We fell onto our asses, and she turned back to me irritably. "Hey, what was that all about?"

"Remember what happened when we touched the last one?" I pointed to the door as she began to stand. "We couldn't get out until it was finished. If there's stronger stuff out there at night, the dungeon could be harder too. We need to come back prepared for it tomorrow. Sound good?"

"Yes. Though I am upset that I didn't get the chance to try anything out tonight." Emerald's crestfallen voice picked up. "Well, that just means we get to come into it fresh! That's exciting, right?"

"Yeah, we can definitely get some good work done in a

dungeon." Sundar agreed as she took out her teleporting stone. "You want to attune it?"

"Can we do that?" I raised a brow at her as she touched the stone to a rocky outcropping by the door.

"Yup, just needs to attune to another stone that it touches. It worked for me." She pocketed the item, then glanced back toward the entrance. "Suppose we should go make sure that no one tried to follow us, or is waiting for us?"

I can go look, then come to you when I'm done, if you like? Vulina offered me silently. *I can teleport to you now, since we're friends.*

I turned toward her. *That would be wonderful, thank you.*

She took off without a verbal command, and the others turned toward me in surprise. "She's going to scout and see, then let me know. You guys can head back now."

They frowned, Sundar casting a more seriously questioning glare at me before shaking her head. "I suppose I'll see you back at the den, then. Don't take too long."

I nodded and looked at Emerald. She crossed her arms and gave me the matronly 'we will speak later' look that every kid ever knew all too well before she teleported just after attuning her own stone to the wall.

I did the same, holding it up to the wall until it emitted a sort of clicking sound that only I could hear, then turned to find Sprinkle staring at me. "Yes?"

"I know that you can hear her voice in your head now." He grinned at my discomfort. "It's common enough among our kind to become friends with a summoner. She just did the thing weirdly. All we have to do is touch the blood. Not consume it. I don't know why she did it that way, but it's between you two."

"Thanks for the heads up?" I could hardly keep the skepticism out of my tone as he chuckled to himself. "I suppose you want more Aether?"

"No. There will likely be minerals or something in this place, since it's below ground, right?" I shrugged, wondering the same thing myself. "If there are, I want to try eating them to see if I can grow from them. Just bits and pieces here and there, to see if it will work."

"Is that even possible?" I scratched my head and considered the implications.

"She's been bathing in lava—a literal mixture of fire and earth—and you worry about me consuming metal?" He snorted softly and rolled his eyes. "It won't hurt me. I just want to see if I'm compatible with any, is all. I don't want to grow into a vanilla creature, like so many of my kind. I want to be different. Help me, and I will reward you."

"Do I have a choice?" I sort of forced a chuckle as he floated closer to me; oddly close.

"We always have a choice, Kyvir." He laid a hand on my shoulder as he stared at me sagely. "You just have to know when to make the dumb one. Like following your summoner into a bug's nest, hoping to get big and strong, so all the chicks will dig you."

He smiled at me and disappeared on his own. As soon as he did, I could feel my summoning Aether returning.

There's a lone rider here waiting. She's asking that you come speak with her. Vulina's voice carried an edge of worry to it, so I began to move toward the entrance.

Is she armed? Can you see anyone else around?

She's armed, but she's not really doing anything other than asking for you as she sits on her horse. She sounded aggravated now. *I'm coming to you. She doesn't feel right. She keeps watching me like she wants to eat me.*

I broke into a jog at that point, a nova of fire bursting behind me as she teleported to where I had been.

"Can you tell me what she looks like?" She shook her head. "Why not, Vulina?"

"She wore a hood and I could only see her eyes." She shivered uncontrollably. "They were so vivid and confusing."

"How do you mean?" I almost tripped over a section of the tunnel that sat lower than the rest.

"She looks predatory somehow." She shivered again. "She watches you like a fire cat watches a mouse. It's creepy."

Picking back up my pace, we made our way toward the entrance where the figure waited on a silvery steed. It wore armor like you would expect to find on some movie mount.

"Ah, here you are." A surprisingly deep voice came from the hood, the figure dismounting and stepping away from their mount.

"Who do I have the pleasure of speaking with?" I called to them as I readied to draw my weapon.

"Probably one of the only other beings in this world like you." Their answer was disconcerting, but I held steady. "You have not realized it?"

"Realized what?" I called back.

They laughed and their hood fell back. A beautiful human woman stood bathed in the fires of the fading sun, her yellowish eyes narrowed at me with a sure grin on her face. As she opened her mouth, I caught a glimpse of her teeth, straight and white, with longer canines that mirrored my own. "We both feed on the Aether of others. I think it is high time that we became acquainted, young one. I am Aertra, an Aether Vampire, such as yourself."

"Fine, I'm Kyvir—what do you want?" I tried to relax a little but, like Vulina had said, she watched me like I was food.

"I want to teach you." She grinned wider and stepped closer. "I know what you are, and I know what you are capable of."

I frowned, blinking and finding that she was gone, until a slight sensation at my back sent a shivering thrill of fear down my spine as her warm breath caressed my right ear. "I can also teach you so much more."

I didn't bother to move. If she wanted to kill me, she likely could. Instead, I turned my head to glance at her. "What do you get out of this?"

"Why must I gain something from teaching you?" She tried to sound hurt, her lips pulling together in a pout that was just this side of believable. I stayed quiet and watched her as deadpan as I could, and finally, she sighed. "Teaching you may lead me to answers as to why I was gifted with these abilities as well. Not to mention, I will have no shortage of Aether to gorge myself on around something as young and lively as you."

"Stop staring at me like I'm food, you weird witch!" Vulina snarled as flames wreathed her hands.

"Lively." Aertra licked her lips, and the motion was enough to make my heart leap in my chest.

"You will not eat my summonings." Vulina glanced at me, her features almost unreadable for a moment before turning back to the other Aether eater with a grimace.

"So long as I find it acceptable not to, certainly." Aertra tapped my shoulder and walked around me. "Come with me."

"Who said I was going to allow you to teach me?" I crossed my arms defiantly.

She didn't stop walking, her steps sure and direct. She mounted her horse and regarded me coldly. "I did." She blinked at me innocently before a cruel smile graced her lips. "Because if you don't, I'll eat your friends until you do."

"All of us are under the protection of the queen of this city. Harming them would be like hanging a steak around your neck and ringing the dinner bell for a couple of pissed-off dragons." Even though the visual was amusing to me, her lack of visible reaction was disconcerting. "You wouldn't live long."

"I would not care." She shrugged and grinned wider. "I've eaten dragons too, child. Regardless, it is not as if you will not benefit from my tutelage. I know for a fact that right now, your body is fighting you, and you are starving yourself. Ask me how I know."

My frown deepened, and I just stared at her. We stood there eyeing each other for more than two minutes, before I finally caved and quietly said, "How?"

She leaned forward and eyed me pityingly. "Because I once did the same. Come, Kyvir. Learn what I can teach you, and you need not be as weak as you are."

If I can benefit from this… fine. "Fine, but you leave my friends alone." I glanced over at Vulina. "All of them."

My summon blinked at me before smiling slyly and drifting closer to me to glare at Aertra.

"So long as I am not *too* famished," she agreed, then patted the spot behind her on her horse. "Come."

CHAPTER NINE

SETH

It was an awkward ride for the distance we had to travel, but it went much faster, thanks to the large horse. Vulina flew above us, not trusting my would-be vampire mentor an inch.

She could eat you as soon as I leave, and besides, you promised to let me meet the former queen to be dragon-fired. I glared at her until she wilted slightly, *Okay, you didn't, but I wanna do it; come ooooon.*

"How did you become an Aether Vampire?" I asked finally, careful not to touch her too much, more out of my own awkwardness than her desire for me not to. I'd only come along to protect my friends, and if I really needed to, I could get away. I hoped.

"Cannibalism." She smiled back at me, and my stomach churned. Then she laughed and faced forward, "I made an ancient being angry by consuming the blood of others to make myself stronger and more beautiful."

"A god?" I frowned at her, and she spat.

"Gods don't exist, boy." Her tone was grave and certain. "If they did, they wouldn't allow the one I upset to do as he pleases even now. They'd stop him."

"Mephisto?" She turned her gaze back at me and stopped the horse.

She eyed me for a moment, silently searching me for something before she asked, "How do you know that moniker?"

"He was the one who took notice of me. He made me what I am." She watched me some more and finally I added. "I see him when I drink enough Aether from someone to get to a hundred percent affinity. He makes me play these wretched games of chance."

"You can obtain the Aether and keep it?" She frowned deeper as I nodded. "This changes much, then."

"Exactly how much?" My body swayed as she kicked her mount into motion, the horse whickering beneath us as it lurched forward into a trot.

"It could be anything from the fact that you might be weaker or stronger than I am, or it could mean that you and I are completely different." She spoke low, and it was hard to hear her over the wind rushing by my head, the plains having been windy even before I'd hopped onto the mount. "Either way, I am eager to see what your limitations may or may not be."

Finding my limitations? That's going to be interesting... I grimaced as the sun fell, the gates of the city in the distance closing slowly. "We need to hurry. I don't know if they will let us in, even if I am a prince."

She snickered and turned the horse so that we moved toward the wall, rather than the gate itself. "What are you doing?"

"Your first lesson, boy." She grinned back at me and motioned to the air around us. "I know that you have fire magic; I can smell the Aether on you. Heat the air around us and make it so that we look like a mirage."

"A what?"

"Are you truly so dense?" She sighed and lifted a flask from inside her cloak and took a swig as she stared back at me. Her eyes glowed a deep orange, and she grinned as she swallowed the contents, then raised her left hand. Her eyes flashed again, then shifted back to their previous yellowed hue. I saw the red and orange aura around her flare, and then the air surrounding us carried that same sort of residue as the heat billowed.

She hit me with a lopsided grin. "There, see how I did that?"

"Not really?" The grin faded a little as her lips fell into an angry sneer.

"Do not think to lie to me, Kyvir." Her low voice held the promise of violence as she leaned back against my chest to bring her face closer. The lines of her face looked a little more defined in her anger. "I can hear your heartbeat, and I despise lies."

How had she known? Granted, I didn't *exactly* know how she had done it; I just knew that it could be done. I would have to practice something like that, and I doubted myself in that sort of thing. "Fair point."

We rode for another half an hour, the heat rising from us as we rode. No one on the wall really noted our entry to the city grounds, though some of them did rub their eyes and blink in our direction several times in worry. One guy took a glance at whatever was in his hands and poured it over the wall discreetly, then shook his head, much to Aertra's delight.

We reached the wall, and she motioned for me to dismount. After I complied, she patted her horse, whispering, "Good girl, Artil. Please, go home and wait for me. Help yourself to a few apples on Eartrid's coin, eh?" The horse tossed her head, mane flipping as she turned and cantered away around the side of the wall toward the mountain. The same billowing heat that had protected us from sight protected the horse as she fled the area.

"What now?" I turned toward the wall and looked up, the dizzying height of it making the massive object seem as though it leaned and loomed over us. I blinked and shook my head.

"Well, as I demonstrated before, we use the magic that we

have at our disposal to maneuver up the wall and over it." She took out a flask and drank from it again, this time, her eyes melding with a brownish amber color. She grinned and stepped onto the wall like it was just a hill, walking up it with little effort. She turned and motioned for me to follow, and I just shook my head.

Fire won't help me here. I corralled my will and intent as I reached for my Ice Aether. I channeled it into my fingertips and the tips of my boots. The ice swirled around my digits before hardening and becoming claws that I used to wedge into the massive mortar lines. It was hard at first, but as I grew used to the hardship, my body lifted and moved with more and more ease.

After a few minutes, my muscles burned, and sweat poured from my forehead. Aertra took another swig of her flask, her aura flaring brown and golden before she took another step. I growled softly to myself and used another bar of Aether to keep my claws.

You're doing well for someone who doesn't normally climb anything like this, Vulina observed softly to me. *It's too bad that you can't fly with this type of use.*

Why can't I? Thinking about it, I could create thrusters under my feet, couldn't I?

Is a hundred foot wall filled with armed dwarves, who are paranoid about their own farts, really *the place you want to try to fly?* I couldn't help laughing at the visual she put into my mind and just shook my head. *Very smart, Kyvir. Keep climbing, I'm watching over you.*

Could you fly me up?

She snorted and flitted closer to me, the heat around her body making her difficult to see, like we had been. *Sorry, pal. These wings beat for one and one only. But if you were to help me grow a bit more…*

I rolled my eyes. *I get it. Thanks.*

She giggled and flapped away as I continued to press myself against the wall, then pushed myself onward. As time went on, my Aether recovered, and I could continuously climb without needing to rest. I was grateful that I didn't need to worry about my only conceivable means of climbing, other than my raw fingers, giving out on me or fading.

Eventually, I grasped the lip of the wall and hefted myself over the side with a shove from the ever-helpful Vulina, her hands grabbing my butt and pushing with an inarticulate grunt of effort that I could have resented, but just was too tired to care.

"Tired already?" Aertra's teasing tone tickled my ears from where she stood bathed in the darkness. The moon wasn't bright tonight, as it was still slim, and she used the guardhouse on the other side of the wall as a hiding place. "You may want to hide. The guards are coming, and they *hate* being surprised."

I heaved a sigh and fought my way to my feet, sore muscles screeching at me as I hid next to her. "Now what?"

"We wait until they pass and slip into the city." She grinned at me, then stilled as her face wrinkled and nose worked. I was about to ask her what was going on when she held a hand up to quiet me.

—*Hey! Are you and Flicker okay?*— Sundar's whisper was almost enough to make me jolt from my hiding spot.

I sent back —*All is well. See you soon.*—

Clanking feet marched our way and drew me from my screen. "I'm telling you, Vler, I heard some'at over here. Had me chilled, it did."

Two dwarven men in the red armor of the city guard clattered into view, the one on the left clearly nervous as he cast his gaze about, while the other simply looked over the edge of the wall. "I don't see nuffin', Wrelt. You sure you heard something?"

The spooked dwarf nodded violently, his armor rattling. The other dwarf just shook his head and grabbed him. "Calm yourself, lad. You'll hear things on the wind more often than not; no need to be so flustered by it."

He shook his head again and shoved the dwarf toward the wall, wagging a finger at his junior, who caught himself well before he was in danger. "*That* be what you should be afeared of. Fallin'. Had two guards nod off just last year and fall over. All the way to the bottom in full armor, mind you. Not how *I* wanna go."

The junior guard, Wrelt, shivered, and they both walked away as Aertra leaned out to watch them go in almost disappointment. "That one had a powerful attachment to earth Aether." She wiped her lips with the back of her hand and blinked to herself a few times before motioning to me. "Come."

We crept forward and around the guard hut, then inside to go down a series of ladders. On the sixth ladder, we paused as I heard something that made a chill run up my spine.

I hopped down onto the floor and moved to the doorway in the room on the right-hand side. I opened it slowly and glanced inside to see a couple figures gathered in a corner with someone laying on the floor at their feet. I was a prince here; I could step in and stop this with no repercussions.

"Get up, lad." One of them spat as if they were disappointed. "You took the beating ya had coming—walk it off like a real dwarf!"

The figure on the floor had wispy hairs on his chin, his leather armor dyed a shade of red just shy of the others' red metal armor. One of his eyes was swollen shut, and the other was already blackened. Blood dribbled from his lip, and I could smell it dripping from the plate gloves of the attackers.

"See if you're late to a shift again!" The other harrumphed and spit on the younger dwarf as I slipped into the room, my anger swelling with the grunts of pain and hurt coming from their victim.

Something rose within my breast, hunger sharpening my vision more than it ever had, and that feral feeling that I had fought to contain raged through me.

I pulled my limbs close to myself as I shuffled closer to the dwarf that had spit on the prone figure. My fingers grabbed his shoulder plates, and I yanked him back. "Wha—ah!"

My teeth slammed into the side of his neck as I reached my

left arm over his shoulder and blasted a simple shard of super-cooled ice into the other figure's thigh. The blood I drained from the dwarf struggling in my grasp recovered my spent Aether instantly, and I fired another at the other's shoulder as he lifted a crossbow toward me.

His finger clenched as he cried out, and the bolt he had loaded fired into my victim's stomach, "Fuck!" I snarled and drank deeper, my Aether recovering again. I could see his health bar draining as the blood pooled inside him.

Rather than leave the meal to suffer, I grabbed his head in my hand and jerked it up, twisting viciously. My anger had over-taken me, and that same swelling sensation in my chest demanded this—whatever it was.

The dwarf on the floor tried desperately to reload his weapon, the bolt slipping from his bloodied fingers as he cursed nervously, "Get up, boy, we're being attacked!"

The young dwarf tried to rise, but I rested a hand on his back and pressed him back down, my voice coming out deeper than I had intended. "Stay down, kid."

"Get up, you useless piece of sh—!" My fingers wrapped around the dwarf's throat, and I lifted. My formerly sore and aching muscles no longer screamed in agony, but relished the exercise.

He choked and coughed, sputtering insults at me as I snarled, " You must be in charge in some capacity, right?"

He just spat and growled wordlessly. I realized belatedly that he couldn't really speak with the grip I had on his neck. I didn't care. He was more of a monster than me. Beating a defenseless kid up. Because he was late?

"Well, I'm here to relieve you of that authority." Something in me snapped as his fist connected with my chin.

9 dmg taken.

"Graargh!" I yanked him forward and bit into his exposed neck, just missing my thumb as his body shook and stiffened. I raised my left fist and summoned my Aether, ice building from my fingertips like a blade that I slammed into his temple.

Soft clapping echoed into the room as I finished my bloody work, the dwarf's body slumping to the ground as I turned to look at the smiling woman. "I had to admit, I was worried that you would be too delicate for what I had in mind, but this? This is *perfect* for my teaching style. What will you do with the child?"

I turned, blood still dribbling down from my chin as I knelt next to him. I took a moment and focused before reaching out to rest a hand on him. With my Lay of Hands spell, I concentrated and pressed a measly three HP into him. He didn't look like he hurt as badly as he had before, the swelling in his eye going down slightly.

"Please…" His voice rasped out from his split lips as he struggled to get away from me. "Don't kill me. Please."

I blinked, realizing what he had to have been going through. "Hey, kid. It's okay. I'm not going to kill you. You get a freebie today, okay?"

He was silent for a time, then asked, "What happened to them?"

"They paid for their crap leadership practices." A rueful smile grew on my face. "They won't hurt you again."

"Leaving him alive could bite you some day," Aertra advised with a blank look on her face. "Are you certain you want to leave a witness?"

My mind raced as I thought of a good reason to do just that. If I didn't, this kid could be killed simply for having the gall to survive. Then, it hit me.

"How is royalty supposed to cement their power if there aren't people to tell tales of their wrath and their benevolence?" I swallowed past the inexplicable lump in my throat and continued. "Those two incurred my wrath, and I took pity on their victim and assisted him. Now, he will do nothing other than sing my praises, won't he?"

As I finished my explanation, I prodded the boy, and he nodded as much as his injuries would allow him. "That's right, m'lord."

Aertra seemed conflicted, then shrugged and turned with a soft grin. "What do you plan to do with the bodies?"

That same feeling swelled in my chest once more, and I suddenly *knew* what I should do. I grabbed them and dragged them toward the room we had entered through. "They'll be proof of my wrath and that we need to keep these folks on watch to ensure this hazing shit doesn't happen again."

She raised an eyebrow and tilted her head as she observed me putting the crossbow into my inventory before taking the body, dragging it to the ladder that led down to the next floor, and tossing it over the edge. The clattering, clanking racket drew shouts of attention and alarm from above and below. I grabbed the other body and repeated the same thing.

Each floor that I threw them down made more noise as the shouts grew closer. After the fourth floor, someone found me dragging both bodies with Aertra and Vulina behind me. Their axe was braced in both hands, voice sounding metallic as it burst from their helm, "Halt!"

"I'm Prince Kyvir; this is my guest and my friend." I motioned to the bodies at my sides, then at the corpses on the floor. "These are criminals."

The figure glanced at them, then me, stepping a foot forward. "Let them go!"

"They're dead," I advised calmly, hearing knuckles popping audibly as their grip tightened on the weapon in their grasp. "I'm moving their bodies to make an example of them."

"That ain't right!" the dwarf asserted, metallic steps and noises coming from other places growing steadily louder. "You wait here until my superior can arrive. Prince or not—no royalty should kill their people like that."

I sighed and shook my head, turning to lift the dwarf who had shot at me with the crossbow. I lifted him as the other dwarf stepped forward and shouted something at me, but I just asked, "This him?"

They lifted their visor and the helmet clattered to the

ground as his eyes took in what they were seeing. They just nodded wordlessly.

"He pissed me off for attacking one of the junior guards. He and this other dwarf,"—I motioned to the other body as I dropped the one in my hands—"beat him within an inch of his life. I don't play that garbage, and they had to die for it."

"You killed them?" he whispered, clearly aghast as I nodded slowly.

"I will not tolerate this kind of mistreatment of my mother and sisters' forces and children." The growling threat came to me easier than I thought it would.

A figure dropped from the ladder behind me with a hammer in his hands, roaring, "What in the absolute goat shite is going on here?"

"They killed the second lieutenant, Sarge!" The dwarf in front of me cried, his axe raising up slightly.

"What?" The dwarf—I recognized him as Vler from the top of the wall—frowned and took in the scene. "Who did?"

"They did!" He took a step closer, and I held a hand up, calling flames into my grasp to light up the dark room.

"This is getting us nowhere, and I'm already irritated." Tiredly, I turned to the sergeant, "Again—I am Prince Kyvir, and these two men had been found guilty of crimes against her Majesty's children, the penalty being my decision."

Vler looked at me in consternation until I held the flames up and pointed to the signet ring on my finger. He scowled. "What was it that they was doing?"

"Hazing," I spat. He looked confused, and I lifted my chin, "It may seem normal to you, but beating a fellow guard almost to death for something trivial hardly seems right. It's one thing if you beat someone in training, and another entirely when two stronger guards gang up on a weaker and younger one. What kind of example does that set?"

Vler looked down at their bodies, the color draining slowly from his cheeks as he muttered, "Not a good one."

"Exactly." I reached down and grabbed the two corpses by

the backs of the armor and turned to the guard that had blocked our path before. "Step aside, guard. I have already shown my lenience twice today."

He looked to the sergeant behind me, whose voice barked, "Move, you witless dolt! You want to die too?"

The guard stepped aside and crashed to the ground loudly in his rush, his feet catching the corner of the ladder leading down. *Vulina, grab him!*

The guard almost fell into the opening of the ladder well, but the draconic-looking faerie grasped his armor and grunted with the effort of holding him long enough for me to get there and finish pulling him out.

I glared down at him, trying to decide what to say, when I just shook my head and went back to removing the corpses. He sat there, watching us as we passed by, the sergeant calling orders to the dwarves that had begun to flood into the area.

"I'll follow the prince out and make sure nothing else of note happens; the rest of you, get your arses back to the wall and your stations!" His howled commands sent the rest of the dwarves careening to wherever they were needed, or wherever was closest. Either way, they were out of our way.

It took another ten minutes to get down the ladders, then a shortcut that the good sergeant showed us that led us toward the barracks. As we passed it, an idea occurred to me. "Sergeant Vler, do the majority of the guards come through here?"

"It's pretty cut off from the public, but aye, the majority of the guard need to come through this area to get to and from the wall." He frowned at me deeply, "Why?"

"I need two pikes, thick and sturdy," I ordered him softly. He just shrugged and walked into a door built into the near side of the wall. Once he was gone, I worked on stripping the two guards of their armor, happy that they had clothes on underneath. A few minutes later, Vler came back out with four large lances that were thinner, and I gave him an approving nod. They would work for what I had in mind.

I used my ice Aether to make a spear that I shoved into the

ground at my feet next to the stair, gouging two holes, three feet apart. Grabbing one of the lances from the sergeant, I shoved it into the back of the lieutenant's corpse before lifting with my entire body. I growled, then grunted and roared, as the strain of it was intense.

Carrying them had been one thing, but this was completely different. Finally, the first was in the air and the haft of the lance sank into the hole I had made, with the second spear pressed into the corner of the wall to support the weight on the original weapon.

Sergeant Vler's already pale face looked horrified. "What is this for?"

"It's a reminder of how leadership is supposed to uplift and support those beneath it." I touched the spears in his hand as I tilted my head to catch his gaze. "I learned this from the histories of my world. There was a leader long ago called Vlad, and when he beat his enemies, he would do this to them as a warning to others who might attack him."

"You think the guard your enemy, Highness?" I could see the fear in his eyes as I shook my head and touched his shoulder. He flinched, and I could feel it.

"I see those who fail the men and women in their charge as enemies." I grasped the next spear and shoved it into the man that had assisted the lieutenant in his cruel mission. "And those complicit are just as guilty! This isn't political; this isn't cruelty. This is a warning to those who seek to abuse their power."

I lifted again as I spoke, the rage in me fueling my efforts as the exertion threatened to overwhelm me. The spear shuddered as it fell into the hole, and the second spear acted in a similar fashion to the first.

"Be certain to pass that sentiment on to every guard who sees these former leaders." I smiled at him sweetly as I passed him, my stomach growling angrily. "And anyone else who thinks that they can just bully anyone they want."

He nodded, ghostly white as he moved away on shaky legs.

"I think I would like to hear more of this Vald man." Aertra stared appreciatively up at my work before turning her gaze to me. "He sounds interesting."

"*Vlad* the Impaler was a very interesting monster," I moved my shoulders in an attempt to ease some of the ache I felt, "as he became one of the most infamous vampires to ever walk my world. His stories have been told for generations, in books and in voice. All over."

She touched the spears whispering, "How wonderful."

Then I realized what I had said, the two corpses hovering above my head casting an even darker shadow down over me. *What am I becoming?*

CHAPTER TEN

SETH

As we walked away from the barracks, Aertra grasped my hand and pulled me into the shadows, her hand clamping over my mouth.

"Shh," she whispered and let go of me. I glared at her, and she just smiled wider. "Tell me, when you fought those men, what did you sense? Did you sense anything about them?"

"No?" I shrugged, trying to think back past the cloud of anger that I didn't really understand. I knew I didn't like hazing, I had a friend in high school who had lost his scholarship for baseball because some *gentle hazing* had torn his ACL and MCL, making him unable to play the game that he loved. It had put him onto a dark path, and even to this day, I still didn't know what had happened to him. He cut ties to everyone and just moved away.

"Tell me what you felt." Her face was expectant as she watched me, almost too eager for my taste.

"Rage at what they were doing." I shook my head as I tried to think it through. "When I fed, I felt stronger." Speaking of stronger, I glanced through my notifications and found that I had gained 23 EXP for both of those guards. No Aether toward my affinities, though.

"Yes, and they had no Aether that they could offer you, right?" I nodded at her question, and she grinned. "Good. Now I'm going to teach you how to find those who have stronger ties to the Aether."

"I can see Aether; does that help?" She stared at me for a moment, then grinned wider. "I take it that's a yes."

"Of course it is, but this would have been a little more difficult and would have involved your other senses." She crossed her arms and leaned against the wall. "Tell me, what are the limitations?"

I don't trust her. I would leave some out—don't lie, but don't tell her everything. Vulina's voice startled me a bit, and I pondered her words of advice.

Finally, I answered, "I can see the color of peoples' auras, and they're usually tinted with the color of magic that they use."

"Everyone?" She raised a brow at me, and I nodded once. "This is exciting. Let's try it."

She pointed to someone, a halfling man walking with a gaggle of children giggling and trailing behind him. He wasn't using any magic actively as I focused on him, there not being any kind of aura around him.

The little girl who was three children behind him, though, was using some kind of deep purple magic that made her levitate slightly off the ground, just enough to make it seem like she was walking when she wasn't. The aura was thicker than any I had seen in some time, almost as thick as Belgonna's when she used magic.

"He's clean, but that little girl is using some kind of magic." Aertra turned her head and closed her eyes as she took a deep breath through her nose.

"Space magic?" She was thoroughly surprised, her nose crinkling. "We should take her. That magic is rare."

"No." I shot her idea down immediately, much to her chagrin. "If we take anyone in the city who doesn't deserve it, Belgonna or her daughter will kill us. Even as strong as you claim to be, you can't take them both."

"Sentimental?" She chuckled to herself. "Even I draw the line at children. Though halflings are almost always older than they look. Now, as we move, I want you to find Aether and point it out to me."

I sighed and moved on, all of us marching through the streets as the other vampire eyed the denizens of the city hungrily. Many of them strayed from wherever they were walking to clear a path for us—mainly to get away from the clearly predatory woman walking in their midst.

As we walked, I would point out the magic that I could see, my Evil Eyes only gleaning so much. But as we drew closer to the den, I began to notice small wisps of magic around a few more people in the streets. As I motioned to them, either with a nod or my hand, Aertra grew steadily more impressed, until finally, I could point out people without her telling me I missed anyone.

Evil Eye (Initiate lvl 5).

Well, that was good, I guess. I turned my eyes to the guards in front of the large door to the den where the queen and Belgonna would likely be.

I turned to Aertra. "What will you do?"

She blinked at the door a few times before stepping close to me and touching my cheek.

You have received a friend request from Aertra Douvin.

Would you like to accept it? Yes / No ?

I accepted it, my lips a thin line as I watched her. "I will be staying nearby. I want to train you more, so come to me when you have time, yes?"

"Fine." I nodded to myself more than her, then turned and walked into the large stone building to see about getting Vulina roasted by mommy dearest. I'd given in, mainly due to her remaining close through all of that.

She took the time to flutter up to each portrait on the wall and ask if I knew anyone. "I don't, no. Though I do like that one. His scowl is particularly nice."

She chuckled at my sarcastic retort and flew down next to me. "How is Belgonna? I've heard stories about her from the more powerful elementals, but I've never seen her."

"She's nice," I started to explain, then frowned. *How do I say this?* "She's pretty motherly. She likes to adopt people and look out for her children. Though I'm certain I'll likely get into trouble. I should go and speak to the queen before we go see Mom."

I chill swept over me. *Mom.* It felt so weird to call her that, knowing my real mother was still out there, helping people alongside my dad.

And why did it hurt so badly that they *still* hadn't reached out to me via email to come back? Or at least get into MMO? I shook my head and continued on.

I knocked loudly on the door to the throne room, and Sinistella's voice rang out, slightly muffled, "Enter!"

I sighed and prepared myself for whatever might come and pressed open the door.

Both Belgonna and Sinistella stood together near the table that had been moved into the chamber on the other side of the room.

"Ah, hello brother Kyvir." Sinistella grinned at me, and my skin prickled slightly. "How can I help you?"

"It's more how I've…helped you and the city." She frowned and cocked her head to the side.

I was about to speak again when she held a hand up and her teeth flashed in the torch light. "You mean those guards you brutally murdered and then hung up near the guard station on pikes?" She crossed her arms and stepped forward. "Please, do explain why I shouldn't have you arrested here and now?"

"Oh, Sin, stop it." Belgonna slapped her daughter's arm softly, much to the newly-crowned queen's distaste. "I'm certain he has a good reason; no need to be so harsh." She glanced over to me expectantly.

I explained what happened to them, the fact that I had a guest and Vulina there with me. She corroborated my explanation, though the entire time, both rulers had their bearing on point to the degree that I couldn't tell if they were pleased or appalled.

Finally, Sinistella made a vague motion with her hand and said, "So, what, you pinning up the men that you believe did something wrong will make others too afraid to do the same?"

"It's a tactic that some find to have worked." *Granted, it's not one that I would have thought of in my own right mind.*

"Is that true, Kyvir?" Belgonna stepped forward, her nose crinkling and scenting the air. "You recently took a job, did you not? And tell me—how is it that you found yourself on the wall?"

"Training my abilities." I deflected carefully. It wasn't a lie, but omission was something I was certain she didn't care for. "And yes, I took the job of Dark Paladin."

Both of them turned to each other, and Sinistella scowled deeply, "Does that mean what I think it means?"

Belgonna nodded, "Yes. It does." She turned to me and walked closer with that look of motherly love clearly visible. "My son, these 'jobs' have a way of… weaving themselves into your being. They sort of gift you with aspects of what they are —what they can become. Did you feel something when you were overcome with these intense emotions?"

I searched myself, trying to put a definition to it, but couldn't come up with anything.

"Righteousness," she growled, her hands on my shoulders clenching a little. "What you felt was righteous fury that bled into you from the job you took, which must have melded with the predatory instincts of what you've become."

"So I'm not going insane?" She shook her head at me and pulled me into a hug.

"No, but you must recognize it so that it will not make you

do anything foolish or dangerous." Her chest moved as she heaved a sigh, then kissed my forehead.

"I see. Then this is not entirely wanton murder, and more a skewed view of justice?" Sinistella posed aloud. "I can't say that I disagree with your verdict, little brother. I do say that it does promote good order and discipline—though I do not need *everyone* to fear me. Just my enemies."

She smiled at me, and for the first time in quite a while, it looked genuine. "I won't punish you for something that I wish I would have thought of myself, so long as I can use it, should it please me?"

I shrugged and scratched my head. "Sure? I don't think anyone owns the rights to Vlad's work?" She chuckled, and I relaxed, looking to both her and Belgonna. "I'm sorry."

"Do not be, brother." It was Sinistella's turn to step forward. "I would have done the same if I were in your boots. Though, I would appreciate a little forewarning next time."

She knocked her fist against my shoulder with a wink. I received a friend request from her that I accepted right away. "Next time, just give me.. what was it Sundar had called it? A 'heads' up?"

I snorted and shook my head ruefully. "Sounds like her. And I will."

"Good." She pinched my cheek. "I will have them taken down and buried in a few days' time. For now, who was it that was with you?"

"A... mentor of sorts." I sighed as she eyed me steadily, until I added, "She's another Aether Vampire. Like me. She's interested in training me to be a better, uh, *me*?"

"I see. And do you trust her?" Sinistella pressed.

"No. But she's the only one I know of who can help me keep myself in check. I think." That last bit had been added, because I genuinely wasn't certain.

Did I want to keep myself in check? Would that make me weaker? Or would losing control of myself make my mission to get to Mona and get her back from the demons a secondary thought?

"You'll find her, my son," Belgonna whispered. "I will see if I cannot suss her out, and this mentor of yours, as well. If I find anything, I will let you know."

She turned to Vulina and smiled. "I see that you have been practicing your summoning magic. Who is this precious little thing? And so beautiful!"

"My name is Flicker, ma'am!" the faerie answered politely as she ducked her head. She straightened and bashfully clasped her hands together. "I had a question that I was saving until after you were done talking, if it wouldn't be rude?"

Belgonna chuckled and held her hand out to the smaller figure. "I think I can manage that. Though I do not know exactly what my breath will do to you. Are you certain about this?"

"Yes I am!" Vulina gushed, her smile absolutely massive, then she paused as she realized that her question hadn't even been asked aloud. Then she gushed anyway, "I'm going to get *so* big!"

I snorted at her, and she spiraled around Belgonna as the dragon beckoned me to her. "Sinistella, we will be in my room for a bit. Please, let us know if anything is needed?"

"Yes, mother." The queen nodded and then gasped, "And brother? Here."

She tossed me something that I caught easily. It was my short sword with the golden blade, her father's presence probing toward me as soon as I touched it. "Try to find a better weapon for him to inhabit some time soon, won't you?"

"Yes, my queen." I bowed my head, and she turned toward the paperwork on her table.

"Kyvir?" I stopped and looked back at Sinistella, "You know that I can't just give you everything, right? Even though I would love nothing more than to be able to give you a weapon worthy of him?"

I shrugged, "We're capable of doing it. I know you have constraints and people to care for."

I excused myself after she nodded more to herself than me. Belgonna walked us out of the room into a large courtyard that had the roof carved out. The night sky was plainly visible, the myriad dots of white light visible in the air. The yard was warm, and shrubs and grass grew plentifully, as well as fungi of differing types that almost reminded me of a play set.

Various wooden weapons littered the ground, the former queen sighing deeply, "They never put away their toys!" She snorted and just continued on. "Children! Hah, I knew what I was getting into, but they are just so adorable."

I found myself grinning. It was no wonder that she and Emerald got along so well.

We left the yard through another, larger doorway the size of a garage door. The massive room inside was hotter than anything I had felt before.

Magma circulated the room like brick would make up a wall, while the center for the room held a large pool of lava that flowed in a circular pattern like a whirlpool.

"This is my private bath." Belgonna shifted her form to that of her ancient dragon body. The towering crimson-scaled behemoth filled the majority of the room with ease. "Would you like a bath, Flicker?"

"Yes. I. *Would!*" The faerie hopped into the pool of lava as if she were a kid doing a cannonball off the diving board. Lava splattered softly against the side of the pool and melded back in.

"Prepare yourself, child; it will be *much* hotter momentarily!" Belgonna reared her head back and drew in a deep breath. Blazing orange, red, green, and blue auras flared around the crimson dragon in waves that started near her stomach and radiated upward toward her gullet.

Flames spewed forth from her gaping maw and rained down over Vulina where she waded in the lava.

"Oh, it's so warm and pretty!" Vulina sounded like she was experiencing pure blissful relaxation as she spoke. It was so difficult to make her out under the scope of the flames and the purity of the Aether I was seeing that I had to actually shut my eyes, it was that intense. Luckily, my mutated body was a little more well adjusted to the heat itself.

The heat that drowned the room turned up a notch and finally died down after a few moments. I was thoroughly impressed that Belgonna could hold her flame that long, but as I opened my eyes to view the scene, I found myself even further surprised.

The flames that had flooded the lava continued to swirl around the pool and the faerie inside it as she laid in the center of it all, gently spinning with her eyes closed. "You alright in there, Vu—Flicker?"

"I am *so* good!" she groaned delightedly as her arms stroked the lava like water.

I chuckled to myself and turned to find Belgonna staring down at me, her gaze curious. "Do you truly think yourself a monster, my son?"

Her question gave me pause and made my heart race as I tried to find an acceptable answer. I noticed that her nose wasn't working like it normally did when she was trying to learn about someone or something.

"I don't know." I scratched my head as she motioned for me to come close to her massive draconic form, her clawed hand palm up extended for me to rest against. She ended up scooping me up like a newborn babe so that she could hold me close. "You know what happened. What I've done, and what I did to those two guards. What do you think?"

"I think that for centuries, we dragons were viewed as monsters, and there are some still today who see us as such." Her warm breath and presence pressed around me, familiar and alien at the same time. "I can also see how some people choose to call those with a certain degree of pragmatism and differing views 'monsters', because it is easy to fear and fight the monsters if they are the bad ones. I think the important thing for you to decide is, if you embrace that title—what kind of monster will you become?"

I snorted, the corner of my mouth lifting wryly. "If I'm a monster already, does it matter what kind I am?"

"I think so," she offered softly, drawing my attention to her eyes. Their ageless wisdom, bathed in orange, stared down at me with nothing but adoration and care. There was no judgement, no pity. Just...love. "I think, if you must be a monster to give yourself the strength to do what you feel must be done, that you must be one of your own design, and not that of what people may try to make you out to be."

Oddly, that made sense. "But, if I choose to travel this path, don't you worry that I could become a danger to others?"

Now it was her turn to smile ruefully. "My love, we dragons have always been a danger to others. I would prefer my children not be your victims, but if there are those who stand in your way—end them."

My jaw dropped at the callous order and finality of her last statement, but she leaned forward and placed the scales around her maw against my shoulder affectionately like a kiss, "That is what we dragons do, dear."

CHAPTER ELEVEN

MONA

"Again." Bardif's indifference and annoyance only made the task he expected me to accomplish that much more annoying and oppressive.

The metal in my hands twitched and bucked as I filtered the new demonic Aether I now carried, thanks to taking the job of Harvester.

Use the demonic Aether as your furnace, then pull and shape the metal to what you see it becoming in your mind, I muttered internally as the mounting frustration of my many previous mishaps and failures began to sap away my will to go on trying. *Perfect practice makes perfect, child.*

I honestly couldn't tell anyone in the last day and a half how many times I had heard that from the surly Reaper.

I took a steadying breath and rubbed my fingers over the metal, feeding the Aether into it steadily until I could visibly see that the metal had grown hot enough to be pliable.

My bottom lip ached from biting and chewing it to try and remain in control of my emotions long enough to truly grasp what the metal wanted to be. Pulling the metal with my mind, I started to finally glimpse what the ingot *wanted* to be. What it desired.

Shaping it with my will and intent grew steadily easier, and then the shape began to curve and twist, the demonic Aether warping it and stealing the image from me as the metal blackened and charred in my hands.

"Gah!" I snarled inarticulately and whipped the metal into the air, the ruined mass clanging on the pile behind me as mild cursing from off to my right was drowned out by Lira's light laughter.

"You'll get it some day," she teased, her mouth hidden behind her hand.

"I see my time will be wasted again today." Bardif crossed his arms, his large wings flaring behind him in his irritation. "I have better things to do. When you finally learn how to make your harvesting tool, call my name."

He touched my head, and I got a friend request just before he took off and flew away, the wind from his departure whipping at my face and fur.

"I don't understand why I can't get this!" I tried desperately to keep the hopelessness out of my tone. I'd learned early on that the demons in proximity tended to get a little excited about that, and they got too close as it was.

Lira stood up and stretched, her every lithe movement drawing ample attention from anyone in sight, much to my annoyance. "I don't know, but I've been called to a meeting and I have to go for a little bit. Keep trying?"

She didn't wait for me to answer before she just blinked away from me. I rolled my eyes. "Yeah, I'll just chill here with all the demons and whatnot while you two are off doing whatever."

I sighed again and thought about my best course of action. I needed true mentoring, and there was no way I could afford to pay the souls to have someone here teach me what I was doing wrong.

Watching all the demons around me glaring in my direction hatefully, I muttered to myself, "Not like I could trust them to teach me correctly, anyway."

I was on my own in a city I didn't know, and I needed help learning to craft. *Think, Mo. Where can you turn? If only there was a smith…wow, you're really dense when your entire world comes crashing down on your head, kid.*

I rolled my eyes and walked over to the corner of the street we had been practicing on, pressing the large stone to the cornerstone of the building. A pulse reverberated up my arm, letting me know that the stone was set, and I thought about traveling to Belgonna's Hold.

One blink later, and I stood in the center of the city, bustling dwarves and the scent of clean, fresh air passing my nostrils. For once, since I had gone to that forsaken hell hole, I could breathe without the scent of sulfur accosting me.

Now, where did master Ori say that this smith was? I took the leather object he had given me and read the note that Ori had attached before making my way toward the shop. Some people stared at me intently, long enough that I eventually found an alley to go into and found someone's laundry hanging in the brief breeze. I grabbed a rather small blanket that was still a bit damp and wrapped it over my head and shoulders like a shawl to make sure I didn't stand out as much.

Once I was ready, I stepped back out into the streets again.

It was a new day here, the sun having just risen over the wall in the East. Children and other people milled about the streets tiredly, their yawns and subconscious scratching of heads and rumps leaving me more and more at ease. The entire time, I couldn't help thinking, *These people aren't really real. Nor are they NPCs. They're something in between, but they can't be trusted. I hope I don't run into Kyvir or Mom… that'd be awkward. Especially Mom, after having finally seen dad after so long?*

I shook my head and made my way to the smithy, carefully watching the roadways and buildings for signs of my former party members and the royalty. Luckily, it wasn't a long trip from where I had teleported in. Twenty minutes later, I stood outside the entrance for a moment, collecting my courage, when the door opened and a surly-looking dwarven man trundled out.

"You just going to stand there all morning, girlie?" The broad-shouldered, older dwarf scowled at me and crossed his arms. His nostrils flared abruptly and his eyes sparkled. "It's you, then!"

"What about me?" I glanced around to make sure it wasn't a trap, but he just came out to usher me inside. "What's going on?"

"That boy with the horns, the Kin one, what was his name again?" He scratched his beard, then shrugged happily as he began to whistle a tune and shove me toward the door.

"It's Kyvir, and what are you shoving me for?" I growled as his hands pressed against my back once more. I whirled on him and snarled, "Would you stop it and tell me what is going on? I don't even know you."

"Well, I'm Master Gretlen, and Kyvir must have sent you to me. Did he give you those tomes?" He blinked, then shrugged again, "Don't matter anyhow, seeing as you're here. Well! Let's not be wasting time, and get you smithing!"

I blinked at the older dwarf in shock and awe of just how chipperly he completely ignored me.

"Master Ori told me to give you this." I offered the object to him lamely, and he took it. He flicked his thumb over the cap and popped it off with a smile, pouring out a letter and several large chunks of dark metal.

He glanced at the letter, his lips moving, and a grin spread over his cheeks. He touched the metal and began to probe it with his fingers, holding it up to a candle and the grin widened even further.

"What's that?" I frowned at him, and he glanced up as if he were surprised I was still here.

He held it up for me to see. The dark ore still had flecks of dirt and stone on it as he moved it in the light. "Oh, this is a new ore that was found in the mines over at Iradellum."

He slammed it on the counter, and a small man screeched as he flew into the room with a tiny crossbow, "Intruder!" He found me, his eyes wide and wild as his finger pressed the release mechanism.

The bolt arched at me and I flinched, but when I opened my eyes, the bolt had stopped mid-flight and hovered in the air before my nose.

Gretlen scowled at the little man. "What did I tell you about that thing and sleeping in, you lazy dolt?"

The other man stammered, "Forgive me, Master Gretlen, I was up all night inventorying the wares, and I lost track of time."

"Stop firing at my apprentices," the dwarf growled, flexing his fingers. The metal portions of the contraption crumpled and the small man cried out, throwing the crossbow down.

Gretlen turned back to me. "Ori says you understand the basics, but I know better. You could have stopped that bolt if you understood everything you should. Come with me."

He scooped the metal into his large hands and walked into the next room, the crimson glow within warm and almost unbearably oppressive, compared to the heat at Master Ori's forge.

"We can skip the preamble of me having you forge something by hand—I know you can do that from Ori's letter." Gretlen stood by the forge and crossed his arms. "Metal magic is different from a lot of others because of the depth of control it allows us. Tell me what you know."

I blanked, then shook my head and took a deep breath. "My magic allows me to shape and mold metal, not only to any shape I desire, but also what the metal wants to become." He stayed completely still, as if he were waiting, so I continued, "I can also control metal objects in a similar manner to you, just like you stopping that bolt."

"No, you can't." He snorted and rolled his eyes, and I just

blinked at him, the indignation of all of his antics welling within me. I clenched my teeth and tried to smile, but he laughed to himself and shook his head. "Listen, girlie, you have immense affinity for metal magic. You could be *better* than me. Surpass me. Surpass us *all*. That's what I want."

I opened my mouth, then closed it again, unable to think of anything to say to him. It had been a while since someone had disarmed me so handily.

He turned and found an ingot of metal and threw it into the forge above the cherry red floor, opening a section of sorts below it that brought lava into a bowl. The metal heated so swiftly that it took almost no time at all.

He brought it out with a flick of his wrist, then began to pinch and pull the metal with his will. He folded and cut and molded the ingot until it was roughly the shape and length of a short sword. Once the basic outline was set, he put it on the anvil before him and dragged his nail across the actual blade portion.

Metal shavings split from where he sharpened the edge and landed on the floor at his feet as he hummed a tune to himself. The blade was superbly made, and as he allowed it to heat once more, he motioned to the shavings on the floor that fluttered into his grasp.

He clenched his fists so tightly, I heard his bones crackling before he opened his palm to show me a line of metal that he then put into the forge for a second. He brought both blade and metal globule out and shaved down the other side of the blade. The shavings flicked to the cherry-red line of metal to add themselves in. He then molded it and made a cross guard that he fit to the bottom of the blade with ease.

The final addition was to carve runes into the spine of the blade before filling them with flakes of gold.

He lifted it with his bare hands and dunked it into the oil barrel he had off to the side of the room, his ears perking up intently.

He nodded to himself after a moment and pulled it out to

inspect his craft. It was beautiful—expertly made, and I wanted to do that too.

"This is what centuries of dedication can do." He smiled to himself before motioning to the blade. "Quicker than I normally do them, and only because I hone my craft the normal way, out of respect for my gods and my ancestors. I expect you hold no such compunctions."

I shook my head, still mute as I took in the sight of the beautiful rune work on the weapon.

"Good." His smile was genuine as he dusted off his hands. "Good. Let's begin then, shall we?"

I nodded, and he pulled out another ingot for me to work with.

"This is all you." His confident voice assuaged some of my nervousness. "You don't need to do everything I did, nor how I did it. I want you to see the metal's desire and bring it out. Don't worry about perfection just yet."

Closing my eyes, I steadied myself and reached out with my metal Aether, lifting the ingot from his palm to put it into the forge.

The ingot glowed red and I pulled it out, focusing on what the ingot wanted to become. *Fold me.* It could have just been me thinking too hard, but I wanted to make sure I did it right.

So I lengthened and folded the ingot several times slowly, the process much more difficult for me than a seasoned veteran smith. It took me more than half my Aether to get even get close to finishing the piece, but as the process went on, I found that the smithing process was easier.

Eventually, Gretlen started gently prodding me with ideas and ways to improve what was being made. Little tidbits of information that were nothing like how Ori used to teach. Not that I had hated that, but this was just so…different.

By the end of it all, I had recovered some and used more of my Aether, thanks to his guidance, and had completed a long, thin-bladed dagger.

Gretlen picked it up and checked it for flaws before putting it into the forge and motioning to the barrel.

I gritted my teeth as I used my last bar of Aether to pluck the cherry-red piece out of the forge and plunge it into the barrel. Flames gushed out of the top and I withdrew it to place on the anvil.

Gretlen held it up again and smiled, "Been a while since I've seen someone make a stiletto like this; rare weapon of at least common make. Needs to be filed and ground, but otherwise? Good work. We can truss this up in a little bit."

His hands treated the metal weapon with respect, and he took it to a small hanging work table attached to the wall and suspended closest to us by chains.

He set it there and placed a few files next to it before turning back to me. "Let's go again as soon your Aether recovers."

"Okay." I watched as he worked, slowly filing away imperfections in the blade and cross guard. Finally, I worked up the nerve to ask, "Is it possible to infuse other Aether into an item that you're making?"

His hands, perfectly steady in their task, continued to move as he turned to look me fully in the face. "Yes. It is. But it's not something I recommend doing until you're much better with your magic. Why?"

Wringing my hands as I realized just how screwed I was, I explained, "Well, I have a job that requires that I do that with a specific type of Aether. If I can't make the weapons I need, then I can't get any stronger."

He frowned, putting the file down onto the table before scratching his heated chin. "Never heard of a job like that."

"It's pretty rare," I offered mildly, a soft smile on my face as I attempted to distract him from thinking too much about that.

"I have no issue teaching you how to do it, but it will take dedicated practice." He wagged a finger at me. "You'll need to be prepared to fail, and fail drastically."

I set my feet, lifted my chin, and growled, "I hate failure, so I will do my best to be better than that."

His stern look faded and a lopsided grin replaced it. "Good. Let's go."

We worked tirelessly on creating as much as we possibly could. I made knives, a sword, and even something that Gretlen called a blackjack, which was basically a small club.

None of these had been created with any different Aether, as it was hard, and I lost control immediately.

All of the weapons took hours, and I was so happy to be getting this sort of personal attention.

"Do you think we could make something with different Aether?" I asked finally. The shrapnel on the floor was still there and would no longer respond to normal metal manipulation.

"We can try again." He sighed, his nod making his beard shake. He had been offering advice while he made a few inquiries on the ore that he had gotten from Iradellum. He grimaced as he shut another large book. "I want to try something."

He tapped the stone and rock off the ore and placed the clumps into a bucket that he used for smelting. He glanced at me and winked as he closed it and opened a section of the floor. Sweltering heat surged through the room as he uncovered lava that bubbled and flowed beneath the floorboards.

"Wow," I whispered to myself in wonder.

He put a long metal rod through a special hoop on the lid to the bucket and dunked it into the lava. As the bucket glowed red, we worked on the theories behind adding different Aether to what was being made.

"Now, when you do this, never make the Aether fully go into the metal." I frowned; that was exactly what I had been doing before in the demon city, though the fell magic was a way for me to heat the metal so it was easily more malleable. "You want to douse it, but not push it *in* to the metal. Surround it, and bathe it at first."

He pulled out a piece of greenish metal and began to mold it, sweat dappling his brow as he worked.

"As I work the metal, I add Aether to it, and once the process begins, I can stop easily." He stared me in the eyes, "You need not finish it right away, or in one go. I will now add earth Aether to this; watch."

The metal was pulled and tugged as the process began anew. As the weapon grew, brown and gray stone covered it and shifted along the forming blade.

He stopped and dabbed his brow with a handkerchief. "See, you can stop at any time. The interesting thing about all this is that the added magic begins to radiate around the metal and further manipulate it in a way that is true to the magic itself."

"So if someone were to use, like, ice or water magic, there may be icicles or condensation?" He nodded and I smiled, happy to have understood. "But how does that manipulate it?"

"In the same way that you would manipulate the metal, the additional Aether sees the image and tries to assist." He touched the budding weapon and pointed to a section of gray and brown stone slowly thickening in the area where Gretlen had stopped, the metal rising and moving with it, albeit painfully slowly. "To use your example, ice Aether could take to making a blade sharper by crystallizing along the edge, or by adding to the length of the blade. Though, with water Aether, it may try to remove impurities from the metal, or carve runes in the metal to make it different. Magic is odd like that."

The way his face scrunched up made me chuckle. After a few minutes, he started again. The metal of the blade broke through the stony addition, but it sort of flowed back into place and thickened again so that the blade appeared to be bisected by a section of stone that held the two pieces together.

Thinking about all of this talk of magic and how it changed things, I had to wonder how Seth was taking all of it. Was he having fun, or had my absence affected him at all?

You know it is, Mo. I rolled my eyes and shook my head, then focused back on my own predicament. I couldn't help him without being stronger first.

He worked some more, and as he did, he talked me through it. "As you close on the finishing of the item, you have to begin slowly pressing and channeling the Aether into it, so that the Aether permeates it."

As he finished forming the tip of the weapon, a longer and broader blade, a sort of barbed bit of stone burst from it and radiated downward in a cascading shower of pebbles and dust. As all of the debris hit the floor, it melted away, and the bladed edges of the sword appeared to be made of pure diamond. Gretlen grinned and patted the sword. "This is a great weapon. Sometimes, I surprise even myself."

"Is there an addition of damage or properties to the blade?" He raised a brow at me and tried to offer me the sword, then sighed before setting it down as I shook my head. "I don't want to touch it. I want you to explain it better than telling me it just affects the metal."

"Sorry; I forgot you wouldn't yet be able to see the statistics of it until you're stronger or have the appropriate level of proficiency." He touched it and paused thoughtfully. "There is additional damage, yes, as the blade is sharp and hard as diamond. There is also an added bit of earth elemental damage because of the Aether, and a rather sizable amount of durability as well."

"That's amazing!" I breathed, and I had to fight not to touch the blade. I couldn't wait to make weapons for myself to use as a Harvester.

He started to speak, but closed his mouth and tilted his head to sniff the air. Abruptly, he turned to the lava flowing through the floor and the glowing red bucket.

He quickly popped over to it and lifted the lid. Taking a small scooper out, he skimmed the top of it before pulling out a setting to make an ingot. He lifted the bucket and poured the molten metal into the mold before setting it onto the anvil to cool.

As he observed the quickly cooling metal, he frowned deeply. "This is an odd metal."

"How so?" I stepped over to join him, and noted with surprise that even though it was fresh out of the lava, it looked almost completely cool. The metal was black and dark gray with spikes and veins of crimson red shooting through it.

"There are only a few metals that will cool so quickly." He touched it and grimaced as he left his hand on it, turning the setting over and slamming it onto the anvil, the ingot left behind on the top of it. "Those that do typically have heavy influences from the elements of either ice or water. But this is neither of those things."

"So what should we do with it?" I touched it, and a shock of familiarity ground up my arm. I flinched, my hand flying back of its own accord. "What was that?"

He blinked at me, his rough and calloused hands dwarfing mine as he grasped my wrist to check my fingers. They looked perfectly fine. "Tell me what you felt."

"A sense of… familiarity?" I shook my head, as it truly didn't feel right.

His jaw dropped, and he picked it up and placed the metal in my hand. The same sensation flowed up my arm, discomforting me completely until it reached my mind. The shock of it jarred me, forcing my eyes to shut so I could refocus my vision.

When I opened my eyes again, the ingot in my hand had the clearest opaque outline overlaid on it.

Gretlen pulled me to the table and laid a sheet of paper and a piece of charcoal in front of me with the order, "Draw what you see."

I obeyed, setting the ingot down so that I could better express the vision I saw.

It looked like a knife, but it was longer and curved deeply, almost like a scythe. The blade came down and thickened into the hilt, with a thorn-like protrusion extending from the back, just above the hilt. Below the hilt was another sharp-looking thorn.

As soon as I was finished, Gretlen took the sheet and glared at it. "This looks… difficult. And cruel. You're sure it was from the ingot, and not you?"

I nodded, frowning. I stared at the ingot, and even from where I stood, I could see the item it wanted to be as if it were already tangible. Nothing I had ever dealt with was *this* intensely desired by metal. Other ingots and metals showed me what they wanted when I touched and held them. This? It *wanted* to become this weapon. Needed it.

I touched the ingot again, and a thrumming rose from it as the weapon outline pulsed.

"We can make it, and I will make certain you do it properly," Gretlen breathed, then cracked his neck loudly, the sound making me flinch. "It will be hard, but we can do it. Are you ready?"

I lifted the ingot in my hand and nodded. "Let's do it."

CHAPTER TWELVE

SETH

Vulina had finished soaking in the flames hours ago and had gone home, so it was time for me to rest. I "slept" in the rooms that we had been given.

The next morning, we woke and ate, Emerald and Sundar joining me for the meal. They were quiet for a while, but we gradually began to talk about what the dungeon could hold for us.

"If it's bugs, we're in trouble. Especially if there are more of those armored beetles." Emerald scowled down at Zanjir when the massive dog whined for food. "You know better. I will not feed you when you whine at me, and you know we plan to feed you in the dungeon, Zanjir."

"Eh, dogs whine." Sundar's stifled laughter drew Emerald's ire, but the larger woman held her hands out to keep the peace. "It's just my modicum of experience speaking. Not to tell you how to raise your pets."

"Zanjir is a companion and tool—not a pet." Emerald

rolled her eyes and offered a lopsided, knowing grin. "That's like telling a soldier that their rifle is a toy."

"Oh, that's very true." Sundar grinned back and winked at the older woman. "I like you. I know I've said it before, but I mean it."

"I hate to interrupt the love fest, but we need to get to getting." I polished off the bread and cheese on my plate happily, grimacing because it was absolutely disgusting. My stomach rolled violently, and I breathed deeply in an attempt to dispel some of the urge to vomit.

"Are you all right?" Emerald whispered to me as we prepared to leave.

"No," I replied honestly as my stomach revolted. "But I plan to visit someone later to help me learn about all of this. Right now, we need to focus on leveling up and improving ourselves—I'll go see if the coast is clear."

I was the first one to teleport to the tunnel and the dungeon entrance hidden within. Once I appeared inside the darkness, my eyes scanned the area for auras and lingering Aether residue. I found nothing; not even a beetle had come in here since we had left.

This is weird... I scowled around and finally decided that it was safe before sending a Whisper to both of them.

—*It's safe, you can 'port in.*— A second after that, both of them teleported next to me, Zanjir looking a little green around the gills for it.

—*Vulina, we're going into the dungeon. Are you coming?*— I blinked as I sent the message and prepared to summon Sprinkle, but she answered, and I paused.

—*Do not summon us yet.*— I blinked at her answer and shrugged to myself, then she sent another. —*The dungeon will force you to summon us again to get inside.*—

"Oh, that's lame as hell." I rolled my eyes and looked at the two confused women next to me. "We ready?"

They nodded, and I touched the door first. "Enter!" Air

rustled around my body, unseen energy pulsing, and then I stood on the other side of the door.

Emerald, Zanjir, and Sundar popped over a heartbeat later and took in the sights.

The tunnel was much the same as it had been on the other side. Deep-brown dirt, carved as if by a singular creature meandering its way through the earth for more than a hundred yards.

After that followed a mass of tunnels that looked to be jumbled together.

Vulina, come to me, please. I whispered through my mind. Out loud, I called, "Sprinkle! We need you!"

A wash of cold hit me, and the faerie burst into existence with an infusion of ice into the surrounding air. He grinned, his features a little more handsome than baby-like now, and he stood slightly taller and broader. Little icicles studded his ears from the tip to the bottom, like some sort of elven punk rocker.

"Hey, glad you called me here." He grimaced and eyed our surroundings warily. "Seriously hope it isn't bugs."

"Same." Vulina's voice surprised me, as there hadn't been the usual rush of heat from her entry.

I turned to look at her and was stunned. She was taller than me now, horns sprouting from the sides of her forehead, just next to her flaming hair, that came out and up in a more traditionally demonic-seeming way. Her once-red scales had shifted to hues of blue and green, which if I was right, meant a hotter flame.

She watched me, her once-fiery eyes now glowing an eerie white. Her skin was a warmer tone as well, a more tanned look than it had been previously.

You'll make me feel self conscious if you keep ogling me like that, Kyvir. She muttered through my head. Her wings were massive now and spread slowly to reveal that she no longer wore a dress but scale-like armor that made her look more draconic and ladylike than before.

Sorry. My cheeks burned hot, and I looked away.

Sundar whistled low. "That's some mighty big upgrading

you've been doing, little lady!" She stepped closer and touched the faerie's wing appreciatively. "How strong are you?"

"Very strong, but nowhere near as strong as some of the biggest of my kind." She looked around bashfully until her eyes fell on Sprinkle, who watched her with jealousy plain on his face. "Hey there, little guy."

"I will *so* kick you in the face." He snarled and launched himself at her, but Emerald was suddenly behind him with her hands under his arms to hold him back. "Unhand me, woman!"

"Shut up, or I will cut you." Emerald's growled threat did nothing until the elemental creature felt the blade that suddenly appeared in her hand. Then he stilled and stared sullenly at me.

"You going to do something about this?" he asked me in a snarky tone.

"I would if you two were capable of getting along." I shot them both a withering glare to drive home my disdain. "We need to be a well-oiled machine out here, people. Stop screwing around. Sprinkle, the usual payment, unless we find a source of acceptable ice Aether."

He nodded and flitted away up the tunnel, knowing I planned to send him ahead to slow anything down that could attack us if he could. I turned to the others. "Ladies, behind me, if you please?"

"Love me a man who takes charge." Sundar winked at me before waggling her eyebrows, then stepped behind me as I equipped my shield and elven sword. I didn't want to use the golden sword if I didn't have to, and I still had my glaive if things got too crazy.

Emerald shook her head and had Zanjir go ahead of us in the middle ground, sticking to the abundant shadows along the side of the wide tunnel.

Vulina walked closer to me. "You should have had me scout ahead. I could tell you what I see while making no noise."

"I need you closer to me to help keep things civil," I told her politely. "You and Sprinkle aren't the closest of friends, and the fact that you tease him as you do is irritating to him. I could lose him if he doesn't grow more powerful soon."

"I think you're wrong, but I also wouldn't mind someone different, either." Her demure shrug made me frown in her direction, so she added, "You're my friend. You deserve to have powerful allies."

Rolling my eyes and shaking my head, I faced forward and continued to scour the area in search of whatever the dungeon would throw at us.

It wasn't long before three medium-sized humanoid creatures chased after Sprinkle, identified by his cry of, "Gnolls!"

Rather than waiting for them to get to us, I glanced back and growled, "Get ready!" My shield at the fore, I sprinted ahead and ducked under Sprinkle to clobber the first creature in the chin and throat with the shield.

4 dmg to Gnoll Omega

Lvl 15 Gnoll Omega – Hostile

My blade bit into the lower leg of one of the other gnolls as it growled, their stinking fur making me gag. The frenzied baying echoing in the tunnel hurt my ears, but I kept moving. Ignoring the damage notification, I hefted my shield in time to block a clawed attack rocketing toward me, the strike doing little more than making my arm rock a bit.

A flaming sword sliced the arm of the gnoll off, and suddenly, I stood next to Vulina, the large fiery weapon casting light and shadow around us, "Stay close to me."

"I'm the tank here," I grunted, stabbing my sword at a gnoll just as Sundar's mace sailed over my head into the creature's chest.

"Just focus on keeping the aggro, Ky. Worry about party dynamics after this pull." She grunted and stepped back, her totem slamming onto the ground hard enough that it actually pushed the gnolls away from us. "Oh, I love that!"

"Traditional party tactics!" I snapped myself out of it and back into gaming mode. Back to basics. "Tank pulls the aggro and faces the mobs away from the party so they can max out damage and flank."

Those times that Sundar had beaten that into my head were finally coming in handy.

"Sprinkle, crowd control; you keep them too cold to move while the others work." I turned my gaze to Vulina. "If you want to be off-tank, fine. Make sure anything that isn't trying to kill me stays away from the others; got it?"

"Yes!" She smiled at me, then backed up as I pressed forward with my shield raised and smacked it on my blade to make noise. The gnolls' eyes turned to me as I growled at them.

One of them, the one missing an arm, tried to back away, and Zanjir pounced on it from the shadows just as Emerald emerged from her stealth. Her blades flashed, slicing the gnoll's throat as it cried out.

I rushed forward as my two targets' attention wavered and shifted from me to her, slamming my shield into the gnoll on my left then kicking with my right foot at the other's leg.

3 dmg to Gnoll Omega

The creatures came at me, their slavering jaws widening as I fought. They managed to avoid the most damage from me, but the rest of the party got to work.

Ice flew over my head, chilling the gnoll on my right as the other swiped at my exposed knee. I pulled it back but took a shallow cut for my troubles. Hissing as the pain flared, I stabbed my sword into its stomach and twisted, flames roiling from my hand into the wound.

10 dmg to Gnoll Omega
5 flame dmg to Gnoll Omega

Aura spiked in one of them, making me freeze on the spot as a green burst of color spread from its stomach, out the chest, and up. Roses sprouted from the bloodied wound and wound themselves around the upper body swiftly.

"What the hell is that?" I cried in wonder, my left arm lifting swiftly to stop a fist from hitting me. Vulina's flaming sword sliced through the last creature's head, the wound not even bleeding, since it had been cauterized on the spot.

Each death gave us 37 EXP, which was nice. Closing in on that next level was beautiful.

Emerald went through the corpses, their bodies disappearing slowly to leave behind small sacks on the ground. "That didn't happen last time," Sundar observed with a little bit of a grin. "Granted, I am happy that I don't have to rip open a body."

"That is nice, though I wonder what I will be able to feed Zanjir?" Emerald seemed disappointed, and the large hound, who had been contentedly chewing on one of the severed arms, whined as his meal disappeared. "Now, now, don't whine like that. You should have plenty of other chances at eating something. Maybe next time, I'll bring more for you than just jerky."

At the mention of jerky, the dog sat immediately, his tail thumping the packed earth as drool dripped from his jowls. I hid my mouth as I snorted; she had him better trained than I had thought.

Sundar opened a satchel and poured out the contents. Some copper coins, teeth and a patch of fur, and a small chitinous chunk of something.

"This does seem odd, but there's nothing that can be done. Maybe this was some kind of patch?" I blinked at them, and they shrugged. Both the faeries watched us with interested confusion, but decided to leave it alone. "How was the tanking; any suggestions?"

"Could have done better myself." Sundar grinned at me with a slow wink. "But I can't complain too much. If you see something or need something to happen as the tank and you feel it will benefit us in the fight, call that audible."

My mouth thinned in a frown, but I nodded once and turned toward the openings down the tunnel. "Move out."

The others fell in behind me, but Vulina stayed by my side, walking close enough that the warmth of her presence fended off the slight earthen chill around me.

Once the tunnel naturally opened up, copper scents littered the air around us. Large bugs had been butchered and strewn about. Some of them were the same sort of centipede-like creatures that had chased us in the rain when we had first arrived at the city.

There was nothing but insect corpses in this chamber, but as I continued to look about, I noticed those same kinds of satchels we had found when the gnolls disappeared.

Dungeon quest available – Dungeon at War – The dungeon your party has entered is currently at war with an invading force. You have several options available to you, all of which carry consequence and reward. Would you like to view the options?

"That's new, too." I blinked at the notification and shrugged to myself before opening the options portion.

Leave and allow the dungeon to fight for itself – Reward: unknown, enemy: Winner.

Defend the dungeon – Reward: 500 EXP, loot from the invaders, and access to the dungeon once more. Enemy: Gnolls.

Invade the dungeon – Reward: 500 EXP, access to the corpses of the dungeon residents, and access to the dungeon in seventy-two hours. Enemy: Insects.

Take it all – Reward: 500 EXP, the spoils of the fallen, and more.

"I would ask what you all think, but that fourth option seems like it could have a lot of benefits," Emerald sighed and grinned at us slyly.

Sundar laughed, her hands on her stomach as she heaved with mirth. "Was there really any other choice?"

I just shook my head and scanned the room. "Let's get what we can from all of this, then move on."

Sundar began to dig through the corpses as Emerald gathered the satchels. Three of the large bugs had monster crystals inside them that were torn out and added to our inventories. I'd talk to them about making dyes later.

"Which way do we go?" Sundar grunted as she pulled a little of the chitin off one of the beetles we had found in a corner of the room.

I wasn't sure; we really had no way to know which way was what, unless.. "Emerald, can Zanjir track the scent of the Gnolls?"

She knelt next to him as he worried at a centipede leg like a stick and spoke softly. He stilled and put his nose to the air. Emerald rolled her eyes and pulled the leg out of his mouth, drool dribbling from it disgustingly, but he kept the scenting up. He began to move in circles, tight at first, then slowly loosening until he found something.

"He has a workable scent. He says that they're all over, but that the strongest scent comes from this tunnel over here." She pointed to the third tunnel off to our left and began to walk toward it.

"Em!" Sundar barked once, her voice carrying the weight of authority. The other woman flinched and stopped, looking back curiously. "I know that you have stealth and everything, but let's have Kyvir go first."

She blinked at me, then at Sundar, before nodding and motioning for me to move. "Sorry about that."

"It's okay." I tried to offer her a soft, reassuring smile, but I just didn't feel it. If she had been killed, she'd come back, but her growth would be stunted until she doubled all the experience she had lost. Impatience was no excuse.

I took the lead, with Sprinkle flying ahead and Vulina remaining next to me, our route much less simple than it had been before. It was longer and wound downward in a sort of spiral. Off that spiral were smaller tunnels that looked to have been dug out by smaller insects, like ants. In these areas, we found a few gnoll satchels, and one actually alive gnoll that Emerald got the drop on. It seemed to have been a lookout; the dagger that she found on it was trashy but could be thrown, so she kept it.

After slowly going down this section of tunnel another

fifteen minutes, we came to the sounds of battle. I motioned for the others to slow down even more, then stop, until I could figure out what was happening. A rat skittered over my foot and continued down the path swiftly.

I almost jumped out of my skin in surprise, but when I looked back at Sundar, her eyes were ghostly white and wide open like she was staring at something. Her aura was thickest around her eyes, and I could see a line of energy running from her that appeared to be connected to the rat.

So she's using her rat friend to scout ahead? Nice.

I backed up closer to her as her mouth began moving, finally hearing what she was whispering, "...A lot of them. Like, twenty gnolls, and so many insects, I can't count them all."

"What kind of insects?" I whispered back, but she didn't seem to have heard me. I glared at her and realized that her ears glowed the same ghostly white. "She's pouring her senses into the animal? That's intense."

"Zanjir can hear it all, too, and he is less than thrilled at the prospect of going into that." Emerald's low tone held a note of uncertainty as she stroked her hound's head slowly.

"Ants the size of chihuahuas, more centipedes, and a few beetles." Sundar's brow crinkled as she focused, then the ghostly aura around her ears and eyes faded. "It went too far. It'll come back."

She turned to me, an unreadable expression on her face as she said, "The gnolls have some kind of caster with them."

A thrill ran up my spine. "Then I get to *play* with my food."

Emerald frowned at that, but kept quiet about it as we carefully crouched our way forward to the room, with me whispering the game plan to the others.

Things were about to get real chaotic.

CHAPTER THIRTEEN

SETH

A beetle screeched loudly as its scythe-like legs sliced a gnoll in half, only to have two more replace the fallen beast and pull the insect low to the ground so others could swarm it.

Ants crawled up another gnoll, its screams and cries of fear soon cut off by a centipede biting its head off.

"Go ahead, Sprinkle." The faerie growled to himself and flew into the room as swiftly as he could, then began to gather as much ice in front of himself as possible before one of the gnolls barked and pointed up at him.

The caster gnoll scowled up into the air and lifted his gnarled staff as his mouth moved.

"Now!" My hoarse whisper to Vulina let her know to fire off her own spell, the heat of the fireball leaving me cold as it sailed along the floor.

The timing of it was a little off, but when the large shard of ice met the fire, a gout of steamy fog billowed from it, which allowed us to get into the room without everyone surrounding us.

The two summons went wild, their indiscriminate castings burning, cutting, and carving into the two battling sides as we moved along the edges. A thrill of warning made the hair on the back of my neck stand on end, and I grabbed Emerald in time to pull her out of the way of an ice shard that shattered against the wall in front of her.

"Thanks," was all she said before entering stealth and going off to complete her own task.

Me and Sundar now, I muttered to myself. I couldn't even see Zanjir, and the caster was all I could think about. I wondered what kind of Aether he had access to, and the thought of it made my mouth water and my stomach gurgle.

A gnoll beset upon by a trio of ants stumbled into the wall as he fought to get them off, and my sword lashed out.

12 dmg to Busy Ant

I allowed the attack to stop and focused on killing the ants, then stepped aside and let Sundar's massive mace crush the gnoll's shoulder and chest partially before stuffing the tip of my sword into his mouth and throat, killing him.

I stepped on another ant, doing minor damage before cutting its head off and moving on. So far, the plan was working well. The insects weren't taking much damage from the spells, but with the openings the chaos created, there was little time for either them or the gnolls to think while we moved through and Emerald did her dirty work.

One such bit of nasty business was creating an opening to get to the gnoll caster.

She fought like a lion, her commands to Zanjir the only thing that separated her from the shadows, until just after someone died. Zanjir worked as mysteriously as she did, weaving in and out of shadows to fell anything his master turned him to, and he took great pleasure in chewing and shaking his head to add injury to his victims.

After just three minutes, the steam had begun to subside, and there was enough of a gap for me and Sundar to get to the caster. He hurled a bolt of lightning from his staff at us, and I ducked under it just in time.

"Ouch!" Sundar growled, and I mentally berated myself.

"Old habits die hard, sorry!" I called and brought my sword to bear on the caster.

The nasty creature chanted something, and a faint, sickly green glimmered around in his aura before a dart of pure lime hit my metal armor.

No damage notification? Sweet.

My shield came up, and I bashed his head at the same time that I stabbed forward with my elven sword. Rather than go for anything important, I went for his leg, pinning his foot down on one of his comrades. Then, I abandoned my sword to grab his arm and twisted it.

Sundar's mace clobbered his shoulder and exposed elbow, breaking the limb so that he was forced to drop his staff. I let go, kicking his uninjured leg in the back of the knee before I sank my fangs into his shoulder. Emerald appeared in front of us and lashed out with her blade, slicing my lip along with his throat.

I drank as much as I could as the blood flooded from his body, both into my mouth and out of the wound taking his life.

Aether Stolen - Earth Affinity at 73%
50 EXP received.

"Love that," I muttered to myself and let the body fall from my grasp. The majority of the fighting was over, as the victors of the various fights that had been the worst were either trying to kill something else now, or they rested and hoped we wouldn't come for them.

Like that would ever happen. "Don't kill the gnolls right away, if you can help it." My voice was deeper, hungrier.

My sword lifted and stabbed down into the carapace of a Busy Ant, the head falling to the floor before I moved on and began to kill more of them. If it even looked like it could have survived, it died.

There were only four Gnoll survivors at this point, and Sundar brought them to me one at a time to drain them of their blood. The first couple gave me nothing, but the last three gave me a couple percentage points each, putting me up to 79% Earth Affinity. So close with a couple of the affinities I had. Wonder what I'd get for them.

The larger bugs, like the beetles and centipedes, gave us about 40 EXP, while the Busy Ants only netted about half as much, so we were well over what we needed to level up. Total, we had killed about fifteen of the bugs ourselves, and of the six centipedes, we'd killed four and all three of the beetles. With the amount of gnolls, we'd killed seven, and that hadn't included the caster, so 50 EXP, plus the 37 EXP from the Gnoll Omegas, gave us a grand total of 889 EXP for this room alone. Some of it had gone to waste when we leveled up, not all of the points carrying over, since they weren't enough to bring about another level—probably around a hundred to a hundred and fifty or so —but we still got a good chunk toward our next one.

"Take a minute to look over your stats and place your points." I glanced at my stat sheet and opted to put an even number of points into all my stats for now, except for presence, which meant my Knowledge went up by one. "Twelve in all but Serenity and Presence. You?"

I watched another small chunk pop into existence and even out my dual-colored Aether bar. Six fire, six ice. And an even twelve summoning Aether.

"Point to Strength for twelve," Sundar said, smiling and looking a bit beefier.

Emerald cracked her neck and sighed contentedly. "Skill for twenty one. Love min-maxing."

"Fucking broken is what you are," Sundar growled and smiled, then looked over the bodies surrounding us. "Not that I'm complaining. Nothing in the way of real loot from these guys. No cores. Nothing. So where do we look next? This place isn't like the first dungeon we entered."

"No, it isn't…" I looked around for any kind of clue as to where we could go next, when we all got a notification.

Warning!

The boss room is under attack, and the door to it will close in approximately five minutes.

A timer burst into life in the top right hand corner of my vision and started to count down.

"Well, we know what we have to do now; let's go!" Sundar grunted and turned toward the side of the room that we had come from. "That's toward the exit, so let's go the opposite way."

"Duh, Sunny," Emerald laughed. She sounded so much like Mo that it was kind of scary. She took off toward the next hall and entered a stealthy manner of stepping that she liked to adopt. I followed, with Vulina and Sprinkle fluttering overhead.

We ran for a little bit, the blood along the walls and fallen corpses a sign that we had to be heading in the right direction. We made it to the next open area, which revealed a large selection of tunnels to go through. Some of them were fresher than others, and a large centipede lay dead in the center.

"Mini-boss room." I called to the others, more a statement than anything else, but Sundar agreed with a soft *hup* and a nod. We ran on, since the chest at the other side of the room had been opened and emptied, it seemed.

The halls contained more dead or dying mobs that we took care of with flames from Vulina while Sprinkle flew ahead. He came back at a fork in the tunnel and pointed left. "That way."

Zanjir started to whine, and Emerald comforted him while saying, "He says the scent is stronger the other way."

"Because there's a pit with about forty dead and dying gnolls in it, and an acid trap, so by all means go check it out." The sassy summon sarcastically stepped aside and motioned to the tunnel.

Emerald walked toward the left with a huff and a softly muttered, "Dickhead."

"I heard that!" Sprinkle jeered, and she just flipped him off. I rolled my eyes and motioned for him to go ahead of us again.

It was a few seconds later when a notification I hadn't expected popped up.

Optional Quest Completed – Master Gretlen's request that, in some way, either by bringing Mona to him, or his knowledge to her, you pass on his teachings. Reward: Go back to his shop to find out, 1,235 EXP.

I blinked, suddenly hot. Mona was in Belgonna's Hold. She was there, somehow, and we could go get her.

"Exit!" I bellowed, stopping where I was, but nothing happened.

"Kyvir, what's wrong?" Emerald asked, appearing at my side with concern on her features.

"Mona's in the city. We have to get there; we need to go right now." I tried to open my interface, and a message appeared from the system.

You're currently taking part in a dungeon war and cannot leave until one of the factions either wins, or the dungeon is defeated.

Someone had to be fucking with us, right? "Let's leave; come on."

Sundar shoved me further down the hall. "If the boss room closes, we can't leave until it's over, and who knows how long it will take to make it out of here after that. The only way out is through—let's go."

I screamed, the rage the most intense thing I had probably felt in days, and turned toward the boss room to sprint on.

———

Somewhere inside the city I'd only been to a handful of times, heat from the magical lava below the smithy makes my charge sweat. The young woman's body is rigid as the attuning between her and her weapon is finally complete. She wipes it off one last time, a single tear escaping from her eye as she looks over what she's done.

Whispering to the air around her, as if to atone for what she did, she mutters, "Sacrifices must be made."

Got your work cut out for you here, Lira, I grin to myself as I watch Mona leave the building and teleport back to her new master. I step over to the old man, but something shaking behind me forces me to teleport myself. *Things are growing more and more interesting; better let the master know...*

———

The door to the boss room was seconds from closing by the time we reached it and barged our way inside, only to see two factions clashing in a circular room with eggs all over the place. The boss arena was a circular section of floor with a small pit to the sides, a small gap between it and the eggs. The ceiling looked to be similar to the floor, though the eggs weren't on the ceiling, and there were stalactites hanging above us dangerously.

"What do you want to bet that those hatch at some point during the fight?" I grumbled and glanced up at my two summons. "Time to really earn it, you two. Sprinkle, I need you to freeze the ones on the floor along the side of the ring, Flicker, you go up and burn it all."

They nodded and went on their way as we watched the fighting between the bugs and the gnolls.

These gnolls were larger than the omegas, though only by a bit for some of them. A couple of them looked like they could be considered betas. Their leader had to be the alpha, if that was what you could call it. He was about eight feet tall and easily thicker than Sundar. He carried a massive greatsword and used it with ease, while his minions scuttled about and kept the lesser bugs off him and attacked the incubating bugs on the far side of the circular area.

The bugs were interesting, all of them ants, but they carried weapons, so they had to be the queen's guards, right?

"Mona, raid pla—" I started, then closed my eyes and clenched my teeth. "Sorry."

Sundar stepped closer and spoke in a low tone, "We get it; let's get this over with." She pointed to Emerald and Zanjir.

"You both are going to go after the stragglers who are close to death—if it looks healthier than a single blow to kill it, use some sneakier stuff on it and get it to Ky. Keep them off balance and kite them to us if you have to, but don't get greedy."

She pointed to me and said, "Do what you're supposed to as a tank, and I'll keep you healed as best as I can. I'll have a buff on you to make this a little faster, but it will wear off quickly, so use it to the best advantage, okay?"

I nodded and put my shield away, Emerald asking, "What are you doing?"

"There are enemies all over. You stay away from me, and I'll cut a path with my glaive." I pulled out my separable glaive and made sure it was tightly attached. "Let's go."

I jogged forward as softly as I could, twirling my glaive, and sliced the back of a gnoll's neck. The blade bit deep, and I yanked back, stabbing at the knee of another. Every time I attacked, I twisted my hips and spun around, dancing like Thea's friend had done with her glaive. The blades bit and slashed, slicing and stabbing as I moved, until one of the gnolls managed to get close enough to grab the shaft of my weapon, snarling victoriously at me with teeth bared.

I just pressed forward and twisted the handles so that it separated, and my forehead slammed into its canid nose with a satisfying crunch. I lifted my foot and kicked the inside of its knee and stabbed the now-split glaive sword in my right hand into its throat, followed by a savage twist to free the weapon.

I focused on the heat of my fire Aether and let it build in my throat before I breathed out a gout of flame three feet long. Two bars of my fire Aether was gone, but the smoking and flaming fur of the gnolls around me made me smile.

Spell obtained: Dragon's Flame (racial) – Caster may spew fire from their mouth like a dragon breath weapon. Cost: 2 Aether. Duration: 3 seconds.

I blinked and prepared for an attack, but the gnolls backed away from me, and Vulina screeched, "Roll left!"

My body reacted to her voice; I threw myself left and just

barely missed being bisected by the massive sword which the largest gnoll carried.

It growled something, and the other gnolls rushed to the large incubation chamber where the boss slept, but it looked to be waking up.

Sundar tackled the Gnoll leader and sucker-punched him in the jaw. I sprinted at him and reattached the swords in my grasp to form a glaive once more. He used the sword to hide behind and kicked out at Sundar, her club taking the brunt of the attack.

I quick-slotted my sword into my right hand as my left slid my glaive over my shoulder and let go, the weapon disappearing back into the hidden "sheath" there. I wouldn't be able to get my shield out in time to use it before I attacked him, but I needed my hand free for my plan.

My sword slashed at the gnoll leader's face, and he lifted a clawed hand to parry the weapon as my free left fist clocked him in the stomach with a small blade of ice over my knuckles.

Gnolladin lvl 17 — Hostile
2 ice dmg to Gnolladin.

The hell is a Gnolladin? I growled to myself, but he kicked at me again, and I had to step closer to avoid getting hit.

Reddish energy radiated from his fist, and I could smell sulfur as he swung it straight at my chest.

Something grabbed me by my armor and yanked me backward, the heat from their nearness nice and comforting as Vulina said, "Job's done, boss."

Ashes fell from the ceiling above us, and I realized she was still there, after all.

"Off-tank for me?" She grinned and shoved me aside as the sword once more tried to cleave me in half.

"Thought you might ask that." She summoned her flaming sword in both hands. "Hey, muttly! Come and get me."

The gnoll roared and went for her as I pulled my shield out once again and checked my surroundings. The gnolls were occupied with the queen's egg, but every heartbeat, one of them would yelp and look around for something that had made them bleed.

One of them had fallen due to an injury and Zanjir was busy dragging the whining creature to the shadows away from the fight with his furiously shaking head.

Just as I stood to re-enter the fight, Sundar was behind me. "Go; I'm going to buff you."

I nodded and launched myself forward, crossing the fifteen foot gap between myself and the Gnolladin easily. My sword slashed into the back of his leg, just behind the knee, and he yelped.

14 dmg to Gnolladin.

Hamstring debuff added, all movement lessened.

I would have tried to slice and dice again, but a booming detonation and the ensuing wave of magical force drove me off my feet. Something screeched, and my ears felt like they could start bleeding at any second.

Paralysis debuff resisted

Good for me. I struggled to my feet as quickly as my now-aching body would allow me, and saw that it was only the bug boss and me standing at this point. Good. It took a step, and I fell at the impact and crawled over to where the Gnolladin lay, tucking into it for a mid-fight snack.

Blood sprayed into my mouth as the paralyzed monster growled at me uselessly. My earth affinity went up by five, and my demonic affinity by two. Once I had my fill and my Aether had refilled some, I stood and began to attack the bug boss, which was eating the dead gnolls and ants alike as it moved forward slowly.

I hacked at the Gnolladin with my sword, arms, shoulders, anything I could reach, until the strength returned to my body and I started to slash and stab at vitals. His right eye was a bloody mess by the time he was able to move again, and he bled heavily from his right arm and the right side of his neck. I prepared for the killing blow, but the bug boss screeched, and a sharp leg pierced the Gnolladin's chest in a fountain of blood and lifted him bodily.

I stabbed and slashed some more, hoping I was doing enough damage to kill him, when I got an idea. I threw my sword like a javelin, and it pierced the invading boss's back.

8 dmg to Gnolladin.

Lvl 17 Gnolladin died.

78 EXP obtained.

The bug boss reached its head down with its pincers and bit the Gnolladin's head off just above me, the blood dropping rapidly. Some splashed against me, but I hadn't been quick enough to get any into my mouth, so I settled for trying to figure out where to look for a critical spot on this thing.

It was just one large ant with a massive ass, right? How hard could it be to figure out where to attack?

Gluttonous Queen lvl 17 – Hostile.

Ah, shit. "Sprinkle, try to freeze its legs!" Vulina shouted from somewhere above.

The little ice faerie bellowed back, "You're not my supervisor!"

"Just fucking do it!" I howled and slashed at one of the six legs that I stood between. No damage to it whatsoever, so there was no luck on the bottom.

Sundar hobbled forward, slamming her Totem onto the ground next to where I stood beneath the queen, as the massive woman joined me. "Your resistance is so good."

I laughed, and she swung her weapon at a leg, the crunch making the Gluttonous Queen scream above us. The noise wasn't so bad from down here, but there was a growing sense of dread in my body that just wouldn't dissipate.

The Hell Cat buff screamed to life over the Totem, and the soreness in my muscles lessened to the point that swinging my sword wasn't such a burden anymore.

I decided it would likely be a good idea to work with Vulina and Sprinkle together. Sprinkle dropped in just as I was about to remind him about what he needed to do, his hands clasping the closest leg to me at the joint. The joint froze over slowly, the ice cracking as he worked, while the Gluttonous Queen just kept walking to collect her meals.

Vulina dropped and sliced at the newly-frozen joint, the ice shattering and the carapace-like armor cracking and falling-away slightly.

"Em!" I bellowed as my sword sliced at the wounded limb.

4 dmg to Gluttonous Queen

"Damn it!" My sword would be useless for this. "Sprinkle, you work on freezing the armor under her chest, and then let Flicker super heat it to weaken it."

Sundar was there suddenly with a grin. "You think it'll work?"

"You hit it with your blunt weapon hard enough, we might be able to crack it," I sighed, and suddenly Emerald appeared and *hammered* her Soul Dagger into the injured joint at the seam as the queen screeched violently. "Crit?"

She nodded and grinned before clambering up the leg and shouting, "Up here!"

I frowned and tried to follow her up, but I just wasn't agile enough and got bucked off.

"Distract it!" she hollered down to me as I glared up at the ceiling. "I think I can make some stuff work from up here!"

I glanced toward Sundar, and she gave me a thumbs up, so I made my way out between the legs from the side and bellowed, "Hey!" My mind blanked on an insult, so I just spat, "You! Yeah, down here!"

The Gluttonous Queen's antennae twitched in my direction, and I could kind of see Emerald clutching onto her back and stabbing with her weapon, but that was it.

"Oh, shit!" I dodged out of the way as she lunged toward me with her mandibles clacking together loudly.

Emerald called out, "It's not working too good up here!"

Sundar shouted much the same, though she added, "If we had some serious force, we could get through the shell."

Serious force? I looked around and nothing came immediately to mind, until I glanced up at the roof while dodging her jaws once more. There were large stalactites all over that we could use, right?

"Em, get down. I have an idea, but it's going to take some maneuvering." She grabbed a leg at my request and slid down with ease. "Flicker, Sprinkle, new plan. The nearest stalactite up there? I want you both to focus on dropping it onto her."

Vulina sped toward me with a grin on her face. "That sounds like fun!"

She raced up to the ceiling and began to hack with her sword into the tip, but Sprinkle just rolled his eyes and chased after her. "Not there, you imbecile. Further up, so the weight might crush her. You may be the brawn, but you clearly need brains, too."

The two of them bickered while I switched places with Emerald. "Keep her here in this same spot, while Sundar and I work the legs from beneath."

"What about the crash?" Sundar called to me from where she beat on a joint mercilessly.

Vulina, call out just as it's about to give, okay? I turned and rammed my shoulder into the nearest leg and replied, "Flicker will call it to us."

"Timber!" someone yelled from above, and my eyes flew open.

I dove to the side and got nailed in the leg by one of the massive chunks of stone that fell to the ground beside it.

29 dmg from nature.

Broken leg debuff added – movement decreased.

"Little help, Sunny!" I grunted and tried to stabilize the wounded limb in ice, but the stone just rolled back and crushed the ice. I had to push the blocky projectile away before I could stabilize the wound.

Sundar appeared over me and grabbed my leg; her tug made me scream and draw the attention of a very injured and angry Gluttonous Queen. Sundar pounded the wounded leg with healing energy, and the broken bone icon began to flicker and fade, but it wasn't gone yet.

The queen ant speared a leg toward Sundar's exposed back, and I brought my shield up to block it for her, reinforcing it with ice as I could, but the limb went straight through it, just clipping her shoulder and missing me.

"Move back!" I snarled and tried to stand, the boss creature wrenching the shield from my grasp painfully. "Get to the next one!"

Sundar grabbed me by my wrist and hauled me away from the reaching grasp of the Gluttonous Queen until I was far enough away to try standing. She had healed me for about half of what I'd lost, and though tender, the break was gone now.

I hissed at the soreness in my limbs and wished that Mephistopheles hadn't fucked me with the pain, but it was what I got for playing those stupid games of his.

"She's hurting, but not badly enough, and we're wasting time here." I glanced around and pointed to the next one that Flicker and Sprinkle had started, "There. Let's go."

I limped until the leg was loose enough to allow me to walk normally and stood just on the other side of the improvised hammer while we waited for her Highness to get off her ass and come after us.

"Any day!" I shouted, and the Queen screeched and began to convulse. "What the hell is she doing?"

"Giving birth!" Emerald hadn't joined us, opting to keep close to her so she could make use of the distractions to get some added damage in. "There are three ant eggs back here, and they're growing fast."

I blinked, and suddenly Zanjir launched himself from the shadows and began to bark loudly at something. Then he stopped, and there was a crunching sound. "Two eggs!"

"Crush them!" I called, hobbling toward where they were. "Guys, leave that and help us kill the eggs!"

Sprinkle flew down and spewed cold air onto the one that Emerald was stabbing, then at the other. I pulled out my glaive and jumped to give myself the added benefit of my weight and gravity to the strike, making just the right kind of hit to crack the egg. There was no ice Aether left for much, so I used my flame Aether and spewed fire inside the shell until I got a notification.

Ant Prince dead.

No EXP.

"They're summoned mobs!" I called and noticed that the last one was dead, thanks to Sprinkle putting in work.

The Gluttonous Queen stood once more, the broken rubble forcing her to move it aside to get to us. That gave us time to get back to our spot where we all called out and jeered at her.

"As soon as she gets close," Sundar huffed and stared at the coming ant, "I want you to blast her in the face with the fire."

"Why?"

She pointed with her head, and I stared at the ant dumbly, finally forcing her to say, "She's looking up, now. She's expecting the attack that hurt her to be replicated."

"Good call." I muttered and took a steadying breath. "After this, I'll have a few bars of fire left, but nothing substantial other than Summoning."

"Why don't you summon more creatures to fight for you?" Sundar asked quietly.

That would be risking my Aether and having to fight another summon for control in the middle of a fight, but I just said simply, "Not an option that I want to take right now."

She nodded once and grimaced. "Get ready."

"On it." I held my hands up and launched a ball of flames up into the queen's face, and then another. Two more bars gone. Two remained.

A cracking and a wordless shout were all the warning we got in order to get out of the way. The ant reared back, avoiding the worst of the blow, but she didn't expect Sundar and me to rush the stone that stayed where it was for a heartbeat to push back onto her.

A satisfying, but sickening *crunch* echoed through the

chamber just before her scream, and the notification we got was sweet.

89 dmg to Gluttonous Queen from nature.
Broken leg(s) debuff added.

"On her bad side!" Em called out, then gasped, "I think she's trying to give birth again!"

"Sprinkle and I will handle the eggs, you guys kill her!" Sundar screamed wordlessly after that, as a solid *smack* of her weapon sounded against the egg.

I thought about it for a heartbeat and put my glaive away, summoning the golden sword that Orthanus called home into my hand as he spoke into my mind, "A dungeon? Very well. That carapace will be hard; swing me true."

I nodded and used my will to cover the blade in flames, my Aether mixing with Oranthus' will. The fire intensified, and the golden dragon laughed as I swung toward the exposed neck. My blow didn't land, the struggling bug moving just out of the way, but I corrected and stabbed forward, drawing a line of blood that gushed onto the floor.

12 dmg to Gluttonous Queen.
8 fire dmg to Gluttonous Queen.

Emerald stabbed her Soul Dagger into the queen's eye nearest me and snarled, "Now, Ky!"

I roared, righteous anger swirling through me as I slashed once more toward the neck and used Wrathful Smite. The weight of the weapon could have been nothing short of a ton when it landed, and the blaze burned hotter than I thought I was even capable of.

Flames washed over the carapace, and she screamed again, Emerald joining her as the fire burst in a wave of heat and pain.

CRITICAL STRIKE
40 dmg to Gluttonous Queen.
Lvl 17 Gluttonous Queen died.
100 EXP received.

I didn't even look at the level-up information that I had

available. Nothing else mattered except getting back to the city to find Mona.

"Emerald, you coming with me?" She nodded and brought Zanjir along to stand close as Sundar watched us. "Can you collect the loot for this?"

"If you leave, I don't know if it will go to you." She grimaced and ran off to the other side of the room from the door and yelled, "Chest is open, it's good—go!"

I bellowed, "Exit!"

I blinked and found myself standing at the dungeon entrance, waiting for Emerald to appear. She blinked at me and asked, "Where to?"

"The center of the city; we will go from there." I teleported, thanks to my stone and the weight of the transport settled on my chest.

CHAPTER FOURTEEN

SETH

Emerald and I raced through the city, avoiding the crowds and passersby as much as we could. She was much more nimble than I was and raced ahead of me by yards, but I didn't care. One of us getting to Mona first would be better than nothing. Better than losing her again.

Even if I wasn't sure of what she had been talking about, I still cared about her. Losing her had been like losing family all over again. Without her around, I felt like I was half of what I could be. What I was meant to be.

And the thought of falling short of what I was meant to be frustrated and enraged me more than it felt like it should. Why was I so angry?

We arrived on the street where the forge was, and I caught a glimpse of Emerald hauling herself through the door so fast that it almost knocked her back out of the building. I made it within ten feet of the door when I heard a deafening, piercing scream.

I sprinted through the doorway, expecting a demon to be

holding my friend hostage, but instead found the old smith laying on the floor with his chest split open and a dull, lifeless look on his face.

The blood wasn't fresh, the carnage coagulating at our feet, but the act was done. Who had done it? Was it Mona?

I looked around for any clues and found nothing, minutes spent frantically turning the whole building upside down for even the most remote mention of a *clue*, and yet still came up empty-handed.

I roared, rage making my bones ache as unquenchable fury ate at my insides.

This man had been kind to me. Fair. All he had wanted to do was to pass on his art, and now he was dead, and we were no closer to finding Mona. She was slipping through my fingers, and there was nothing I could do about it.

I grabbed a hammer and threw it as hard as I could, the wall on the other side dinging in a way that was almost satisfying, so I looked around to find another hammer to lob. There, in the old man's hand, was a hammer.

I had to pry it from his grip, and once I did, a small sheet of paper fell out. A cold chill washed over me, but my fingers couldn't get there fast enough, Emerald having gotten to it first. She unfolded it and showed it to me.

It looked like a weapon with no handle.

Which would be perfect for someone who didn't really need one—like Monami.

"She was here," Emerald muttered, blinking around the room, as if seeing it truly for the first time. "We missed her."

"Yeah, we did." I motioned to the corpse. "And she must have done that, too."

Emerald looked up at me, her face severe, "You don't know that. It could have been the succubus, for all you know."

"It could have been, but that weapon was made specifically for someone who uses Metal Aether to manipulate their weapons." I sighed at the accusatory glare she brow-beat me with. "It could be a coincidence, but the quest I received was for her to come and learn from him, or give her the tomes that he gave me. I still have them, so that leaves it pretty clear what happened."

She closed her eyes and tears fell, then a soft voice piped up from behind me. "He asked me to give this to you after she left."

"Raaaaa!" I snarled and whipped around, Oranthus whooshing forward and over Oleg's head where a normal person's stomach would be. "Oh! I'm so sorry, Oleg."

Oleg sniffed, not even phased by the violence, and held up a parcel for me, but his eyes fell to his former employer. "He was a cruel man at times, but he was always fair and hard working. He taught me the finer points of business, and I'll always remember him."

I frowned, touched by the sentiment, but it was just a little much at the moment. I took the parcel and opened it to find a new sword, the blade thick at the base but slowly tapering to a thinner point, then widened a little more before the tip came to a point like a teardrop. Honestly, I wasn't certain how the sword would hold up in a fight, but it looked like a good weapon, if only a little large.

"That's a holy sword, Master Kyvir," Oleg whispered reverently. He pointed to the base of the dully glimmering blade, and I found runes that appeared to have been carved out and filled by something liquid. "It wasn't one he made, but it was something he modeled a few of his weapons after, trying to get a feel for the design. As much as he hated to admit it, it always eluded him, and the weapons were too weak at the bend."

I couldn't imagine a better weapon for Orthanus to inhabit than this. I realized that there were no stats as I touched it. "Why aren't there any stats?"

"Well, I'm not exactly sure about that." He scratched his head. "It could be that someone of a *holy* order has to wield it? I'm just a lowly merchant; I don't know the ways of these things."

I narrowed my gaze at him, and he just flinched, then I

nodded and figured I would just ask around about it later. "It seems that the forge here is closed?"

He nodded, sadness overtaking him, but I asked, "Would there happen to be any kind of throwing weapons available? Or well-balanced knives?"

He stared at me for a second, and I looked over to Emerald. "Upping your arsenal." I turned back to Oleg and added, "I'll need you to also put out your finest blunt weapons, maces, and other things for my other friend. She would be about level fifteen."

He nodded and scurried off, so I called after him, "You have time!" He came back and blinked at me curiously. "You have time. Take care of your master, and then when you're ready, send word to us that you're done. We will come then."

He nodded, and I frowned, uncertain as to what to say to the small man, but it was Emerald who spoke. "Send the bill for his funeral to us at Belgonna's Court. We will see his family compensated."

"You're too kind, madame, but I will." He bowed to us and went to see to his master, sniffling as he crouched over the dead dwarf's body.

I turned and left the room immediately, the holy sword safely stored in my inventory without a second thought. The emotions running rampant through me felt muted now, all except for rage. What was going on?

"Are you okay?" Emerald asked me, and all I could hear was a detached sort of numbness to her question that made it seem almost as if it were an afterthought.

I turned to look at her, and I could see the stress in her eyes, plain as day. She was worried about Mona, and she had lost her too. I wasn't the only one dealing with this, and she had even more of a right to feel the way she did. The fact that she cared enough to ask was proof that she actually gave a damn.

"Not really?" I shook my head and finally said, "I don't know. It's like, every emotion I have but anger is being dampened. It's hard to really gauge how I feel about anything."

"That's got to be hard." She frowned and stepped closer, her arms open for a hug that I just wasn't sure I wanted to give right this moment. But it was Emerald. Emma. The woman who had basically helped raise me. Was I really so callous now that a hug for *her* benefit was something I wouldn't allow?

I reached out and pulled her into a hug, allowing her to bury her head into my shoulder for a moment as I just stood there and bore it for as long as she needed.

Eventually, she broke away with another sniffle and wiped her eyes with the heels of her hands. "We should go and talk to Belgonna." She blinked up at me and cocked her head to the side. "She should know that we plan to move on and chase Mona down, right?"

"Probably, yeah, but I have something that I've been neglecting that I should probably start doing." I tried to offer a smile, but she saw through it, and I let it fall as that decidedly *mom* stare radiated from her face. "I wonder if it's the job influencing me, or if it was the sacrifice I had to make in order to get my magic. Either way, I only know of one person who can help me, and that's Aertra. So I'm going to go and see her for a bit, and maybe get some training. I'll meet you and Sundar at the Den, okay?"

Her lips pursed, then she nodded once and turned her back to me before saying, "Don't make Belgonna wait too long to see you." I raised an eyebrow after her, but otherwise just nodded more to myself than her and watched as she fled into the crowd that gathered down the road.

I sent a whisper to Aertra, —*Hey, are you busy? I think I need some more…guidance?*—

Her answer was discomfortingly quick, —*Just in time to join me on a little hunt. Come to the mines. (X,Y)*—

I blinked, wondering why she had included that last bit, but saw that it was red and it could be clicked in the chat logs, which was weird, because there had been another way that we had shared locations. Once I did, my map pulsed, and a red arrow led toward the mines, which were very likely where she waited for me.

As I began my trek, Sprinkle and Vulina found me, though his demand came first, "Time for my payment!"

I rolled my eyes and studied my Aether. Sure enough, I had all of it, save for the two summoning bars and one each of fire and ice. I looked to Vulina, and she just winked at me and mentally told me, *Later.*

"Fine. Here you go, Sprinkle." I willed all of my remaining ice Aether to him, and then the remaining eight summoning to him, as well. "A belly full? I'm sorry we didn't really have the time to look for any sort of metal."

"So incredibly much so." He smiled at me genuinely and winked. "It's okay. Summoning Aether is nice, too. Much more malleable, and less of a crunch."

I frowned at him, "So, do you need to stay here to digest it, or is there somewhere you plan to go with it?"

"Oh, no. I don't need to stay here at all, now that I'm a little stronger than I was." He smiled again and poofed out of existence.

"Why is it that he doesn't have to stay, but you do?" I turned to Vulina and stared at her for a moment, but she just carefully avoided my gaze.

Finally, she glanced at me and bashfully held her hands in front of her stomach, explaining, "I like being here in this world with you rather than being at home." She must have caught my confusion, because she nervously added, "It's just so much more interesting here! There are things to fight and kill and eat!"

I just shook my head at that, tired of the nonsense. "Come on, then; we'll likely be doing all of that here soon."

———

Soon enough, Vulina lit the way through the tunnels of the mines, the walls cast with a bright orange glow under her gaze, as though she were a gigantic flash light.

I was right on top of the point that Aertra had sent to me, and had found nothing.

"Where the hell could she be?" I stared around and finally got frustrated enough to yell, until a hand appeared over my mouth and held it closed. "Mmf!"

"I just taught you how to use the Evil Eyes, and yet you fail to use them. Why?" Her voice was a whisper next to my ear, then her hand was gone, along with her presence.

I turned and focused all my senses on searching the darkness as Vulina darted this way and that, looking for the person we searched for on her own.

"Stop moving around and lower the light you're putting out for a second." I growled at her, and she did so while pouting.

I allowed my gaze to relax and search for the Aether. There was none at first, until a certain spot on the wall radiated darkness and shadow more than the other pools of shadow in the room. I smiled and pointed. "Hey, Aertra."

Vulina shot a bolt of fire into the corner just above the shadows, and the shadows dropped, the predatory Aertra glancing from me to the summoned flame creature with me. "Ah, you brought a snack with you."

"I am no such thing!" Vulina snarled, and her hands began to glow violently.

I huffed and spat, "Enough!" They both turned their sights on me, and I simply ignored the animosity they both held for each other. "What is wrong with you two?"

Aertra smiled and said, "She's food," at the same time that Vulina said, "She's a jerk!"

It was almost enough to make me laugh, but I just didn't feel like it. Instead, I stared at the elder Aether Vampire and asked, "Why are we here?"

"Hunting, as I said." She tilted her head toward the tunnel leading away from where she had been standing; it was smaller than the crevice made it seem. If she hadn't pointed it out, I wouldn't have known it was there. She sniffed the air. "Something is off about you. You feel stronger than the level above your head appears."

"I haven't spent my level-up stuff yet," I grumbled, and she made a shooing motion, as if I should. So I checked everything and found a single notification.

Level 15 Acquired – would you like to split your Aether?

Yes? / No?

Mephistopheles had said that this was something that would happen at level fifteen. I should do it, right?

I mulled it over and finally accepted it, then blinked before another prompt asked:

Please choose an Aether bar to split, or the choice will be made for you.

The Aether bar containing my fire and ice Aether began to glow a dull white; then in the middle, the glow began to fade and travel outward slowly.

If I chose this one, it would make it so that I got more, right? So it would make sense to have more Aether for both my offensive and defensive capabilities. But if I had more Summoning Aether, what could I do? Could I steal weapons out of people's hands? Could I force their limbs from their bodies?

I wished that the others were here to help me make this decision. At least they would be able to make sense of it all, or allow me to bounce ideas off them.

Rather than the what-if reward, I did the smart thing and chose the fire and ice bar.

My back arched, and it took all my strength, and even some help from Aertra and Vulina, not to scream bloody murder as the Aether in my body was torn in two. As the two new bars settled, ice on top of fire, they began to rebuild until they reached twelve each, same as Summoning.

"Fuck, that hurt," I whispered raggedly, my eyes closed to escape the pain.

"I've killed many of your kind since coming here for the fun of it," Aertra said and scowled at me. "Mephistopheles doing this to you seems to be an isolated incident. I am sorry."

I growled and spat up some blood, gasping. "Fuck, that *really* hurts." I closed my eyes again and focused on my stats. I had one point to put into something, and I chose Strength, bringing it up to thirteen and raising me up to 180 HP.

"Are you well enough to continue?" she asked. I shrugged, and then decided, with a nod to indicate my choice. She smiled. "Good. Follow me."

"Oh, wait," I called out, an idea occurring at the last minute.

She turned impatiently and watched me. "Yes?"

I brought out the holy sword, and she hissed at it, "Put it away!" I put it back into my inventory, and she stared at me. "How did you come across that thing?!"

"It was given to me," I told her the truth, but she still eyed me grimly. "I can't see the stats it imparts, and I wanted to use it. I was wondering if you might know anything about it?"

"It's a holy sword, Kyvir." She pointed to me. "You are not a holy paladin—you are a *dark* paladin. A job that is innately just, but to the wielder's sense of justice, and nothing else. That sword is meant to be used by someone who is a paragon of truth and light. It is the bane to evil."

"I thought the only evil thing in this whole place was just perspective?" I crossed my arms and watched her patiently.

"It is, but there are many perspectives that mesh what *we* do and what *we* are into what would be considered evil, because we steal the vitality of others for our own needs and causes." She once again jabbed a finger at my chest. "Add in the job that makes you rage at what you think is wrong, and you have someone who even the gods themselves would consider 'evil' or selfish."

"Okay, so there have to be unholy swords, right?"

A certain look of glee flitted over her face that she failed to rein in. "No. Only tainted holy ones."

I frowned. "How would you do that?"

She grinned now, not afraid to hide it. "Killing innocents."

I sighed. "I don't kill the innocent; I kill to improve myself, and those who stand in my way, or deserve it."

"The innocent don't necessarily have to be those who take no part in what goes on. They need not be *pure* beings." My frown deepened as she spoke on. "They just need to not have done anything to *you*."

She laughed to herself and motioned that I should follow her. I squeezed through the entrance she used and came out into a cramped tunnel which forced me to remove the armor I wore in order to move through without making any noise.

As we came upon a ledge that overlooked what could have been a serious drop, I saw something that made me smile almost as evilly as Aertra had. An underground city of sorts, buildings made of carved and hewn stone that reminded me of ancient civilizations, nestled together. Within them was a camp of goblins and gnolls living together in what could have been the most tenuous peace I had ever seen in my life.

The gnolls stuck to one side of the city, and then the goblins stayed in the other. Roasting insects and other creatures turned over spits and boiled in stews. There had to be hundreds of them down there.

"Look at all that food." Aertra all but drooled where she crouched, then turned to me hungrily. "Eye them, Kyvir. See what we have to work with."

"We're going to need back up for this," I grumbled, and she pointed insistently, so I turned my gaze on them all and focused.

For the longest while, I would catch brown and gray glimmers from the gnoll side of the city. Every now and then, something would catch in my peripheral vision, but I couldn't quite hone in on it.

"What do you see?"

I sighed and closed my eyes. "Brown; earth affinity. Gray aura that I'm not familiar with. And then something else that doesn't want me to see it."

"Shadow." She pointed to a swathe of shadows that was

darker than the rest, in the area with all the fires and whatnot. "The gray? That smells of undeath."

I didn't know if I even wanted to taste undeath. "So, let's go and get my friends, then come back."

She shook her head, "No. I'm hungry now, and you need to learn sooner, rather than later." I started to object, but she stared at me and closed the distance between us. "We aren't going after all of them, and if you listen to me now, I will allow you to return with your friends under my guidance. We will kill many of them before they realize we are here. But you *must* learn to hunt as I hunt."

Torn, I just stared back and nodded once. "Fine. In and out, as fast as we can be."

"We do it right, and you will grow stronger from this." She was smiling again, and her fingernails clacked against the stone as she tried to think of a way down.

The drop wasn't *too* far. Definitely not as far as the wall to the city was tall, but it was enough that the fall damage alone would kill me.

Vulina, are you big enough to glide down there with me? I turned to find her still hanging back in the small tunnel, kneeling where she was.

I would light up the sky down here if I were to go in there and try to fly with you.

There went that idea. Though, it wasn't necessarily a bad one. Since Sprinkle had gone home, I had been slowly regaining some of my ice Aether, though it seemed like the six I had given him weren't returning just yet.

Enough to get myself down there if I just slide, but it'll make noise. I scanned the area until I saw something on the goblin side of the camp that made me smile.

I narrowed my gaze and focused my will before summoning the item to my palm. Three summoning Aether drained from me instantly, then another and another. Finally, the length of rope that had been tied to the ground was in my hands. Using my ice Aether, I made a grapnel and secured the rope around a large toothy-looking rock on the outcropping we were on, tested it against my weight, then froze it to the edge so the rope wouldn't fray against the stone as well.

Aertra nodded with approval, drank from a familiar flask, and stepped over the edge of the outcropping with nary a care, floating down in the darkness as if it was the easiest thing to do for a deadly Mary Poppins.

I slid down the rope in increments, making sure it would be enough to get me down—it wasn't. But it got me close enough to the ground and to a rockier area that hid me from view, which allowed me to clamber down the twenty feet with icy claws, and no one came looking for me.

Aertra found me, dragging a young gnoll behind her with her hand crushing its muzzle shut. It was unconscious, thankfully. "Here, feed so you're stronger."

I frowned at her again, and she just thrust the creature at me, blood already dribbling from its neck. I bit in and drank my fill, the small amount of Aether that coursed through the veins under the furry flesh just enough to give me a couple bars of each Aether type. Nothing added to my affinity, though.

A heavy sigh, and I took out the holy blade, thinking *Do I really want to do this? Will this really help me get Mona back?*

Vulina flew behind me and I could see myself in the blade, like a reflection in a mirror. My eyes glowed orange, burning with hunger and rage, my fangs and jaw bloody, and I looked gaunt. Driven.

Yes. A sudden realization steamrolled any doubts I had, *Power is the only way to attain what you need in a timely manner. And with the update coming soon, I need to make as much progress as possible.*

The holy blade dipped and turned, then plunged into the body at my feet.

You have sullied the blade of a holy weapon. Cleanse it at a shrine, or the weapon will lose its holy properties.

"Good," Aertra purred again. "Follow me. We hunt."

Following the elder Aether Vampire was like following an

expert thief through a museum filled to the brim with valuable treasure and well-made fakes. She would watch, sniffing and tasting the air ahead of us, and shake her head, then turn a corner and stealthily move down a roadway to grab a gnoll whose aura glowed strongly brown.

"You see this? Earth." She held the gnoll's muzzle while I fed, then I kicked it in the back of the knee and stabbed it through the back with the sword. The same notification persisted from it. And three percent more added to my affinity for the element. "Hide the body."

I frowned at the task and decided that hiding it on the Goblin side of the city might be beneficial, at least to hide our presence for a short time. Dragging it closer to the goblin side, I found a rock and started to bash the head with it, then threw it behind a closed door under some trash and made my way back to Aertra.

Three more gnolls fell to my hunger and the holy sword before one of them noticed me, and we had to kill them and back off a little bit to watch from the shadows. The sound of water drew my attention and made me wonder if there would be anyone else that we could get to without drawing any more gnolls after us. The experience was negligible, due to the difference in levels.

Following the noise, it grew steadier and louder, until an underground river that fed into several smaller ponds and large puddles came into view.

There were a few divided camps of goblins and gnolls which guarded certain wells close to their respective sides of the city, but there were loners who strayed from them. Whether they sought to get water that they weren't strong enough to get from the others, or they just weren't welcome, they were isolated. And some of them were just *ripe* for the picking.

Aertra fed on one of them, having snuck her way closer to it, then snagged it in a headlock to snap its neck so it was helpless.

Normally, that sort of brutality would have rubbed me the

wrong way, but here in these full hunting grounds, there was nothing I enjoyed more than growing stronger.

My footsteps, drowned out by the rush of the water, failed to alert the lone goblin in front of me, its back turned. Rather than grabbing him outright, I wanted to play.

I threw a rock at his feet, gently enough for him to think it was something coming closer, and he turned to look for whatever it could have been. Goblins were a hateful sort down here; his beady little eyes were distrustful and narrowed into the shadows where I stood, but I knew he couldn't see me. If he had, he would have screamed or panicked. He would have been right to do so.

He slowly made his way into the darkness, with a poorly-made stone knife as his only protection, and cautiously crept toward me where I stood—waiting hungrily.

I reached out and gripped him loosely by the throat, sliding the dying holy blade into his stomach slowly, before yanking him close enough to feed from. The ebbing flow of his life's blood was enough to finally push me over the edge to a hundred percent affinity to Earth Aether.

100 % affinity for Earth Aether completed: Would you like to collect your reward?

Yes? / No?

Knowing it would be the roulette, I heaved a soft sigh and nodded, "Yes."

The world faded, and once more, I stood before Mephistopheles and his wheel, his sweet voice ringing out around me, "Hello again, *Mageblood!*"

His cackling sent a chill down my spine only the way he could.

CHAPTER FIFTEEN

SETH

"That's the first time you've said my name with so much emphasis, I think. Mephisto," I ventured carefully as I watched him. He no longer went to the pains to hide his truly grotesque demonic form anymore. His bald head had since elongated and looked almost liken that of an alien as he stared at me. "Well, not since the first time we met."

"Well, I do love that one of my favorite little monsters is out creating such a delicious smorgasbord of chaos for me to thrive on." He licked his finger and touched the wheel, the last options that I'd had fading away, until eventually the wheel itself began to turn to dust. "Times are changing, my young, naïve, and *murderous* little friend. As much as I would love to sit here and spin the wheel of fate, I find that I grow tired of that little game. So how about a new one, eh?"

"I liked the old one just fine."

He pouted and poked me with one sickeningly long finger. "Don't be like that. You have so much more change coming—getting used to the way things are only makes it easier for me to create and sow chaos, sure—but you're different." He tilted his head a little to the side and smiled, his teeth sharp even with his creepy car-salesman style of speaking. "You and that little fiery hell-cat, Monami."

I looked him in the eyes and held his gaze. "Give her back."

"No," he stated simply as he folded his too-long arms at his waist with a self-satisfied grin. "You won't play my games—I won't play yours."

I growled, "Fine!"

He clapped like a child, and the ground lengthened behind him, almost like a jumping pit. A net rose from the ground on each side, and a batter's tee burst from the dirt. "This one ought to be fun!"

He pointed to the tee, and a large, yellow softball appeared. To the left of the mound, where the ball and tee waited, grew a giant scoreboard, with the amount of distance and the prizes written in a language I couldn't comprehend on the side.

"Simple concept, though this one relies a little more on you for the results, and I am *dying* to see how it works out." He manifested a comedic-looking bat into his hand and swung it at the ball, just barely missing. "You swing, you hit it far enough, you get a prize."

His head snapped around so impossibly fast that there should have been a break in his neck, but instead, he stared at me and actually hit the ball this time. "You manage to hit it farther than me, and I'll tell you *right* where she is and what she's up to." The ball sailed into the distance and finally stopped somewhere. He spoke again. "But if you *don't*, not you or anyone else is going to know a single thing."

"What do you mean 'anyone else'?" I frowned at him as he chuckled. "That makes no sense; who else would care?"

"Aside from your little party?" He looked strangely over my shoulder, as if someone was standing there watching him. "Loads of people. More than you would likely ever care to know."

He twirled the bat like an expert, dropped it to let the end hit the ground and then bounce back into his hand. "Whaddaya say, slugger? Wanna give it the old college try?"

"Fine," I grumped and held my hand out for the bat. "What are the rules?"

He tossed it to me, and I caught it easily as he grinned manically, "Hit the ball and let it fly! Fall just short, and you'll die—but hit far and watch it sail!" He spun and sat on a set of bleachers that popped up, filled with more than a dozen demons that clapped and cheered like fans in a stadium. "You just might make those prizes... okay, I'm bored; hit the ball."

Popcorn appeared when he snapped his fingers, something red drizzled all over them that reminded me of blood. "No other rules?"

He scooped up a handful and grunted, "Nada."

I picked up the bat and focused then, making the air around me cool with my ice Aether, slowly dropping the temperature, then introduced my fire Aether into my blood and body to heat my muscles, hoping this would work. I continued until all of my Aether was gone, then focused on the popcorn in the demon's hand.

I tried to summon it to me, but much like I had thought and hoped, he held onto it and just grinned as he shoveled another bite into his gullet.

Spent and nearly out of time, I readied myself at the bat and swung for all I was worth while using Wrathful Smite. Bat connected with ball just below center and gave it some higher drive than I thought I would even be capable of.

The ball flew, and a screen above me burst into life as a small, winged imp with a magical camera took off after the flying object.

We could all hear his panting as he struggled to keep up, and suddenly I wasn't alone, Mephisto standing directly to my left, closest to the prize board. "Cleverly done, my little monster. Cleverly done."

I shrugged, used to this part of things. My only hope was that it wouldn't be a waste. And that it wouldn't kill me.

The ball and the imp started to slowly sink in the air, dipping toward the earth, then I turned to ask, "Does the roll count?"

Mephisto grinned, "What roll?" Then waved his hand at the camera where the imp and ball touched the ground around the same time, but the imp and camera rolled on the ground past the ball. "Ah, I see. Was that it?"

I grunted, "No, but whatever."

Mephisto's grip tightened slightly. "Don't be that way, Kyvir —this is meant to be fun!"

He waved his hand again, and an unseen force grabbed the imp, who grunted and puked violently before wrenching it up to look at the ball.

A tape measure appeared in Mephisto's hand, and he winked before the tape shot from it like a bullet from a barrel.

The imp looked toward us, and all he saw before the metal nub hit him was something shiny that pierced his gut with a disgusting squelch. He fell forward onto his knobby little knees, and Mephisto grunted as he read the information.

He snapped his fingers, and the score was updated on the prize board. At the top was the distance his ball had flown, and beneath that, by two hundred yards, was where my ball had fallen.

"Too bad." Mephisto looked genuinely saddened by the results, turning to me. "You still win a prize, though I know it isn't what you wanted at all."

He smacked me on the forehead, and a searing pain ran through my skull as something burst through my skin and grew. "Tell us what he got, Azriel!"

A massive demon lurking behind the bleachers spoke as if he were the announcer for a bad game show, "It's a set of new horns!"

"What?" I snarled and whirled on Mephisto, who just chuckled. "What are you playing at, here?"

"Did you think I would just allow you to collect all the Aether you liked and give you limitless power?" He laughed, the volume not matching how wide his mouth stretched to do it. "No. I like chaos; I feed on it. Allowing you to grow unchecked like that just creates a much more linear route to balance, and I cannot abide that."

"You're afraid I'll win." I'd have to admit I was trying to goad him into giving me more power, but he just laughed again, joined by his horde of followers.

"I fear nothing anymore but boredom, my little monster." Mephisto clapped his hands, his audience gone from our vicinity and replaced by slowly encroaching darkness. "Your secret quest is almost finished, and who knows? I just might allow you another, as a show of just how little I fear you."

He lifted a finger in the air and turned to me with a grin. "Do pass on my warmest regards to my dear old friend Aertra, won't you? How I miss the way she stirred things up." He tickled my chin with two long fingers like an elderly person tweaking a loved one's cheek, and I couldn't move as he waved. "Ta-ta!"

The darkness swallowed me up, and I opened my eyes, finding myself exactly where I had stood before being pulled into his game.

Aertra flitted across the small shadowed area and flinched when she saw me. "Kyvir?"

I nodded, and she slowly let herself ease out of whatever instinctive reaction she had. "You look…different."

"I went to see that clown of a demon," I growled. She frowned, then realization dawned on her. I nodded again and confirmed, "Mephistopheles."

"He gave you those god-awful mossy, green horns?" I reached up to understand what she was talking about and sure enough, the horns he had given me were covered in something that felt almost like fur to my bloody fingertips. "How lovely of him."

"He said to tell you he said hi, and that he misses the way you would stir things up." She froze at my comment, her body stiffening until you could have painted her and she would have been easily mistaken for a statue. "Called you 'old friends'."

"I never cared for him as much as he thinks, but it was he who told me that drinking the blood of others would keep me young and beautiful." Her admittance didn't surprise me much, but her sudden sadness did. She sniffed, "Then he destroyed my world and brought me here. Made me a monster anew. And he plans to do the same thing here."

"What do you mean?"

She shook her head and muttered, "The locals call it the Merger, but when it happened on my world, the magic that was here pulled my planet into it and melded it with itself." She frowned and shrugged. "After that, magic was stronger for a time, the Aether more prevalent. But the demons were stronger, too."

So *that* was the play. The "change" that was coming soon was the Merger. After that, the chance we would be stronger was unlikely, but the demons would be, almost guaranteed.

I snarled and punched the wall, damaging my fist and making noise that drew some attention.

"Hide," I growled at her, and she stared at me indignantly before I shoved past her and grabbed the goblin who scouted into the area. I lifted him bodily and drank from his shoulder until it felt like my stomach would burst, then crushed his skull against the wall to my left with a heaving motion.

His body fell, and I turned to her, tapped my stone against the wall where she stood, and asked, "You going to wait here, or do you want to come and introduce yourself to the rest of the team?"

"I will wait here and ensure that no one finds the bodies until you return." She frowned and added, "I do not work well with others. I will meet them, but I do not plan to function with them as a 'team.'"

"Fine by me." I grunted and activated the stone to take me back to the city with a message to the others via whisper, —*Meet at the den in a few minutes; we're going hunting.*—

They tried to send me responses but I just ignored them. I hadn't eaten anything in a while, and I should. I *knew* that I should. But I just wasn't in the mood. We needed to prepare. We needed to be ready. As soon as we got word of Mona from anywhere, we had to be ready to rush off.

And to get there, we had top be strong enough that no one could fuck with us.

That meant leveling and gearing up.

I made it to the guarded entrance to the Den, where the others waited for me, "What's going on?" Emerald asked with no preamble, then glanced at my new horns, "and what are those?"

I glanced at the guards, knowing they would report anything they heard to the other authorities. The Talons would effectively ruin any advantage we had with stealth by sending an army into the tunnels that would ruin our hunt.

We couldn't allow that. All of the creatures that I had encountered down there had been too weak to offer much of anything as far as experience was concerned, but the ones that weren't the stragglers and weaklings?

Those ones would be worth it.

I motioned to the entrance, and we walked inside, waiting for the doors to close behind us before I muttered, "There's a city of gnolls and goblins in the mines, and I found the way in with Aertra." I pointed a thumb to my horns and added, "These are from Mephisto after I got a hundred percent with Earth Aether. He screwed me over big time, and he knows more about everything than he's letting on. More on that later."

"I want to know more *now*, Kyvir." Emerald held her hand up to stop me, then cleared her throat as I attempted to speak anyway.

"I really don't know how much he could possibly know, but I do know this…" I glanced down the hall to ensure no one was with us and spoke a little more clearly, "Something big is coming, like 'merger of our two worlds' big, and I don't know what that will mean for us, but it can't be good. So we need to go down there and wipe them from the map and move on as fast as we can."

"Are we ready for something that size?" Sundar scratched her head and stared intently at both of us. "We're only a tank, DPS, and healer, Kyvir. If this is really a whole city, that sounds like it might be better suited as a raid."

"The gnolls' leader likely left to go and invade the dungeon to take over, so they're currently leaderless. The only reason that the goblins don't move on them is because the gnolls are better equipped and larger than they are." I frowned, trying to remember the layout of the city, but I had been in a fugue state, and it was fuzzy. So much blood and feeding. "I don't think they like each other and are only tolerating each other for now. If we do it right, we can subvert blame to the other side and make a getaway, if needed."

"What of this Aertra you brought?" Emerald crossed her arms. "She useful?"

I nodded, "She's an Aether Vampire like me, so she can kill just as easily as we can."

"And she's not a threat to us?" The motherly figure raised an eyebrow at me, and I just shrugged. "That's not good enough, Kyvir."

"She's not a team player—her words, not mine—but she knows that if she hurts you guys, she has nothing to lord over me anymore, and I'll try to find a way to kill her."

Sundar nodded and after a long, silent moment, and Emerald pointed to the doors to the throne room. "We should at least let Queen Sinistella know what's going on in her mines, so she can prepare."

I wanted to tell her no, but the way she looked at me brooked no argument, and we made our way toward the throne room.

Sinistella was seated at the desk that she'd had brought into the room, an older-looking dark wooden monstrosity that could have been more table than work station. She worked her way through a pile of paperwork while seated in her throne.

"Ah! Brother, sister, and surrogate daughter." She regarded all of us keenly. "I trust things went well in the dungeon?"

"We beat it," Sundar stated calmly. "It was a dungeon at war, though."

Sinistella paused and blinked at us, "A what?"

"Dungeon at war," I repeated grimly. "Gnolls had come in and invaded the dungeon before we got there, and we had to kill everything inside."

"Gnolls," she flipped open a book on her desk and thumbed through some pages before quoting, "A canid species whose society is hierarchy-based. In order to be considered stronger, or strongest, you have to be able to do something worthy of merit for the group." She closed the book, her pensive face concerned. "I wonder where they came from."

"We aren't fully sure where, but Kyvir and his…tutor managed to stumble on a city full of goblins and gnolls in the mines."

Emerald's statement made her stand and slam her hands on the desk. "What?" Some of the papers that had been stacked on the wood precariously pitched over the side and fluttered onto the ground.

Sinistella's sudden worry wasn't out of line; she had just been given the throne by her mother. Something like this would be scandalous, at the very least. "We plan to take care of it as best as we can."

She turned to glare at me. "You've known this all of *how* long?"

"A few hours. I was hunting there before I came here, picking off some of the stragglers." The truth.

"Why didn't you send me a whisper or something?" She grilled me, the heat in the room growing, like her mother's fury had mildly touched her.

"I honestly wasn't myself." Thinking about it, I wasn't sure if that was the truth or not. "I was there to kill and feed, and wasn't really considering too much. But now that I am, I see it as an opportunity for us to grow and for it to be taken care of quietly."

She stilled once more and stared at me, openly confused. "Quietly?" She came around the desk to stand in front of me and cross her arms. "You find a city of monstrous races, and you want to take care of it *quietly*?"

"Think of the advantages that taking care of an entire city of enemies would net you, then add to that the fact that your people may never be the wiser." She frowned at me and narrowed her eyes further, so I went on. "You send warriors down there just after your coronation, and they'll cry scandal— even the ones most loyal to you. If you send *us*, you minimize the risk to your people, and the risk of them finding out."

"You'll even be able to use the city as a mining camp under-ground that could allow you a chance at rarer finds, and a way to watch what's beneath you," Sundar nodded her head sagely. "There are some things that the dwarves could build and create to make this place hugely successful and easily accessible, provided we don't let them destroy it."

"There are other Wanderers in the city now, as well." Emerald leaned down and picked up some of the papers that had fallen, but the dragon queen twirled a finger and all of the mess flew from her hands into the air, where it stacked itself and returned to the desk. Sinistella nodded in gratitude and bade her continue with her thought. "You can ask that they be rounded up and brought to you, swear an oath of silence, and then you could give them a quest to further eradicate the gnolls and goblins in the mines and the city over the next few days, if it proves to be too much for us."

"But all of you agree that you want to be able to take a crack at it alone, is that it?" She stared at us with a complicated look spreading over her beautiful features. "What if they over-whelm you? Kill you? See your presence as the will of those above and launch an attack on the city?"

"What if grasshoppers had machine guns?" Sundar huffed, and all of us turned toward her with apparent confusion on our faces. She chuckled to herself and pointed to Sinistella with a knife in hand. "You spend too much time with the what ifs, and they'll walk all over you until they *do* decide to come up here. At least with us, there's a definite possibility that we could turn them on each other and come out alive. We need the experience and you need them gone. The only sweeter way for you to come out of this with less heartache is if you have people on standby for if we do take the hit."

She pointed to me, then Emerald. "If one of them bites it, I can get them back up quickly, and we can keep kicking ass. All it takes on your part is patience and trust."

"We did it once before," I added for her, and Sinistella turned toward me with a hiss.

She pointed a sharp nail into my chest. "You got lucky before, Kyvir. We had more warriors on standby, in case things went tail-up."

"Let us do this, and then we're out of your hair," I pleaded, her face now a blank mask. "We mean to do this: kill as many as we can to keep the city and her people safe, and then we go for the front lines—wherever they may be."

She bit her nail, something I had never seen her do, then sighed and relented her worrying. "You have six hours' head start before I send every able-bodied and sworn-to-silence traveler I can muster down there. If any of you fall, one of you is to immediately send a whisper to me so that I know what your status is. If you fail me in this, I will be very displeased and may decide to kick you out of the city."

She eyed us all and stared directly at me. "I know why you work so hard for what you do, and I know that she thought of you equally. Don't fail."

She turned and raised a hand to dismiss us so she could go back to her work, shouting commands to parties unseen. We had the green light, so we wasted no more time.

"Zanjir!" Emerald bellowed with the authority of a trainer who knew dogs better than anything else. Her massive dog stepped out of her shadow, and I nearly fell over at seeing how big he was now. His head was easily up to Emerald's shoulder as he stood alert, watching the surroundings.

"Was he supposed to grow so fast?" I leveled my gaze at her, but she just shrugged. These new breeds were going to be interesting.

We raced down the street to the mining area that I had left from and worked our way into the tunnels using the same link to the previous location in my chat log.

I whispered to Aertra that we were coming, and she just sent me, —*They have yet to find their dead, but the gnolls have someone interesting with them, I think. I will await your arrival to investigate.*—

"She said there's someone down there with them that she finds interesting, so we will likely be checking them out before we start the killing." They nodded as we entered into the darkness of the tunnels, and I followed the arrow to return to the buried city.

CHAPTER SIXTEEN

It took us a moment to get down from the outcropping, seeing as it was dark as hell down there now, and the rope was no longer secured to the stone by the ice that had since melted.

Eventually, I was able to summon the rope back with a glimmer of light that Vulina allowed me, since she had thought of this happening and offered to meet me there.

What did she do while we were away? I watched my summon down below as Sundar efficiently sealed the rope to the stone and made her way down it with the ease of a trained soldier who had rappelled before. I didn't dare leave them to go straight to Aertra, so I instructed them to wait until I could guide them safely.

She skulked around the shadows and watched for anything she could kill. That made sense for Aertra to do. *She also kept the more curious goblins and gnolls from finding the corpses you left behind. You know, you're kind of brutal when you kill.*

I raised an eyebrow at that and almost chuckled wryly. *That going to be a problem?*

Not for me, she replied with a snort of her own. *I'm here to help you with that. I am literally made of fire, Kyvir. It's my job to destroy.*

I grabbed her shoulder when I made it to the bottom and reassured her, "You do it well."

"Do what well?" Emerald asked quietly as she joined us. She was hard to see in the darkness, given the dark clothing she wore to hide herself.

"She destroys well," I said, unphased. "Let's go see what we can see, then get started."

Sundar had already secreted ahead slightly, so I had Aertra give us her coordinates once more, and we made our way to her.

It was slower going this time, both Sundar and Emerald wanting to get the lay of the land before moving along. They stopped and watched the gnolls and goblins at their various fires and dens, how they interacted and treated each other. One of them even got the bright idea to pitch a rock at the goblins from the gnoll side to see if they would squabble.

The struck goblin hit pitched forward, stunned, and came back up confused. The goblins around it turned and began to yell at the more beast-like denizens of the city, who milled about nearby, but they didn't take that well at all.

One of the larger gnolls crossed the distance between the two groups—easily twenty feet—in two long bounds and jammed its clawed hand through the loudest goblin's throat.

The two groups got into a fight, with more goblins streaming into the area. It would have been a good time to step in, until we heard a sharp, piercing whistle.

The gnolls straightened up, and someone shouted in a thicker southern drawl than I had heard in a long time, "Now, y'all knock that off, y'ear?"

The figure walked through the gnoll line and pointed at the aggressors, who whined and flattened their ears at him, but he took it in stride. "Doesn't matter who started it, I'm endin' it!"

He huffed and stepped closer to the goblin side of the city, their fire casting light onto his fur. He was more grey in areas than some of the other gnolls, a chunk of his right ear missing, and he walked with the kind of swagger that some older people used when they needed others to know they were in charge. But this didn't seem like it was meant to be a challenge, just his natural gait.

He leaned down and peered into the area around the fire and said something in a high-pitched squeal that could have been goblin, for all I knew, but they just let their jaws drop and cleared away from him. They looked terrified.

"I thought I said 'sorry,' but that ain't the right direction for someone to step for an apology." His drawl had dissipated a tad, now that he seemed more contemplative than angry. He shrugged it off and turned back to the gnolls. "Now, y'all go on and git you somethin' to eat. We gotta be patient 'til the boss gets back." He eyed the gnolls lingering and barked, "Git!"

"What do you wanna bet that's who she was talking about?" Sundar muttered softly to us, and I had to agree. I couldn't see an aura around him, so I couldn't see what might bear investigating, but who knew. "Do we follow him, or go find Aertra?"

"She has found you," Aertra whispered, and Sundar's fist streaked toward the Aether Vampire like she was trying to kill her. Aertra just stepped aside and stopped the larger woman from traveling further., "I like this one. Good instincts."

"Please don't startle her again," I muttered, then pointed to the retreating gnoll. "That the interesting person?"

She nodded and smiled excitedly. "He has life and gravity Aether inside him."

My eyebrows shot up; that was an interesting combination, for sure. If I ate him, could I get those kinds?

"I wonder what he's doing down here with the gnolls?" Emerald looked puzzled. "I remember that some of the more monstrous races were choices, but it makes no sense to have them be enemies like this, and have a player be here, too."

I shrugged. "We could always just go ask."

"We could, but we have about five hours left until the cavalry arrives." Sundar frowned and thought for a moment, "Life and gravity... that sounds like it could be a crowd-control healer, and if we had that kind of oomph with us, we could do damn near anything we wanted. I think we need to go about this in a way that will get us on his good side. Or him on ours."

"What're you thinking for it, then?" Emerald's gaze flicked toward the goblins. "They aren't enemies right now."

"Right, but we could drive them to be," Sundar smiled. "Or we could warn them about the coming raid after we cut a swath through the goblins."

I smirked. Sinistella was a lot of things, but she was flustered as the new ruler and hadn't sworn *us* to secrecy. "Emerald, you warn the player about someone coming to kill them all in a few hours, and see about getting on his good side. Sundar, Aertra and I will come in kicking ass stealthily, and when you give us the word, we'll make a big show out of it."

"Why the last part?" Aertra asked in confusion.

"Lends more credibility to what we say, and the faster they're gone, the better for us, because smaller numbers are less likely to turn on us." Emerald said before she smiled and turned to me. "You've become very crafty, Kyvir. I'm proud."

I nodded in thanks, and she took off, fading from view in a matter of a few strides. I motioned for Sundar and Aertra to follow me, and we were on our way as well.

Moving to the opposite side of the city as the gnolls wasn't hard at all, but I made sure to be as cautious as we could manage so that no one was alerted too soon. It seemed that more and more of the goblins on this side had moved here expressly to fall asleep.

We walked until we came to an open area with about ten of them sleeping in little piles under furs and whatever other coverings could be scavenged.

I sent a whisper to Sundar and Aertra, —*Take them quietly, and make as little sound as possible. The more we kill, the easier this goes.* —

Both of them gave me the 'duh' stare, so I just pulled out my dying holy blade and took a steadying breath as the tip of it hung over the throat of a goblin that was too weak to give me any EXP.

I stabbed down, the metal of the sword passing through the neck cleanly enough to sever the spine before the creature could make any noise.

I took a step and slid the blade along the same height into the side of another one's head and then flicked the blade into the third one in the open area that I could reach. All of them were dead in a matter of seconds.

Aertra, covered in gore and blood, looked even more hungry than when she had begun. "They have no Aether, it's like drinking salt soup without the pleasure of the salt."

I frowned at the analogy and turned back to our work. If anyone came here, they would see what we had done, and then there would be a panicked call for a search. We needed to hide the bodies for now.

Searching the area for a place that might work, I found one and smiled. A small house that actually had a door in the frame would serve perfectly for the sort of hiding we needed to do.

I could *just burn them to a crisp, you know…* Vulina crossed her arms as she leaned against the wall of the nearest side of the cavern.

The smell might alert the gnolls and give us away too soon. I lifted a couple of the bodies easily and walked toward the house, then thought to check inside to be safe. There were half a dozen sleeping goblins inside, and several smaller bundles in the corner furthest from the door that one of the goblins had dozed off against. If I had opened it, that would have woken it up to shout for the others.

The window was broken and little more remained than two wooden sticks at a cross section. I used the bodies like a stepping stool and pulled the sticks out with dull snaps.

The goblin inside at the door stirred, waking up a little, so I ducked down and heard it get up. Something flatulent and gross came to my ears and nose in a wave that made me gag. I heard a sharp intake of breath above me and instinctively slid my holy sword straight up. Blood dribbled down it and onto my shoulder, as well as something else that was a little more solid.

"You've gotta be shitting me," Sundar snickered and almost vomited all at once. "Oh, my god."

"Goblins are vile little creatures." Aertra smiled and actually tried not to laugh as I flung my sword sideways, and the body plopped onto the ground.

"Someone, please, just get it off me," I muttered through gritted teeth so I didn't breathe too much of the stench in. "Or I will burn the whole fucking city down."

Sundar came over to me and smiled. "Now, now—no need to get shitty with us."

Aertra snorted and began to laugh with a soft wheeze. This was going to be a long massacre.

I cleared the house with Aertra's help, the blood and excrement on my sword just going a long way to dirtying it up. I wondered how many more I would need to kill, until one of the bundles in the corner of the room began to squirm.

Aertra cautiously made her way over to them and grinned. "Kill them."

"They're babies," Sundar growled. Everything else, she had been all for, but this one thing, she actually stood in front of me to prevent.

"They are babies who will either be starving soon, or be killed by the Wanderers who make their way behind you," Aertra insisted, bending down so that she could touch one of the bundles, then motioned from them to my sword. "This is the ultimate act of sullying something pure and holy."

"The ultimate act of destroying your principles and soul," Sundar corrected vehemently, her eyes coming back to me as she openly pleaded, "I've seen what this kind of choice can do to someone, S—Kyvir. You may be going through some shit, and we do need to be stronger, but I don't want this for you."

Aertra watched me in a way that almost called to the dark paladin in me, but the way that Sundar watched me, as if she would launch herself at me if I did something wrong, resonated with my sense of justice.

I nodded at my friend and just put my sword down. "I'm

not going to argue with you; I don't want that on my soul either." I turned to Aertra. "I'll kill a thousand sleeping goblins before I stoop to that demon bastard's level."

She stared at me hard, the contempt plain on her face before she shrugged, "Fine. At least I know how far you won't go for power." She walked out of the room, tapping my sword with a red-stained nail that left a mark. The mark glowed red and black, the red streaking out along the blade slowly. "It's begun; the real work starts now."

I frowned and turned back to find that none of the bundles moved, and all was quiet.

CHAPTER SEVENTEEN

It took everything I had to stop Sundar from trying to kill her. "If we try it down here, we're surrounded by enemies who will rip us apart, and she thinks she could go toe to toe with an ancient dragon. I don't want to test that." She strained against my grasp, and I doubled down, adding Vulina to the mix to grab her. "We keep on with the plan, and then we get the hell out of here."

She stopped struggling as Aertra came back into view with more blood dripping from her hands, then turned to me, muttering under her breath, "We find a way to end her as soon as we're able, or we leave her ass behind. I will not travel with her if I don't absolutely have to."

I nodded in agreement. "That's fine."

She seethed for a moment, but decided to act cool, so we let her go. She walked off a short distance and motioned that we should carry on.

From then on, we worked quietly through the ranks of those sleeping around the camp until we got to the stronger goblins. These ones were only level 13 or so, but still, the points were nice and added up at 20 or more EXP per goblin. We probably killed more than two dozen before anyone even found a corpse, and that one barely got off more than a drawn breath before Sundar clubbed him so hard that his eyes popped out of his head.

The deaths continued to pile up, but then we got sloppy when we ventured too close to the gnoll side of the city.

A baying call went up, and six or seven gnolls stared straight at me as my sword burst through the back of a patrolling goblin. "Shit."

"Get in front, Kyvir," Sundar snarled as she threw down her totem, the glow of it pulsing through the area in a way that was new to me. The energy flooded the area, the Hell Cat buff roaring through me as I hefted my sword.

A howl of sorts ripped through the air, and the gnolls turned tail and fled with their tails tucked between their legs. The unusual gnoll that we had observed earlier swaggered through the street toward us with a deep, rippling glow around his left hand.

"I appreciate y'all not comin' after my kin, but I'm gonna to need you to stop killin' these little fellas." He paused a little outside the range that someone should have been able to make out his name above his head, but my eyes were stronger than that.

Elder Berry Lvl 16

"Elder Berry?" I called over to him, my sword tip falling so that it rested against the ground. "They call you their elder, or is that actually your name?"

He sighed, and the shadows behind him released Emerald. She chuckled to herself and muttered something to the gnoll, who huffed, "Well, my name is Elder Berry, but y'all are young, right?" I nodded, though Sundar just stared at him. "Your mother was a hamster? Father smelt of elderberries?"

I blinked at him confusedly, while Aertra slowly stepped toward the gnoll. He just shook his head and explained, "Too young; they made me split it, 'cause I guess you know that they have to have a first and last name, for some reason. You really don't know about Monty? The Holy Grail?"

"The dragon chicken?" Sundar perked up and pointed at the gnoll.

He growled happily and pointed back at her, "Yup!" A crushing weight pushed the air out of her lungs, and she fell to her knees. "Oh! I am so sorry; I forgot all about that."

The rippling around his hand ceased, and she stood to her feet slowly. "Y'all come with me and the gnolls, and we can get out of here before the other Travelers arrive. It'd be a shame to have to fight all of 'em. Though, they can have what's left of the goblins, angry little folks."

"We would much rather leave the way we came, if it's all the same to you." I put the sword into my inventory and watched how Elder Berry reacted to my statement. He just nodded sagely. "Are you planning just to stay with them forever?"

He shook his head. "Naw, was gonna go out and see the world eventually, after all these folks got settled somewhere safe." He shrugged and motioned to all of them vaguely as we made our way through their side of the city unmolested. "Their leader, Fangory, was supposed to secure a dungeon for 'em nearby, but he never returned. Guess y'all saw to that?"

Sundar rubbed the back of her head. "Sorry about that."

He just chuckled. "Ain't no thing. He was a brute, but he cared about his people, and he wanted what was best for 'em. If he had to choose how he would go out, it would be either that way, or huntin'. You did him a favor."

"So, since they're leaderless now, what does that mean for you?" I was genuinely curious as to his position.

"Well, they'll pick a new one once they know he's gone—likely one of the stronger betas—and they'll go from there." He whistled at one of them and barked, "Go on and get the other betas! I need 'em."

"They understand you when you speak like that?" Emerald raised an eyebrow at him, and even Zanjir watched him.

"Well, yeah." He shrugged. "Been talkin' to 'em their whole

lives, for some of 'em. They understand the common tongue easy enough, they just prefer to speak their own language. Same goes for a lot of the more monstrous races."

"That's … good to know." So then they were just dumb, allowing us to communicate to each other and plan, then falling into the traps we laid. I sighed and shook my head; horses and gifts. "So, once they're taken care of, any plans? We could definitely use someone of your skills and ability."

He glanced over at me. "And what would those be? You've only seen the one."

"Crowd control like that could come in handy with training," Emerald offered politely, but his gaze stayed on me.

"You have two kinds of Aether: Gravity and Life." He frowned at me in his own animalistic sort of way, like he was considering something. "I can see Aether. It's an ability of mine."

"I see." He relaxed considerably, but didn't totally let his guard down. "So you'd like me to tag along?"

"If you wanted to." I shrugged, and Emerald and Sundar acted as if they were about to hand me my own head for being so indifferent.

"What he means to say," Emerald growled at me and then turned to more adequately face Berry, "was that we could all benefit by you joining us. See, we're looking for my daughter, and we think she might be working with the demons against her will."

He stopped and turned to her, then to the rest of us. "Demons?" His eyes blinked pointedly, and he motioned to Emerald. "Your daughter is with the demons?"

"Not because she wanted to be, I don't think," Emerald admitted, then shook her head. "She had to make a terrible choice, and I believe she made it because she thought she was protecting the rest of us."

He spat and snarled, the gnolls around us beginning to growl threateningly. "Demons were what ran us out of our forest dens." He pointed to Emerald. "Your kid is a patsy to one of 'em? She make a deal or somethin'?'"

"Not that I know of, no—but Monami is nothing of the sort!" Emerald was offended now, her hands clenched at her side, and her mountain of a dog Zanjir growled menacingly. "She did what she thought was best, and now she's alone without me to watch over her. She was kidnapped by the demons at home, too, and we have to find her."

"If anything, we can offer you the chance at revenge that you seem to want." I felt that idea would likely be enticing.

"I'm not one for revenge—my dear wife abhorred the idea of it, and never cared for what it made people do." He put his hands on his hips and frowned at all of us, staring intently at Emerald as Zanjir growled softly at her side. Finally, he offered her his hand and mumbled, "But she was always one to say thanks and offer a helpin' hand to a neighbor in need. You folks saved my folks, and you're hurtin' for one of yours. Least I can do is offer to help, in return for gettin' to see more of the world here."

Emerald took the proffered hand and shook it in return kindly. "Thank you." She tilted her head at the gnolls around us. "How soon can they get out of here?"

Three of the second-largest gnolls I'd ever seen made their presences known to us, and I had no doubt they were the betas. They growled and whined at the gnoll, who stood there and nodded slowly before turning to us. "They have a way out, but it will take 'em a while to get to it. They'll make it if they leave now, since they know how to cover up their trail. So I'll head with y'all now."

The three betas all looked at each other before the one in the center stepped forward and licked the player version of them. Berry just chortled and muttered, "Stop that; you're actin' like dogs now." The others, tails wagging, circled around him and sniffed him, rubbing their heads against his shoulders and neck affectionately. One of them even nipped at his ear, and he just hauled off and kicked the gnoll in the butt, hollering, "You already took a chunk once, you greedy thing!"

The gnolls took off as one and raced through the city, rushing across the underground river, and diving into a tunnel that I had put off as only an optional exit if things went particularly bad. I motioned for him to follow along and led everyone to the small getaway with the outcropping above us. Getting up to it without alerting the gnolls was no longer an issue; however, the goblins were still a threat, and without the rest of the gnolls to back him, they would likely go straight for Elder Berry.

"We need to try to get this rope up there." I pulled the rope up and started to make a grapnel with ice, but there was no chance of it.

My whole body was weightless, and I slowly lifted off the ground as Elder Berry muttered, "Grab the wall, and you can make your way up. Don't leave more than twenty feet away from me, though; it'll get heavy if you do."

I snickered at the pun, but he seemed oblivious to it. We clambered up the side of the wall and crested the outcropping easily. Once we arrived, there was a moment of indecision. We hadn't gotten enough experience to level up, but we had to leave something for the others to hunt, in order to lend credence to our claims. I looked around and noted that Aertra wasn't with us.

"We return to Sinistella and move on, as we said we would," Sundar decided grimly. "We keep our word, and we need her backing if we're going to figure out where to go next."

"Wait; you said that demons had come to your dens in the forest, right?" Emerald turned to Elder Berry and looked excited. He nodded, and she glanced back at us. "Now we know where we can go on our way to the front lines."

"The front lines are somewhere further away, aren't they?" Sundar frowned and looked to me for confirmation. I wasn't sure either, and shrugged.

"They're anywhere the demons are," I growled after thinking about it for a moment. "Maybe someone there knows something. Someone there could have heard of a succubus taking a human with her somehow, and we could learn something about it."

"I'm not against goin' back to my old stompin' grounds, though I do wanna say that goin' there is dangerous." Elder Berry scratched his head and pointed above his head to his level. "The monsters there are dangerous, and the elves aren't exactly kind to my kin. It was thanks to our numbers that we survived as long as we did, takin' on bigger and more powerful monsters, and then hidin' from the elves that searched for us."

"I thought the elves came from another continent?" I frowned at him, and he just shrugged.

So there's even more to figure out now… I did promise Thea that I would come find her on the front lines. "We need to get there, but leveling up so we can be of greater use is a priority, too. If there's a way to the front lines through the forest and we can keep the demons from encroaching too far toward here—we should take a shot at it."

The others nodded in compliance after a moment of thought. Suddenly, Aertra spoke up, appearing next to the larger woman with fresh blood on her lips. "If you're going to fight demons, they will be rich with different types of Aether, but they are harder to hunt. You'll need to be able to dispel their magics quickly and efficiently before they can trap you or attack you."

"Is that something you can teach us?" I stared at her as she stood behind Sundar and watched the large woman as she mouthed, *The hell are you doing? No!*

"I can, to an extent, but it is something that, until you see it for yourself, you won't know how to defend against it." She grasped Sundar's shoulder. "I know that what I did affected you, and that does not bother me—I am a monster and will do as I will. What does bother me is watching your thinly veiled attempts to separate my student from me prematurely."

"You killed children," Sundar snarled and shrugged the other woman's hand off her shoulder with a mighty effort. "You have no place here among us. You're no better than those demons that we're going to fight."

"I can assure you that I am," Aertra replied with a hefty sigh, then looked up into Sundar's eyes. "Those children, if found by the demons, would have been consumed, then made into demons themselves. Forced to be hosts to parasites that would eventually eat their fill of their souls to become lesser demons like imps. Once the imps are born, the corpse is cast aside and becomes something called a carrion."

"They the little critters that consume everythin' in their path, growin' and becomin'g somethin' soulless and empty?" Aertra nodded at Elder Berry, a chill clearly running down his spine at her confirmation. "We had some of 'em with us when we fled the forest. Them baby gnolls that the imps had come from… they ate their parents, their families, and anythin' else they could, includin' each other. The thing that was left still looked like a gnoll, but it was too consumed by its need to feed and kill that it was just…wrong."

"And as it grew—impossibly fast, I presume?—it became deadlier than its kind normally were?" Aertra asked, but she didn't even wait for his nod before she added, "They kill with little conscience or desire to preserve themselves. That makes them so much more dangerous than their souled counterparts."

"What did you do with it?" I blinked at him, and he just shook his head. "Did you kill it?"

"We were going to: me, Fangory, and the other betas, but by the time we found where it had been holed up, it was gone." He shivered again. "Like I said, it was much too smart."

"That will be a dangerous foe if left unchecked," Aertra spat as if she was warding off evil, then turned to look at Sundar. "I killed them for a goal; that would be wrong of many beings, but it could have been so much worse. To me, their deaths served a purpose and were a mercy. Hate me, if you must—if your honor demands it—but you should know that they would have suffered needlessly if left alone and they would have found death anyway."

Sundar grimaced and turned her head away, her eyes clenched shut. "Get away from me." Aertra nodded, but didn't move fast enough, so Sundar whipped around and slammed her fist into the vampire's chest.

She didn't so much as bounce from the pressure of the blow; she just stared at Sundar with pity. "To be so young again." She patted the arm that was still there, like a mother patting a child on the head. Sundar took her arm back and silently raged, her eyes almost glazing over with fury. "If it will make you feel better, I will allow you a chance at vengeance on their behalf."

"What?" I spat and blinked at them both. "You're going to allow her to try to kill you?"

Aertra glanced down at the fist that was backing away from her. "Yes."

"I don't need your pity." Sundar heaved a growling sigh as she turned, crouched into the tunnel, and moved on. "I messaged Sinistella; she knows we're coming."

With that, she turned and stalked off into the tunnel ahead of us, ignoring all attempts to get her attention, even going so far as to ignore whispers. She just moved on.

After a time, we were up and out of the tunnels, making our way through the city, with Elder Berry in the middle of our group. Any of the other players who were dumb enough to try to get to him through us received the business end of a pissed off and hungry Aertra.

It seemed she hated traveling with a group quite so noticeable toward creatures who might be able to take her, like the dragons. She talked a big game, but words only got you so far.

The streets were quiet aside, from the grumbling of those who could see us from where they stood. The dwarves who knew us looked shocked, and those who didn't at least recognized that we were of Belgonna's ilk, thanks to our appearance and the signet rings all of us wore except for Aertra and Berry.

"Wonder if they mean to execute him?" One of the closer

dwarves muttered to another, with his wide eyes fixed on the gnoll. "Good riddance, I say."

Elder Berry took it all in stride, but I could tell it sucked to be talked about that way. "We'll be there soon."

He nodded in my general direction at the same time that a host of guards in red plate mail clomped down the roadway, coming to a complete halt just in front of us as the first one to the right of the group bellowed, "By order of the queen, we are here to escort you to her presence."

Sundar frowned and glanced over her shoulder back toward us, "Any of you understand why this might be going on?"

"Nope." I crossed my arms, and Emerald's hands fell to her waist like she was reaching for a weapon. "You want to explain why?"

The speaker blinked a couple times, then answered curtly. "I am not beholden to you, my Prince;, we are here to escort you, and that is all you need know." He snapped his fingers, and the soldiers with him spread out and surrounded us. "This way."

Emerald was about to say something, then decided against it and complied, motioning for all of us to do the same. Except Aertra had vanished, and I had no idea where she could have gone.

I closed my eyes. *Vulina, where are you?*

We walked quickly but smartly, making it about a block, before she finally answered. *You forgot that I was with you when you went to fight all those creatures. So when you were leaving, I went to see about getting into the fire one last time, if I could. Your mother has been very helpful with my growth, you know. She's so nice.*

That explains a lot. I blinked and thought about it some more. *Has she asked you any questions, or have you heard anything?*

There was a fight that broke out here; someone shouting something about there being a raid boss here, and that they could all band together and kill it?

"Shit." The others looked at me. "There's been an attempt to overthrow them, someone tried to say there's a raid boss in the throne room or something." The guards around us just carried on with their duties, but we weren't going to get there in time if there were others. "Let's hurry this parade up."

One of the dwarven soldiers glanced at me and muttered, "These men were sent to ensure that no one attacks all of *you* to try and get to the throne room again. Stick with us, kids. We'll get you there."

"But the queen—" I started, and he shook his head. "What do you mean by that?"

"She killed a score of them before they could even touch her, and she has an army—you don't." He winked and turned forward so that none might be the wiser. "Don't know how you found that out, but the queen is safe; don't you worry, young Prince."

We moved as quickly as the large group of soldiers could, the population of players growing steadily. Some of them wore piecemeal armor, patched and poorly matched, but the benefits would likely be better than nothing.

The way they watched us, though…something wasn't right.

An arrow whizzed through the air, and I bellowed, "Ambush!" All hell broke loose around us as Travelers drew weapons and began to cast their various spells.

CHAPTER EIGHTEEN

The dwarves roared as one and turned on the nearest combatants, attempting to thwart the attacks on them and civilians too close to themselves. My shield had been made useless by the Gluttonous Queen kicking through it, so I just pulled the dying holy sword from my inventory and called out for Vulina through my mind.

On my way! she snarled, and I could feel her moving.

The Travelers off to my right, closest to where Sundar and Elder Berry were, fell to their knees, the radiating heat-like aura around the gnoll flaring as he focused on controlling the crowd.

I burst through the line of soldiers, and my sword sang through the air to sail through the neck of the closest Traveler.

Element Pwns died.

95 EXP received.

City Renown increased.

I grinned and, though the strain of the gravity against me was taxing, it wasn't nearly as bad as it was for all of these guys.

Gravity change resisted.

"That explains it." My sword lashed out once more, and another Traveler fell. More experience flooded through me.

I turned to avoid an arrow that dropped from above, and just barely missed being pierced by another, when a red, roiling rage slid through the air and sped straight into the archer above us with ease. Vulina had arrived.

My sword slashed at those still caught in the crossfire of the flames and gravity, and where it cut, limbs and heads thumped onto the ground while we raked in the experience.

Glancing around, the Travelers who still remained, standing over the fallen dwarven warriors that had fought for their people, sent a thrill of rage so pure and unadulterated through me that I had to let that bloodlust out of myself.

I screamed, roaring so loudly that all of my Aether bars shook, and two of my Summoning Aether dropped instantly.

Job Ability unlocked: Dark Paladin's Rally.

I didn't need to glance at the description of the ability to know what it was doing. Everyone on our side who heard my shout for almost a hundred feet glowed with a murky red aura, and their eyes glowed with a crimson that hadn't been there before. They all roared, and their attacks grew stronger and much more frenzied.

Dwarven warriors all around us wove into attacks that otherwise would have been impossible, and their health bars appeared over their heads, slowly draining away point by point.

That was alarming, but Vulina abruptly shouted in my head, *Duck!*

I dropped my stance and lowered my body as a massive plume of flames roared over my head, but these ones were green and burned differently.

I turned and found a woman smirking at me with a staff in hand, her robes billowing around her and a set of horns of her own.

Lvl 15 Demon Bread—hostile.

"Nice name," I grunted as I pushed up to stand in front of her. I took a quick tally of my Aether; I had nearly full flame, and my ice was slowly returning. The two summoning that I had used were still gone, but that was okay, because I had plenty more.

"Bit of fun, and it paid off." She grinned a little wider. "You know you have a bounty on your head?"

That caught me off guard. "Yeah?"

"Yup!" She spun her staff in her hands and slammed the end on the ground, and a wolf made of ghostly green fire appeared next to her. "Seems the princes don't like how much attention daddy is giving you, and all the characters in the world can cash in on it, no matter their alignment."

I blinked. *Shit.* The wolf lowered its head and put a foot forward.

Sundar put a hand on my shoulder, and a thrill of energy ran through me.

Priest's Blessing received.

+1 to physical stats for one minute.

The wolf launched itself forward, claws outstretched to slice me as the maw opened wide to bite. I snarled and lashed out with my sword, the flames washing over me.

14 dmg taken by Arcane flame construct

I hissed as the flames licked over my head and shoulders, then looked up at the woman standing before me with a cocky grin. "Seems that resistance doesn't hold up all the time."

"You know about that, huh?" I tried to smile at her, working on planning the right angle to get to her.

Demon Bread just laughed and nodded before she spun her staff and let it fly out of her hands and up into the air.

I almost scoffed at how easy she'd made this. I lifted my hand and summoned the weapon to me, two more summoning Aether draining away.

The weapon appeared in my hand, and her eyes widened as I grinned. "Can't trust everything, but I am happy that they know I'm a threat."

I tossed the weapon behind me and grinned wider, knowing that it was closer to Sundar or one of the others who would use it a little better, then launched myself forward with my blade held straight out toward her. *Vulina, grab her!*

On it. The flame elemental creature rocketed toward the now-backpedaling caster, grasping her around her neck with her hands. "Hold still, you flaming bitch!"

Green sparks spat from her skin in a protective cloak that merely washed over Vulina in a wave of color that she cared little about. The elemental creature's nose crinkled in disgust. "This stuff is gross."

My sword slashed through the flames and cut the caster's stomach, dropping her life heftily, judging from her reaction and bitter groan. From the look in her eyes, she knew she was about to die—she just didn't know how bad a death it might be.

I grabbed her by the throat and pulled her close before I grimaced and muttered, "Sorry, but this is a bit of a necessary evil for me."

She frowned and started to buck, the sword wound opening and bleeding a little. "What're you doing? All I wanted was the money and extra levels. It's just a game."

I sighed, "Not for long." I glanced into her face and added apologetically, "And I'm so hungry."

My fangs lengthened as my mouth opened, and she screamed so loudly, I thought my ear would start bleeding, but I thrust my head forward and latched onto her neck as I shoved my gauntleted fist into the wound across her stomach and rooted around for her heart. I drank greedily until she died.

It occured to me that some of them would realize what I was, to some extent, but the fact that I was taking Aether wasn't common knowledge, and I wanted them to fear me.

The battle had quieted somewhat as I lifted my blood-soaked face and took count of the spoils I'd drank.

Aether Stolen - Demonic Affinity at 100%
Aether Stolen – Arcane Affinity at 12%
92 EXP received.
City Renown increased.

The travelers who survived stared at me in shocked horror,

though they couldn't afford not to pay attention to their attackers.

I felt a hand on my shoulder, and life flowed into me, the damage I had taken nullified and reverting slowly as Elder Berry sidled closer. "My spell is wanin'; better get the rest of 'em taken care of, or hit the ol' dusty. Understand?"

"Not really?" I frowned, and he chuckled and pointed toward the way we had been heading. More dwarves in armor flung themselves down the streets, and a few good Travelers with green names above their heads were with them. I sighed gratefully. "Cavalry's here."

"You get *that*, but not the ol' dusty trail?" The man threw his hands up in defeat, and the gravity on the remaining people lifted. "Shoot!"

"I got 'em; just start healing the dwarves and others who need it." He nodded at my orders, and I launched myself forward with my sword out, ready to pierce someone's chest.

Massive wings spanned the sky and swamped us in darkness, a booming draconic roar sending a chill down my spine as my adoptive mother dropped into the street we occupied.

She shifted mid-fall, so as not to destroy her surroundings, but as she landed, the flames that roiled around all of us from the spells burned hotter with her presence. She didn't even so much as whisper as, all around us, elemental flames burst into existence.

The majority of them were merely humanoid-looking flames, like the one she had shown me before, but some of them had draconic features that reminded me of Vulina and what she was becoming.

Her beautiful almost-elven features twisted in a rage so primal that even I felt like running to hide, but she just bellowed. "Every red-named being in this place is to die—no mercy!"

The elementals hissed and popped in their own language and hurried to comply. Their proximity was enough to char some of the Travelers where they stood. Those with water or ice affinities stood a slight chance against a single elemental, but none against the sheer numbers and power that Belgonna had at her command.

No matter how many ice lances or arrows whipped toward them, they melted and burned uselessly as the tidal wave of flame crashed over the whole of the place in seconds.

The flames died down just as quickly as they had come, and the elemental creatures surrounded Aertra uncertainly, as she had finally reappeared again, her arms covered in blood.

Belgonna stepped closer to the Aether Vampire, then looked to me, the gnoll standing with us bashfully staring up at her as if he had never been in the presence of someone so strong before. The weight of her gaze was heavy, but I just shrugged and offered a soft, "We can explain?"

"I know you will." She motioned that we follow her as she turned and moved on.

The trip back to the queen's den, where Sinistella waited for us, was uneventful, though smoldering marks on the ground littered the stone cobbles everywhere we walked, not just where we had been ambushed.

"They were all over the city," Belgonna hissed angrily, her steps measured and regal, but the heat that rolled off her in waves from her displeasure were enough to force everyone but Sundar and me to stand back away from her.

Elder Berry had his own set of guards, all of whom seemed displeased with their assignment. However, they were careful not to act not too terribly over-burdened, what with the former queen so close by and ready to mete out justice to any who displeased her.

People collected themselves, injured and confused—some of them even going so far as to call out to Belgonna in their time of need.

She would stop here and there to tend to those she could, or to allay their fears as much as possible, while more than fifty dwarves combed the streets with her elemental summons, searching for any who could have survived her wrath.

At one point, Elder Berry shoved his way through his guards and attempted to lift a wall that had collapsed onto the street. He strained, and when the dwarves tried to herd him back toward the safety of their numbers, he turned on them. "Any of you idjits touches me, and I'll slam you so hard, your outlines will make puddles—now help me lift this damn thing!"

Sundar and I went to help him before any of the dwarves decided that it would be to their benefit to assist, but eventually, a couple of them did. We counted and heaved in unison, lifting the broken stone and wooden wall away from a mother and her child; they were cut and bruised, but they were whole.

The mother sobbed quietly, and finally, all she could manage was, "Benan…Benan was in there."

I blinked and shoved Elder Berry out of the way as the former queen rushed forward to lift the wall and toss it aside with minimal effort, her muscles barely straining as she cried, "Benan!" A crowd began to form, but they didn't dare try to get any closer as Belgonna slowly lost her humanoid form in favor of the massive bulk that allowed her to lift more of the rubble away.

"Benan!" She roared again, and finally scooped away a doorframe to find the boy unmoving.

The low, mournful scream that rose from her mouth was enough to crush the spirits of everyone in hearing distance, but Elder Berry just surged forward to get to the small form before she could scoop him up into her grasp.

"Don't touch my child!" Belgonna screeched, reaching for his still body. The gravity around the two of them shifted, and she moved slower, if only for a heartbeat.

Elder Berry touched his neck for a second, then lifted his hands into the air with his palms facing upward. A nimbus of white and silver swirled in his grasp as he suddenly slammed his hands into the child's chest, making our adoptive mother scream again and rear up to gather her breath in a low rumble, her eyes wide.

The child coughed, stirring and then coughing more before

the gnoll helped him sit up, muttering softly to the boy, "Take 'er easy there, little guy." He patted the kid's shoulder gently and grinned at him. "Gave me a heck of a scare; your mama, too."

The child looked up at Belgonna with wide eyes. Her rage slowly melted away as he stared at her, tears falling from the sides of her eyes and slipping onto the ground from her scaled maw to sizzle as they hit the stones and evaporated. "Benan?"

"Ma?" The little dwarven boy peered up at her as if in disbelief, and she stooped low to nuzzle him with the side of her great maw, then shifted her form and stooped to lift him to her chest where she clutched him. "You're warm, Ma."

She sniffed and said, "I know I am, my love. I know." She kissed his head and turned to the dwarves who had been guarding the gnoll. "Take up arms and keep this one safe." They started to come for the boy, but she just growled, "The gnoll!"

Elder Berry raised a furred eyebrow ridge at them, but otherwise just shrugged it off, consigned to whatever she wanted to do. He had seen her power. I didn't blame him for it.

I tried to speak to Belgonna, but she took off toward the den, and that was the end of all chances to talk.

As we moved, she listened for any names being called and pointed to men and women who were able bodied to help in any kind of search. Luckily, the worst of the fighting had taken place nearest us. That one spot had just been the unfortunate site of one of the more powerful fire Aether users throwing his weight around when he'd come upon a group of soldiers.

The child clung to his mother's shoulder and watched the furred man who'd saved him with open interest as we walked. Benan finally asked, "Mister, can you move your tail?"

Elder Berry just chuckled and nodded, "Yup! Sure can. See?" He turned and wagged his tail for the boy, his delighted giggle making all of us smile slightly.

I snorted, glad I didn't have a tail to protect every time I sat down, nor something to brush against my leg to annoy the hell out of me.

We soon crossed the threshold of the hall to the throne room. Elder Berry stared around, vibrantly ecstatic about all the paintings and history behind this place. Soon, we stood in the presence of the queen, who looked less enthused about our presence, especially with one of the gnolls we were supposed to have been hunting.

"It's nearly time for the hunt to begin; what is he doing here?" Queen Sinistella stared pointedly at Elder Berry.

"We've adopted him into the party for his skill, and because he's adorable." Emerald crossed her arms and leaned back onto her left leg to watch the queen's reaction to her obvious disdain. "We need him if we're going to have a chance out there on our way to the front lines. Also, the demons appear to be moving on the forest north of here, because that's where the gnolls came from."

"I don't care where they came from; I have more problems at present." Sinistella closed her eyes and kneaded the muscles on the side of her head.

"Sorry, ma'am." Elder Berry stepped forward and held his hands clasped in front of him. "I know that things are rough right now, but I'm a Traveler, as well. I'm sorry that our kind caused you any strife. My people tried to claim the dungeon here to keep the rest of our kind safe and to make the whole of 'em stronger to face what chased us off. We'd have done it, too, if it weren't for these meddlin' kids and their dog."

The Queen stared at him, Belgonna tilting her head with her daughter, as Emerald snorted and Sundar threw her hands up in exasperation.

"Sorry, I was just excited." Elder Berry \chuckled and cleared his throat. "If I could make a request, I know how we could help each other."

Sinistella scoffed, "Help each other?" She blinked at the earnest man who simply stared at her. "Your kind tried to take over a dungeon in our lands, then occupied a city in the underground beneath our hold. How can we help invaders such as yourselves?"

"My kin need somewhere to stay, and they like to dig a lot." He shrugged and looked around the room. "Dwarves made this place, I'd reckon, but gnolls could out-mine almost any of the miners you've had. We can smell the ore and metals in those mines, sure as your people can feel 'em in the air. We can help you mine, and stay out of your way."

"How so?" Now the queen was curious. "How do I know that, if I were to allow you to stay, you wouldn't keep what you find for yourself? Or allow other monsters in?"

"The entire time I lived with 'em, the gnolls hunted other monsters for their raw materials. They like to craft and create just as much as the dwarves." He pointed down at his clothing, which was well made, though dirty. "They strive to make and do with their hands, too. Hell, they loved livin' in dwarven places that had been abandoned, and they even worship one of the dwarven gods of creation. Though they prefer to think he was a gnoll, since his beard was so wild."

Sinistella just stared at him as he spoke. Finally, he got to her question, "They might keep some of the materials to worship their god, but anythin' that comes through them tunnels, what ain't themselves or the dwarves they'd allow, will die simply for breathin' in their territory. They all speak common languages, though it's a little hard for 'em to speak it, but they can. They'll work hard for you; all they need is a place to be."

"And what of the goblins?" Sinistella crossed her arms and raised her eyebrows questioningly at her gnoll guest.

"If they hadn't outnumbered us six to one, we would have killed 'em all, but we came to an agreement—just like we would with you." He motioned back to us. "I know that you planned to kill us, and I know they would have, if it weren't for me. Y'all got people to protect, and I respect that. But please, ma'am, don't kill 'em. They'll work hard for you."

Sinstella considered the proposal for a moment longer, looking to her mother, which surprised me. Belgonna glanced at all of our tense faces and only stated, "He brought Benan back to life. For that alone, I would at least hear him out—but I owe him so much more. If I need to, I will carve his family out a home with my own claws."

The way she lifted her chin and the set of her jaw meant that she was hardly kidding around.

"Who leads your people now?" Sinistella sighed and pulled a sheet of paper from the side of her desk, staring at the gnoll. "Who would I benefit from negotiating with the most?"

"There are three betas who would be more than happy to speak to you, and I can offer to be a liaison of sorts." Elder Berry looked supremely excited, but grunted, "Ah, the alarm is goin' off for me to get ready for bed. I'll message 'em for you, and I can have 'em meet back here in the mornin', I think?"

Sinistella blinked at him. "It's nearly morning now."

Emerald cleared her throat and advised, "He means morning for us."

"How long do you plan to be gone then, for our time?" Belgonna asked softly.

"Time travels three times faster here than it does in our world," Emerald explained, then looked to Elder Berry. "We've been doing four hour naps between gaming sessions. Can you do that too?"

The gnoll frowned and scratched his head., "I'm an old man, ain't no pup like y'all, so I need some sleep. Four hours, though?" She nodded, and he just blinked, "Ain't got nothin' better to do, I s'pose. Might be a bit of a grump, though. I have time for some coffee?"

Emerald smiled. "Let me give you my email address before we log out, and I'll ensure you have something strong enough to keep you more chipper than any of us."

He grinned, and they both stepped aside, though I moved closer to the Queen and our mother. "There's something that will keep us from this world the day after tomorrow in our world. I don't know what it is, but we will be back as soon as we can, okay?"

Sinistella nodded and sighed, "We don't know when the Merger will be upon us, but I expect that will be a time of great turmoil. Please, little brother, be safe?"

"I'm immortal. I think I'll be okay." I grinned at her and tried to appear confident. "We'll be back in time for the meeting, okay?"

"And what of your Aether Vampire friend?" Belgonna eyed me. "Will she be a threat to our people while you are away?"

I shrugged, because I really didn't know what she would do while I was gone. "If she's a threat, kill her. She's a wily one, though, so be careful."

Belgonna's eyes narrowed, but she said nothing, Sinistella just smiled. "I'll have something ready for her, should she decide to be a nuisance."

I raised a brow at he "Care to share?"

She rolled her eyes, "Not with you. I need all the advantage for it to work, and I can't risk her finding out."

I nodded my head once and decided that would have to be good enough for now. "What does our renown with the city raising have to do with anything, by the way?"

"It's something that royalty has, to know how their people think of them." She frowned at me, "Does this mean that you have earned some?"

I nodded and looked into my stats to try and find it. There was a new one called Royal status.

Iradellum – 000/000
Belgonna's Hold – 247/100*
?????
?????
?????
?????

The list of unknown and yet-to-be-visited places annoyed the hell out of me, but the star next to the one for Belgonna's Hold was enough to draw my attention. I touched it and read the notification.

Belgonna's Hold – You are a prince, and have

shown that you care about the people who reside here. As such, they revere you for more than just your title. Speak to the Queen to receive your reward.

I grinned and said, "I've been asked to speak to you about a reward?"

Sinistella stilled and stared at me for a moment, a wry look on her face as she appeared to be reading something, then turned to her mother and grumped, "So this is what it felt like for you to let me and Balfour rummage through your hoard as children?"

Belgonna laughed and nodded, then looked at me. "Forgive her; this is the dragon in her coming to the fore."

"I just *got* this hoard!" I didn't blink as I stared at her. Sinistella harrumphed and crossed her arms, sullenly saying, "Fine. I guess."

CHAPTER NINETEEN

She led me into a large room and pointed in with her thumb. "This is our treasury—my hoard—you and Sundar, as well as Emerald, will be permitted to take one item each." She put her hand on my chest and stated again for emphasis, "One."

"What if it's coin?" She pointed to satchels lining the walls on hooks. "Just fill one of those, then?"

She nodded tersely, and I smiled, glad to be freed to roam the room of riches, to ravage and revel in the revoltingly far-reaching piles that would need to be rummaged through cautiously.

Mountains of gold and silver that attempted to touch the ceiling loomed overhead in a manner that made my vertigo act up. I left the coin alone for now to peruse the piles of weapons and goods. We hadn't had a chance to really look to see if any of the Travelers had left loot, but that staff that Demon Bread had so graciously allowed me to swipe would make a fine addition to either Sundar or Elder Berry's arsenal.

Probably the latter, since he wasn't royalty and couldn't get in here for gaining renown.

The swords were lovely. The weapons, all of them amazing

and splendidly kept, seemed like someone had taken special care to organize these over all the others.

They were okay, but I had a soon-to-be not-so-holy sword in my possession and didn't plan on giving that up any time soon.

There was glorious armor, but much the same as the set that I had recently been given. . I was below the level required to wear it, some of them requiring level thirty to sixty to even get a piece of it on. Jesus. So that was a no. Looked to me like I would need to go and get some armor elsewhere until I was strong enough to wear mine.

That left either finding a replacement for the shield that I'd lost, or another glaive. That, or a trinket for me to use for anything else.

Which reminded me. I needed to go and see Mephisto about my demonic affinity.

"I hope he doesn't get cheap on me like he did last time." I grumbled to myself and closed my eyes, then thought better of it, and instead called out, "Sinistella?"

She appeared next to me so quickly that I lost my balance and fell into a pile of gold and silver as she asked, "Yes, little brother?"

"I need to go and see a certain…demon about power and potentially finding out about Mona." I motioned broadly to the room around us and asked, "Can I come back to this?"

"Yes. But do be careful about deals and demons." She smiled and helped me rise from the golden encasement that began to form around me. "They're hardly ever good for you, even where power is concerned."

She started to turn away but stopped, "Your little friend Flicker has been here a time and is with Mother. I would make sure that she hasn't frayed Mother's patience, asking her to breathe fire all over."

I nodded and sighed inwardly. *Vulina, are you bothering Belgonna?*

Heavens, no. She's telling me all these stories about you from when you were a baby. I frowned at that, and she just laughed. *Turns out she saw a lot of your memories, more than you even were aware of.*

Oh, god. I opened the notification and selected yes to get away from her incessant laughing. Good to know being embarrassed was still something I could feel.

The same sensation of fading out then back in made me feel nauseous, and I stood in front of the same set of bleachers that had been summoned to the room last time.

This time though, I was behind the bleachers, and Mephisto wasn't there. I was alone, and it was only me, the bat, and the game.

Rather than calling out, I decided to check around a little— see if there was anything behind the curtain that the demon didn't want me to see.

I walked for a time. I couldn't be sure how long it was, but it was long enough and far enough away from the scenery he had created for my benefit that I was sure this had to be the same area where I had made my avatar for the game originally.

Soon, whispers echoed through the space. I couldn't identify them, and there was no real way to really see anything out of the norm, other than to just keep moving forward and hope that I could find something. Anything.

After what could have been hours, I heard something. A fraction of a sentence that made my blood run cold.

"…ead of schedule, my Lord." The voice was familiar, too. Reminded me of someone. Who could it have been?

"Excellently done, Practus." Mephisto's voice was soft, almost smug as he spoke, and I came upon a room that looked vaguely similar to a shady car-dealership office, the poorly painted walls and tragic décor down to the last detail of what one might think. It was just gross, and he sat with his long legs up on the desk, where they partially hung over the side, and his arms twice folded behind his head. "As always, your managerial skills are above your office. Who knows? Someday, you may even become a prince."

Wilhelm! That greasy little... "I live to serve, master." He bowed at the waist and looked up. "I see that the newest recruit of Abbadon's is making quite the splash near the Sentry Gates; she's very impressive to watch."

That piqued my curiosity.

"She is good, isn't she?" Mephisto smiled and waved a hand so that a screen blinked into existence on the side of the room closest to me. I ducked back far enough to stick out less, but I could see everything as if it were mirrored.

Mona tore through a battlefield like a bat out of hell with a weapon that soared around her and sliced anything and everything it touched. She danced and swayed and as she moved, her other weapons flowing effortlessly around her. She touched nothing for a while, then more of the soldiers that marched on her began to fall.

Something massive with wings dove in next to her, and his own scythe slid into someone and raised them up.

"Bardiff is her trainer?" Wilhelm chuckled. "No wonder she's such a monster."

"I know." Mephisto cackled to himself before his eyebrow raised. "Had a pleasant traipse through my realm, Kyvir?"

The creature I had figured out was Wilhelm turned and lunged at me, his slight figure swift and efficient. He caught me around the throat with fingers that reminded me of a creepy pasta nightmare creature and lifted me off the ground. "Sneak! How dare you come here uninvited?"

"Release him, Practus," Mephisto sighed, his trademark smile beginning to split his face once more. "I knew he was here and did nothing." He stared at me for a moment, then made a motion as if for me to turn around.

I stared at the screen and watched as Mona savaged the remaining soldiers near her, and silvery-dark blobs began to flee from the bodies and gather near her. Mephisto put his creepy hands on my shoulders and stooped impossibly low so that he could stare at me as he asked, "How does it feel to know that she does this right now?"

"She's doing what she thinks is right," I asserted, not really sure what to think. "She's making the best of her situation. We'll get her back."

Mephisto snorted once, and Practus just laughed outright, muttering, "Naïve."

Mephisto glared at him through my head, and the other demon quieted; then the head honcho spoke again, sickeningly sweet, "I'm sure you'll try."

"You have no idea where to go, with powers you can't control, and you have no one to coddle you anymore." He laughed at me as I stared at him in confusion. "Did you not know that the attack on your city was orchestrated by your fellow Travelers? That they succeeded in taking your queen and Belgonna?"

Now it was my turn to laugh. "Are you smoking something?"

He blinked, clearly unused to someone laughing at his expense, so I just said, "Where did you hear that?" I turned and pointed at the demon Practus, who was Wilhelm. "Him? Because if so, he's wrong. Both are alive and well."

Mephisto turned on his subordinate, "Is this so?" He didn't wait and instead bellowed, "Show me!"

Practus jumped and slammed his hands on the desk, where a live feed of the dwarven city burst into life. Sure enough, the citadel stood, and Belgonna roamed the streets with one of her many dwarven daughters at her side while they oversaw repairs to those places that had been attacked. A small boy sat on Belgonna's shoulder, pointing a few people out and laughing boisterously.

"What is the meaning of this?" Mephisto's voice took on a higher, more annoyed pitch. "You assured me that you had this under control."

"I did; everything was supposed to be according to my plan." He shook his head and tapped a few invisible buttons. "The call to the demons and their pets was put out, and they sent their numbers to infiltrate, and then they attacked. It should have been enough."

"What about the bounty on my head?"

Mephisto's head slowly twisted until he stared at me with full-blown rage on his face, "The *what?*"

"Bounty?" I scratched my head for effect and pointed to Practus. "Did you not tell him about that?"

Maybe this could be used to my advantage? "Seems that some of the princes don't like me and have put out a bounty on me." I crossed my arms. "And here I thought you liked me, Mephistopheles."

"Demonic affinity, right?" The great demon stood to his his full height as I nodded. "Your reward."

He held out his hand and was about to touch me when I decided to kick him while he was down. "Aww, no games?"

He seethed, "I have a headache." He touched my shoulder, and I was back in the treasury hall with Sinistella.

She jumped and her fist nearly collided with my nose before she realized it was me. "Do *not* scare me like that again!"

I shook my head, "Not my choice!" I touched her shoulder. "You gotta get all the help you can,. The demons are actively trying to kill you and Belgonna so they can take the city."

You have been logged in for an excessive amount of time. You will be logged out forcibly in five minutes.

"That's never fucking happened before." I blinked and tried to make the notification go away. It did, but there was a timer in the middle of my vision that moved everywhere I looked, so I just chose to ignore it for now. "You have to warn everyone."

The timer dropped to three minutes in a heartbeat.

"Mephisto, you motherfucker!" I roared into the sky, and the timer dropped again. I growled and glared at Sinistella, "Can I come back here once I come back?"

She shook her head, "I have to be here with you to keep the innate spells and wards from killing you, and if there is an attack on the horizon, it could be a little while before we come back in here."

I shouted, "Shit!"

I turned and looked around, there was nothing that I could

immediately see that would greatly benefit me. There were baubles and items all over. I turned again and spied some accessories, choosing to run for them. Seconds counted down cruelly, and it was all I could do to dive for them before I logged out. I grabbed blindly, and then the system logged me out by force.

Please come back in a little while after some rest and relaxation. You can return in 07:59:47...

The statement was enough to make me angry, but it was Wilhelm's voice that caught me off guard. "Congratulations, Mister Ethelbart—you have brought up the time of the update. I hope you enjoy it."

I opened my eyes to the dark room of my real world home and screamed in rage and frustration.

How was I supposed to do anything stuck out here? And what the hell did they mean about the update? How could they just move that up?

I lowered my head, irritated, and shuffled out of the portal, the ambient glow of Aether permeating the air where it had grown around the fixture in the time that I had been inside, and there was no hiding it now. The portals would play an instrumental role in the merger. And there was nothing I could do about it out here. Shutting off the systems or telling anyone to unplug them would just give the demons the advantage.

I picked up my shorts and put them on out of habit, then shuffled down the hall and into the kitchen. I turned on the news and quickly shut it off again. There was nothing I wanted to see there; just more demon attacks, and nothing good.

I tried to eat. Nothing. There was nothing even remotely appetizing in the house, and I just needed to get outside. It was dark out; for some reason, darker than I thought it had ever been. The stars didn't even seem to be twinkling in the night sky. The air, cool and somewhat soothing, felt good on my bare skin.

Once I'd had my fill of the fresh air, I made my way back into my darkened home and stared around bleakly. My clocks read that it was after midnight, so that had to have been why. I rubbed my eyes. There was nothing I could do. I was exhausted and alone. I texted the others, but there wasn't much to be said, other than that they had been forced to log out as well.

I trudged into the bathroom to relieve myself and took a shower, long and hot like usual, but this time, I just stayed in there for a while longer with my eyes closed so I could process.

Even that was too much. *Maybe after some sleep, you'll feel better?* I questioned myself, but went to bed regardless. I set alarms and laid in the bed awake for a little bit, unsure for how long. I knew if I checked my phone, I would just set myself up to stay awake longer.

Finally, with thoughts of nothingness and trying to do my best to make things count, I passed out.

———

Beeping and alarms rang throughout the room that the developers and programmers usually worked in, as they frantically tried to figure out what was going on with the game world they had just been inside of.

I did my best to stifle the yawn building, due to the boringness of it all. Hart bellowed at his crew to get everything possible done, screaming, "Purple banks! Make sure that's done!"

"It was done hours ago; he's locking us out of the system. We failed!" one of the others shouted back, throwing their headset across the room to land at my feet.

I drummed my fingers along the wall as I exited the building and faded from view. "Let the merger begin."

CHAPTER TWENTY

I woke up some time later, with no sound reaching my ears, other than the sound of birds in the sky. Which was odd, because I never heard them anymore. My room was sound-proofed against things like this.

I blinked up at the roof, a cool draft coming in through the window I nearly always kept shut.

I froze, thinking I could be the victim of a robbery or even about to be kidnapped. When no sound came to me immediately, I chanced a glance outside and saw nothing other than my fenced-in backyard, so I just shrugged it off and glanced at my phone, wondering why it hadn't gone off hours ago.

As soon as it touched my skin, it crumbled into dust that blew away in the cool breeze that flitted through my window.

"Oh my god, no." My eyes widened and I launched myself out of my window. *No, no, this can't be it!*

People were screaming somewhere as I crossed my yard and clambered up onto my fence to look toward the city. People milled about, moving away from cars and buildings that they had been in as they crumbled and fell away as dust in the breeze. I shook my head in disbelief. "There's no fucking way."

I clambered back into my room, threw on a pair of jeans, a T-shirt, and a loose gray hoodie. It was the only one I owned that wasn't an extravagant color, and if people were freaking out like this, I didn't want to stand out as much as I normally would.

I was back out the window and moving toward the source of the screaming in an instant, angry that I hadn't had the time to collect those weapons that I had ordered. Honestly, I wondered where they could be, but that wouldn't matter soon.

I gritted my teeth and sprinted forward harder, jumping and launching myself over my fence with an ease that I had never had before. I'd never really tried to do it before, either. I landed on the other side in the community park that bordered my house, and I ran toward the woods.

People sobbed and screamed, calling their children close to their houses as the wildlife grew around us. The grass steadily grew taller and more vibrant, even though I was pretty sure that the grass here was just a high-grade sod, and the blades wrapped around the play equipment of the park like they would consume the metal and wood where it stood. The woods sounded more alive than they ever had.

Birds sang and flew all around, and deer that were usually cautious enough to only venture out at night ran alongside me for a time, then split away as I ran even further.

My breathing slowly grew more and more labored, but by the time I was almost too tired to take another step, I had made it to the other side of the strip of trees and watched in horror as the merger began to take place in earnest.

The sky darkened with clouds of a metallic gray cast, and the wind picked up tempo, marked by the swaying of the trees behind me. I stared up in the sky over the street and watched helplessly as the buildings began to fall to vines and the power of nature, as if they had never been less needed. And I could have sworn I saw that bastard Mephisto standing in the open sky with his arms held wide open as if to welcome us all into this fresh new hell.

The apocalypse of Earth had finally come, and instead of zombies, we got an asshole demon and his cronies.

A baying growl unleashed from somewhere off to my right, and I blinked. "And his little dogs too."

Sighing, I tried to figure out where it was coming from, when a piercing screech and the wailing of a child meshed with the rabid barking that rose up with it. My adrenaline spiked, and my body moved without a second thought.

Down the crest of the hill and over the slowly growing grass, commands and shouting broke out around me as people began to appear out of their homes to investigate the new world and the commotion.

I found them behind a building that slowly crumbled and gave way to trees that grew way too fast, a small family of three. A woman protected her two kids, a boy and girl who both looked to be under ten huddling behind her, as a dog shook itself out in front of them.

Blinking, I glared at it, trying to decide what was it and what its aura was. The dog had the body of a Labrador, which appeared to be slowly mutating and changing as the Aether permeated it. It shook its head again, its teeth growing sharper and more feral. The shoulders began to grow as well, but that must have been too much stress on its body as it yelped and growled before darting forward.

"Hey!" I roared, and the dog didn't seem to care at all. "Come and get me!" I picked up a stick and threw it at the dog without reserve.

The projectile slapped against its back legs, barely doing more than slightly drawing it away from the attack that seemed more and more likely. "Come on, you stupid mutt!"

It turned suddenly and barreled toward me, slavering jaws opening wider and wider as it lunged, and here I was, with nothing to protect myself with.

I set my legs wider and decided that taking the bite on the forearm would have to be better than it going low, so I offered up my left arm as bait and waited.

As soon as it was close enough to jump at me, I moved to the side slightly, like Emerald had taught me and Mona as kids, and tried to grab the neck. The dog managed to catch my arm closer to the wrist as I wrapped my right arm around its throat and let the momentum carry us both into a sprawl. The dog wasn't able to let go because I forced my forearm further into its mouth when it tried to adjust and move on me.

"Ah!" I gave a guttural growl of frustration and anger while I twisted and threw the dog under my body so I could squeeze it and use my body weight to lock the grapple in.

Flecks of spit and sweat dripped from me as the pain roiled through my body, and I had no choice but to just deal with it until the dog was no longer a threat. It whined, and I almost wanted to let go of it, but the transformation looked to be nearing completion, and the mutt was getting stronger and more aggressive by the heartbeat.

Claws swiped at the air and dipped closer and closer to my arms and elbow, since the legs were blessedly aimed away from me. Steps drew my attention, and a man I didn't recognize sprinted forward and drove the stick I had thrown into the dog's stomach like a spear. It yelped and thrashed, and my grip tightened to the point that lactic acid began to build and threaten to cramp my arm.

"Stab it again!" I spat, grunting as the teeth ravaged my flesh once more as it squirmed and bucked against me. He shook his head and leveraged the stick into the dog's mouth, shoving it in as ruthlessly as he could until it snapped, and the dog yelped one final time before it stilled completely.

I waited another couple seconds just to see if it was just stunned, but it didn't move whatsoever. I grunted and let go of the hold, letting the dog's head loll off my arm, then rolled the opposite direction before slowly climbing to my feet.

I looked up at the man, slightly balding and overweight. He huffed wild-eyed and alarmed at something he saw over my shoulder. I turned, ready to defend myself from something else, but this time, all I saw was Mephisto. He was tall and stood in all his creepy glory, but he wasn't just here in the flesh.

He was everywhere.

He spoke, a smile on his face, "People of Earth, darling, dull, and delightfully unaware of the happenings around you, I would like to introduce myself as your new benevolent benefactor." He bowed; the one standing in front of us mirrored the copy in front of the family I had fought for. "I am Mephistopheles, or Mephisto, if you would like to call me, and I am the demon in charge here now. Some of you might have heard of the game that bears my name? Well, that was no mere game. And this is not truly the end."

He looked me in the eyes, and I could swear that I felt his evil presence as he continued, "See, my game is just beginning. I want you to struggle. To fight. To grow strong, so that you can survive my army's arrival. I'll even give you all a week to wrap your tiny little minds around it."

The man next to me sputtered, "What are you talking about?" He grew a little bolder, stepping forward so that he could have reached out and touched the demon copy. "What is all this?"

"This is the beginning of your demise." Mephisto smiled, reaching out to touch the man's face sweetly, but leaving bloody cuts behind. "No one here can stop me, and your lives as you know them are over. Now, you must adapt and learn how to fight back, or perish, and your souls can nourish me until I find another world to take."

"One week for humanity to learn how to use the system?" I crossed my arms and glared at him. "How is that fair? And how do we know that you aren't lying?"

"Have I lied to you yet, Kyvir?" He turned to me, and I knew that this was less a copy of the real thing and more something different as he cocked his head to the side. "There are millions of you who played my game, and did you think the souls who were locked within it were just going to disappear?"

He waved his arms and motioned to the world around us.

"Everything is going to change, and in a day, you'll hardly recognize yourselves or the world you once knew. Humanity won't be alone for long, and you'll be back to the war you never knew of before. The trip to the front lines was never about you getting there."

He crossed his arms, then pointed to me with one wickedly long finger, "It was always coming to you." He pointed again at the older man. "And you. To all of you. So it will be up to people like you to either teach them how to use the gifts of the new world, or let them fall and your chances dwindle."

He grabbed me and yanked me close to him, spinning me so that I was looking at all of the people in the vicinity as every other copy turned toward me with a vicious grin. He leaned down and whispered softly into my ear, "Or you could kill them all and grow stronger yourself. You could slake the hunger in that belly of yours and then do what you want. I'm not picky."

He laughed as I fought free, standing up to his full height as he called out, "Changes are coming, people of the dying Earth. Welcome to the new Earth. Let's call it…Eden, for irony's sake."

He turned and began to fade away, but held up a finger and turned back toward us all. "Oh, and a little heads up? Just because I'm holding back my demons doesn't mean that there aren't monsters out there in the wings just *waiting* to have some fun. I might be a benevolent guy, but I'm still a demon."

He faded from view, and it was all I could do not to chase after him and try to kill him then. But all I had was what I could go on, and that wasn't much. Even now, I was a ways away from Emerald's place, and who knew where she was or what was going on.

I closed my eyes and tried to imagine the status screen, but all I got was a notification that was basically someone spitting in my eye.

Ah, ah! You're not ready yet. There's still an update going on, you know.

I growled softly to myself and shook my head. Okay, so the

update was still processing, but there would at least be access to the system when it was over? Good. That was a start, at least.

"So what do we do?" the man closest to me asked, his sweat-covered forehead glistening as he watched me and huffed. He looked like the poster child for an entitled dad who just didn't give a shit about anything but drinking beer and getting paid to do nothing all the time.

I was honestly surprised that he had tried to do anything like help me with that dog.

"What're you asking me for?" I wanted to walk away, but the mother had chosen now to walk closer to us and seemed to be trying to catch my gaze.

"You obviously knew that guy, and you played that game before, so you have to know what's going on!" the man insisted. "I helped you with that dog, so you owe us an explanation."

"Listen, I appreciate that, but I don't owe you a thing. You heard what he said; the world has ended, and it's up to us to save it." The woman had joined us, and honestly, I just wanted to run off at that point, but instead, I continued to speak, including her too. "When you can gain access to the system, you'll be able to try and figure it out for yourself, but my friends and family are in danger, and I need to go."

"Take us with you, please?" the woman with the kids asked softly. "What are we supposed to do if one of those things attacks again?"

I shook my head; it would take me too long to get to Emma as it was, without a car, and now this random woman wanted me to take her and her kids with me, too? "Listen, it's cool that you want to come with me and all, but I can't protect you and worry about them. Go into the woods, and get them up a tree where they'll be safe."

"What about after that, huh?" The older man growled and took a menacing step toward me, and I was already starting to get more and more annoyed at him. "We have no food or water, and he said that you would be able to help us."

I rolled my eyes and looked at the woman once more,

ignoring the man. "I'll come back to check on you once I have my ma, okay? You'll be safe if you get up the trees and stay together." I nodded to the tree line. "Find anything slick you can pour on the wood *after* you climb up, and secure yourselves how you can. We'll be back as soon as we can."

I turned away, and a large hand grasped my elbow, "Now see here, you little punk asshole, I've never had someone be so rude and disrespec—"

I wheeled on him and threw my fist into his throat, crushing his windpipe more out of rage that he had thought he could stop me, than anything else.

The woman cried out as he gasped and held his throat, face turning purple as he struggled to get a breath in. She pulled her kids back and put herself between me and them.

I glared at him, then att the slowly growing number of people around us, and raised my voice. "My name is Kyvir, and I played the game he spoke about. I get that this is all new, and I know that you're scared." I jutted my chin toward the older man that had fallen onto his back, still trying to get a breath in and failing. I guessed I'd hit him harder than I'd meant to. "Don't let yourself be fooled into thinking that the power and status you once held is anything other than a distant memory now. You'll need to work hard to have a hope of being anything more than bait for the demons when they come."

Another man, dark-skinned with dreads, that I recognized as someone who went to the same gym that I did, stepped forward. "Then if you know what's coming, stay and help us."

"I can't stay when my friends are in danger. I need to get to them." I thought for a moment, then sighed. "We will need each other, but there's no way I can travel with all of you without drawing attention and putting you all in danger. Stay here, get to safety in the trees, and do *not* go anywhere alone or move after dark. You'll likely die."

I closed my eyes, thinking a bit, then opened them and added, "Some of you are likely going to gain powers that you can't even imagine. Just experiment with them, do what you can to learn in safety, but don't get too cocky." I turned my gaze and slowly looked from eye to eye to eye as I spoke on. "If you have to defend yourselves, use overwhelming numbers until you can level up or I come back with help."

With that, I turned and walked back into the wood toward my house. I needed to make sure that things were okay there, and then make my way toward Emma's place to ensure she was safe. And figure out what the hell we were going to do with all these people.

If we do anything for them at all, I grumbled more to myself than anything. I could leave them behind and feel nothing. Now that we weren't in the game, we would likely have to try to find Sundar and Elder Berry before going back to trying to find Mona.

And if she was working with the demons now, like I had seen, chances were good that she was somewhere with them, right? That gave us a week to get our shit together to attempt to find her.

Something barreled into me, and I pitched sideways with a "Woah!" I went down hard and felt something pierce my right side as I hit the ground. I turned in time to catch a cat no bigger than a medium-sized dog gunning for my throat.

It clawed at my bicep and tried to rake my eyes to blind me, but I grunted and slammed it onto the ground next to me and stunned it. The only way to prevent it from coming after me, or the other people in the area again, was to kill it. So I did.

I reached into its mouth while it was still stunned and grasped the upper and lower portions of the jaws, then yanked as hard as I could. A sickening pop and a soft hissing yowl sprang from the broken jaw; then I gripped the back of the head as steadily as I could and beat it into the ground next to the tree that I had fallen against.

It tried to fight back, but every new crack on the ground stunned it again, and I just kept going until it stopped moving.

Someone whistled, and it turned out to be the man with the

dreads, who was watching me with a look of horrified amazement on his face.

"Any reason you're following me?" He blinked at me as I tried to stand up, and he stopped me, the pain in my right side close to my hip more than enough to keep me perfectly still.

"Because I was a player, too; I just didn't want anyone doing me like they tried to do you." He reached down and grasped the object that was just outside my range of vision and stared me straight in the eyes. "This is going to hurt."

I gritted my teeth, and he yanked as soon as I gave him an acknowledging nod. "Ah!" I hissed and was finally able to move. "Thanks."

The stick he held up was sharper than it should have been, almost like it had been placed there on purpose. "No problem. Sorry; I knew you had to go, but I needed to sound convincing."

"So you're out here now to apologize, but look like you're trying to convince me to stay?" He nodded, and I just shook my head. "Smart, but futile. Lead them yourself."

"That's the key to the whole 'look like it' part—I don't care if you stay." He shook his head and grinned, shrugging as he added, "I'm capable of leading, and I would like to. Having you and your friend or whoever here would just help with protecting us and adding teachers and tutors for those who need it. We don't *need* you here."

I blinked at him with surprise as he shrugged again. "It would simply be beneficial for you to be here. So you're welcome to return, so long as you don't go attacking and killing my people. Okay?"

I blinked at him again and growled, "Whatever. You and your people behave, and I'll be content to leave you alone." I turned to walk away, and he put a hand on my shoulder. For the second time that day, I turned in rage. "What did I just tell you? Are you trying to get your ass handed to you?"

The guy scoffed and rolled his eyes. "I was going to warn you about that." He pointed to a nest of something that writhed on the ground not twenty feet in front of me. "But it seems that you're letting your inner edgelord run rampant today."

I closed my eyes and sighed; the pain and confusion of all of this happening so fast wasn't helping my already dark mood. I grumbled, "Thanks," and moved on my way, carefully avoiding the nest of writhing bodies on the ground that looked like snakes.

Everywhere I walked, I surveyed my surroundings carefully, more than I ever had before, and it felt like every step I took brought the fact that more and more of the world around me was changing and becoming something it had never been before.

What it should have never been. Had there ever been a way for us to stop this?

I shook my head as I stepped on a branch that cracked loudly and paused to listen to see if there was anything coming for me because of it. The sun was in the sky by now, and a lot of light was still getting into the area, despite the fact that the trees seemed to be growing faster, and the roots doubled as roots for new growths as well.

Green Aether that could likely be attributed to nature magic permeated the world here, every branch and root—every budding leaf on every minuscule branch—lousy with it, as each plant flourished in ways unimaginable.

If they have Aether to use, and it's all over the place here, maybe I can use it too?

I'd felt the magic before, the movement of it through my being in the game, as if it were as much a part of me as anything else. As real as my own limbs. So I reached for it, even if there was no system to guide me.

I closed my eyes for just a moment and willed the blood in my veins to carry heat to my muscles like I had when I'd played the demon's stupid game. It had made me slightly stronger then, so here was hoping it would make me slightly faster now.

I took a step forward and the heat was enough to make me break into a sweat immediately without my ice Aether to cool me down from the outside. I made it a hundred yards in seconds, faster than I had even thought that I could go, when my muscles began to shriek and cramp.

"Okay." I grunted and leaned up against one of the last trees before open ground to stretch my calves experimentally. "Not a long term kind of thing; got it."

My stomach began to rumble softly, and I rolled my eyes. No food around, either.

After a few minutes of stretching and looking around, the walk to the other side of the street went well. No one tried to accost me, nothing tried to kill me, and the majority of the looting and ransacking looked to be happening in the nicer houses down the road.

People shouted and blubbered at each other in the streets, some banding together and helping their neighbors defend themselves; others betraying their friends, and even families, in this time of utter chaos.

"I bet you're having a grand old time, aren't you, Mephisto?" I muttered to myself angrily as I watched the demon's favorite meal unfold all around me.

I moved on. Nothing I could do, unless I wanted to kill them all.

Passing through the streets without glancing at anyone was good for a time. At least, until I got closer to my house, having taken the long way to ensure there was nothing crazy that I would run into, and saw a group of three or four humans in hoodies with bottles of liquor and lit cigarettes in their mouths. At least some things were still sticking around. Though I wondered how long it would be until everything would change. Like our clothes.

I blinked, *Did I just refer to them as humans?* I shook my head and got onto the sidewalk closest to my place, ignoring their calls to stop and come back. One of them actually had the stones to shout, "Or else!"

I chuckled and kept walking until I heard them start running toward me. I could use Aether; it was stilted a little, but still usable, to a degree—I wasn't afraid, and I wouldn't give them the satisfaction of thinking they had spooked me.

I stopped and turned, sighing, "What?"

All of them pulled up short, having likely expected me to ignore them or something.

The leader of the bunch, a guy in a red hoodie that tickled something in my memory for some reason, grinned at me and motioned to his pals. "We wanted to know if you had any smokes, or something to drink for us, since you're infringing on our territory."

He chuckled a little bit manically, "I was dying for it anyway; may as well tax my new peeps."

I raised my eyebrows, blinking exaggeratedly. "*Your* territory?" I glanced around, tired of people being assholes already. "I don't see your name on it."

"It's in the works, friend; just pay the toll, and you can fuck off." One of the cronies rolled his eyes, and something caught my eye—he had a knife. The plastic was gone, but there was a bit of wood that had been placed over it to act as protection for his hand and serve as a makeshift handle.

The one in front glowed ominously in red, and I recognized him, saying as much, "You must be Blasik!"

He blinked and frowned at me, then tried to shove off the sudden paranoia with bravado. "You must have seen me playing in the game and recognized my voice. Cute *and* creepy. Hand over whatever you got, and we'll let you go."

I laughed, shaking my head. "No. I remember you being a petty criminal in the game, and now I remember where I recognized *you* from. You tried to rob a diner a little while back, and I was there. You didn't get anything then, and you won't now. I suggest you all leave before you get hurt."

I didn't turn my back on them like I was sure they were hoping; I just crossed my arms and stared them all down.

Blasik growled and held his hand out to his buddy, who deposited the knife there. "Give us what we want!" He brandished the blade toward me, and his aura began to mount and flow outward clumsily. I could feel the intimidating aura wash over me with no effect, like last time, but I let him come closer to me as I pretended to freeze where I was.

As he closed the distance, I could see that his human features appeared to be giving way to the orcish ones that he had sported in the game. So we were changing too, it seemed. Weird.

He lifted the blade toward my throat and chuckled darkly, "There's a good piss-ant. Now, go and get all the valuable shit left from wherever you were heading, and I'll think about letting you go with only an ass kicking."

He was close enough now that I lashed out at him with my foot, kicking in his knee hard enough that it collapsed inward with a snap. He screamed and tried to cut me, which was smart, but I moved aside and grabbed his wrist, snapping his elbow inward with my knee. The knife fell, clattering to the ground.

"Fucking get him!" Blasik snarled, but the others just froze. I had a new toy to play with once again.

I turned and looked at the others, allowing his ability to leak from me toward them, "Stay right where you are and don't move a muscle."

Their eyes widened, and only one of them looked to be unaffected. I kept my eye on him for a second longer before I glanced back down at Blasik, who was trying to go for the blade with his good hand, but he fell forward onto his now-broken arm and screamed again.

The hood on his head made a good handle to haul him up by, and I used it to painfully position him between me and his cronies. "This is my place. I lived here, and I'm not going to tolerate you assholes making a nuisance of yourselves. So let me show you what you'll be dealing with if you decide to keep doing dumb things around me, eh?"

I leaned down and grabbed the knife, making a cut on Blasik's neck that I leaned down and sniffed. His blood actually smelled good. Like a medium rare burger.

It called to me, and my stomach grumbled loudly as I grinned at the panicking man. "Thanks for the meal."

"Get your pervert ass away from me!" He bellowed and tried to use his ability again, but I'd already struck. The blood flooded my mouth, and his Aether refilled me, feeding me and replenishing the Aether I had yet to get back on my own, this being the first time I had gathered it in this body and all.

Better yet, it seemed to have jump-started my HUD, as well. I could see my health bar, Aether bars refilling, and everything else, though my mini map still appeared to be offline.

I took the knife and slammed it into the man's still-beating heart as I looked up at the others, his life ending and giving me a minuscule amount of EXP, it seemed.

But that was fine, because I was still hungry, and there were three more snack packs right here for me to have.

CHAPTER TWENTY-ONE

I belched, full to the brim and feeling much better now on Earth than I ever had. By the time the second crony had fallen to me, the other two had taken off, but I was fast enough to catch them.

The one that hadn't been taken by the intimidation had been stoic enough to actually fight back instead of begging, since he had tried to rally the others against me. I respected that.

But I couldn't leave someone who knew what I was alive right now, because that was just asking for some kind of witch hunt.

I picked my teeth, some of their flesh remaining, for some reason, and noticed that I had my fangs now. That would make things a lot easier.

Once I made it into my house, I searched for anything that I could use as a weapon or to defend myself with. There wasn't much that I could touch that didn't turn to dust almost instantly, though I did have one cast iron skillet that remained. That had been a gift from Emma for a birthday or something. She knew I liked to cook and had more talent at it than Mona had ever had, so she'd wanted me to have it. It had been her grandmother's, and now it was mine.

There should have been a crushing sense of loss and remembrance at all of that, since I had known the woman, but it was just...not there. I felt next to nothing, other than just needing to get to Emma so I knew she was okay, then getting the group together to go after Mona.

Even that seemed like it was moot at this point. But the front lines held more than just her. I could go and hunt the demons down. Make them pay for all this. Make Mephisto pay for it. Eventually, we would hunt him down and kill him if we could, but for now, that meant getting strong enough to be a threat.

I grabbed the pan and went to find a bag to put some clothes into. I didn't have access to my inventory yet and borderline wondered if there would be one now.

How much of the system would be brought over? How much would remain unmolested by the demons, and how much would it cost us all to be able to fight back?

I shook my head and gathered what clothes I had, stuffing them into a bag that I found in my closet. It was a little black thing that would barely fit a few outfits and some other minor items, but that was all that mattered for now. I left the house without lingering for too long, knowing that I would have a bit of a trek ahead of me to make it to Emma's place before nightfall.

I put the straps over my shoulders, carrying the knife in my right hand and the skillet in my left like a shield. I was about as prepared as I could be for the apocalypse. The door to my place opened, and I could hear footsteps before I came out of my room.

More looters? I sighed softly and checked around the door frame into my hallway. Short as it was, it would give me some kind of insight into who was coming into my home. I heard breathing, and a dog I didn't recognize trotted into the hallway. It was massive.

At the shoulders, it could barely fit into the hall and had to slink forward. There was more movement in the living room and more clawed feet hit the ground. I closed the door slowly, so as not to give myself away to the pack outside in the hall, and instead moved to my window and used it once more.

Only to find two more dogs standing guard at the entrance to my backyard. The gate was open, and they did *not* look happy to see me. They looked like different breeds of dog completely. Demonic, even. The one closer to the fence was tall enough that she could have rested her front paws on the wood easily. The one closer to me was blockier and more muscled, the massive head that could have been more alligator with a dog-like body than any kind of canid I'd seen before.

Their heads lowered, and they began to growl. The one closest to the house began to bark at me and closed the distance slowly.

The blocky wood that was the handle of the knife dug into my palm as I readied myself for a fight, the metal of the skillet digging into my hand, too. First, I'd beat the dog with the skillet and then stab it, then turn on the other one and repeat.

The one closer to me scented the air greedily and paused before his tail began to wag as he crept forward. The muscles in his back and chest bunched as he crouched and began to whine as his black eyes found mine. I blinked. "Seamus?"

The dog barked once and launched himself at me as I howled, "Not the face!"

He landed on my chest, and there was a crunch as my ribs bowed in; he was so much heavier than he had ever been before. He chuffed and sniffed at my body, licking me greedily in delight as the other dog went wild and joined him in sniffing me. "Ah! Hello, which one are you?"

"Seamus, Losa, *pfui!*" Emma's voice carried softly, and then came the follow up, "*Hier.*"

Both dogs slunk away from me and went to the window, where Emerald hopped out, followed by the dog that had been in the hall. "Seth?"

I nodded, and sat up with my hands out. "Do you not recognize me?"

She shook her head, "No. You look more like your avatar than you do my son."

I blinked back at her, "Seriously?" She nodded. "That's why I felt so different. I thought it was more slow, just the nails and fangs."

I lifted my hands and felt my face; the horns had come back, and I grasped them both. "Never gonna really get used to those."

"How new is the tail?" I blinked at her again, and she pointed to my rump and grimaced. "It moves?"

I turned in tepid horror to see what she was talking about. There, attached to my lower back in a way that I'd had yet to notice, was a demonic tail. The kin were demon-like, but what made them different from the enemy was the lack of a tail.

Now there was nothing that separated me, other than my actions, and based on my last meal…I was likely little better than some of the demons, anyway.

"Goddamn you, Mephisto!" I snarled and lashed out, my teeth gritted and my fists beating the ground. I glanced up at Emma and noticed that her hair was much the same as it always had been, but the rest of her features were slowly shifting toward what she had been in-game as well. "Looks like you're on your way to being like me."

She nodded, and I just shook my head, "How long have you been here?"

"I came here with the pack, because I was worried about you and the others." She was quiet, looking down at her pack; there appeared to be a couple of dogs missing. "We lost Tialca and Remi."

I stood up and moved toward her, my arms down so the dogs wouldn't attack on accident. "Em…I'm so sorry. What happened?"

"Someone attacked my house; it was someone who wasn't from the neighborhood." She shook her head, and tears began to fall of their own accord. "Tialca wasn't taking the change well, and she attacked them. She killed a couple of the attackers, but there were other wild animals nearby, too."

"What kind?" She shook as if in shock from trying to recall.

"Remi went after one that looked like a fucking *bear*, and then a man came out of the wood with an axe," she seethed, her rage, coupled with the loss, making her grip her hands tight enough that her knuckles cracked and popped. "Tia killed him too, but the bear got her and dragged her into the woods. I need your help to find her, Seth. Please."

"Why would you even ask me that?" I spat at her as I turned toward the fence and walked around the dogs. "We should have been on the way there already; let's go."

She sniffed a little and chuckled. "Sorry. Figured I'd better ask." She moved with the dogs taking their places around her, Brom sniffing me a little more intrusively than usual. "With how one-track your mind has been lately, I figured anything else but searching for Mona would be out of the question."

I blinked and frowned…mulling over whether I should say something or not to her. How she might take it. Finally, I figured that the truth might be a better option, as it would help us keep things simple and allay her worries.

"Listen, you don't have to worry so much about her." She flinched as if I had struck her and looked taken aback, almost as if I was betraying her. "I still want to find her, but I saw that she was safe recently. Or at least, about as safe as any of us, and she was doing well enough on her own."

She grasped my shoulder hard enough that the dogs were uncertain what to do, and I knew that I'd bruise if she held me too long. "What do you mean?"

I was about to answer her when the dogs turned and growled in unison as something stepped around my house and moved toward us.

"It's one of them!" Emma snarled, and a shimmering blade of light appeared in her hands. "More later."

It reminded me of the bears that we had seen at the zoo,

but it was somehow wider and more dangerous looking. What was it doing here?

I stepped in front of the woman who helped raise me, and raised the skillet out in front of me with the knife held back. "You ready?"

"I'll kill every last one of these things in my way, if Tialca and Remi are out there." Emma's savage reply goaded the beast in front of us into charging. "*Fass!*"

The dogs between us charged the beast, snarling and barking as they threw themselves at the thing's legs. It roared and whined as it tried to swat at the more agile animals, but they wove in and out of range in perfect harmony as Emma and I moved in.

She went around the far side, pinning the beast between herself and the wall. It glanced at her, and Losa bit it on the cheek and skidded away before it could swipe at her.

I braced the skillet in my right hand and waited for the right moment to strike, when the bear reared up and slammed its front paws into the ground with enough force to throw the dogs backward and make Emma and I flinch.

The bear lumbered forward and bit at me, but my wits returned and I walloped it over the head with the skillet as hard as I could.

A fuzzy notification for damage tried to come from the strike, but it just wasn't legible to me, so I ignored it and stabbed with the blade in my left hand.

The blade screeched against the fur as it shifted color from a mottled brown and tan to gray and silver. Finally, the blade bent entirely and snapped, leaving the bear's fur completely untouched.

The bear heaved a sigh and bashed the back of its paw into my chest, flinging me sideways into the wall of my house with a thick *thud* that nearly put me out like a light.

A groan escaped my lips as I tried to figure out if the blur I saw was the wall in front of me or if I'd lost my sight, but that didn't matter, as pain that nearly split my mind apart erupted in my stomach.

Claws burst through my front as the bear attacked me, pain taking my ability to think. As excruciating as it should have been, I couldn't help feeling as though Mephisto had made it so I felt pain a little more harshly here, too.

The bear lifted, and I screamed, slapping the skillet against the claws that still burst through my flesh in an attempt to force them out of me. It just continued to savage me.

I groaned and reached back, grasping fur as hot breath blew over the nape of my neck, and cast a wisp of flame onto the furred arm. The heat of the flame intensified, and Emma appeared right next to me to stab her blade over my head as spittle flecked onto my cheek from above.

Vulina! My mental roar seemed to echo in my mind, and my summoning Aether bottomed out instantly. A single flame Aether joined it, but when it did, heat bloomed into the area to a degree that took my breath away.

"Get off my *friend!*" a husky voice snarled, and the claws in my stomach were yanked out. Searing heat passed through the air in a whistle like a tea kettle, and the bear crashed away from me. Emma wrapped her arms around me and kept me from falling to the ground.

I gasped and tried to close the wounds myself with ice, but the blood was too hot to allow it to freeze shut properly.

"Don't move too much; I got you," Emma hushed me as I coughed, and blood gushed anew over the crimson-dyed ice. "I stabbed it in the eye before she came in. Is that Flicker?"

I nodded without needing to see her, my hands pressing against the wound in my gut uselessly. Dark spots began to ring my vision as my health bar slowly lowered past a quarter left. "Need to heal."

"Lay down; we'll get you some help, okay?" There was a crash, and Emerald muttered a curse under her breath as the dogs rejoined the fight. "They're on our side, Flicker!"

I grimaced and gritted my teeth, fighting the encroaching

darkness to survey the fight. The dogs attacked the bear and harried the impressive creature that was Flicker now. She was larger and more muscular than she had been, but nothing close to the orcish woman or some of the people I had seen in the game either. However, she was taller and stronger now.

Half the bear's face was melted away, and some of its chest and shoulders smoldered as it tried to swipe at her and the dogs.

She clenched her fist, and a lance of flames sprang to life in her grip. She twisted it and speared the bleeding and burning animal in the chest, and it stilled, then dropped a bit before it fell to the side.

Emma howled a command, and the dogs backed away from Flicker and toward her, but they kept their eyes on the newcomer, just to be safe.

As she turned toward me, my vision darkened even more, and my sight faded completely.

———

I woke up some time later to the darkness of my room, the hallway lit up for some reason. I stirred, my stomach burning to the point that I felt like I was on fire. I clawed at the blanket over top of my body, but someone put a hand on my arm.

"We couldn't move you far, and we had to do something to staunch the bleeding," Emma whispered softly as she put her other hand on my cheek. "You don't want to see it right now."

I grunted an "okay" and sighed as I took inventory. My health was up to half by now, and I had a small flame symbol pulsing under my health bar. "I've been burned?"

"To staunch the bleeding, dear." She gripped my shoulder, a sad and tired look taking over, and I knew she was worried about something. Likely Tialca and Remi.

"I'm sorry about the dogs. If I hadn't been so stupid, we could have gone straight after them." I attempted to say more, but she shook her head solemnly and didn't say anything as she lifted an object and placed it in my hand. Then another.

Tialca and Remi's collars.

"Emma…" She shook her head and sniffed. "Emma, I'm so sorry."

"So am I." Her eyes looked haunted. "It wasn't the same one, I don't think, but it dropped both collars, for some reason. There are other creatures out there, Seth. So many others."

"I don't know what we're supposed to do anymore." My admittance of that little fact surprised me. There had been purpose to all of this before. Now, with Mona working with the demons, there was nothing left to do but get stronger and wait for them to be unleashed.

That, and reunite the party.

"How do we find Sundar and Elder Berry?" I shook my head, and she seemed just as daunted by it. "The system is supposed to come back online at some point tomorrow. But the topography of the world is changing. Everything is changing. How do we know what way is even fucking north at this point?"

"We do what you kids taught me to do in the game," Emma growled, shoving my shoulder a bit as she turned her cool gaze on me. "I've lost almost everything to this shit, Seth. The love of my life, my daughter, my home, and two of my dogs."

She prodded me in the chest, "But I still have you, and I still have the hope that we can fucking do something about this." She cracked her neck, and I noticed that her body was getting a bit more furred, even as I sat there and watched. "So quit your belly-aching and get with the program. We're going to get stronger, find our friends, and go look for my girl. You with me?"

"God, you could give me a speech *any* day." Flicker stepped into the room and towered over both of us as she glanced from Emma to me. "Sorry for the mess I made on your stomach, Kyvir. Or is it Seth now?"

"Seth is…gone," I decided, touching the horns on my head and the wounds on my stomach that were covered with cloth bandages. "Seth died today. I'm Kyvir now."

She nodded and looked to Emma, "And I only know you as his friend."

Emma smirked. "I watched his mother give birth to him. The only person in this world who knows more about him than her or me is possibly Belgonna, because she's been in his mind."

I frowned. "You knew about that?" She nodded, and I rolled my eyes. No point in secrets, then. "Will you be Emma, or Emerald?"

She touched her darkening face. "I think Emma's time has come, as well."

"Emerald, it is." Flicker grinned and turned back down to me, her bulk bending low. "There are people outside hunting for someone who killed them earlier. I get the distinct feeling that they may mean you."

I blinked and frowned at her. "That can't be possible. I killed them here on Earth; they should still be dead."

"This is Eden now," Emerald corrected me thoughtfully with an evil, contemplative look on her face. "We might not be able to die here."

"What if it's someone else?"

Emerald just gave me the look that said *really?* "Someone claims to die? Four of them? And they're hunting you for shits and giggles?"

I shrugged sullenly as she stood. "It's possible?"

"We will see." Emerald grinned savagely before turning to Vulina. "Watch over him. If anyone who isn't me comes in here—"

"I'll kill them." The draconic woman spoke with little hesitation and all the malice she could muster.

Emerald nodded and put the hood up on her dark hoodie, then left the room, closing the door behind her.

The dogs were up and moving, based on the sound of their paws on the floor padding down the hall and outside.

There was nothing left for either of us to do but wait. I thought about ordering Vulina to go after her, but instead opted to obey Emerald.

"You know, before, it was kind of hard to care or really get to know her, but I think I might be starting to really like her." Vulina smiled, catching me off guard. I chuckled, and she turned to look at me. "I really am sorry for having to burn you like that."

"You saved my life; consider it a hazard of the job." I winked at her, and she smiled more, her sharpened incisors flashing at me. "How's being here for you?"

"It's different." She frowned and closed her eyes in thought. "It's hard to be here, but easy, because it's you. I think that's going to change soon."

"What makes you say that?" I blinked at her, then again in surprise, as one of my summoning Aether returned.

"It's getting easier to remain here for me." She looked a bit more chipper and was about to speak, when a barking growl and a horrid scream rent the somewhat peaceful calm.

Pleading cries continued to ring out and get closer and closer to us. Moments later, the door opened, and Emerald walked in with one of the men that had died at my hands earlier in her grasp.

It was Blasik, and his eyes went from terrified to enraged, then back to terrified as soon as his gaze fell onto the massive woman standing protectively over me. Behind him, I could see his three groupies. Emerald made them kneel in the hallway, and the dogs stayed trained on them.

They weren't going anywhere.

"What happened to you?" he sneered, trying to sound like he was in charge, but I just ignored his question.

"What happened to *you*?" I returned, and he just stared at me until one of the dogs growled behind him.

He flinched and muttered, "I don't know."

Emerald's hand moved, and he hissed in pain, the delicious scent of his blood wafting into the air from his forearm. "I don't!" She moved again and he shied away from the weapon. "We died, and some time later, I woke up in bed. I don't know what happened, but that's it."

"Any loss of experience?" He blinked at me as if he wanted to tell me to shove it, but both women closed in on him, and he wilted.

He held up his hands and shouted, "I don't know!"

"What do you know?" Vulina bellowed and backhanded him hard enough that his lip split open.

"Flicker, you have to let him answer the question before you beat him," I muttered to her with a hint of the chuckle I wanted to let loose.

"Oh." She frowned at him, and when he didn't answer her after a few seconds, she slapped him again. "There we go."

"Would you two dumb bitches just stop *fucking* hitting me?"

I grunted as I sat up, intent on getting into the interrogation myself, but Emerald's arm blurred and her Soul Dagger slid across his throat in a shallow line. "*Guc!*"

"Better." She looked at me. "Snack?"

My stomach rumbled wildly. "Yes, please."

He tried to fend me off with his one free hand, but I just punched him and Vulina caught his arm and held him for me to drink from. My health recovered slightly, and I decided to try Lay of Hands on the man as well, but shaping it to my benefit.

His cheeks sank in, and I could feel myself getting stronger as I drained the blood from his body and his HP by hand. As soon as the first round was done for the spell, I did it again, since there was no cooldown for it and there was no cost. I just had to remain in contact with him to siphon his life force into myself. Of course, that was after lifting my hand away to cut off contact.

I drained him until my stomach was full, and I was almost at full HP. He stood as barely a husk, and I just glanced at Emerald, "Think he's in any condition to give us answers?"

She grinned evilly. "Certainly." She turned him as he gasped and said sweetly, "If you come back to life, stay away from us."

He started to gasp something, but her dagger slid into his chest just before she tossed him backward into the hallway. I heard a faint sound and caught sight of a stream of liquid before she snorted, "Seamus!"

The stream stopped, and the massive dog poked his head around the doorway to blink at her questioningly.

We laughed, and the other guests just stared in shocked horror as we turned our attention on them for answers to our questions.

CHAPTER TWENTY-TWO

The morning sun rose, and with it came a stream of notifications that made me smile.

Welcome to Eden, Earthlings. The transition is still underway somewhat—but it won't be long until they finish.

Here, I return to you your inventories, items, gear, and spells. Everything you had in-game, you now have returned to you.

You'll need it all soon.

Love,

Mephistopheles.

I just shook my head and opened my inventory to equip my gear once more. My armor felt good on me again.

I thought about something for a moment and decided that it may be for the best to at least try for it, or ask about it beforehand.

I pulled my golden blade from my hip. "Oranthus?"

"I had wondered where you had gone to, child." The golden dragon spoke tiredly.

"Things got a little weird; sorry."

"I sense a question, how may I guide you?" His wisdom knew no bounds, it seemed.

"I have a holy blade in my possession that I'm in the process of corrupting so that I can use it with my Dark Paladin Job." I took a breath and added, "I wondered if you wanted to be used on it, since it seems to be a more appropriate weapon, and I need to know more about it."

"As much as a holy weapon would suit one so formerly just and glorious as myself, a fallen weapon would corrupt me and my intelligence, I think." I could almost feel him spiritually shaking his head. "I would be useless to you then."

"Thank you." I frowned and thought of the weapon. It looked like it was closing in on becoming fully corrupted. Maybe I could keep sacrificing innocents to it, and still get what I wanted?

Maybe that could be something that we could do first.

I glanced through my inventory and found that there were a couple of new items. One of them was a ring that looked unassuming, a sort of copper color with an intricate design, called the Ring of Soliadad.

Ring of Soliadad
Quality: Rare
Effect: Gives user skill of Minor Telekinesis.
Durability: 47/40
Worth: Unknown.

That was weird, so I pulled Oranthus from his sheath once more and asked, "Do you know what it means when something has more durability than it should?"

"It means that the item was in a dragon's hoard and was well-maintained by their residual magic." He sounded like he was frowning. "Normally, that means that it can be upgraded if you know how to do so."

"Could you do that?"

"I am a dragon, you know."

I laughed at his sassy retort and opted to look at the other item, the one that Sinistella would claim that I stole. If she was around anymore to accuse me.

This one was a silver chain of some kind, which looked like it had a ring attached on one end, then another one at the other end. Oranthus's voice was excited as he spoke, "I recognize that from my hoard!"

"What is it?"

I touched it, and he cackled as I did.

Fafnir's Gaudy Horn Ornament

"Are you serious with that name?" He just laughed some more, and I continued to read the stats.

Fafnir's Gaudy Horn Ornament
Quality: Mythic (Soul Bound)
Effect: Offers the wearer the treasure senses of the Dragon.
Durability: Cannot be broken.
Worth: ??????????

"So this means I can sense treasure if I wear this?"

Oranthus actually cackled and bellowed, "Pull me from this worthless weapon and place me on it before you don it."

I shrugged and did as he asked, pulling the original vial that the dye had been stored in from my inventory and touching it to the blade of the weapon.

Dye Separation available.
Would you like to remove the dye from this item and return it to the vial?
Yes / No ?

I selected yes, and the dye beaded up onto the weapon, revealing that the true metallic sheen beneath was dull and pitted, unlike the smooth surface the dye had covered. Some of it even looked scorched.

I turned and put the vial to the horn ornament and began to pour, the dye beading and covering every inch of the accessory. Once it was done, I had to try to decide which horns needed some bling. I decided on the left two, so that the item wouldn't dangle into my vision.

"Ah, that's much better!" Oranthus sounded like he was stretching out as he spoke to me, the chain jingling a little as it swayed over my eye. "Now, let's see if we can't get you up to snuff a little bit, shall we?"

My eyes, ears, nose, and mouth throbbed a few times, then burned, until I could almost smell the meat of my flesh cooking. "Oranthus, what the hell is going on?"

"Your senses are being purified and strengthened; it would have been worse had I not been here to soften the transition for you."

Evil Eyes upgraded to Eyes of Avarice (Expert Lvl 43)

The colors in the world took a dramatic shift, and I doubled over with the vertigo it gave me, vomiting onto the floor until I could barely see or feel anything other than the throbbing pressure of blood in my head.

"Open your eyes slowly, Kyvir, and allow the differences in the world to come to you." Oranthus sounded like he was trying to be gentle, but there was just so much levity to his voice that it grated on my raw nerves. "You've only been down a few minutes. Come now; the dragon must advance."

I rolled my eyes, the act irritating them, but otherwise, they were open now at least. Gray casts lay over most things, which confused me. "What's with all the gray?"

"Things of no value do not have colored aura, nor do they smell or taste as enticing," he explained as I reached out to touch the bed in front of me. "Dragons are born with Master-level Eyes of Avarice, and can automatically filter this information, so it will be a little much for you at first, but I will attempt to guide you through this."

"Will I be able to see colors again?" It was hard to hide the slight thrill of panic I felt at the idea of no longer being able to see the very things I enjoyed so much. "Magical auras?"

"Disengage the eyes, and you should be able to see things normally." I focused on not seeing the value of things—hard—and after a few seconds of consternation, I was able to make out the bedding on my mattress. "As for the auras, that gets a little trickier. You will see them, and you might develop other sensory information to associate with them, too. But dragons inherently place value on magic as well, so those values may bleed into what you see."

A sigh of relief, and I could close my eyes, just as a scent wafted under my nose. This one was new, and I couldn't place it. "I smell something."

"Follow it." Oranthus advised, and I found the trail easily. "Use your eyes too; you'll be able to track the scent visually if it is connected to something of value."

The colors once again faded, and this time, I could see the scent in the air wafting from the hallway, then down toward the door to the outside.

I moved past Vulina and Emerald, who sat with the dogs to get them used to her, and out the door. They called after me, but there were things out here that had value.

And I wanted it.

The air outside the house was clear, and for the first time in a long time, I thought of it as fresh. The sun seemed brighter as well, lighting the world in a new and refreshing way.

I followed the scent through the neighborhood. Eventually, the ladies caught up with me, following along quietly when I wouldn't answer their questions. I was too lost in the hunt.

Four houses down, I found my neighbor June's front door had been kicked open, her place ransacked and trashed. Luckily, she had left for Florida to visit her grandchildren and brother Franky.

I followed the scent upstairs and into the main bedroom, the scent and sight cloyingly sweet, with vibrant gold and silver auras in the wall just behind the head of her bed. "There's something there, Oranthus."

"It's a hiding spot, most likely." He chuckled to himself. "Find a way in."

I lifted the bed frame easily and launched it aside, with a splintering crack of wood. Seemed to me that the head of the bed had been bolted to the wall and floor. I took out my dying holy blade, then thought better of it and put it away, instead using the damaged sword that Oranthus had been coated on to try to pry my way in.

Burning hands reached out next to mine, and the wood was engulfed, Vulina silently attempting to help me. I piled ice onto my palms and shredded the wood as it burnt, pulling it aside to find a small cubby nestled in the wall.

Inside lay four bricks of gold like you would see in the movies, a folder and a small, torn piece of paper with what looked like a combination on it.

"That means there's a safe somewhere around here." I blinked and tried to judge where it would be, based on how little I knew about June, other than what had come up in conversation.

"Who keeps gold bricks in their wall?" Emerald whispered and picked up the folder that wasn't exactly worthless, but didn't hold any immediate value to me. "I guess the kind of woman who keeps evidence in her wall for blackmail?"

I blinked and snorted. "June? No." She turned the folder around to show me photos of the same old bulbous man I had throat-punched in front of the kids. They didn't look like they were *his* kids. "Oh my god, I know him."

She snarled, "Where is he?" I was stricken by her sudden animosity, but she just shook her head when I reached for the folder again.

Vulina's hand rose to her mouth as she stared over Emerald's shoulder, a look of disgusted horror falling over her face that suddenly left no doubt in my mind why Emerald was so angry. "I'll lead the way."

"You can't be serious." Vulina asked, shocked but angry. "I know that the messaging isn't working right now for you to reach out to your friends, but there's no way you can be seriously thinking of hunting this guy down."

I glared at her, and she blanched. "There's no thinking involved." She blinked and started to back away as I turned my gaze back to Emerald. "He's likely in a new group or something; this other guy was leading it, I think. He was going to make the place into a refuge for people. He had been in the game too. But I doubt that he knows this monster is there."

"Sounds like we need to let them know what kind of monster is in their little community." Emerald's teeth flashed; now that her fully Kitsune features were evident, she looked much better than she had in her half-transformed state.

"Let's." I turned on my heel and made my way back outside to lead the way into the wood.

There were more trees now. So many more. And all of them were beginning to encroach upon the street I called home.

Birds screeched and sang above us in the branches, flying through the beams of light to other branches and hiding spots.

"Keep your wits about you; this place is dangerous." We walked for another ten minutes when I finally asked, "You tried to get ahold of Sundar and Berry?"

Emerald nodded, the dogs plodding protectively around us in a triangle, with us in the center. "I tried to summon Zanjir, too, but he's not answering."

"Things aren't fully done, I guess." I blinked and stilled as I heard voices, the scent of something valuable wafting toward me. "Call the dogs close."

"*Hier.*" Her voice was soft but firm, and all the dogs stilled, then moved toward her. "What's going on with you, and what's with the decoration?"

"It's a mythic accessory that allows me to find valuable things like a dragon would." I blinked, and the aura around me began to shift and hard line in a way that scared me. "Run!"

I grasped her and Vulina, throwing them back in the direction we had come from as a building burst into existence. The bricks shoved the earth and trees away from us with a violence I had never experienced before.

Trees ripped from the ground and fell in directions untold, and there was nothing we could do but ride the wave of earth that sprayed out around us.

79 Dmg taken

"Jesus!" I groaned and tried to sit up, groaning again as my leg popped and adjusted so that I could stand.

"Buses and horses fucking threw a train at us," Emerald muttered incoherently, and I wondered what the hell she meant or was trying to say.

"Ouch." Vulina sputtered a bit, leaves falling from her open mouth as she extricated herself from a partially destroyed tree. "I hate that."

A voice echoed out from the other side of the tower, "Someone over there?"

"Your mother!" Emerald jeered, and I snorted as I tried to help her stand. Suddenly, she wasn't smiling. "The dogs!"

She whistled in a shrill piercing tone, and the dogs made their way closer, Losa limping and leaning on Seamus a bit. "Good boy!"

I closed the distance with them and put my hand on her, using Lay of Hands to heal her a little bit.

Branches cracking and voices ringing out in the distance brought my attention back to the present. *Vulina, hide in the trees up top and wait for my signal to attack if we need it.*

What if you don't? She retorted quickly as she did my bidding.

Then stay hidden until we know what's going on. I'll let you know. Someone stepped around the side of the tower and brought up a weapon that looked more like a stick than anything else. "Hey!"

"Who are you and what are you doing here?" the man called out, and I could see that it looked like a kid, but I couldn't be sure. I started to step forward, but he raised the weapon to his shoulder and whipped it forward. A stone smacked against the armor on my chest with a ding. "Stay right there!"

"I was asked to come back here by a guy with dreads?" I called again. He paused, and I heard another shrill whistle from the other side of the tower. "He said I could come back?"

"Did you drop this tower on us?" someone else asked, their voice entirely too close.

I blinked, and I could see someone standing three feet away with a short knife drawn. They were blurry, but I could tell from the way the dogs and Emerald were acting that they were supposed to be invisible or stealthing.

I tried acting like I couldn't see them. "Do I look like I could drop a tower on someone?" They seemed to consider the question and came closer distrustfully. "I mean, my mother and I were trying to come back so we could help the community that it seems you all have started. We're players."

"Players?" The first one called and rushed forward; it was a face I hadn't seen in a bit.

"Antonio?" He blinked at me, his wooden weapon up at his shoulder. "It's me, Seth."

"Mister Seth?" He put the weapon down and peered into my face. "You look so different!"

"This is the avatar I had while I was in the game." I blinked at him and stared him down. "Are you going to stay human?"

"None of us knows." He shrugged, then looked over at the tower. "Some people started to change yesterday shortly after that creepy guy showed up. Others, this morning. But it's not consistent."

"That's really weird." I shook my head and glanced at him, inspecting his aura. It was a deep purple, sort of like the child that I had seen while training with Aertra. "So, have you tried magic yet?"

He shook his head, "We don't have anyone who can awaken our Aether." He sighed and whistled, "Garren says that should come sometime soon, but in the meantime, it's kind of shitty having the capacity to do something but lacking the ability. You know?"

"I can imagine." I smiled at him and then tilted my head. "So are you going to take us back to your camp, or are we just going to stand here awkwardly?"

"Garren said that you might come back, and he's probably

going to want someone to come back and check this place out." Antonio frowned at the tower. "Let's go."

"You aren't going to check into the potential threat that just happened to appear in your front yard?" Emerald raised an eyebrow at him, and he just looked uncomfortable.

After staring at us pointedly for a moment, he muttered, "The last guy who went against what Garren said was killed."

"I know it sounds callous, but you'll come back to life if you die." He stared at me as if I had grown a fifth horn shaped like genitals on my forehead. "We've seen it."

"Then what happened to him?" I could tell that he was beginning to waiver, but the invisible guy stepped forward and stabbed his blade toward Antonio's throat.

I growled and grabbed the wrist in front of me, moving forward with icy claws to tear into him, then bite his throat. "Oh my god, what are you doing?"

I allowed myself a chance to breathe and said, "Saving your life." I turned back and launched my mouth back into the bleeding wound before I tore the attacker's throat out savagely.

Antonio backed away a couple steps. "Mister Seth, what's going on?"

Aether Stolen – Light Affinity 8%

96 EXP obtained

"So close to leveling up again." I seethed for a moment, then looked over at Antonio, his eyes wide and horrified.

I closed my eyes and turned to the kid. "People aren't that nice around here, Antonio, and this one tried to kill you. You know him very well?"

He shook his head. "He was a gamer that Garren knew." He shrugged and said, "There was another guy like that, too, and when he did something that Garren didn't approve of, he gutted him in front of all of us."

I blinked, "Who was it?"

"Some kid in a red hoodie." He shrugged again. "I don't remember his name, but some other guys disappeared after that, too."

"It's been a little over twenty-four hours since Seth was with all of you; how does he have such a tight grip?" Emerald crossed her arms and stared at him. "Is he threatening you with death?"

He nodded, then seemed confused. "Yeah, but he also does a lot of things for what he calls the greater good. He runs lessons on using weapons, and he's also giving out quests. More gamers who knew him have begun showing up, too."

"Players can't give out quests," I grunted and stared at him.

"It always says, 'Guilty GameZ was the quest giver,' for some reason." He shrugged, and I started to see red.

"That son of a bitch!" I seethed, and both Emerald and Antonio flinched at my sudden rage. Emerald looked ready to ask a question, and I just stopped her. "He's one of the players who was robbing and killing NPCs in the game. I caught him and his buddy Blasik in the act and got kicked off the game for a bit because I broke the rules to stop them."

I blinked and tried to wrap my head around it all; how the hell was he giving quests?

Then it dawned on me. "He's a plant by one of the demons."

They looked at me as if I were deranged, but once again, I told them with my hand to hold off. "When I was with Mephisto, just before he gave me this tail, there was a talk about the demons sending in their pets to try to take the city. The ones who attacked us were the Travelers, right?"

Emerald nodded once and said, "Right."

"So then it would make sense that, if the demons now run the system, they can pick and choose who can give quests and whatnot out, right?" She looked horrified, and I continued, "So they send their pets to lead the survivors and gain their trust by helping them level up a little bit."

"Yeah, but what are they getting out of it?" Antonio was trying to act as if he was abreast of it all.

"Probably protection when the time comes for the demons to be released, or something; I don't know." I crossed my arms and thought for a moment longer. "I don't really care, either. He's going to die, and so is the guy we came here to get in the first place."

"What guy?" Antonio asked.

Emerald put herself between us and held up a photo, "Have you seen him?"

He frowned at the photo, then nodded. "Yeah, he's one of the guys who is helping Garren keep everyone…uh… understanding. Watches the kids while the rest of us are working."

"Fuck no!" Emerald bared her teeth and turned to her dogs. "*Hier!*"

I already knew we would be going toward the little community now, and there was no stopping us, so I turned to Antonio, "Find whoever hates these guys the most and get them together to form a riot or something. Go now. And tell no one we're coming."

He ran off, and I turned my face up to Vulina. *Can you fly over the place unseen and tell us how to get in without being found before we get what we want?*

I'll try to. The branch she was on shook, and she took off in the direction that Antonio had run.

I walked with Emerald and the remainder of the pack around the tower; the thing had to be at least sixty feet tall and looked more like a guard tower than anything else. There was a wooden door, but it was locked from the inside.

"We can come back to it later, but for now, there are kids at stake," she prompted. I nodded, and we continued our trek slowly.

Not much in the way of fortification, Vulina told me softly as we walked on. *A fence and a few trench-like holes in the ground closest to the tree line. They have guards posted, but they aren't equipped all that well. Basic weapons, like simple sharpened spears that would barely scratch you. All of them lower levels, mainly twos and threes.*

Layout? I returned, and she grunted and dipped.

Three buildings that look to have been hastily bridged by unseasoned wood planks. Those are the central hub, it seems. Most people look like they're trying to get some sort of farming facility going, and then after that, there are more, tilling fields of grass. She paused, seeming to focus on something. *I see children being led into the steeple of what could be the local church or something. Seems holy; it has crosses on it and stuff.*

Who is with them? I pointed to a flash of heat above, the burning red and orange of her aura shifting to follow along. Emerald and I adjusted course and walked through what could have been a logging camp, for all I knew. Most of the felled trees were stacked high and gave us great cover to move behind.

I can't see; they look miserable, though. She grunted, and I could hear the anger in her voice as she added, *There are guards with weapons that look to have been brought from home. They aren't letting anyone in after the children.*

"Chances are high that they're holding the kids hostage, and we need to stop that, too." I grimaced, wondering how the hell we had gotten pulled into this.

Then I remembered what was said about jobs: the Dark Paladin cared only about justice and retribution. That sick fuck was hurting kids, and there was no way that could be ignored.

The fencing on this side of the community was really just a series of sharpened logs and branches dug into the ground and placed at an angle to keep things out. It would have been great for a defensive countermeasure, if it wasn't for the fact that we could jump up onto one of the logs and walk down unmolested.

The people nearby didn't really know us, but with the way some of the more well-equipped people watched them, it was easy to tell that they feared the guards enough not to stop their various tasks.

One of the overseers glanced our way, and I just kept walking. until he yelled, "Hey!" I just turned my head toward him as we continued on. "Where do you think you're going?"

"Extra hands at the chapel," I called back. He walked closer, and when he was close enough, I chanced a try at a hunch. "Guilty sent for us to boost the guard there."

He nodded, frowning before muttering, "For your sake, I hope that guy doesn't try the shit he's known for again."

Emerald's stride broke behind me, and she wondered aloud, "What happened?"

The overseer shook his head, feline eyes staring back at me in disgust. "He's not right. He's good with the kids, but one of those people who's like…*too good* to them, y'know?"

"So he hasn't …" I left the silence to hang in the air, and he just shrugged.

"Good luck." He shivered and turned back to his job, yelling at the people he had been watching. "Get your lazy asses back to work!"

I watched him walk back, jaw clenched in rage. *Vulina, when it all starts—he dies painfully.*

With pleasure. She returned to her quiet observance, but I could feel the eyes of a predator watching the man as he took a sip of a flask he pulled from his pocket.

"How are we going to get in there?" Emerald muttered, and I sized up the building as it came into view.

It wasn't as big a church as it could have been for the area it was in; the mega churches I drove by regularly were almost stadium-sized. This was a building roughly twice the size of Emerald and Mona's house, and the most room would likely be in the chapel itself.

"We go in the same way; we assuage his concerns, we mention Guilty by name, and hope for the best."

She grasped my shoulder and made me look at her so she could ask, "And if the best doesn't happen to be what we get?"

I clenched my fist and let the Eye of Avarice rampage through my senses, her breath freezing as I said, "Then we kill anyone in our way."

CHAPTER TWENTY-THREE

"Halt!" One of the guards raised his large great axe and slammed the base of the haft with a dull *thunk* on the stone of the steps that led up to the entrance to the church. "Who are you?"

Emerald spoke up for me. "We were sent to collect the children and Jarrett." She paused to let him puzzle out what that meant, using the man's name from the file. "Guilty sent us."

His eyes widened, and he started to lower his axe toward us, fear on his face. "How do you know that name? No one is supposed to know that name!"

"He used it in the game." I shrugged but clenched my hand and let it go in an attempt to appear normal. "Guessing you didn't play with him?"

"No one here did." One of the other guards lowered his bow toward us and nocked an arrow to point at us.

Vulina, now!

Flame rocketed into the air in a plum that left the overseer screaming until his vocal chords were crispy. The other guards around the church broke toward the commotion with weapons drawn. The dogs, having been summoned by the blast as well, bayed and attacked those who came to help.

I'll watch over the pups until you need me. She grunted, and more fire spewed down onto the warriors below. *Might be a good time to summon Sprinkle.*

I closed my eyes and called mentally to Sprinkle. I knew my summoning Aether dropped down by one, surprisingly, but this time my ice Aether went down by two.

A thin young man in a cloak of frost appeared in the air over the two guards with his arms spread. "Finally, he summons his most powerful friend!" Sprinkle's gaze flicked down to me. "His summoning who worried if he would ever come back, because he's not a woman with voluptuo—"

"What the hell is that thing?" The guard with the bow screeched and loosed the arrow he had pulled back.

The projectile skittered off the cloak, but the piercing white gaze from within the hood of the cloak flared angrily. "You dare interrupt the reunion of my glorious self with my friend?" A scythe appeared in his hand, swinging down to slice into the man's chest and lift him into the air. "I don't abide rudeness."

"Sprinkle, kill all of the better-geared people you see, and if anyone takes a hostage, make it especially brutal, to set an example." I stepped up the stairs toward the man with the axe, who looked like he wanted to challenge me, but he had been too preoccupied for far too long.

Emerald's blade burst from his chest and I rolled my eyes as the weapon in his hands fell from his grasp onto the ground.

The door was locked from the inside, and I didn't want to risk burning the place down, so I tried to figure out how else to get in, but soon heard grunting behind me. Emerald had the haft of the axe in her hands but it looked too heavy for her.

"What are you doing?" I raised an eyebrow at her, but she just grunted again, her eyes closed as she fought to lift the weapon.

"This is the key to a lot of good things in the books I read when you guys were kids." She grunted and dragged it forward.

"He was kind enough to leave it for us, so I think we should use it. It's how Zeke would have done it."

"He always struck me as a bit unbridled when you let me borrow that." I snorted and took the axe from her. It wasn't a sword or a glaive, and it was very unwieldy, but it was okay for this, I guessed.

I hefted it behind me and focused on the door, the Dark Paladin's rage springing forward into my chest as I bellowed and Emerald snarled, "For Storm Company!"

The axe struck the center of the door and splintered the damned thing to hell before sticking into the ground, where it stayed. Both of us moved past it into the chapel entrance area, where a set of guards rushed forward.

"Oranthus, what is it that I'm seeing around their joints?" Everywhere I looked the joints of the guards glowed brighter with their auras. One of them was a deep blue that reminded me of a crystal, the other, orange and fiery. Both of them showed brighter spots near the bases of their skulls that were like beacons.

"Those would be valuable places to attack." He chuckled, and I dodged an overhead chop from the fiery guard. "Dragons see value even in combat. Strike them there, and you should see great results."

I cracked my neck and thought about it, but didn't have too much time, since the blue guard decided to start sending bubbles of water toward us in that same moment. Emerald stepped forward and yanked the red guard off balance before I willed shoving him toward his friend and activated my Telekinesis. It pushed him into his friend much harder than I had thought it would, the bubble washing over his shoulders and face before popping.

Acidic hissing made him scream and screech as the liquid continued to work itself lower on his body. The blue guard shoved his friend away and took off his shirt to try to get rid of the liquid, but it didn't seem to be working well.

I reached down and grasped the back of his neck before

biting down as hard as I could near his spine. Little blood trickled out, but this was mainly about the spot that I had seen there.

I drank what came from the wound. The man froze and began to groan in agony.

Aether Stolen – Water Affinity 10%

I blinked at the huge boost in stolen Aether and killed him on the spot with a savage jerk that severed his spinal cord. Sadly, no more notifications after that, other than the 98 EXP I got for killing him. His friend, slightly less, after Emerald put him out of his misery.

Adding those who were dying outside and the experience we were getting for them, it was a good little rake.

Level up!

I smiled and thought about it for a moment, then looked at Emerald, "Ding."

She blinked and frowned at me. "How did you level up so fast?" I rubbed my stomach and grinned until she shook her head, "You had killed those kids before, too. I was too far to get any of the experience for it, party or not. Spend your stat, then."

I nodded and opened my stat screen, wondering what I should add my point to. *Screw it, this sword is kinda heavy, so strength should be it for now. I'll add more to my magic later.*

*Kyvir Magebloood**Level: 16 Race: Kin (blooded)***
HP: 185
Strength: 14
Skill: 12
Heart: 12
Knowledge: 12
Serenity: 5
Presence: 5
Unspent Stat Points: 0
EXP to next Lvl: 123 / 1600

"Better." I sighed and focused my eyes on the ground,

searching around. I couldn't see too much of any value here, but I did hear whimpering nearby.

I closed my eyes and listened intently, following the noise as best as I could to the door of the chapel, and peered inside the place. Pews lined the sides and led up to the area near the altar where the pastor or whoever it was would speak and pray.

The children were there, at least a dozen or more of them standing there with their arms around each other as the fat old man stood over them. There was a haze over him that I didn't recognize until I got closer.

"He's got a demonic aura around him," I muttered to Emerald as we closed the distance toward him cautiously. *Vulina, if you guys are done out there, get Sprinkle and come to me.*

A little busy out here! An explosion rocked the ground, and I heard manic laughter coming from outside. *Whatever you fed him really amped him up.*

I frowned; it had only been summoning Aether. Was it that potent?

One of the kids cried out, and I saw all of them looking in front of the altar in horrified shock as the fat man raised a dagger and plunged it down into something that screamed long and low.

A cruel laughter echoed from him, but I was already moving toward his back with my left hand raised and an icy spike soaring through the air.

Something roughly chest height rammed into me like a runaway train and slid a blade into my stomach twice before disengaging and rolling away. The creature sprinted back into the pews and disappeared once more.

15 dmg taken.

Bleeding Debuff added.

Lvl 4 Carrion – Hostile

I snarled and bellowed, "Carrion!" I glanced up toward the parapet and saw Jarrett reaching for another child as he tossed the one he'd stabbed aside, only for the body to start to jerk and flail. "He's making more!"

"Zanjir!" Emerald howled, and the shadows between the two pews closest to where she stood exploded outward, with the massive dog appearing near her. "Losa, Seamus, Brom, *hier!*"

Zanjir ducked his head and began to growl low in his chest as the first of the other dogs began to make their way into the church through the door.

The dog, Brom from the looks of it, began to take offense to Zanjir's proximity to his mistress, but after Emerald barked something, he stood shoulder to shoulder with the massive canine. His ears flattened at the same time as Zanjir's did, and they both lunged forward as the Carrion speared forward with its weapon. The creature screamed and tried to stab them, but Losa appeared out of nowhere and bit the soulless creature's arm, ripping it off at the elbow with a sickening, wet snap.

The screaming died down as the children began to beg and plead for help as yet another Carrion rose and darted down the center aisle toward us.

"Go deal with Jarrett; I'll take care of the Carrion," Emerald snarled as she sprang over me and plowed into the creature that had been coming toward me.

I grunted and lifted myself from the ground, superheating my hand to stem the bleeding.

Bleeding debuff countered.

I grimaced and gritted my teeth; the 5 HP I had lost since it had taken effect was a drop in the bucket, but still annoying to lose.

My first shot at the monster's back had gone wide, thanks to the Carrion that had attacked, and now I was on a time crunch, as the third one he'd made was beginning to jerkily pull itself into a sitting position.

Time to really move. My blood began to boil in my veins, fire Aether eating away so that I could bound the distance to my target even faster. Imps burst from the second and third rows of pews as I passed by and crashed into one another, still too uncoordinated to truly be a threat to me.

I took out the dying holy sword and stabbed it at the

demonic being's back, only to have the nearest Carrion launch itself inhumanly at the sword. It was cut in half. These creatures didn't seem nearly as concerned with self preservation as Aertra had made them out to be in the slightest.

The children screamed again as the rotund man turned around, and I kicked him in the chest as hard as I could. My foot met his body and almost bounced away, but I held firm, using Telekinesis as well to assist.

He slammed backward into the altar, smoke rising from where he touched it, an unearthly scream filling the air. I grinned, another burst of speed bringing me to him so I could slam him back onto the altar.

"Get off me, you pathetic worm!" he seethed and snorted, as if he had any choice in what I was doing. "You're stopping me from creating my army!"

I rolled my eyes. "Duh?"

He blinked, then realization hit him, "You're him, aren't you?"

Now it was my turn to be confused, but he just chortled, "Oh, this is rich; you—here. Now? Of all times? My luck is terrible."

"It's not a stat that can be raised, so yeah, it is." I blinked at him, and he just stared back in angry contempt. "Are you a demon?"

He shook his head, and I blinked at him. "Are you lying?"

"Demons have been expressly forbidden from operations in Eden for a week from yesterday." He grimaced and watched as something landed on my shoulder. "That only counts for his demons, though. And these ones are *mine*."

One of the imps slapped me in the face, more irritating than actually painful. So I grabbed it with the hand that was on my sword and slammed it onto the altar, where it burst into flame, screaming in agony.

"My baby!" Jarrett cried and tried to struggle free, but I was much stronger than he was, since he appeared to only be level 11 himself.

I grabbed a fistful of his shirt and yanked him off the altar so that his stink would stop wafting into the air. I turned to the kids who were still hiding. "Look away, kids."

They stared in rapt horror, so I repeated myself a little more forcefully, "Look away!"

They did as they were told, Emerald joining me near the altar. "Where's your respawn point?"

"What are you talking about?" he sneered. I slapped him across the face, kneed him in the gut, and pressed his cheek onto the altar. It burst into flam,e and he squealed, "I don't know what that is!"

"Your little leader would have told you what it is," I reasoned and let off the pressure just a bit. "Tell me where it is."

He just shook his head and tried to say he didn't know, so I pressed his face down again. He screamed, the cycle repeating again once more before one of the kids hollered, "I can show you where his room is!"

Emerald and I turned toward the kid, my attention on him so that I promptly *forgot* to lift Jarrett's face off the altar. "What's that, sweetheart?" Emerald asked gently and stepped toward him.

"I heard the grownups talking about the response point you said." The six-year-old boy sniffed and pointed toward the entrance where Vulina and Sprinkle had just flown in. "It's near where the mean guy lives."

"Who's the mean guy?" I asked, and Jarrett tried to escape my grasp by punching me in the leg. "Knock it off."

"The one with the tusks like a elephant!" One of the girls explained, jumping to her friend's side to hold his hand. "He's all green and mean, yells a lot."

"Flicker." The elemental summoning flew over to land beside me. "You and Emerald take the dogs and kids to find where this guy lives. You keep them all safe. Anyone tries to stop you that the kids aren't comfortable with, you kill them."

She nodded and turned to Sprinkle. "Keep him safe."

Sprinkle just waved her off. "I'd be more worried about Big Stack here, if I were you." The blue-cloaked creature strutted around to the side where Jarrett could see his face. "Have you always been so pretty?"

I laughed, "He's about to get a whole lot prettier, if I have my say about it." I glanced at the kids, who moved toward the dogs cautiously, despite their wagging tails and relaxing demeanors.

The large man struggled some more, but I just waited until the kids were clear of the door before the interrogation really began. "Who are you all working for?"

"I don't know what you're talking abo—" He screamed as I shoved his face back onto the altar.

"How many times are you going to lie to me today, huh?" I droned as if I were bored. Honestly, I was. I wanted to kill him to move on to the next little phase of what I had in mind for him.

"I swear!" The smell of burning flesh intensified even more.

I sniffed dramatically, "Oh; seems that whatever higher power might be with us is pissed that you swore on their altar." I lifted up his face, the smoldering meat charred enough that a strong gust of breath from Sprinkle removed ash that had begun to blacken with the heat, revealing bone. "Might not want to do that."

He stayed quiet for a moment or two, thinking about it, until I grew even more bored and just rolled my eyes. "Sprinkle, help me load him onto the altar, please?"

"With pleasure!" He reached out and grasped the man's legs, then heaved at the same time I shoved the upper body onto that Altar. The response was outstanding.

"Please stop!" Jarrett begged, "I'll do anything—please?!"

"Was this how those kids begged?" I hissed next to his ear, more enraged than hungry at that moment. "Did you stop for them?"

He whimpered and opened his mouth, but I clamped my hand over it and growled, "If the next words out of your mouth aren't who's behind this, I'll cut some stuff of yours off."

A cool breeze whipped through the room as Sprinkle summoned his scythe and leaned on it theatrically, "And I'll make sure you can't bleed out."

I let him go, and he shuddered before screaming, "You don't have the *balls!*"

—*We found where he's staying; turns out that he was really close to Guilty as well, since it's right next to his rooms.*— Emeralds whisper was lovely news to me. —*I'll sit on the place for a bit, but Guilty's rooms are torn apart and he's gone.*—

I sent one back, —*Thank you. Sprinkle and I will be along shortly.* — I thought for a second as I loomed over the slowly roasting man. —*Don't let anyone come to the church for a little bit.*—

She messaged me back to ask what I was doing, but I just ignored her to focus on the target of my ire. "Good news, Jarrett. I know that you aren't working alone, and that Guilty, or Garren—whatever his name is—is in league with the demons, too."

He whimpered, and the smell of burning flesh grew thicker as his clothing began to burn away. "The bad news is that he's in the wind." I leaned down and whispered into his ear, "And you're in range of my *tinder* mercies."

I stood up and smiled at Sprinkle, unsure if he understood the concept of puns. "If you would do the honors? That left foot looks a little crisp."

"I'd say that would be a *step* in the right direction," Sprinkle returned, and his scythe flashed as it fell.

"Ahhh!" Jarrett screamed.

"Sprinkle, you heel, your other left!"

Sprinkle slapped himself in the face lightly as he grinned savagely, "Forgive me; I have so much trouble when I'm around new people. We always end up off on the wrong foot!"

His scythe fell again.

———

Hello, Mephisto here. I realize that this might seem a bit jarring, but I've come with a sort of… truce from my benevolent self to you.

I would like to go ahead and just warn you now that this is an incredibly graphic and vile act of violence in the highest degree, and while I find it *highly* entertaining, I do know that some of our viewers might not particularly enjoy this enlightening brand of gratuitous violence.

As such, I would like to do the honorable thing and allow you a moment to go ahead and skip to the next bit of pertinent information to avoid such unpleasantness.

I'll pause while you go about that, if you're going to.

Pausing.... still waiting.... pregnant pause with demon babies...

Oh my, that appears to be a mole of some sort on the leg? Well we just cannot have that, can we? That has to go…Oh. Sorry. You're still here?

The pausing thing. *Ahem* yes. Still doing that.

How on earth did they get that to happen, is that from twisting? Oh my.

Forgive me! Forgive me. I just…this is *rather* creative. You know what? Let's just go ahead and all go to the end of this, shall we?

———

I stood there at the altar, bloodied and weary, but feeling slightly better. But the grim work wasn't done yet.

You have defiled a holy weapon in a holy place, along with the sacred grounds, by spilling the blood of a non-innocent on the altar.

The defilement of the holy weapon Wing Brand is complete. Wing Brand has become a Fallen Blade and as such requires a new name befitting its new nature. Would you like to rename this weapon?

Yes / No ?

I selected yes, and a new screen populated my vision with a keyboard. Taking a moment to consider, I thought about all that the sword had really done for me, and it was nothing but a deliverer of death and destruction.

Thinking out loud, I asked Oranthus, "What do you think a good name for this weapon would be?"

He paused for a few seconds and finally stated, "I do not know. The nature of the sword is closer to what *you* desire than anything else. 'Tis a Fallen Blade now. It will work well for you as a Dark Paladin, that is for certain. But the name of things has a way of shaping their destinies and what they are to become. I think you will name it well."

"At the risk of sounding terribly cliché, I would almost name it 'Fate's End,' because of how many I've killed with it."

Fate's End, accepted.

I blinked. "What the hell?" The weapon grew hot in my hands, and even with my fire resistance as high as it was, my palm burned and instinctively let go of the weapon.

It lifted into the air, and the blade faced straight up over the blood-stained altar. Two ghostly sets of ivory wings burst from the surface of the blade, the feathers graceful and beautiful as they fluttered in the air, just before blood began to drip from the inside of each individual feather until they were blackened and crumbled away to dust that blew onto the ground and altar together.

Left behind were the demon-like wings of a fallen angel, or at least what one might assume them to be, since they were all leathery and scary-looking. They folded onto the blade, and it remained the same sort of blackened, charred-looking metallic color with streaks of angry, fiery red shooting through. There were cracks and crags in the metal that, if you weren't looking at it carefully, made it look more like stone than metal, but it was just as sharp as it had always been.

Fate's End
Quality: Legendary
Base dmg: 30-40 dmg*

Durability: ???
Worth: ???????

I clicked on the asterisk to see what it was for and was pleasantly surprised to see that this weapon would scale with me and my level. Nice.

I put it into my inventory, since I didn't want to leave it out and have it get stolen if someone jumped me. Now it was time to go see a fox lady about a more appropriate way to say goodbye to someone.

CHAPTER TWENTY-FOUR

Finding Emerald was easy enough, since she had decided to share the location with me about halfway through Jarrett's removal from the world.

The people who had been working under the banner of Garren or Guilty stared at me with open morbid curiosity and more than a few looks of horror before the urge to vomit got to be too much for them.

I noticed that some of them had their kids with them, the majority of whom gaped at me in terrified wonder as I strolled openly through the place.

Everyone I passed had levels, but they were all low, mainly ones and twos, with the occasional higher one sprinkled throughout. They all watched me quietly, except for one woman, the one who I had saved from the dog when the merger had first happened.

She had tears running down her face as one of the boys I had saved trailed behind her. A sinking feeling hit my gut as she stared up at me, the blood on my body and her lack of the girl.

"Did she suffer?" was all she asked, her jaw clenched, and I nodded. I knew that people respawned—Travelers did, at least

—but I wasn't sure if there was a chance of that if her soul had been taken.

"She'll likely come back soon," I muttered, and her eyes widened. "I can give you a chance at the revenge you want."

Something bloomed in my chest, and I knew that that was the right of it. I would give her the revenge for her daughter's life. She deserved that. Her *girl* deserved that.

She nodded and then faltered, looking back at her son.

Without hesitation, I looked to Sprinkle. "Care to entertain a child?"

He grinned, "It'll cost you, and I have to warn you—I'm not certified."

"I'll pay. Just keep him safe and preoccupied." He nodded to me and as I walked away, I heard the kid scream.

I turned around in dismay to discover that Sprinkle had lifted him into the air, howling, "Let's make some snow!" The boy cheered and hooted as the summoned creature took off toward the church, and snow began to fall in the summer sun.

"Is he going to kill my son?"

I looked back at her, seeing she was clearly worried, "Not that I'm aware of. And he wants to be paid, so he would do well to keep him safe. So..." She took the hint from my silence after that statement and followed me to the coordinates that Emerald had sent me.

I knocked on the door and let myself in at a grunt from Emerald on the other side as she moved something out of the way.

"Move your fat, blubbering ass!" she shouted, and I kicked the door in, the wooden frame splintering as the door slammed into something big and heavy.

The door fell off the hinges and onto our good old friend Jarrett, oddly enough. I grinned down at him, "Jarrett! It's only been about fifteen minutes or so, my friend—how are you back so fast?"

"I don't have to tell you anything!" He sobbed and tried to lift himself to his feet. He didn't make it far before the mother I had brought with me surged through the doorway and barreled into him.

She was smaller, but her rage gave her something poor Jarrett never saw coming—a mother's revenge.

"You killed my baby!" she snarled and continued to choke him with her tiny hands, his arms suddenly pinned by Emerald and Vulina. "You stole her from me!"

I knelt down behind where he had fallen, close to his bed, and grinned wolfishly down at him. "You're right; you don't have to tell us anything." I motioned lazily to our guest, her tears falling onto his face and chest. "I'm just going to give you to her and let her have her vengeance as creatively as she wants to take it."

Finally, his bulging eyes glazed over and his body disappeared. The sobbing woman still clenched her fingers. I whistled softly, passing her my pitted and nearly-ruined sword. "When he comes back, use that on him. However you need to."

Emerald seemed confused until the woman nodded her head, and she saw the look on my face, but I explained anyway. "She's going to need more than just a pound of his flesh for this. And I'm going to let her have it."

Emerald blinked, and her shoulders sagged, so I offered, "You can leave, if you like. Make sure that the others outside are all okay."

She shook her head and lifted her chin. "No. I know how she feels, and I'm going to help her, too."

We waited in near silence for the predator to return, and when he did, he was still kneeling where he had spawned when the blade in the enraged mother's hands bit into his arm. He tried to defend himself, but failed.

So he died again.

He would return, and die again. Soon, the mother grew tired, but she couldn't leave. Not yet. That left Emerald and I to take up the mantle of avengers so that her slain child could Rest In Peace, as they hadn't returned yet, and it didn't seem like they would.

Did I believe that? No. But it was the righteous nature of her revenge that called to the Dark Paladin and forced my hand to fly a little harder. To be a little more brutal every time the screaming man respawned.

Again. Again. Again. Dead. Dead. Dead.

Decapitated. Stabbed through the heart. Bled dry. Burned. Frozen. Crushed, and even castrated once or twice.

After the fiftieth time, he finally just spread his arms and stayed where he was, sobbing quietly.

Fate's End had long since become drenched with his blood, but now it seemed to hunger for it. The desire was almost too much to handle.

"I'm feeling generous," the mother told him, and he opened his eyes, still flinching at the sight of her covered in his dried and still-drying life blood. "Give them the information they need, and I'll stop."

He frowned, disbelieving. "You swear?"

She remained quiet, but stared at him pointedly. He finally got the idea that she wasn't going to swear anything and looked at me. "The demons gave us a shorter respawn time in exchange for being their informants and starting a farm for them. We would purposely only half-ass preparations, then leave the souls here unattended and let the demons have them."

"What about the experience issue?" Emerald's question nearly fell on deaf ears, until the mother turned to look at her and cleared her throat.

"We can't get around that, but it doesn't look like it gets any worse than it was for those of you who played the game." He looked like he was starting to regain some semblance of hope for a life other than constant death. His cheeks had a soft rosy tint to them now.

I nodded and looked over his head; he was still a decent level at seven. Which made me wonder… "Miss?" She looked over at me, and I cocked my head to the side curiously, "Are you gaining experience for killing him?"

She nodded. "I'm level five now from killing him; he gives about sixty or so experience per kill."

"And this last time you killed him?"

She smiled, "I still got some."

"Good." I grinned and killed him with a sweep of my sword through his throat before he could protest. "I think we just discovered the perfect experience farm for all of you."

She cocked her head like I had. "For all of us?"

My grin widened. "Why, yes. Jarrett is going to be generously paying off *thousands* of life sentences in order to pay for his crimes."

CHAPTER TWENTY-FIVE

All of the former guards and overseers were interviewed extensively to find out what they knew, the ones who had been truly abusive to their charges to the point of injury or even killing them being given the same sentence as Jarrett.

By nightfall of the second night we were in the little community, Jarrett had lost his life countless more times to the line of patiently waiting people who had been made aware of what he was and the terrible things he had done.

Those who were in on it all served as the training dummies for casters, like the rats had when I had first logged into the game. They died, then a couple of the higher level citizens would march them back out and tie them to the stake to do it all over again.

"At this point, are we any better than the demons?" Emerald stood next to me with her arms crossed, watching the scene unfold as the grisly power leveling took place. She paused and glanced at me. "I wanted to kill him myself. I wanted it so badly, Ky. But I couldn't do it. So I let you do it, and now I have to live with that. But isn't this so much more than what should be done?"

"The demons would likely think this was smart, but they don't care about us, and all they want is to win." I shrugged. "At least this way, their informants pay for their betrayal, and those who need to protect themselves are learning to do so." I glared at the dying people as one of the citizens leveled up. "Helps that we're evening the odds a little more."

She turned her head so that she could stare at me, then craned her neck a little, trying to catch my gaze, "Is that you, or the Dark Paladin speaking?"

Puzzling over it for a while, I finally answered, "I think we're aligned on this one." I gazed out over the people and frowned. "There's no way we stand a chance against anyone if it's just you and me when the demons are loosed on the world, and we're still going to have to go and find Sundar and Elder Berry if we want to stand any kind of chance on the front lines searching for Mona. At least this way, we can eventually have these guys as backup to fall back on."

She just huffed and crossed her arms tighter. "There's no way these people can do without us, Kyvir. If we leave them, they're sitting ducks." She glanced out over the posts dug into the ground, half finished and still being worked on in shifts but without overseers. "What if something attacks them before they're ready?"

"We just have to hope that we're enough to defend them until they are, and then we can move on to find those who belong to us." She sighed, and I silently watched over the progression of the people for a while. Then she sighed again. "Yes?"

"I can't just sit here and do nothing anymore; I need to go and do something." She looked around the camp, then a spark of fire lit in her eyes. "I'll go and patrol."

"You taking Zanjir with you?" She nodded, and I let a breath of relief clear my lips. "Be careful."

She gave me a curt nod in return and left the area, leaving me alone with my thoughts and Oranthus. Vulina and Sprinkle had already cleared off into the area to scout a bit, but I hadn't told her that.

Secret Quest Alert!

"That's new," I muttered to myself, touching the notification to open it.

Secret Quest Received: A mysterious entity has requested you come to the altar of the nearest church. You have three minutes before you fail this quest.

Reward: Information, possible quest line, ???

Shit. I blinked and started to sprint toward the church. It wasn't far, but people tried to stop me to ask questions, and I hoped that my rush would put people off that, but I had one man actually reach out and try to grab me as I passed him by.

My fist connected with his shoulder, and a meaty crunch met my ears, his sputtering cursing behind me fading from vehement to quiet as I carried on.

I blasted through the entrance to the building and skidded on the blood-soaked floor for a few feet before I was able to correct myself enough to continue on into the chapel.

Up the center aisle, between the pews, I launched myself toward the altar. As soon as I made it, a notification appeared.

Good work, kid.

"Where are you?" I called and looked around the room.

Touch the altar, follow the prompts, and I can reveal myself.

I narrowed my gaze and still couldn't see anyone.

Have a little faith, Kyvir.

That made me stop and think. What did I have to lose by touching the altar? I could get a quest line, too. Maybe this could help us?

I touched the altar, prompts appeared asking me if I would like to dedicate the soiled altar to a god.

"Who do I dedicate it to?"

You can call me Darnath, god of Mercy.

"Okay, I'll bite." I touched the altar again and stated, "I dedicate this altar to Darnath, the god of Mercy." I shook my head and laughed, "Mephisto told me there aren't any gods. So who are you really?"

Someone sighed behind me, and I whipped around and came face to face with Frito. "Hallo dork paladin!"

"Frito?" I blinked at him as he reached down and patted my head before stepping back to show me the man who sat on the altar with one leg up on it and the other dangling.

His simple clothes didn't look godly to me, nor his silver hair and ridiculously blue eye. The other eye was bisected by a scar that seemed to glow red. The man caught me staring and spoke in a familiar, light, and informational tone, "You like that? Mephistopheles gave me this before I had a chance to lay low as one of his."

"I don't understand." I blinked at him, and he just smiled again. "Who are you, and why are you here right now?"

He patted the altar. "You're my chosen, Seth." I frowned at the information, and he just snickered, "You didn't seriously think that he was the one who allowed you the ticket to Dark Paladin, did you?"

I stared at him, clearly confused. "Why would a god of mercy do that?"

He grinned, his teeth whiter than any set I had ever seen before. "My sort of mercy typically means the mercy of the grave, Seth."

"How do you know my name?" I held up a hand as he started to speak. "Do *not* say some stupid god-like bullshit. How?"

"We've met before." He smiled, and his body shifted until Wilhelm stood in front of me, his familiar Germanic accent addressing me, "Do you recognize me now, Mister Ethelbart?"

"How would a god be his right hand?" I thought about drawing Fate's End, but he just waved the question away as he retook his natural form. I added as I shook my head, "This is a trick; it has to be."

"No tricks against you, my boy." He smiled again sadly. "I hid in plain sight. Made myself more useful than his former right hand had ever been and hid things from him. You showing up in that last meeting we had was enough to surprise even me, but you sort of unknowingly outed me, and here we are."

"How am I supposed to trust that?" He glanced over at Frito, who just shrugged and continued to smile.

"Again," he eyed me drolly, "Paladins are supposed to operate off *faith*, my boy."

"Stop calling me that." I gritted my teeth and took a step forward, but Frito's hand shot forward, and he just shook his head at me in warning.

"Fine, I'll refer to you as Kyvir." He stared at me for a small amount of time, then said, "I would prefer to cooperate with you. We need each other, if you and I are to make it through this with any modicum of safety."

"Why are you at risk?" I folded my arms over my armored chest and glared at him.

"You outed me to the big bad, Kyvir." He sighed and threw his hands up. "I'm still under his thumb, but now there's a knife gripped in the hand pointed at my throat. You may not have meant to, but I was trying to keep him complacent, and now he's triple checking my work to ensure there's nothing foul afoot. And there is."

He hopped off the altar and pointed to it. "*This* is how we start to go against him." He slapped the altar now, his flesh making smacking sounds against the stone. "You find any altars in the world, and you dedicate them to me. As I grow stronger, I can give you more help and more advice. Eventually, we'll be able to stand against the asshole who did this to me."

I ignored the thumb he jabbed at his ruined eye and tilted my head, "And you're just doing this out of the goodness of your heart?"

He laughed, and laughed. Eventually, Frito joined in and laughed with him though in confusion. Soon enough, Darnath stopped and wiped his good eye, "No. I'm doing it for the same reason the demons are, but the opposite—souls."

"What about them?"

"Souls how gods eat and grow big," Frito offered sweetly and beamed with pride. "Demons eat souls and make more demons. Gods cycle souls, allow rebirth. Make angles."

"An*gels,* big fella, but he has the right of it." Darnath ran his hand through his hair. "Mephisto's forces were too powerful when he arrived on our planet and began to corrupt our angels with his power. Eventually, they turned and fell, working for him. But with the souls of the Travelers and the fallen of the previous world, combined with the power of controlled altars you make, I could create even stronger angels to combat the demons."

"Does that mean that you're going to start killing Travelers? Or that we won't be able to respawn?" I glared at him some more. "We have a nice little EXP farm going on here, and you'd really be screwing us all over if that happens."

"No." He chuckled and shook his head. "No one will die permanently, but I will take some energy from all of the Travelers who die within a certain radius of this place. There will be a small debuff for a little bit after you respawn, but nothing that wouldn't fade away."

—*We have an issue.*— Emerald sent through a whisper. —*Where are you?*—

—*At the altar in the church.*— I blinked at Darnath, and he smiled, "What do you know?"

"I'm about to have some good food served right up to me." He clapped his hands twice, and Frito moved closer to him. "Do try not to die in this, Kyvir."

He started to fade from view, then snapped back to fully visible with an audible click of his fingers. "Yes, sorry; your reward for this."

He reached out and touched my cheek, and a searing pain roiled from my flesh into my mind that made me scream and fall to my knees. When I could think again, I growled, "What did you do to me?"

"Installed a quest line for you where I'm concerned." He

grinned. "I also leveled up your job class from initiate to basic. Now, you'll be even more dangerous."

I gasped and blinked, the pain ebbing as he faded away. Sure enough, the proof was there as soon as he was gone in the form of notifications.

Job Quest revealed – Darnath has asked that you find and dedicate more altars to him so that he can grow more powerful as well.

Reward: Deeper understanding of the Paladin (dark) job, ??? EXP, increased rapport with your new god.

"Damn it." I clenched my jaw and stood up, shaking my head.

Where the altar had been a deep and rich mahogany color before, albeit stained with blood and vitriol, it was now a deep, dark black color and gave off a cool sense of ease.

Call that the comfort of the grave, Darnath whispered into my notifications again. **Also, please refrain from speaking about me out loud; Mephisto has spies everywhere.**

"Okay, then," I grumbled. This entire time, I had thought there were no gods out there who cared or even existed in the first place, but now here he was. What the hell was I really supposed to believe?

As I stared at the altar, something else popped into my view that I hadn't really expected, but it made my blood boil.

And now the completion of Eden is nigh. To you newfound Edenians, or is it Edenites? Whatever.

That had to be Mephisto.

Your world is about to be wholly changed, and some new topography added, so if you see any falling mountains, I would suggest not standing beneath them.

Or do so, you rascals. See you in a few more days.

I could almost hear Mephisto's cackling as I read the last line. "Kyvir?" Emerald called out to me, and I nearly snarled in fright. She came into the chapel and found me where I stood. "We have a big fucking problem."

"What?" I started down the aisle toward her when I heard the first whistles and chirps outside of dusk falling.

"Garren is coming back with a group of higher level players —our level—to take this place back."

I growled, "Shit; how many?"

"I counted at least ten who were well-armed, and some creatures were following them at a distance." She scowled and sniffed the air, then gagged. "Oh my god, what's that smell?"

"Frito." I replied absently, but she just wrinkled her nose at me, and I realized I had almost messed up. "Sprinkle calls poo that."

She blinked at me, and I was glad that I still had both of the summoned creatures here. "Sprinkle! Come back to me."

He appeared, and with a mental flex toward Vulina, she appeared in front of me in a wash of flames. "You rang, hot stuff?"

Sprinkle gagged, then shot her a withering glare, "Are you serious with that?"

She just crossed her arms and sighed, "My preferences are none of your concern."

"Pay attention, assholes!" Emerald bellowed, and both summoned creatures straightened right up. "God damn... you two have a fucking wire loose in those shit-bird ass brains of yours, or do you just fight like bitches and bobcats for no fucking reason at all?"

Both of them looked thoroughly wounded, Sprinkle even a little impressed, but it was me who yelled, "Jesus Christ, do you kiss your mother with that fucking mouth?"

Her hand lashed out and smacked the back of my head, refreshing my filter. "Sorry."

"Assholes are coming. We need the help., Can you both stay to assist us?" They both glanced at me, and I just shrugged; this was their question to answer for her. They nodded. "Good. We'll need it."

I sighed, weighing our options as best I could, and finally ordered, "Sprinkle and Flicker, go and get all of the citizens who are higher level and those who have longer range, then bring them to us here. While we fill them in, you take flight and try to keep tabs on them."

"Payment?" Sprinkles brows rose slowly. "You owe me one already."

"I do. And I'm a man of my word." I pointed to myself, then him. "You do this for me, you get two days off, and I only summon you again to give you Aether, unless it's a true emergency."

Sprinkle threw out his hand and roared, "Deal!" After shaking my hand, he tore off so fast that it was a miracle the hood of his cloak didn't whip off his head.

"You spoil us," Flicker muttered as she stepped by, batting her eyelashes at me. "I take it I get a reward, too?"

I shrugged, knowing I had the Aether to give her as long as we were okay, and started to say as much, but she just smiled and said, "I'll take mine after you've paid him. Don't worry about it too much."

I watched her fly out of the chapel and just stared after her while Emerald scowled, either at their banter or at the situation itself, I couldn't tell.

After ten minutes, a crowd had gathered, seating themselves in the pews closest to the parapet as they waited for us to speak.

"Intruders are coming to try to take this place back under their banners. Your concerns and fears are correct, if you think that it's a certain troll called Guilty or Garren or Get Over It," I called as they began to whisper and speak among themselves. "He's brought some cronies and is leading some monsters here to attack us. He knows this place better than I do, and if anything, he's still expecting you to be weak."

Emerald stepped up and raised her voice, "That's where the element of surprise comes in!" She pointed to the crowd. "Those of you with long range abilities and spells are going to help us keep them all at bay. There is a cooldown, yes, but it all helps. You'll do that, while those of us with more up close and personal skills are going to raise hell if anyone gets close."

"What about the children?" someone called. "The people who aren't here?"

"They'll be here in the church's lower floors, being watched over," I explained tersely.

Antonio piped up, "What about the tower?"

Emerald answered for me, "It's a good position, but they're out there around it and moving closer; that, and the tower is an unknown. We have no way of knowing if it is safe or not."

"We have one chance to get this right; otherwise, they're going to overwhelm you and bring the fight to a close." I called over the slowly rising voices, rounding their attention back to us and the task at hand. "We can't let that happen. So here's what we do."

CHAPTER TWENTY-SIX

They'll be in range in five minutes, if they keep sneaking as they are. Vulina spoke inside my mind, and I grinned. We had the trap ready to spring at any moment, thanks to both of my summons being our scouts.

When they're in position, blind them. I watched through a crack in one of the walls that we had hastily erected in several places, behind the lower-positioned stakes, as cover and a means to protect those entry points.

We also went ahead and poured out something slick, which one of the men who acted as target practice secreted as a sort of physical defense. Almost like oil, but slicker.

Sprinkle appeared behind me. "My part is done out there. There shouldn't be any reason why it doesn't work."

I nodded once, "Good. Can you help guide some of the better fighters into things? I know you're strong enough to handle most of the Travelers that are near our level."

"Certainly. I won't charge you for this one, since you gave me all that summoning Aether." He snickered at my exasperation and took off the back way to where some of the higher level fighters waited with Emerald in the trees where they could be used most effectively.

They're in position and moving across to the entryway, Vulina hissed at me. *Cover your eyes!*

I ducked my head back behind the wall and closed my eyes as a bright *whompf* of flame burst into existence to blind the attackers and beasts.

Then all hell broke loose.

Spells of all shapes and sizes lobbed over the defenses, haphazardly splattering and blasting the open area before the entrance to the community, and my Eyes of Avarice saw nothing present but the auras that blended together into one big gray mass.

Then I saw a whisper of deep purple in the area and realized something was wrong.

Space Aether? I wondered to myself at the same time that a doorway opened almost on top of the casters, who were still lobbing their personal abilities. I shouted, the din of the spells hitting the ice almost drowning me out, "Turn around!"

"They're inside!" My voice carried this time, and the spells stopped. The first fighter stepped out of the doorway with a sword as long as my body.

The wielder turned and slashed at the casters behind him, the group of them falling as the blade swept by. Another came out of the doorway with a spell that washed the area in something that made my stomach turn.

Fear. Guilty had arrived.

"Put your weapons down, and I'll only kill you once for the uprising!" he shouted, and I just chuckled. Yet again, it hadn't affected me.

—The creatures are the ones being bombarded, and they're mostly dead. What happened?— I couldn't answer Emerald's whisper as I was too busy taking stock of the situation at hand.

The others poured out of the doorway, and finally someone else stepped through that I recognized but hadn't thought to see.

Albarth.

I blinked and looked at him again... no. That wasn't him, he just looked like him. What was going on? The aura was solidly space, and not wind with it.

But that was the problem. He could get them back here or help them leave at any time, and that wasn't okay.

He was my first priority for now. I took Fate's End out and stepped toward them all, coating myself in my Ice Armor (full). Someone sprinted in from the other side of the group, the mother, whose name I had never bothered to learn, screaming incoherently.

The space user, who looked like Albarth but couldn't be him, turned, and a dagger appeared in his hand and sped toward her.

She flashed, her body disappearing, then reappearing three feet to the right, and she came up from the side to stab at him. He was able to dodge her strike and slap the blade away, only to take an ice spear to the shoulder from behind me.

I glimpsed someone behind me winding up for another strike when two people tackled him from behind. He screamed, "He'll get us all killed! He's a murderer!"

"Shut up!" One of his assailants punched him in the face, and I turned to catch the same blade that had missed the woman in the stomach.

20 dmg taken (halved).

Jesus, that was a lot of damage to take. Even if it was halved.

I grasped the blade and tore it out of my armor, whipping it right back at him. The closer I got, the more the similarities to Albarth waned, and I began to notice the thin aura of some other type of Aether covering the man's body.

It had to be a trick, then.

He smiled and closed the distance between us. He threw himself on my sword and grasped me, whispering, "When this is over, go to the tower."

He winked and disappeared without even so much as a trace of blood left behind.

Move! Vulina howled, and something pierced my shoulder painfully from behind as the man shouted in triumph with his arms lifted in celebration.

Flames speared him to the ground where he was, and the ice in my body melted as the other warriors came my way with weapons drawn.

Emerald's pack tore through the street, with Zanjir in the lead, to get the drop on Guilty. The cronies he had with him appeared to be fighting Emerald. Vines with red roses burst from the ground below one woman's legs and pierced her where she was.

My sword crashed down into the woman and slashed her in half, Vulina at my back with a flaming sword in her hands.

Zanjir dragged Guilty onto the ground, and the bastard started to spear him in the neck and shoulders with his long, gross nails. The dog yelped and bucked before running away, which was new, a sickly aura flowing behind him.

The troll hopped up onto his feet and pointed to me. "*You!*"

I grinned evilly and bared my fangs, "Me." When he lifted a small object that reminded me of a gun, I panicked and raised my hand, activating my Telekinesis with the ring on my finger.

The bolt in it flipped out of the groove as the string released and fell away uselessly, his footing rocked slightly but not enough to throw him like I had the guard in the church. The string looked frayed, but otherwise seemed usable still.

He grinned and pulled out a blade, then shoved the crossbow onto a leather thong at his hip. I just shook my head and flexed my will as I readied for the fight.

Sprinkle whirled into the troll from above with his scythe, and then ran off screaming, as if he was terrified.

He's weaponized his fear, I warned Vulina mentally as she and I squared off against the green man.

He sliced toward me with his knife, but I juked to the side and raised my blade to meet his. Instead of actually letting the strike land as a block, I took my elbow and rammed it into the flat of Fate's End, slapping the sword around his knife and into his shoulder.

Vulina surged into the opening I made and stabbed toward his abdomen, but he reached out with his other hand and scratched her arm. The wound and his fingers pulsed with the same sickly green aura that I had seen the first time we'd met in Codgy's shop, and it was clearly what had begun leaking from Zanjir.

Vulina screeched and lashed out in terror, which he didn't seem to expect. Something grabbed my sword, and I turned to find that one of the goons he had brought along with him was interfering.

My skull shoved forward and collided with his chin, forcing him to let go of Fate's End so that I could move again.

3 dmg taken.

Guilty and Vulina were locked in combat, and she was bleeding flames from several small wounds on her abdomen and shoulder. The asshole was laughing about it, too, muttering things to her that I couldn't hear.

Time to use that ability, then. I lifted my sword and roared as loudly as I could, my throat going raw from it.

Dark Paladin's Rally – activated.

The same darkness as before in Belgonna's Hold swept over the people who were on our side. Suddenly, Vulina glowed brighter and hotter than before. Guilty tripped over his foot as he tried to sidle backward.

Now she wore scale armor that reminded me of the dragon whose flames she had bathed in. It covered her wounds and body wholly as she stepped forward.

I took my fist and coated it in ice like a club, then clobbered the woman who had decided she was going to try to sneak up on Emerald on my way to Guilty, Meanwhile, Emerald reached down and grasped his throat to pick him up to toss him toward the flaming elemental creature whose sword burned blue.

She batted him down with a sweep of her tail and he cried

out. He tried to slash her with his knife, the blade flashing with his aura as it plummeted toward her tail.

I gritted my teeth and threw my summoning Aether at the weapon, willing it to appear in my hand. Two, four, seven Aether gone in an instant, and finally I held the blade in my left hand with a grin on my face.

His empty fist slammed into the scales on her tail, and she just stabbed him in the shoulder savagely, a scream passing his lips. "Fuck!"

Emerald loomed over him almost instantly. "Language!"

She slapped him hard enough that one of his long tusks grazed her hand and drew blood. She held her knife over him and looked to be about to kill him, but I called, "Wait!"

She looked up at me, and the dumbass had the gall to look relieved. "We should take him into the church and do it there. That would be nice."

"What?!" Guilty and Emerald asked at the same time. Emerald just looked down at him and punched him in the face again. "Shut up."

"Hit me again, you stupid bi—" Vulina's foot caught him in the chin and snapped his head backward, making his eyes roll into the back of his head.

I leaned forward and whispered, "My patron might like it?" I was hopeful that she wouldn't question it, but I was wrong; it just looked like she had more questions than before. "Just have a little faith."

She frowned at me harder and even managed to look like she was asking herself if I was all right. I reached down and flipped my prisoner over before I created shackles of ice, attaching them to both of Guilty's hands and freezing them together behind his back.

Vulina walked closer, and I just nodded for her to step back a little. She looked mildly hurt, but I explained, "You're made of fire and that's ice magic." She made an O with her mouth and I smiled, adding, "Your armor looks great on you, by the way."

She put her hand on her breastplate and smiled, her flaming hair falling over her eyes a little bit as she looked up at me, "Does it?"

I nodded, and she giggled a little bit before she followed along behind me with her hands on her wounds. They looked to be healing quickly.

Lugging the man wasn't hard, and we had almost made it back to the church before he started to squirm and fight back. His fear magic washed over me, but I just ignored it. I wondered if he had any other kind of Aether at his disposal, and that made me hungry, but I had things to do, and that would need to wait.

Inside the church, the room felt cooler than before. The blood stains on the floor were dissipating little by little, even as we approached. The monsters that we had killed were gone. The altar was free of blemish and grime, which was mildly disappointing since I wanted Guilty to feel the same fear he tried to instill in others.

I dropped him onto the altar unceremoniously and asked quietly, "Wonder what kind of debuff being murdered on top of the altar will give you?"

He looked up at me in shock. I just smiled as I lifted Fate's End and said sweetly, "Let me know how bad it is the next time I come to kill you, okay?"

"Wait!" he screamed, and I stilled my blade an inch from his throat. "I don't know what kind of crazy shit this is; I just wanted to survive. If I didn't work with the demons, they would have killed me, or turned me into a demon."

I nodded, putting my sword down to lean on it like I cared as he continued to beg, "I'm serious. You don't know what they're like. They're pure fucking evil, man. They'll kill anyone who crosses them."

I nodded again and flipped the large sword up onto my right shoulder. "I mean, that sounds about right." My new tail flicked up beside me, and he stared at it in horror. "But you know what? So will I. You tell everyone you know to stay the hell out of my way—or they'll get seventy percent off, just like you did."

He looked confused, then realization dawned on him as my sword passed through his chest where his heart and ribs were, cutting his upper body apart just below the shoulders.

CRITICAL STRIKE
47 dmg to Guilty GameZ
Guilty GameZ died
104 EXP received

Good work, was all that Darnath said to me with that grisly business out of the way.

"Well, we could have grilled him for information, instead of just killing him," Emerald grumped angrily.

I shrugged. "He could have lied to us, and we would never have known it. Better to put a stop to him here and now." I glanced over at her, "Besides, the guy that got them past our trap told me to come to that tower once everything was over."

"You can't be seriously considering going there right now, Kyvir." Emerald looked like she was ready to tie me to the altar right that moment.

So I did the smart thing and just snorted. "Me? No. That'd be absolutely crazy."

She narrowed her eyes at me, and I sighed, "Seriously, I'm exhausted. I just want to pay Sprinkle and go to bed."

Sprinkle erupted into existence beside me. "I heard I was being paid?"

"Jesus!" I snarled and tried to punch him, but he just chuckled and moved out of the way.

Rather than deal with his shenanigans any longer, I willed him my remaining summoning Aether and all of the ice Aether I had. He looked content and bowed before he faded from existence.

I moved to one of the pews and laid down on it for a time, then sat up and called over to Emerald, "Does it bother you that it doesn't really seem like we're any closer to catching up to Mona?"

"All the time," she answered swiftly, then seemed to dwell on it some more. "The front lines sound like a very dangerous place, and now with everything going on, it would be reasonable to say that we should have made it farther."

"Right," I muttered, Seamus finding me and wagging his tail at me before butting his head into my chest so I would pet him.

"But we also had to survive the end of the world, Kyvir." Emerald's voice was soft. "We're alone down here, and there's nothing we can do, other than our very best."

I stayed quiet, and she and I just sat in amicable silence with Vulina sitting in the same pew I was in for a time.

Eventually, I fell asleep, and it was peaceful.

CHAPTER TWENTY-SEVEN

I woke up with my head in Vulina's lap as she slept sitting up, the warmth of her body comforting somehow, instead of overwhelming. Emerald was up already and hardly looked pleased to find me there, for some reason.

I sat up and thanked Vulina for letting me use her lap as a pillow, and she smiled sweetly, "My pleasure."

Without another word, we all left the church and extricated ourselves from the people of the community in order to go and investigate the tower. Vulina had opted to travel with us on foot, which was nice, as she kept the critters that thought they could try us at bay.

It was a little bit before we reached the tower, and by the time we did, slightly more construction seemed to have been added to the top, like a rampart or something. It was weird. The place looked unfinished somehow, even though the tower itself had looked complete before.

The wooden entrance was open wide and dark on the inside. Vulina stepped closer. "You want me to go in first?"

I shook my head, casting Ice Armor (full) on myself, "You bring up the rear and watch our backs." I looked at Emerald,

"You want to stealth between us and have the dogs guard the entrance?"

"Good idea." She turned and began to speak to her dogs, and they all sat dutifully on either side of the door to watch all directions. "They'll let me know if anything comes up."

The entrance led to a set of stairs that curved around the inner portion of the tower, then up and out of sight. Emerald and I both looked at each other and shrugged before stepping up onto the case and plodding upward.

We climbed for a while longer than it should have taken before we made it to the top, or at least found a room. Eventually, we tried to stop and glance outside one of the few windows, but by the time we did, it appeared to be night time outside.

Emerald grabbed my arm. "Do you think this was meant to be a trap for us?"

I shrugged, uncertain. "I saw something like this once before; it was meant to mess with people who had no business climbing the tower. If anything, it could mean that we're on our way toward somewhere we were meant to be going."

She looked panicked, but I just let her hold my arm as I continued up the stairs to find a door a little bit later. I reached out to knock, and the door opened on its own, just as my knuckles should have touched it.

The room inside sped toward us, almost as if it were consuming us, until we stood in a dark room that I recognized as the cave in the grave dungeon under Iradellum. This time, instead of a stand holding a small glass ball that made the place into a dungeon, there was an ornate chair of bone, with glass shaped like wings that wrapped around it.

It looked gaudy, but that was neither here nor there, because it was who sat on the chair that mattered.

He stood up, younger than even I remembered, but I recognized his voice when he opened his arms and spoke softly to Emerald, "My emerald."

"Peter?" Emerald whispered, her hands shaking and

climbing involuntarily toward her mouth. Tears burst to her eyes as she stared at him. He didn't move, just waiting. "Peter?"

He nodded and looked down at himself as his arms slowly came to rest at his sides. "I did my best to keep myself as close to you as I was, but there's just no way to tell how the Aether is going to manifest in someone. Luckily, I made this world, and I know it better than anyone. Well, half of it, at least."

Emerald swayed where she was, and I reached out to steady her, but she caught herself and moved toward her husband, who she hadn't seen in years. He frowned. "Baby, I'm so sorry. I didn't know any of this was going to happen."

She ignored his words and closed the distance between them, throwing her arms around his shoulders and sobbing. He tried to comfort her, but as soon as his hands touched her, it was like a switch had been flipped, and she reared back and slapped him hard enough that he fell back onto the throne.

I flinched, and Vulina muttered, "Oh, that'll leave a mark."

"You had better *damned well* have a perfect fucking reason why you left me and your daughter alone for years!" Emerald seethed, her clawed hands clenching and unclenching at her waist, as if she wasn't sure whether to reach out to touch him or claw his throat out.

"Language, Emerald."

"Piss off, Peter!" Emerald howled, and the man visibly flinched as she raised her hand, then clenched it and screamed, "Explain—now!"

"There's no time, Emma!" He countered and stood up, backing away from her, then side stepping a little to come closer to me. "I know where the demons mean to attack first, and despite what you might think, it's not here, and it's not the front lines."

"Where would they gain the most by attacking, then?" I asked, trying to put him on the other side of me as he moved away from the pissed off woman slowly stalking him around the room.

"Getting rid of the people who know how they operate." He

ducked under Emerald's swing, and Vulina had to step in to keep her from diving at him. "Thank you."

"Explain!" Vulina grunted and growled as Emerald tried to bite her shoulder to get loose.

"They're going to target the former NPCs of the game, the survivors of the first Merger!" His scream over Emerald's baying cries was enough to make her fall still. "They're going to attack them as soon as their leash is pulled, and the demon lords are splitting it all up."

"What's that supposed to mean?" I blinked at him, and he sighed.

"It means that there are four major cities with survivors, and Mona will be heading to one of them." He looked at Emma and muttered, "And I know which one."

"How do you know?" Emma asked, her voice soft.

"We were the ones who took her so that we could put her in a special portal of our design." She looked like she was about to start screaming again, so he raised his voice. "She's lost her ability to control herself, Emma. She operates on pure instinct and drive now. I knew that, based on some of the coding in her avatar. I was able to tinker with that code and add some spyware."

"How did you know that?" I watched him carefully, "Did you look into all of us? Could you help us get back what we lost?"

"No. The magic takes it away permanently, unless some-thing happens that allows you to find an equally powerful kind of Aether to awaken that can give it back, but those are rare. He forced me to make them that way." He stared at me, and I could see the pain in his gaze. "I'm sorry, Seth. I was just trying to give us a chance after I made this mess."

"So you knew that she was more easily susceptible, and you just let her go into the demon's territory anyway?" Emma gasped. "What the *hell is wrong with you?*"

"She was our Trojan horse, Em." He clapped his hands, and screens opened all around the room. "I knew we couldn't stop the merger. There was never any hope of that, but we could spy, and she's been able to infiltrate Abbadon's lair. And according to my findings, he plans for his demons to go and attack Iradellum and all the former NPCs who had been placed there. They were all spawned back in their home cities. So there is no front line anymore."

He grimaced and pointed to the screen where Mona stood in the center of a room surrounded by demons, who cheered her on as she fought against another large creature in what could have been a demonic fight club.

"They're bringing the front lines and the war straight to the cities." He closed his eyes. "And I have given everything that I could to ensure that you all would be able to endure, so that you had the best chance at surviving and getting her back."

"So what do we do?" My voice sounded hollow, even to me.

He frowned and said, "You make your way back to Iradellum with the people in that colony, and you make damn sure they're ready for the fight to come."

"Is there any way to win?" Emerald asked at last. Tears soaked her furred cheeks as she looked at her husband. "Can we ever go back to the way things were?"

He shook his head forlornly. "No, we can't go back." If I'd had the ability to feel anything, I'd have thought that was enough to make me feel like hell. But he clenched his fist and grinned in a way that I had never seen. "But that doesn't mean we can't kick that bastard Mephisto out of here."

I blinked at him, then at Emerald and Vulina. There was hope. It was a long shot, but it was there.

And all we had to do was get to where the ball was going to drop in time to crash a party with a bunch of demons, kick their asses, get our friend back, and then take the fight from there?

That sounded like one hell of a time.

I grinned, "I'm in. Let's go kick some demon ass!"

Both of them looked squarely at me and barked, "Language!" They looked back at each other and smiled bashfully.

This was going to take some getting used to.

ABOUT CHRISTOPHER JOHNS

Christopher Johns is a former photojournalist for the United States Marine Corps with published works telling hundreds of other peoples' stories through word, photo, and even video. But throughout that time, his editors and superiors had always said that his love of reading fantasy and about worlds of fantastic beauty and horrible power bled into his work. That meant he should write a book.

Well, ta-da!

Chris has been an avid devourer of fantasy and science fiction for more than twenty years and looks forward to sharing that love with his son, his loving fiancée and almost anyone he could ever hope to meet.

Connect with Chris:
Facebook.com/AxeDruidAuthor
Twitter.com/JonsyJohns

ABOUT MOUNTAINDALE PRESS

Dakota and Danielle Krout, a husband and wife team, strive to create as well as publish excellent fantasy and science fiction novels. Self-publishing *The Divine Dungeon: Dungeon Born* in 2016 transformed their careers from Dakota's military and programming background and Danielle's Ph.D. in pharmacology to President and CEO, respectively, of a small press. Their goal is to share their success with other authors and provide captivating fiction to readers with the purpose of solidifying Mountaindale Press as the place 'Where Fantasy Transforms Reality.'

Connect with Mountaindale Press:
MountaindalePress.com
Facebook.com/MountaindalePress
Twitter.com/_Mountaindale
Instagram.com/MountaindalePress

MOUNTAINDALE PRESS TITLES

GameLit and LitRPG

The Completionist Chronicles,
The Divine Dungeon,
Full Murderhobo, and
Year of the Sword by Dakota Krout

Arcana Unlocked by Gregory Blackburn

A Touch of Power by Jay Boyce

Red Mage and
Farming Livia by Xander Boyce

Space Seasons by Dawn Chapman

Ether Collapse and
Ether Flows by Ryan DeBruyn

Dr. Druid by Maxwell Farmer

Bloodgames by Christian J. Gilliland

Threads of Fate by Michael Head

Lion's Lineage by Rohan Hublikar and Dakota Krout

Wolfman Warlock by James Hunter and Dakota Krout

Axe Druid,
Mephisto's Magic Online, and
High Table Hijinks by Christopher Johns

Skeleton in Space by Andries Louws

Chronicles of Ethan by John L. Monk

Pixel Dust and
Necrotic Apocalypse by David Petrie

Viceroy's Pride by Cale Plamann

Henchman by Carl Stubblefield

Artorian's Archives by Dennis Vanderkerken and Dakota Krout

Made in the USA
Middletown, DE
20 December 2024